"Do you really think we might die there?"

"Well, *you* might. Me? Been there. Done that."

"Of course. Personal question, but . . . what's it like to be dead?"

I gave him a look, right in his baby blue contacts. "I'm starting to understand why you don't have any friends."

I don't usually talk like that to a client, but I already had two envelopes full of his cash, and I wasn't very happy about being out here at night.

"I don't mean now, Mann. I meant before . . . when you *were* dead."

"Oh, then. There was a bright, warm golden light at the end of a long tunnel and all my deceased loved ones were on the other side, beckoning me forward to everlasting joy."

"Really?"

"No."

Dead Mann Walking

A HESSIUS MANN NOVEL

Stefan Petrucha

A ROC BOOK

ROC
Published by New American Library, a division of
Penguin Group (USA) Inc., 375 Hudson Street,
New York, New York 10014, USA
Penguin Group (Canada), 90 Eglinton Avenue East, Suite 700, Toronto,
Ontario M4P 2Y3, Canada (a division of Pearson Penguin Canada Inc.)
Penguin Books Ltd., 80 Strand, London WC2R 0RL, England
Penguin Ireland, 25 St. Stephen's Green, Dublin 2,
Ireland (a division of Penguin Books Ltd.)
Penguin Group (Australia), 250 Camberwell Road, Camberwell, Victoria 3124,
Australia (a division of Pearson Australia Group Pty. Ltd.)
Penguin Books India Pvt. Ltd., 11 Community Centre, Panchsheel Park,
New Delhi - 110 017, India
Penguin Group (NZ), 67 Apollo Drive, Rosedale, Auckland 0632,
New Zealand (a division of Pearson New Zealand Ltd.)
Penguin Books (South Africa) (Pty.) Ltd., 24 Sturdee Avenue,
Rosebank, Johannesburg 2196, South Africa

Penguin Books Ltd., Registered Offices:
80 Strand, London WC2R 0RL, England

First published by Roc, an imprint of New American Library,
a division of Penguin Group (USA) Inc.

First printing, October 2011
10 9 8 7 6 5 4 3 2 1

Copyright © Stefan Petrucha, 2011
All rights reserved

For Sarah,
because she liked this
even though she's not particularly into zombies

Back to back,
Belly to belly,
Well, I don't give a damn
'Cause I'm stone dead already.

—"Zombie Jamboree"
by Conrad Eugene Mauge Jr., 1953

1

Sixteen pieces.

That's how many chunks the newslady said Colin Wilson was cut into. He was scattered across the desert like bits of burger wrapping and leftover fries. The cops found all the bits. Except the head. That's unusual, seeing as how the police don't tend to get involved with Wilson's type, no matter how many pieces they're in.

Of course, the news didn't play it like a murder. To the livebloods, it's more about litter. Lousy so-and-sos always leaving their body parts around, making the living waste their time picking up after them. The candy-blond anchor shrugged. Must've been an accident. Wilson's type are always getting into accidents. Cut to deodorant commercial. At times like this, you want to smell *nice*.

Accident, my ass. One or two pieces, maybe, and they would have found the head. Seeing as how there's no middle ground between accident and design, that meant something weirder: He was cut up on purpose. That's a lot of work. First, you have to get Colin Wilson into a position where he can't disagree, and then you have to do all that cutting. Human bone, too. Probably needed special tools. It's sure as hell not the kind of thing you do on a whim, or even out of anger. The reasons would have to run dark and deep.

And then there was the head.

I tried not to think about it, to focus on something else, but I didn't have a lot going on. I stared at my desktop, the stains looking like a faded Jackson Pollock. I tried to make animal shapes out of the Goodwill shirts piled on the floor, or see a tree in the cracks on the door.

By the time the news came back on, a late-afternoon light, the dying kind, had intruded from the broken window, making the TV hard to see. It didn't help. I couldn't get Colin Wilson's head out of mine; images of it were crawling around my brain like freshly hatched baby spiders. I didn't know Wilson from a punched hole in the wall, but I kept seeing his severed head in some coyote's mouth, an eye socket pinched between two strong canines, its saliva slapping the skull. Colin's good eye opens and he realizes where he is.

Cut to deodorant commercial.

It didn't make sense. What would a coyote do with a head? Not much meat on that bone. What bugged me made less sense: What if Colin Wilson's brain really was still *thinking*? What if it knew what happened, understood that it was a lot shorter and less mobile than it used to be?

Weirder things are true. The official line is that decapitation ends it, but they don't know shit. Calling my memory bad is a compliment, but I do remember the strangest shit, like how I read somewhere that back when they used the guillotine, a French scientist asked a condemned murderer to blink twenty times after his execution, if he could. He did. When the scientist called his name, the head opened its eyes and looked at him. True story, true as anything.

And that's the living. Wilson wasn't of that persuasion. His functions wouldn't necessarily *ever* stop. So maybe he's still out there.

These days there are so many things worse than death that it's not even high on the list. Thousands of years we look for eternal life and what do we get? Fucking zombies. First I ever saw was in Romero's *Night of the Living Dead*. Scared the crap out of me. These days all I have to do is look in a mirror. Yeah, I'm one of *those*, too. Me, Colin Wilson, a hundred thousand or so others. Livebloods call us *chakz*—a mangled version of *charqui*, or, *en inglés*, jerky—dried meat. If we're still oozing, which is pretty rare, they call us *gleets* or *juicers*. Then there are *danglers*, but I'll leave that definition to the imagination.

It's not like the movies. We don't eat human flesh unless we go feral, and then it's more like we'll eat anything. We *are* tough to destroy, which is why I was so obsessed about that head. Cut off an arm or a leg, shoot us in the chest—we'll keep coming.

Then there's burning. Now, there's another great thought—watching your flesh curl until the heat takes your eyes away. Brr. But that begs the question, Who bothered giving Colin Wilson such special treatment? If they wanted to make sure he was gone, why not just incinerate him?

With all the love we get, why bring us back? Mostly because some idiots figured out how. Mammalian life is based on cellular metabolism, right? Ten years ago, the boffins at ChemBet's research labs came up with an electrostatic something-or-other that keeps cellular metabolism charged *permanently*. They call it a radical invigoration procedure, RIP for short. Ha, ha, ha. RIP a corpse, and hallelujah, the dead have risen!

The rich and famous were falling over their adopted third-world kids in the rush to bring back their loved ones. The feds gave ChemBet some huge tax breaks so the industry could grow and make the process cheaper. Everyone wanted in. Only, once the thrill died, livebloods started noticing how parts of Mom would rot off if she wasn't kept squeaky clean, or how, if you didn't talk to Uncle Stu often enough, he'd get all morose, go feral, and plant his dentures into the dog or a neighbor's kid. People not only wanted their money back, they wanted the process reversed.

That, ChemBet *didn't* know how to do. Neither did the government. They say decapitation is surefire, *D-cap*, but, like I said, I'm not so sure. It sounds too much like something a PR flak cut and pasted from a movie script.

Point being, people stopped ripping for love, but they couldn't just D-cap Grandma, not unless she went feral first. Those early revivals account for about half the chak population. The rest are another story.

Me, I was still obsessing about Wilson's head when I finally got my distraction. Misty, my assistant, walked in wearing a tight blue number with fishnet stockings. She's a liveblood. Nowadays you can see it by the flush to her face. When we met six months back she was a crack addict, picking through garbage to survive and turning tricks when things got really bad. So bad she tried working my neck of the woods, the Bones.

She was such a little, half-starved thing, I felt bad for

her, which is saying something. Usually chakz don't feel much, even physical sensations. Oh, sometimes a sock in the jaw still feels like a sock in the jaw, or a nightmare can rock your world, but everything tends to be at arm's distance. Maybe it was her hazel puppy-dog eyes or the cracked teeth, but feeling for her gave me something to pay attention to. I also figured there were places a live-blood could get to that a dead guy couldn't, so after I got some food in her, we made a deal: She'd try to keep clean; I'd try to keep from going feral.

Our fingers remain crossed.

She strutted toward me, modeling her dress. It was something new from the thrift store, cleaned so carefully you could see only the outlines of the stains. Aside from the fact that she could stand to lose the stockings, she should've known flirting with me was a waste. When I said she moved me, I didn't mean she moved my groin. Hell, I'm afraid to look down there since they brought me back. Officially, chakz don't have a sex drive.

She meant well, wanted to keep me engaged with my environment so I didn't get too morose over, oh, I don't know, my entire fucking existence. I appreciated the effort, and she was sort of fun to look at.

Trying to play my part, I attempted a wolf whistle. It came out more like a spastic steam kettle. Chakz are bone-dry. I should've taken a drink first, but the effect doesn't last long, and the liquids slosh around inside so much you can never be sure when or where they'll come out.

Misty got the idea, though. She winked. Then she flashed a business card.

I leaned forward for a closer look. Nice paper, maybe even linen. *William Turgeon, Esq*. No address, just the name and a cell phone number, like he was a place all by himself.

"You find that in the street?"

She blew a raspberry. "No, stupid, he's outside. Wants to see you."

"Me? Really? He's not lost?"

"Nope. Asked for you by name. Says, 'Is Hessius Mann here'?"

That's my name. The hand-painted sign on the door says I'm a detective. I don't particularly agree with the title, but I keep that to myself. And I do get clients, sometimes among the living. Unfortunately, your average liveblood is about as knowledgeable about chakz as they are about how evolution works, so when one shows up, they usually want me to kill and eat someone they don't like. Then they get all incensed when I say no. Most likely, this was more of the same.

On the other hand, it could be a blackmail case, especially with that fancy card. Those're good, but few and far between. See, it's best to tell your hired dick what you're being blackmailed *for*. Livebloods don't like chakz, but they don't seem to mind telling us everything. Not only are we dead, our memories are so wonky our testimony's not admissible in court. A plus for someone with a secret, a minus for me.

When I was alive, my recall was photographic. It was half the reason I had my job. These days, I remember the weirdest crap. The Beatles' last album? *Abbey Road*. They recorded it after *Let It Be*. My middle name? Your guess is as good as mine. Oh, I can still have a decent conversation. It's the transition from short- to long-term memory that's AWOL.

Misty adjusted my jacket and straightened my tie. I felt like a rotting, life-size Ken doll.

"So, should I send him in?" she asked.

I held up a gray finger. "Keep him busy a minute. Say I'm on the phone. There's something I want to do first."

Soon as she left, I forgot what it was. The television? I clicked it off. No, something else.

Talking head? No. Oh, yeah. The head.

After I was ripped, one of the first things I realized I had to do was buy a little handheld digital recorder to store all those details I used to have at my fingertips. Took a week to remember to buy the damn thing. Now I was always losing it. I felt around on the desk, then my body, and finally found it in my pants pocket. With a press of the red dot I rattled off what I was thinking about Colin Wilson, for future reference.

If I ever remembered that I made the recording, that is.

I was finished when the door swung open. Misty held on to the knob, stretching her thin arm across our guest, putting herself in the doorframe along with him. She knew he'd have to rub against her to come in. Poor Misty, she wasn't very subtle. I understood why she was interested. His suit cost more than the building. It wasn't his looks. He was big, though not exactly fat. The word I'd use is puffy.

Unlike Misty, William Turgeon was not a lot of fun to look at, but it was unavoidable because he took up so much space. He was a six-footer, rounded, not obese, but his proportions were off. Largish head, squat arms, over-size hands. The clothes helped. The lines of the suit matched his body snug as puzzle pieces, but overall he looked kind of like an overdressed, overly large baby.

As he squeezed past her, she tried to make eye contact, but either he wasn't interested or he was real good at hiding it. She gave me a no-playing–*Pretty Woman*–today shrug and made herself scarce.

It was late and my office didn't get much light to begin with. The room was dark enough for his Stetson to keep most of his features in shadow. I could see the whites of his eyes, but that was about it. What I could see of those pupils were all over me. He was checking me out for something. What, I didn't know.

"Hessius Mann?" he said. It was an even voice, not unfriendly, but high-pitched. On the phone I might think he was a woman.

I stood and caught a glimpse of my bony self reflected in the window. The suit was decent, but something stuck up from the top of my head. Hoping it was hair and not a piece of scalp, I nodded a greeting. I didn't bother putting out my hand. Livebloods don't like to touch us.

"What can I do for you, Mr. Turgeon?"

He took off his hat and planted himself in the smaller chair in front of my desk. The old wood creaked loudly, but it didn't collapse. A good look at his face did nothing to deter my impression of him as a giant baby. His head was a series of puffy ovals, fat little egg shapes. As for his hair, well, he should have kept the hat on. It was braided in tight cornrows. Not the fashion choice I'd have made.

"You used to work for the police?" he asked.

He'd done his homework. I didn't like talking about my past, but Turgeon looked like he had money, and I wanted some. "Yeah. It's no secret."

"Until you were accused of beating your wife to death after discovering she'd had an affair with the chief detective, Thomas Booth?"

Nobody likes a show-off. Some things have emotional resonance even with a chak. That, for instance. Really strong feelings are physically uncomfortable for us, like forcing too much water through a thin, cracked tube. We don't like it.

"What's this about, Mr. Turgeon?"

He narrowed his egg eyes. "You can be offended. You're higher-functioning than most."

"You're pretty high-functioning yourself, for a live-blood."

"I'm sorry. I need to be sure who I'm working with."

The apology surprised me. We don't usually get that. It made me relax, but just a little. "Let me clear something up for you right now. I don't kill and eat people."

The puffy lines under his chin wobbled as he shook his head. "It's nothing like that. I have a touchy situation to resolve. I have to trust you first, though. May I ask another personal question?"

"Try it and see how it goes."

The chair creaked again as he shifted. "At work one day you received an e-mail with a photo showing your wife, Lenore, engaged in coitus with your boss."

He looked as if he were going to giggle when he said *coitus*. This time, I wasn't aware of having an emotional reaction, but my body disagreed. My knee started twitching.

"You put your fist through the wall," he went on, "then raced home. Your boss, concerned, followed with some men. They found you hovering over your dead wife. She'd been beaten with your baseball bat. You claimed you found her that way, but no one believed you; you were known for having a temper. You were found guilty and executed."

Point of pride, desire for the job, whatever, I struggled not to react, but my knee just wasn't doing it for me anymore. Fucking memory. It never rains but it pours. Fractured images, burning pricks, stabbed my brain: the color photo of Lenore and Booth together, the side of her enraptured face making a shadow on the nape of his neck, the feel of plasterboard buckling against my knuckles, the twisted, almost clownish look of surprise on Booth's face as he burst into our kitchen and saw all the blood. Then a blur.

The next clear sensation was my execution, the needle sliding into my arm, fishing for a vein, the sense of relief that it was all over. But it wasn't. Next thing, it's a few months later and I'm staring at the herpes sore on the lower lip of a chain smoker. He's giving me my ten-minute exit interview, explaining how I was one of the "lucky" ones. A grave diggers' strike left me on ice, refrigerated for three months. Between thick, wet coughs he says that with the right makeup, if I kept the lights low, I'd *almost* pass for a liveblood.

Never tried it. Kept forgetting.

He hands me my wallet and the little green vial I had in my pocket when I was arrested. Inside the wallet was sixteen bucks and two condoms. Lenore and I had been trying to have a kid, but when I didn't get a raise, she decided to wait.

The flashbacks retreated. Turgeon was still talking in his high, sweet voice. "Your fellow detectives were so eager to convict you, some DNA evidence was kept hidden from the defense. Between that and irregularities in your arrest and trial, you were exonerated and restored. Most people still think you're guilty."

He paused. His eyes flared as if he felt guilty about

dragging all this up, but he didn't say anything else. I figured that meant it was my move.

"Is there a question in there?"

He rubbed the brim of his hat. "Well . . . did you do it?"

I leaned back and twisted my head. Something in my neck cracked. I hoped it wasn't bone. "I'll answer you, but first, I like to know who I'm working with, too."

Turgeon pulled out an envelope and tossed it on the desk. It slid a little before coming to a halt against a crack in the veneer. I didn't have to pick it up to see it was stuffed with hundreds. Decent amount for a live-blood detective. For a chak? A fortune.

"I don't know what sort of cases you usually get, but I'm certain this isn't one of them. Your police background makes you perfect for what I need. I don't care if you lied to the jury, but I can't take the risk that you'd lie to me." He moved his shoulders in what seemed an apologetic fashion, then lowered his voice to a boyish hush. "So, did you kill your wife?"

"Honestly?" I told him. "I don't remember."

"In the court transcripts you say you were innocent."

"Did I? I've read them a few dozen times, but a chak's memory, right? I get flashes, but the actual moment? A total blank."

That's why I never went looking for her real killer. I'm afraid I'll find out it's me.

He zeroed in on my eyes. Like that would help. *Idiot, you can't read chak eyes.* It's like watching someone zoned in front of a TV or video game. They don't call it a zombie look for nothing. You can't tell a thing by looking at our eyes.

I met his gaze nice and steady, but it was like that lame wolf whistle I gave Misty, going through the paces out of politeness . . . acting, like a friend of mine says, *as if*, in this case as if I were still alive. Turgeon's eyes were a weird baby blue, the color so consistent he must have been wearing contacts. Funny thing to be vain about, but beauty's in the eye of the beholder.

Finally, he said, "I believe you," as if we were in his no-girls-allowed tree house, making some kind of pact.

A man of many pockets, he pulled a photo from one. It was a head shot, posed, showing a square-headed forty-year-old with close-cropped curly hair, a few lines on his face, and a decent smile. The top button of his blue shirt was loose, the collar not completely ironed, so whoever he was, he wasn't anal. Into himself enough to pose for a head shot, though.

"Frank Boyle," Turgeon said. "His father, Martin, was a close friend of my firm's founder, Mr. Trent Derby. Martin Boyle passed away last week from lung cancer and left all his money, a considerable sum, to his eldest son. I have to find him and let him know about his inheritance."

It was starting to make sense.

"Let me guess. Frank's a chak, right? On the streets somewhere, no known address?"

Turgeon nodded. "Exactly."

"Even so, why hire me? Why not a liveblood, or go to the cops?"

He rubbed his hat again. "It's complicated. He has a living brother and sister who are both contesting the will. They're people of influence who wouldn't think much of . . . getting rid of a chak to preserve their fortune. Mr. Derby is concerned that they may have already reached out to the local police and any real . . . uh, liveblood detective in the area. Sorry, no offense."

"None taken. I get your point. They'd never hire a chak, right?" I drummed my fingers on the envelope and tried to look as if I were thinking about it. "You're leaving out the other complication. Frank might be feral."

Turgeon made a funny little swallowing sound. "Naturally, that's a concern."

"Natural's got nothing to do with it." I laid my palm on the envelope. "I get paid whether he is or not, long as I find him for you before the sinister siblings?"

He nodded at the money as if embarrassed it was too little. "That's for accepting the job. I'll pay the same if you find him first, feral or not. Time is of the utmost. You have to start now. I need . . . I . . . *expect* immediate action. They can't be allowed to find him first."

I flipped through the bills. It was more than I'd guessed. I looked up into Turgeon's eyes, trying to suss him out. Mostly he looked nervous, which pretty much matched his story.

I picked up the envelope. I started to put it in my jacket pocket, forgetting there was a tear in the bottom. Before it fell into the lining I pulled it out and shoved it into the top desk drawer, trying to make it look like that had been the idea all along. The drawer stuck. I cursed under my breath until I got it closed.

"You'll take the case?" Eggman asked.

"Hey, you're the Eggman. Goo goo g'joob," I said.

I don't think he got the joke.

2

When Turgeon said *now*, I didn't realize how much he meant it. I offered to do some digging and call him in twenty-four hours, but he crossed his arms over his belly.

"I need results *tonight*. Frank Boyle may be in immediate danger, Mr. Mann," he said. After a beat, he lowered his head and tried to suppress a giggle. "Mr. Mann . . . Sorry . . ."

Yeah, the name Dad left me gets big yuks sometimes. I got into so many fights when I was a kid, they mistook me for the neighborhood bully. At least, I like to think they did. Part of the reason I joined the force was because Officer Mann or Detective Mann sounded better. Didn't always help. Once during a bust, a dealer, all buff and full of tattoos, saw my badge and said, "Jeepers, Mr. Mann!" He and his buddies had a real laugh riot until I coldcocked him with my nine-millimeter. He nearly lost an eye.

Police brutality? Nah. *Mr. Mann* brutality. Maybe I *was* the neighborhood bully.

These days, no pride to hurt. Hell, I had a hard enough time thinking of myself as a *real* detective. I sat there until Turgeon composed himself. I figure if he pays me enough, he can call me whatever he wants.

"I've got a couple of sources I can check out," I told him. "Misty can make you some coffee. I'll be back soon." That seemed to satisfy him.

Maybe the big rush should've set some bells off, but between wincing about my name and thinking about the dead presidents crammed in my desk, I was distracted. I snatched the head shot and left Misty to babysit. I kind of wished she had some car keys to jangle in front of him.

I trudged down three flights of interior squalor to get to the squalor on the street. The sun had pretty much said *screw this* and was headed home. A yellow Hummer was parked right in front of my building, a piece of gold in a toilet bowl. I figured it belonged to Turgeon. The only working streetlamp crackled like it was spitting the light on the sidewalk.

This was the Bones, the kind of place even crack heads see as a step down, six blocks of half walls, barbed wire left over from WWI, and vacant lots. Since we generally don't have jobs, homes, or most of our faculties, any Fort Hammer chak who doesn't hole up in a shantytown stays here. It's the better choice, but not by much. We're a city park away from a gated liveblood neighborhood, so the cops keep things relatively quiet. Not at the shanties, though. *Hakkers*, bored, disaffected livebloods, pick one every Friday and go play whack-a-chak, beating, cutting, and otherwise not letting the dead rest in peace. It's like a live-action role-playing game, only you can't tell who the monsters are.

Turgeon hired me probably thinking all chakz know one another. Truth is, he may have been better off on his own. Finding a particular chak was no easy trick. Yellowed finger bone in a haystack. There were four shantytowns everyone knew about: two in the desert, one near an old iron mine, and the biggest, Bedland, in an abandoned mattress factory. When I first came back, I stayed there a while, until a bad raid wised me up.

Since I barely remembered anyone from yesterday, my best play, my *only* play, was to find Jonesey. I'd known him long enough for the name and face to stick. Before he was wrongly convicted of childnapping, he was a motivational speaker. If you want it bad enough, you can have it; just act *as if*; that sort of horseshit. Had some books published. Somehow I don't think he was found guilty because he didn't want his freedom bad enough. Ha. When it turned out a year later that the kid was living with his aunt in another state, they brought him back. Oops. So sorry, Mr. Jones. Now he's a small-time dealer, and he knows not to call me Mr. Mann.

The dead make okay street dealers. They can't get hooked, and in a pinch they can take a bullet or three. Sure, eventually the damage gets too severe to patch with thread and Krazy Glue, but who cares? So what if pieces dangle, rot sets in, things fall off? Eventually they go feral, but by then there's not enough left to do much damage. It's a win-win.

A couple of cars trolled the field of potholes that passed for a street—most likely liveblood druggies hoping to score. If you're not an addict, alive, and here at night, then you're a whole new breed of pervert, into *chakking up*: a quick one with an animated corpse in the alley, or a drive back home, giving a whole new meaning to the phrase *dry humping*. And they know what they want. Back when Misty tried passing as a chak, it earned her a beating or two from disappointed johns. She showed me the bruises.

My dad once said to me, "There ain't a single thing in all creation someone hasn't tried to fuck." I was five or six at the time. Had no idea what he meant. Now I wish I didn't.

Then again, I've never heard of a chak, male or female, going feral from what pervs do to them. I guess there are some things we really just don't care about anymore.

Jonesey usually hung at the third lamppost down Cruger Avenue. Just my luck, tonight he wasn't there. That was a little weird. He was a regular guy, for a chak.

In his place, a real Romero type was leaning against a building like he was holding it up. The left side of his skull looked like it'd been caved in by an anvil.

Hoping his remaining ear still worked, I sauntered up. "Jonesey around?"

I got some grunts. He twisted his shoulder to the right, the arm dangling, useless. At the end of his hand, bones poked through blackened skin. I knew what it was, but a whiff of something putrid told me how bad.

"Hey, pal, watch the rot. Soak that in some bleach before you lose the muscle."

He gave me another grunt. I hoped I wasn't talking to myself.

"Bleach? You know? Kill the rot? Keep the fingers?"

Nothing. At least I tried. There's not much you can do for the low-level types.

I hoped Jonesey was all right, but I was starting to worry. The feral thing's hard to predict. I knew a chest, arm, and head that had its act together for years. Others go with a finger snap. The fastest was under thirty seconds, Tanya Felding. Funny story. She was a cover girl who died in a car accident. It was the early days of the process, so her agent figured he'd have his cash cow ripped. A little makeup, some plastic surgery, and he'd have the first living-dead model. The look was *in*. But the stupid docs, typically arrogant, thought they'd done such a great job, that right after she woke up, they shoved a mirror in her hands. It wound up embedded in one of their skulls. After tearing off another doc's face and swallowing it, sweet little Tanya was subdued and humanely D-capped. Her agent sued. Dunno if he won or not.

Jonesey was always a bit on edge, but I never took him for someone who'd go wild. That'd be bad news. If he'd picked tonight to fall off, I'd never find Boyle. Aside from which, I kind of liked Jonesey, insofar as I liked anyone. When I first moved to the Bones, he taught me some of his memory tricks, using weird images to remember people, like that baby-Eggman thing for what's-his-face.

Oh, yeah, Turgeon. See? Works sometimes.

If anyone could find Frank Boyle, it was him. The problem was finding Jonesey.

I tried turning my back on Anvil Head, but he grunted again, real loud, and kept it up. It was like Lassie trying to tell Mom that Timmy was trapped in a cave. I thought he wanted money, so against my better judgment I pulled out a buck and pressed it into his good hand.

He didn't want it. He pulled away quick. The loose arm fluttered like a bird wing.

All of a sudden I realized what he was trying to say.

He was answering my question about Jonesey, pointing as best he could toward the alley.

"Much obliged."

He nodded.

I pulled out the recorder and made a note to have Misty come out with the bleach. Could've called her, but I forgot my damn phone.

The alley was a car-wide slot between half-standing walls. Stepping in meant leaving even the sickly yellow streetlight behind. It'd been a hot day and I still felt it on the sidewalk, but as things went from dark to darker, it got noticeably cooler.

Takes longer for chak-eyes to adjust to lighting changes. I could make out a Dumpster, and the fact that there was more garbage outside it than in. I kept going, farther back, toward what looked like a fire escape.

I stepped on something. It was big, slightly soft, and when my foot hit it, it moaned.

Not a sound you want to hear in this neighborhood. Better to hear a snake rattle. Moaning is what chakz do right before, and after, they go feral.

This one obviously wasn't feral yet, or it'd be chewing on me. It looked like he was under some cardboard. Poor bastard probably felt it coming on and crawled in here to be alone when it happened. We have an instinct for that sort of thing, like dogs.

I didn't think it was Jonesey, but I had to be sure. Jonesey had a red flannel piece of crap he called his lucky shirt. They buried him in it. When they rip you, they give you a cheap new set of clothes, generally prison gray, but Jonesey turned it down and kept his lucky shirt. It was the only shirt he ever wore. I think over time it melded with his skin, and he couldn't get it off anymore.

Not that I'm one to judge. Besides, it made him easy to spot.

I lit a match and knelt for a better look. The moaner wasn't him. I snapped the match out before it reached my finger. Odds are I'd feel the burn, but no sense in taking chances.

My big plan was heading nowhere. I put an elbow against the Dumpster and tried to gather the few thoughts I had. This is often a bad move. I never know what I'll get. This time, a picture of Wilson's head popped into my mind. I'd only seen the guy on TV, and here he was eye-balling me like I was supposed to do something about his unfortunate situation. Like what? Buy him a hat?

It wasn't ESP, more like my brain was a cave about to crumble. Strong picture, though, colors vivid enough to make you puke. I'd been thinking about the head too damn much, the way I used to close my eyes and see cards if I stayed up all night playing poker.

It was starting to get to me. And I never knew which freaky obsession would be my last. If I wasn't careful about my mood, I'd wind up sharing a cardboard quilt with the moaner at my feet. If I had a happy place I'd try to go there, but I don't.

What was wrong with me, other than the usual? Maybe it was all that talk with Turgeon about Lenore. Lenore. There's a famous poem about someone named Lenore, real famous, but I can never remember it. I wonder if the guy who wrote it knew whether he'd killed his Lenore or not.

Damn it, Lenore!

I may have started moaning right then and there. I'll never know, because a big distraction showed up. A shadow flew down from the fire escape, right at me, looking like a dark sheet hurled out of a window. One second there was building and sky, the next, just black.

It wasn't a sheet. It was heavier, and it caught me at just the right angle. I went down. My back slapped the asphalt. I didn't quite feel it, but I heard the crunch, so I knew it was bad. Praying I hadn't broken my ribs, I brought my hands up and grabbed what felt like an empty leather wineskin.

It was a neck. I heard teeth gnashing, dried lungs wheezing. Then I caught a flash of red flannel.

"Geez, Jonesey!"

Like I said, any of us can go, and it's hard to predict when. Once you're feral, the cops *do* get involved, especially in the Bones, since we're so close to that gated neighborhood. They'll hunt you down, shoot you until you can't move, then cart you off for a quick D-cap. So they say. More likely they'd need fire or a meat grinder. None of it sounds pleasant.

Feral chakz aren't much of a threat unless they come at you in numbers. Sort of like a poodle with rabies. You can kick it away, but you really don't want it to get ahold of you, with its teeth or anything else. They do get all animal, as the name implies, like the body suddenly remembers it has instincts.

I tossed him off—I still have some muscle left. He rolled into a crouch. As I lumbered to my feet, he came at me, mouth open, teeth like rotting bits of a yellow moon.

The reason you don't want them to get ahold of you isn't that they'll infect you. Once a chak grabs onto something, feral or not, he doesn't let go unless he wants to. If Jonesey grabbed me, I'd have to break his hand off to get free, and unfortunately, I liked him.

I stuck one hand out, open palmed, and planted it in his chest. It stopped him in his tracks long enough for me to give him a good hard slap. His eyes rolled in their sockets. Good sign. He felt it. There was still a light on in the attic.

I slapped him again, harder. "Jonesey! Jonesey! You in there?"

Third time I whacked him so hard I was afraid I'd pulled off some cheek skin.

"Come on out of there, Jonesey!"

Maybe the shirt really was lucky, or maybe it was just another random act of the universe, but he closed his mouth and shivered. I stepped back to put some distance between us, but his head bobbed like I was still slapping him. He brought his hands up to steady his skull. He blinked six or seven times and then aimed his pupils in my direction. They were still vibrating, but after a second they settled down.

"Mann, that you? I am so sorry. . . ."

"You and me both."

Low-level chakz tend to go feral and stay that way. The "lucky" or smart ones drift in and out first. It's never a good sign. If a gun would work on him, and I had one, I'd be tempted to put him out of his misery.

I didn't tell him that. "Christ, Jonesey, if I'd been a liveblood you'd be . . ."

He twisted his lips into a familiar shit-eating smile. "What? Dead?"

"Well, in a lot worse shape than you are now."

"Worse? Oh, Mann, I know, I know. Funny, I used to tell people that death was just another form of consciousness. I had no idea. No fucking idea. What day is it?"

He had big eyes, the kind that looked soulful back when

they had some meat around them. Now they popped like the googlies on a cheap doll. You could still see it, though, the whole charismatic-motivational-speaker thing. Once that grin was exactly the sort a lost soul would trust enough to hand over his hard-earned cash on the chance Jonesey really might teach him the secrets of the universe.

I hate con men. I'd have hated Jonesey when he was alive. Not a problem now.

I checked my watch. "Tuesday. You need the date?"

He nodded, so I checked my watch again. "August twelfth."

He looked up and groaned. Groaning is better than moaning. It's intentional. "Six fucking days, Mann, that's how long I've been out."

I took a step closer. "What happened? You're usually Mr. Positive Thinking. Someone forget your birthday?"

I was half kidding. Jonesey thought in extremes. He was either a self-styled superhero or a bug lying against the wall too worthless to crush. I don't know if that was a result of being ripped or if he was bipolar before-hand, too.

"My birthday? Hah. *I* don't even remember that! I had a . . . uh, professional setback. One that interfaced negatively with my life plan."

I gave him a look. His grin widened, his roller coaster on a definite climb.

"Fine, my *after*life plan. Two livebloods in a blue SUV stole my stash. I lost a half gram of meth. I tried to picture a positive outcome, focused, meditated, tried to make it real, y'know? But when it came down to it, I couldn't face my supplier. He says I'm the only chak in the world he can count on, and I just couldn't go there, not with him. I crawled in here to meditate and . . . zoned out."

"Six days ago. Ever happen before? The feral thing, I mean."

His brow crunched. "What feral thing?"

I gave him another look. My memory wasn't *that* bad yet.

The grin faded a bit. "No. That was the first time. I swear."

He was lying, but I let it go. Making him think about it too much could send him off again.

"Anything I can do? I've got some cash these days."

"Really? Good for you! I knew you could do it. Were you putting the vibes out there? Acting as if? Faking it until you make it?"

"Sure. Something like that."

He pushed his head around like he was trying to snap it back into place. "Spot me five for a double espresso? Helps me focus. I know those two addicts. I know where they live. If I really bring the right attitude toward it I can talk them into giving me the stash back, or at least paying something for it. If not, at least I can go feral on someone who deserves it, right?"

"Right. Espresso, huh? That . . . you know, work?"

He shrugged. "Seems to. Maybe it just reminds me." He tapped his temple. "Head game. But it's all head games, right?"

Head was the wrong word to use around me at the moment. I pulled out the photo, if only to change the subject. "This is why I was trying to find you. Know him?"

He took it between his fingers, moved it around in the scant light.

"Hair's a little different, and he doesn't have all that flesh anymore, but . . . of course I do. What was it? Pimple. Boyle. Frank Boyle. Lives in Bedland. Last I heard, anyway. You got that five?"

I pulled out a crumpled bill, the last I had on me, and stuffed it in his pocket.

"I thought the doubles were only four bucks."

"I like to tip the barista," he said. "Keep a good thought, Mann!"

I watched him shamble off, hoping he didn't go feral in Starbucks.

Then again, he wouldn't be the first.

3

Mr. Turgeon was full of surprises.

"Tonight? You want to go *tonight*?"

He could laugh his wobbly ass off at my last name all he wanted, but I wasn't getting maimed for a few bucks, even for a lot of bucks. I tried to put it politely. "Look, Mr. Turgeon, I admire your tenacity, but even armed liveblood cops don't go to Bedland after sunset on a Friday."

"I understand the risk."

"No, sir. I don't think you do. Every meathead in Fort Hammer gets the weekend off from his shitty job. They spend it looking for more exciting ways to get off, and hakking is the number one sport. If the hakkers don't kill us, the ferals they leave behind will. Add to that the fact that we don't even know if your boy can still answer to his name. . . ."

Pursing his lips, he looked out the window. The flighty evening glow had vanished into a more honest dark. "I told you. We *have* to find him before his siblings. There are four shantytowns, aren't there? And the hakkers only attack one? Doesn't that put the odds in our favor?"

One in four. I looked at Misty. She shook her head, no way. I agreed.

"Sorry, Mr. Turgeon. Bedland's the favorite, the biggest target. They just use the others for practice. Unless you want to wait until morning, you're on your own. Believe me, it'll be well worth the wait, if only because you get to live another day."

I wanted to put the fear of God into him. He did me one better and summoned Mammon. He reached into his jacket pocket and pulled out another envelope stuffed with cash.

"Take it. There's a third just like it if we find him."

Crazy son of a bitch. I reached for the bills.

"No," Misty said.

I owed her, I should have listened to her, but the money would be too good for both of us. For that kind of cash *she'd* take the chance if she could. I nodded for her to step out into the little anteroom that doubled as her bedroom. She grimaced, but did.

I hefted the envelope and finally asked a decent question. "How much is Derby paying *you* to find Boyle? Take it from someone who knows: It's not worth being dead for a bigger flat-panel TV, even if it is HD."

If he was afraid, his face didn't show it, but he rubbed the rim of his hat, turned the Stetson like it was a little steering wheel and he was trying to avoid an oncoming truck. Appearances aside, I got a strong sense of naïveté from his demeanor. He knew what he wanted, but so does an infant. I wasn't even sure if he'd been out at night by himself.

Finally, he spoke. "You know how some men slave all their lives in a job they hate to give their wives and children a better life?"

I shook my head. "You don't strike me as a family man."

The hat stopped moving. "That's the point. I'm *not*. I don't have a wife, children, or friends, just this job I do. Mr. Derby made it clear that if I *didn't* find Frank Boyle, I'd be fired. I don't want to work anywhere else. I just don't. I can't. I can't let him fire me. I'd rather . . ."

His voice sounded distant, but I didn't have any reason to doubt him. It was pathetic enough to be true. If I didn't go with him, he could toddle out there all by himself and get hit by a car.

I tossed my hands up. "Your funeral, my mutilation. Do you have a gun?"

I was still trying to scare him, but, surprise, surprise, he nodded. Maybe he wasn't as stupid as I thought. If I didn't know it'd come out more like a hiss, I'd have sighed.

"Then let me get mine. Assuming that yellow Hummer outside is yours, I'll meet you at the car."

He smiled like Mommy had pinched his cheek; then he rolled up to standing and ambled on out. The second the outer door clicked, Misty rushed back in, all teary-eyed.

"No fair—you know I can't cry," I told her.

"Don't go, Hess. Even if they don't chop you up, you shoot a liveblood, even by accident, and they catch you, it'll be worse than death."

"Like this isn't?" I said. When she didn't react, I grimaced. "I wasn't going to tell you, but half an hour ago, Jonesey went feral and nearly had me for dinner. I shook him out of it, but it's just a matter of time now."

Misty lowered her head. "Shit. He's one of the smart ones."

I poked a thumb into my chest. "Smarter than me, Mist. So how long do I have? And who even knows if ripping is permanent? We could all go, any minute. I don't make some kind of move now, I might never be able to, right?"

She didn't say anything.

"Right?" I asked again. I sounded angry. I *was* angry, taking it out on her just because she was worried about me. It's so much easier to think about not existing if you can be sure you won't take anyone with you.

She made a face. I let it go.

I opened the lower desk drawer and removed the false bottom. I had two things hidden there, both contraband: a little vial of green liquid and a Walther P99. The vial's its own story. For now, I took out the gun, a nice combo of stopping power and low recoil. Too little of the former, whatever I shot would still be coming at me. Too much of the latter, I could tear my arm off by firing the damn thing. It's totally illegal for a chak to own a weapon, but you never know when breaking the law might suddenly become the best idea in the world.

"You're doing this because of the money?" Misty wasn't finished yet.

"Partly," I said, checking over the gun. "It's also something to do. I'm curious about this Boyle guy. Being curious is good. Better than watching TV."

Satisfied he'd perform, I shoved Walther between the back of my pants and the small of my back.

I turned to Misty, looked in her eyes, and touched her cheek. The last of her tears, a big one, rolled onto my finger. The dead flesh sopped it up like a sponge. "We have to be realists, right? We have to be. More than likely, I'll be back this time. But do me a favor, Misty? If and when I do go, make sure my head's totaled. Crushed or something. Not just a D-cap. And definitely not fire."

"I hate it when you talk like this, Hess."

I forced my lips into a smile. It hurts to do that, ever since I died, but I had to show her I was still in here. "Me, too. But I'll feel better if you promise. So?"

"I promise."

I turned her head side to side, studying her a bit. Her cheeks were so hollow when we met, from the drugs, that her face had no affect. Now it was easy to see how worried she was. I was her lifeline. I really was risking both of us. "You're looking better. Try not to worry too much. I like to think I'm not an idiot. And you heard the big baby. We've got a one–in-four shot at a quiet night."

I took a hundred from the envelope and held it out to her. "If you want to keep busy, you can get some more bleach and go down to Cruger. Flat-headed guy there has some finger rot. Can't miss him if you follow your nose."

She eyed the bill. Depression meant one thing for me, something else for her.

"Got anything smaller?" she asked.

I looked in the envelope. "Nope."

"Too much temptation. Keep it. I still got some bleach left. Should be enough for some fingers. We'll go pick up some more when you get back. And you'd *better* get back in exactly as many pieces as you are now or I'm taking that envelope, buying a shitload of crack, and smoking it until I get to see God face-to-face so I can demand an apology from his almighty ass for this fucked-up life. You got that?"

I gave her a salute and headed for the door. "Deal. Say hi for me."

She tossed me my cell. "Call him yourself."

There's better than the Bones, but Fort Hammer's generally crappy. The city used to have a manufacturing base and a big insurance industry, but when hard times hit, it was just like that little old lady on the commercial who'd fallen and couldn't get up. You couldn't blame anyone here. The citizens were all doing exactly the same things we did during the boom years. But sometimes it rains, and sometimes it rains hard.

These days Fort Hammer's two big claims to fame are one of the highest murder rates in the country and *the* highest execution rate. Cheers went up in bars across town when we pushed ahead of Texas. One town, ahead of Texas.

That's where the rest of us chakz come from, myself included: the death penalty.

It makes perfect sense, as long as you don't think about it too much. The same year they started ripping the dead, improvements in DNA testing revealed an embarrassing number of wrongful executions. Ethically, the biggest argument against the death penalty was that it could never be undone. Thanks to our caring friends at ChemBet, now it could be.

Sure, most livebloods decided real fast that it was better to leave their loved ones resting in peace, but the state saw it as a way of rectifying what was euphemistically referred to as "certain inadequacies in the judicial system." Thanks to the Revivification as Restitution Act, (RAR), the wrongfully executed were brought back as chakz. Oops, sorry! No harm, no foul, right? If anything, it made it *easier* to give someone a lethal injection in the first place.

Not that anyone ever asks the deceased. I've yet to see a new chak run around screaming, "It's great to be back, Fort Hammer!"

But here we are.

I gave Turgeon's car a once-over. I don't go for gas-guzzlers, but the Humvee was probably the only model that'd make him look normal size. I opened the door, surprised to hear some particularly misogynist gangsta rap on the sound system, the lyrics going on about there being one less bitch to worry about. I gave him a look as I climbed in. After a little giggle, he shut it off and our great buddy movie began.

Sure to be a classic.

Other than the damage to the environment, the drive was uneventful. It's a straight line to the outskirts of town, so it even lacked the excitement of turning. Soon, with the city lights behind us and a single-lane highway ahead, Turgeon made a stab at conversation. If only he'd decided to talk about the weather.

"Do you really think we might die tonight?"

"*You* might. Me? Been there. Done that. Got other problems now."

"I'm not afraid of dying, you know," he said. Then he asked the question every chak loves to hear. "But . . . what is . . . what is it like? Being dead?"

I stared into his blue contacts. "What's it like? What's it look like?"

I don't usually talk like that to a client, but I already

had two envelopes full of his cash, I was risking my neck, and he had a habit of pushing the wrong buttons.

He shrugged. "I don't mean now. I mean before ... when you *were* dead." He kept his voice soft, as if that meant he was concerned about my feelings. "You know, *really* dead. Right after the execution."

I leaned back and stared at the headlight beams. "Oh, then. Everything went dark for a little while, and then I saw a bright, golden light at the end of a long tunnel. It felt warm, welcoming. I could see, on the other side, all my deceased loved ones, beckoning me forward to everlasting joy. I've never been happier."

His lips parted. They stayed that way a while, like his nose was stuffed and he had to breathe through his mouth. "Really?"

"No."

"What, then?"

"I don't remember."

"Do you know ..."

"And no, I don't know any other chak who remembers, either. One of us would have written a book about it by now, don't you think? Had the money stolen by a publisher or an agent?"

He wasn't about to let it go, though. "So it was quiet for you? A big nothing?"

"I don't know means I don't know."

"So strange. They conquer death and still don't know what it is."

"Yeah, a real laugh riot, like Woody Allen's early films."

I hoped that was the end of it, but no. He was like a kid asking why the sky was blue, just so he could ask why again.

"Is it different?"

"Is what different?"

"The *way* you don't remember death. Is it the same as not remembering whether you killed your wife?"

Now he was back to pressing the other button. And here I had so few.

"For the love of . . ."

"I'm sorry. I'm only curious. Please tell me."

I squirmed in my seat, wondering if there was any other way to get him to shut up. Something told me there wasn't. "Fine. Whatever. Yeah, it's different. I don't *miss* not remembering what death was like."

He had to think about that. "So . . . that means you *do* want to know about your wife?"

"No. I didn't say that . . . but with Lenore, I feel . . . a gap."

"Ever try to push at it, try to get it back?"

"You *should* be a lawyer, you know? All the questions? There are some things you don't want to push at."

He didn't like that answer. "I don't understand. What do you mean? Why not?"

I felt like a rat trying to get out of a maze. Images started clawing at me, Lenore's face turning into Colin Wilson's head.

Maybe I should tell him a bedtime story, distract both of us. "There's something I do remember. It's a story, but if I tell it to you, you've got to stop asking."

"Why?"

Jeez. "Because if you can't figure it out from this, I can't explain it to you. Okay?"

I'd never seen a grown man pout before. Frankly, I never wanted to see it again.

"All right," he said. "Tell me your story."

Satisfied we had a deal, I went into it. "Back when I was a cop, there was this suicide. Guy named Flitwick stuck a garden hose from his exhaust into the driver-side window of his Lexus and closed his garage door. He climbed behind the wheel and let the engine run until his heart stopped beating and his brain stopped doing whatever the hell it is a brain does. According to his friends and family, though, he had everything to live for. He didn't suffer from depression, business was great, and he'd even brought his wife back from the dead.

"Booth thought it smelled funny. He never liked chakz, so he had me take a look at the wife. She was my first chak interview. Quiet little thing. Wouldn't say mousy so much as still. Didn't move or talk much. Detectives have, like, a radar for liars, but the cues are different with the dead. I didn't know what to make of her. I didn't think she'd killed him, but I couldn't tell whether she felt guilty or didn't feel much at all.

"For her part, she didn't have a clue why we were suspicious about her husband's death. I had to spell it out—if he didn't have a reason to kill himself, maybe she did. That, she seemed adamant about. The idea made her shake, like it hurt to think about. She didn't hurt him, she said; they'd always loved each other deeply.

"When it dawned on her how important it was, though, she did tell me something she hadn't told anyone else. Mr. Flitwick kept a journal. He wanted to keep it private, so she'd kept it from the police and hadn't even read it herself. It's a chak thing, especially among the low-levels, taking things too literally. Private meant private. But with a little coaxing, she did give it to me, and it did explain things.

"According to what he'd written, ever since he'd

brought her back, Flitwick felt something was missing. Nothing crass, like sex—he understood the limits of the process—but there was, in his words, a sense of intimacy missing. He thought it had to do with the fact that she'd experienced death and he hadn't. So he kept asking, like you, what's it like? What's it like?

"She told him what I told you, she didn't remember, but that wasn't enough. Flitwick was convinced she'd had some mystical experience, and that was what was keeping them apart. If only he could feel what she'd felt, they could love each other the same way again, whatever that means. I'd seen that kind of thinking in rape or violent crime cases. It's a variation on survivor's guilt. Some spouses even put themselves in dangerous situations, trying to get the same thing to happen to them.

"In Flitwick's case I don't know if it was guilt, curiosity, or exactly like he said, but he decided to kill himself. He didn't tell her why, though, didn't want her to know he doubted their relationship. He figured that of course she'd bring him back. Then they'd be together like in the old days. Cue sappy music. So one fine morning, he kissed her on the cheek, headed to the garage, and sucked down some exhaust fumes. But she didn't bring him back. As far as I know, she never considered it. Once I knew the whole story, of course I told her about her husband's expectations."

Turgeon was wide-eyed, but I let him hang until he asked.

"And did she? Did she bring him back like he'd wanted?"

"No."

He looked angry. "Why? Why not?"

"I asked her the same question. Even had the same

look on my face you do now. She had a hard time phrasing it, and I didn't really understand until I came back myself, but it was something along the lines of she'd never do that to anyone, let alone someone she loved."

He exhaled, made a sound like a word. I think it may have been *bitch*, like from the song he was listening to. No wonder he didn't have a family.

Whether the story satisfied his curiosity or not, the conversation was over. A dull glow to our right told me we were nearly there. Dim orange fingers poked through the maze of dead branches. I tapped him on the shoulder.

"Slow up. You'll miss the turn."

His head twisted. "Is that a fire? Does it mean the hakkers are here?"

"Nah. All it means is that they don't have electricity."

Even so, I rolled down the window and listened carefully. Nothing.

"The real thing to worry about is a motorcycle whine," I explained. "Hakkers love riding in on rice grinders. Makes them feel like they're playing polo or something. Your hearing's probably better than mine. Keep your ears peeled and don't keep any strange sounds to yourself."

He nodded. "If you don't mind my asking, then, you've seen an attack?"

"I never mind smart questions. Not usually, anyway. Yeah, I did, once. It's why I moved back to the city. Look, Mr. Turgeon, I was against it, but we're here now and things look quiet. Do what I say when I say it and I think we'll have a decent shot at getting out of this in one piece. Okay?"

He didn't answer. He was so mesmerized by the dark

rectangles of the buildings above the tree line that he missed the turn. We had to back up.

Not a good start.

Once we were pointed the right way, the Turgeon-mobile took the buckled asphalt and rocks easily. I started thinking the Hummer wasn't a bad idea. It could probably even handle its share of machete and crowbar blows. Worse came to worst we could take cover in it. Wished it wasn't piss yellow, though. Aside from being embarrassing, the gaudy color was easy to spot.

After a few curves, the road straightened on a nice postcard view of Bedland. Years back, Mayor Kagan and the board convinced Bedland Mattresses Inc. to open a factory here. Everyone thought it'd bring a ton of jobs. Two thousand, they guessed. In the middle of construction, the recession hit. Bedland went under, and I don't mean under the blankets, and stiffed a bunch of local contractors. One wound up throwing himself off the main building so his family could collect on his life insurance policy. Nobody ever brought him back either. Lucky bastard.

With the girders, concrete, and drywall in place for three buildings, it made a perfect home-away-from-home for a certain class of pulse-challenged undesirables.

The banana-mobile crunched along, its halogen headlights hitting makeshift tents and tin-and-cardboard huts. They usually housed the overflow crowd, but they were dark, lifeless, to coin a phrase. The fire lights we'd seen from the main road were inside the buildings. Funny.

Funnier still when, as we watched, one by one, those lights went out.

They'd spotted us. It dawned on me that there was

another really good reason coming here at night was a stupid idea. Mistaken identity. Nobody ever visits shantytowns at night except hakkers, so that's what they took us for. How could I be so stupid?

"Slow down!" I said.

Too late. The air in front of the Hummer exploded.

Turgeon slammed the brakes so hard the shoulder belt nearly crushed my collarbone. As the heat blast hit the windshield, an enormous fire flower blossomed a few yards ahead. I could barely make out the shape of the wrecked car behind it.

"The chakz are getting more aggressive in their defense tactics," I said. I was impressed. I opened the glove compartment and found a flashlight. With a click the light came on.

"Are you sure it's the chakz?" Turgeon said. His voice had gone up half an octave.

"Pretty much. Relax. Kill the engine and get out of the car, slow. Once we're outside, don't say anything; just stand behind me."

He was busy staring at the fire, so I had to tap him and repeat myself. Once he cut the ignition, he pulled a large piece from the same jacket pocket that used to hold the envelopes.

Looked like a forty-five.

"Put that away," I hissed. "And don't take it out again unless I say otherwise."

He hesitated.

I put my hand on the gun. "This is what you paid for, right? My expertise?"

He gave me that pouty expression again, but shoved it back in his pocket. I wanted to pat him on the cheek and tell him what a good boy he was.

Instead, I got out, my eyes half on the fire, half on Turgeon. Once I was certain he was between me and the Hummer, I faced the burning car and held up my arms.

"Hey! We're not hakkers, you idiots! You think those lowlifes could afford wheels like this? You think if they *could* they'd drive it out here and scratch the finish? Hello?"

Nothing. I pointed to my face.

"I'm one of you! I'm a chak! Hessius Mann! Any of you out there with half a brain left know me?"

Again, nothing.

Turgeon nudged me and whispered, "Ask about Boyle."

I waved him off. "Shh! They heard me. They're thinking about it. Keep quiet and watch."

I trained my eyes on the edges of the flames, trying to peer into the long, flat darkness between the burning car and the main factory building. That's when I saw them. They'd blended in so well with the shadows, the dead bushes, the broken bits of concrete, they were as good as invisible until they moved. It was as if they'd planned it that way.

Chakz. Lots. Five. Ten. Twenty. All shambling toward us. A field of rotting flesh and gnashing teeth.

"Oh, my God," Turgeon said. He whimpered and staggered backward.

I kept my eyes on what was coming and muttered, "You think?"

4

The closest was a real walking-dead poster child—a gleet in a construction jumpsuit with a juicy hole in his forehead the size of a golf ball. Arms out Frankenstein style, he looked as if he was leading the others like a parade marshal.

There's a song in there somewhere, but I don't know what it is.

As they came forward, I was more worried about Turgeon. He held his ground, but shook so badly I felt a breeze at my back. I was afraid he'd do something stupid that'd require quick thinking on my part, or at least a phone call to Misty to say good-bye.

If the shambling didn't freak him, the moaning would. It rose above the crackle of the car fire, one sandpaper-dry voice overlapping another, making a steady rush, like the ocean on a white-noise machine.

When a chak moans in torpor, I take it for sorrow, profound sorrow. That doesn't explain it in a feral. At that point, why moan at all? There's also the weird fact that when a feral shambles, he moans louder, as if there's a gear connecting the diaphragm and the legs, like the way a pigeon's head bobs when it walks. Human body is a complicated mother. The dead ones more so. Sometimes my left leg shakes like it's hooked up to a vibrator.

Sure enough, soon as Frankenstein was three yards off, Turgeon went for his gun. I grabbed his elbow. It was a breach in living/dead etiquette, but too fucking bad if he didn't like a chak touching him. The fat moved loosely aside under my fingers, as if I hadn't gauged my own strength correctly. The elbow was surprisingly bony.

He yelped and tried to pull his arm free.

"No!" I said. "Listen to me. If they're feral, it won't help. Kneecap one and you'll only piss the others off."

His face went blank. "You said to bring a gun."

"For the hakkers!" I said. "But I guess we should have gone over that in the car, huh?"

"What *do* we do?"

I was about to tell him to dive for the Humvee, but something caught my eye. The minute I'd said "hakkers," Frankenstein blinked. Blinking is not something ferals do. It could've been a trick of the light, but I didn't think so. Plus, they were already close enough to charge, but hadn't.

I raised my voice so anyone listening could hear me. "Mr. Turgeon, I know you're scared, but please put the gun away for now, nice and slow."

The moment it disappeared into his pocket, the crowd slowed. I heard a relieved hiss.

Damn.

I rolled my eyes. "Who the fuck do you think you're playing with?" I yelled.

"What? I did what you asked!" Turgeon said.

"Not you, *them*!"

I took a step toward the crowd. "I already said I was one of you!" I shone the flashlight up into my face. "You think I need this crap?"

When Frankenstein stopped and squinted, it was obvious even to Turgeon they'd been faking. It was a setup. They'd taken us for hakkers and hoped a mass of ferals might scare us off. If we'd been a bunch of drunks on motorcycles it could've worked. Nice.

Frankie held up his hand. "False alarm! Everyone back to places!"

More moans. Not desolate, just annoyed. He jerked a thumb at the burning car. "And somebody put that thing out!"

I stuck my hand out open palmed and took our new friend's paw in my wrinkled mitt.

"He's just nervous," I said, pointing back at Turgeon.

"He's not the only one, Mann. I'm Thornell. Word is Bedland's getting hit tonight."

I let go of his hand and punched the air. "Shit! Shit! Shit! That's what all the theatrics are about?"

"Hell, yeah," Thornell said. "It's not like the cops are going to help." As if it itched, he rubbed the rim of the hole in his head, then wiped his fingers on his arm. "You're so worried about it, what're you doing here? We figured you had to be hakkers. Who else?"

I'd hoped to play this close to the chest, in case anyone working for Boyle's siblings was here ahead of us. But with the hakker odds ramped up, my strategy shifted.

"Long story short, I've got some good news for a chak I heard stays here."

Thornell laughed. That meant that he was high-functioning, and that he was easing up on us. "Good news? Didn't know they made that kind."

"Yeah, there are probably snowballs in hell, too." I pulled out the photo. "Frank Boyle. Look familiar?"

Thornell stared and scratched his forehead hole again. "We've got a Frank, but that's not him."

Maybe he wasn't all that high-functioning. You never know which parts of the brain are working, and that hole meant at least some was missing.

"Look again. Picture him dead a few months."

He squinted, shook his head a while, but finally nodded. "Yeah, yeah. That *is* Frank. One of our community organizers. Lives in a room off the front hall of the admin building. Shares a space with Ashby."

I raised my eyebrows. "Shares? I didn't think we went for roomies."

Thornell gave me a good-natured shrug. "I don't, but he does. It's company, I guess. Rumor is the kid reminds Frank of someone, maybe a younger brother."

"Kid?"

"Oh, yeah, yeah. Ashby's a juvie. They tried him as an adult for shooting a cop with his own gun during a convenience-store robbery."

Having been a detective means I heard a lot of the local RAR stories. This one rang a bell because it sucked so much. "Right. Didn't bother with ballistics, then found out the cop's gun misfired. He'd accidentally shot himself. Hey, I do remember things sometimes."

"Good for you," Thornell said. "Good for Boyle, too, I guess. Hope he stays. This whole thing was his idea. He's one of the smart ones. We don't have many."

That bit of news lowered my threat level from panicked to anxious. Not only was Boyle here, but we'd be able to talk to him. I nudged Turgeon, but he didn't look as happy as I thought he should. He was probably still thinking about the hakkers.

Thornell looked over his shoulder at the smoldering car fire. "Better get back to my spot. Whatever business you've got with Frank, be quick."

He trudged off, calling the names of a few stragglers. Some tripped, bumped into one another, backed up, and bumped into one another again.

The smart ones are pretty rare. It must have taken hours for them to set that trap up.

Turgeon still seemed out of it, so I said, "We could come back in the morning."

Stunned as he was, he shook his head no. Right answer. One, we were too close to give up now, and two, by morning, after the hakker attack, Boyle might not be one of the smart ones anymore.

I didn't feel good about leaving the Humvee behind, but the smoldering car was blocking the road. Pointing the flashlight at the broken asphalt, I nodded for Turgeon to follow. He stayed so close behind me, if I so much as slowed down, he'd smack into me. I had to tell him twice to give me some space.

Like the dead, the place had yet to be completely reclaimed by nature. We made our way along a concrete path shattered and cracked a thousand times by years, neglect, and pretty thick weeds. Whenever we passed some chakz, they'd moan, not stopping until I pointed the light up at my kisser and mentioned Thornell. Then they cursed us out.

Admin was a smaller building sitting to the right of the massive factory, the upscale Bedland neighborhood, compared to the middle-class factory and the makeshift shelter ghetto. By the time we reached it, all the fires inside had gone out, leaving the place as pitch-black as it gets.

Back when I lived here, I'd managed a spot in the factory, but admin was where I'd want to hole up in case of attack. The concrete walls were so thick and strong, they seemed smug. The windows were tall and narrow, more for light than air, not wide enough for a man to pass through. The only spot that might be vulnerable was the front entrance.

Still, even as we walked up to it I couldn't see inside. The dirt on the glass doors was so thick it sent the flashlight beam bouncing back empty-handed. There could be an army or a toy store in there and I wouldn't know until it was too late. Good for Boyle. If he was really lucky there'd be a rear entrance and a basement.

Turgeon was getting too close again. I put a hand back to restore some distance, then pushed the door open with my foot. It swung in noiselessly. Someone kept the hinges oiled.

I turned the beam to the four corners and crept into the tomblike reception area. It was surprisingly intact, with a front desk, still-life paintings on the wall, and one or two plastic potted plants. There was a big cracked coffee table surrounded by cushioned seats and couches. Some chak who was either anal or had kept his sense of humor had put a few magazines out on it. Far to the left there was a wide hallway with closed doors. Offices, I figured.

But no sound came from anywhere.

Turgeon whispered, "Now what?"

"Call him?" I suggested. I was going to try it myself, but he beat me to it.

"Is Frank Boyle here?" His thin voice didn't even echo.

"Connect the dots," I whispered. "Give him details. Little louder wouldn't hurt, either."

"Mr. Boyle, I have a message from your father!"

Nothing.

"More."

"Your dead father. I mean . . . I'm sorry to say that your father passed away. That's why I'm here. It's unusual, considering your condition . . . but he's left you a lot of money. His name is Martin Boyle. That's your father, yes? I'm his attorney. Actually, I work for his friend. . . ."

Turgeon sounded like a bank manager from Ghana who wanted to transfer $62 million directly into Boyle's bank account if he'd only kindly supply his social security number and blood type. I guess I should've done the talking.

He was about to say something else, but he didn't have to. A sound like crinkling paper, but heavier, slower, came from that left-hand hall. The third door down, barely visible from where we stood, opened.

I aimed the light and caught a chak stepping out. My flashlight beam made his dilated pupils glow. He had a shock of curly hair I recognized from the photo. Half the skin on his face was gone, though. From the look of the other half, it may have been what scared it off.

He was of average height, good shoulders, and definitely Frank Boyle.

"My father's dead?" he said in an even tone.

Turgeon smiled widely, way too pleased with himself to realize it's not particularly appropriate to wear a shit-eating grin when you say, "Yes. Lung cancer."

Before I could tell if Boyle cared, a string-bean shadow appeared behind him, shorter body, longer hair. It had a nasal, whiny voice that was even more annoying than Turgeon's.

"Okay if I come out, Frank? Heh-heh."

Boyle looked at Turgeon, then at me. I gave him a nod.

"Yeah, Ashby, it's okay," Boyle said.

Ashby stepped into the flashlight beam. He was a good half foot shorter, blond hair and aquiline nose. His smooth features made me think his bones hadn't fully matured at the time of death.

"You tell 'em I didn't shoot that cop? Heh-heh," he said. I could tell by the way he twitched as he spoke that he wasn't one of the smart ones.

Boyle grimaced like he was embarrassed.

"Yeah, we know all about that," I said. "We know it wasn't you."

"Good. Heh-heh. Because it wasn't. Heh-heh."

"Sometimes he thinks he's still in prison, waiting on his appeal," Boyle explained.

"Good of you to take care of him," I said. I meant it.

He looked at Turgeon. "What's this about my father?"

Baby Head cleared his throat. "I'm sorry, but he passed on a week ago. You were named as the sole heir."

Boyle twisted his square head. "Nothing for Marty Junior or Cara?"

"No. I don't know the details, but it seems they had a falling-out."

"They must be pissed."

"Oh, they are," I added. "But what with the hakkers coming, maybe we could all hop into Mr. Turgeon's Hummer and continue this conversation anyplace but here?"

"Can Ashby come?"

"Heh-heh. I'm going, too? Heh-heh."

Turgeon hesitated, maybe annoyed by the laugh. Bugged me, too, but I figured he couldn't help it. Probably just as eager to leave as I was, after a beat he said, "Certainly."

"Cool, oh, cool. Heh-heh."

As Boyle stepped toward us, I felt a weight lift. For a second there, I was stupid enough to think the evening might end well. Maybe the good guys could win sometimes. Maybe that bank in Ghana really did transfer millions into your account now and again. But then Boyle stopped short.

"I've got some notes I have to give to Thornell. Come on back with me. It'll take a second."

"You mean the maps, heh-heh. He makes maps. He's a mapmaker. Heh-heh."

"Yes, Ashby. The maps."

Not wanting to slow him up with any questions, I followed them down the hall. A few more doors creaked open, chakz sticking their heads out.

A woman with one eye hanging from the optic stalk, a dangler, said, "You're not leaving us, are you, Frank?"

"Just for a little," he told her. I couldn't tell if she thought he was lying.

The kid straightened. "We've got some business, heh-heh."

He sounded proud about the *heh-heh* part.

I was afraid there'd be a big social scene, or someone would want to throw a farewell party. But chakz are slow thinkers, so we made it to Frank's room without much ado.

It was pretty big, an L-shaped deal with a couch, a

couple of beds, even some shelving with old photos. Ashby threw himself on the couch and bobbed his head. Boyle headed straight for a big drafting table set up against the wall. On it, I made out plans for the factory complex, full of notes in colored Magic Marker. Boyle wasn't just one of the smart ones—he was doing better than some livebloods.

I pulled out my recorder, thinking I'd make an entry, then forgot what I'd wanted to say. Wouldn't be the first time. Instead, I looked over Boyle's shoulder. Using thumb and forefinger, he peeled up the masking tape holding the paper.

Curiosity got the best of me. "Still got a lot of dexterity in those digits, too. Grave diggers' strike? Kept refrigerated until use?"

"Uh-huh," he said. "My IQ only dropped fifteen percent. I could work a real job if someone would hire me."

Turgeon cleared his throat. "You won't have to work anymore, Mr. Boyle."

Still peeling, Boyle asked, "How much are we talking?"

"Roughly? Forty million."

"Whoa! Heh-heh!" Ashby said.

The kid was happy enough, but something about it bugged Boyle. "And not a penny for Marty and Cara?" Was he regretful? Certainly confused. "What could they have done?"

"I'm sure I don't know," Turgeon said.

Boyle straightened, ready to go, then slumped into the chair in front of his drawing board and muttered, "Forty million."

"Buy a fast-food place! Heh-heh!" Ashby said. "Lickin' Chicken! Merger Burger and Fries and Lies! Heh-heh."

Turgeon blinked with every *heh*.

Frank was more contemplative. "I could open a home for chakz. Someplace safe."

"If that's what you want, easily, Mr. Boyle," Turgeon said. "My firm would be happy to help you manage your finances, as we did for your father."

While Eggman yammered, I scanned the pictures. The glass was clear. He cleaned them regularly. There were a few self-portraits, no surprise, given the head shot Turgeon gave me. Others had him arm in arm with a slightly older, taller man, likely his significant other.

I thought maybe he kept Ashby around because he reminded him of an old lover, but the kid looked nothing like the man in the photo. Then I spotted a three-shot, both men along with a fair-haired cherub with an aquiline nose. Bingo. Boyle smiled in all the photos, but in the individual shots he had a practiced expression. Those with the older man put a real smile on his face. In the shots with the boy, his grin was widest. He looked really . . . happy. The boy was the one Ashby looked like, or would've if he was younger and still alive.

I tapped the frame. "Son?"

"Duncan. Adopted from Russia."

"Can I ask . . . ?"

He rolled up the plans. "I came home one day and found Kendrick, my husband, beaten to death. We'd had some problems, fights that got physical. The police knew I had a temper. I was found guilty and put to death. Duncan was deported."

"And some suppressed DNA test showed someone else was there?"

I don't know why I said it, but he gave me a look. "It wasn't suppressed. It was botched. My father had the samples retested, but it took a long time. The results came in after the execution. He tried to stop the RAR, but it was the law."

"Huh." Except for the choice in gender, Boyle's story sounded familiar. Not really unusual, though. Crimes of passion are big on the hit parade. What was weird was that Boyle, like me, wasn't guilty.

"They catch the real killer?"

He shook his head.

I didn't know if the story awoke any uncomfortable feelings for him, but I felt something. I don't know what, but it didn't feel good. Antsy about the similarity, maybe.

Boyle stood, rolled plans under his arm. "Let me give these to Thornell. He has to reposition the scouts."

"They spotted us easily enough," I said.

"In a Humvee with headlights," he answered. "The hakkers have taken to walking their cycles in the last half mile. That way you can't hear them until it's too late."

Turned out that was exactly what they did. Even rats learn how to run a maze.

We were halfway down the hall when a series of shrill whines made the stale air shiver. What nerves I had left vibrated in tune. The dead stumbled from their rooms, trembling.

Boyle barked orders. "Back inside. Stay quiet. Remember, this is the last place they'll come."

The whining increased. The rats wanted cheese.

Boyle pointed at my flashlight. "Turn that damn thing off!"

I clicked the switch and we all stood there, wrapped in the dry, dusty dark. The whine grew denser, wilder, morphed into a whirring like a robot-locust plague. I could hear the loose dirt and rocks kicked up by their wheels.

Ashby said, "Heh-heh." The others huddled around Boyle.

"They have to use the main road," he whispered. "If there aren't too many, Thornell and the others will scare them off."

Half a minute later, moans mingled with the whining. They'd met the fake ferals. If the plan worked, the swarm would turn tail and head home.

"Heh-heh."

We heard a mash-up of engine revving, moans, crunches, and some inventive liveblood cursing, but the swarming sound never returned. They'd broken formation.

"Boyle?" I said. "Sounds to me like they're running everyone down one by one."

"I know."

"A couple of us might be able to make it to the Hummer."

He clenched his teeth. "I can't leave everyone."

"Don't go, Frank! Heh-heh."

Not wanting anyone else to hear, I shifted nearer to Boyle and whispered, "You could do a lot of good with that money, but only if you stay in one piece."

He exhaled, which, since he didn't need to breathe, meant he was thinking. I'll never know what he would have said next. Thick beams flooded the windows, lighting us all in an eerie blue-white. It matched everyone's skin except Turgeon's.

The lights spun this way and that as the bikers oriented themselves. The hall looked like a crazy discotheque, but instead of dancing, we all froze as only the dead can.

My flashlight had bounced back from the filthy glass, but their cycle high-beams were ten times brighter. There was hope, but not much. Even if they could see inside, we could be taken for trash. They might leave, move on to the factory.

Or . . . they *could* check in here first, for the hell of it.

I was praying for the first option when the glass doors swung open. But it wasn't the hakkers. It was Thornell. He stumbled in, carrying something thick, long, and dripping under his right arm.

Turned out it was his left arm.

Boyle rushed to his side. "What the hell happened?"

"Car wouldn't burn twice. Not enough light. They only saw a third of us, decided they could take us. They were right."

The door was still open. No one followed Thornell in, but when the cycles passed again, their headlights came through unfiltered. Cradling his arm, Thornell dived for cover. Boyle pushed Ashby behind him.

"Heh-heh."

"There a basement?" I asked.

Boyle shook his head. "Yeah, but it's a dead end. One way in, one way out. They come in, we're cornered."

I tried counting the headlights and gave up at seven. "We're *already* cornered."

Turgeon looked at me, eyes wide like he was ready to bawl. Instead he said, "Now?"

I nodded and he pulled out his gun. I pulled my own piece from my waistband. Some old cop instincts still intact, I crept across the reception area.

Moving up to one of the narrow windows, I took a look outside. It was real chiaroscuro, a play of dark and light. The dark part wasn't so bad, just a bunch of abstract silhouettes against a blasting sound track of horrid cries, screaming engines, and macho whoops. It was the light that got to me. Every now and then a cycle headlamp threw a neat circle on some chak, man or woman, their face twisted in agony as they watched some piece of their lifeless body hacked off.

And why? Because some demented, drunken childkings thought they were fighting the good fight for truth, justice, and sick fucks everywhere.

I had the gun, sure, but if I shot one of those idiots, if I so much as clipped him, *I'd* be the one they tore up next. And it wouldn't just be the hakkers after me. If I got away from them, it'd be the cops, the army, all society. The next morning, the cable-TV pundits would be yakking about me, how I was the one who finally gave them the excuse they needed to round up and destroy every chak in the country.

There were screaming, buzzing engines, and moaning bodies everywhere. Like a camera flash, a headlight lit one of a dozen nightmare scenes. An old chak, cotton white hair where the skull wasn't exposed, knelt with his head down like he was praying. But he wasn't; he was staring at his two severed arms on the ground in front of him.

A liveblood, white safety helmet and brown outfit making him look like a plastic bald eagle, saw him. It all went to silhouette again, but I could still make out what happened. The liveblood braked, spun, and headed for the old chak. The LB's machete was out, aimed at the old man's neck. The chak didn't notice.

A pain bubbled in my gut. I knew it well. Utter helplessness. Utter helplessness with one difference: I had a gun.

Before I realized what I was doing, I'd aimed and pulled the trigger. My first shot cracked the window glass. The second entered the liveblood's head. As it snapped back, the rest of him followed, flying off his bike. Riderless, the rice grinder fell sideways, skidded, and stopped. Its spinning front wheel knocked one of the severed arms. It twirled like a bottle in an adolescent kissing game. When it stopped, the fingers pointed my way.

It was loud; it was dark. By rights, no one should have spotted me in that little narrow window. But hunting in a pack is an old, old instinct. Everyone has it, especially the ones who look stupid. It's like they give up on things like reason and individuality in exchange for group instinct. When one of their number falls, the whole pack senses it.

Out of nowhere, five, six of the dog-men zoomed up to the body. His fresh blood glistened in their headlights like liquid ruby.

"Shit! Cyrus!"

So he had a name. Good for him. Bad for me. One looked at the way the body had fallen, then snapped his snout toward my window.

I ducked, but not fast enough.

"There."

The pack came toward me, toward all of us. I'd brought them. They burst through the entrance, rode into the lobby, popping wheelies, gunning engines, their machetes up and ready. And there wasn't any door I could slam, not even to keep them out of view for a while, just a solid concrete wall against my back.

5

What's that Tom Waits song where everything's broken? Wasted and wounded? Can't remember. What came next was something like that, though, an apocalypse in a broken teacup. It wasn't important to the universe, or even the next town over, but it was intimate, and messy as hell.

Hakkers swarmed the space like rats entering a bakery, giddy from the smell of food, mad with hunger. A chain saw, teeth whirring, grunted in my direction. I stood there, dumb as a post. The blades made contact with the wall, inches from my head. Cold bits sprayed my face. Plaster or dried flesh—I didn't know which. I only knew I was glad it wasn't part of me.

I'd be next. No reason to think otherwise. So this was it, or as close to "it" as a chak gets. What do you do in that moment? Me, I closed my eyes. I pressed my hands into the wall behind me. I tried to focus on the concrete's feel against my palms and fingers. I tried to think about anything except what was right in front of me. Common sense tells you it's better not to be paying attention when they cut you up.

And they say if you really, really work at it, you can do that: slip out of your body, away from the here and now, especially if you're a chak, since you're half-gone to begin with. But instead of working with me, taking me to my happy place, or at least a cheap motel, my brain came up with something I probably read on a bubble-gum wrapper:

That which does not kill us makes us stronger.

Right. Fuck you, memory. Just fuck you.

No chain saw, though. A hand grabbed my shoulder. When it pulled, I followed, stumbling along. I kept my eyes shut until a low voice said, "Basement. It's all we've got."

It was Boyle. Somehow he'd managed to keep his head, arms, and legs when all those about him were losing theirs. Did he serve in a war? He acted like he'd been trained, yanking me with one hand, pushing Ashby with the other. All I could think was that he was saving the wrong guy. He should've been helping Turgeon. He was the one who could get him the money. Not that I was planning to mention that.

Bit by bit we stumbled through the Mixmaster of a lobby. There was one thing in our favor: The hakkers, bless their tiny brains, were too stupid to get off their bikes. For every lug wrench swing or chain saw swipe, they spent twice the time repositioning their grinders, as if staying in the saddle were a rule of the game. That gave Boyle the time to steer us down the hallway.

Ashby moved like a pull toy with a broken axle. With every shove he'd take a few steps, slow, and then stop. As we neared the end of the hall, a steel fire door came into view. Boyle let go of me and gave Ashby a final push that sent him teetering along like a penguin.

"Run!" Boyle shouted at the kid's back.

Then he did something that made me think he wasn't so smart after all. He turned back toward the lobby.

I grabbed him. "You nuts?"

He tried to twist away, but I dug in my fingers and locked the joints. Like I said, once a chak gets hold of something we don't let go unless we want to. That got his attention. He growled like he was planning to drag me along.

"Let go," he said. "Stay with Ashby, please. I've got to get the others."

"There's nothing you can do! It's over for anyone out there."

Before he could argue, a new sound rose through the mix of whining engines, screams, chops, and whirs. In a way it was like it'd been there all along, but someone had just plugged in a subwoofer so you could hear it better. It was a keening, deep, low, abject. It sounded so bereft it made you want to weep along with it.

It was the chakz.

Not the ones still struggling, the ones who'd been cut down and left to writhe. Even shredded, they couldn't die, head for the other side, or melt into an existential nothing. The magic of ChemBet had seen to that. All they could do was abandon what little they had left, their souls, if you like to pray. As they felt it slip away, they cried for it, like it was a baby they couldn't feed anymore. Once it was gone, they'd be feral.

What was left? A predator honed by millions of years of evolution, or worse, designed by God, hungry, but severed from its higher functions. One after another, the

maimed chakz bowed to their inner lizard kings, then
lashed out at whatever moved.

You'd think the hakkers would be scared, but they
weren't. They were thrilled. This was what they were
waiting for, the moment that justified these little soirees.
Ferals proved that chakz were dangerous, that we *should*
be destroyed, that we deserved it. Safe and smug on
their bikes, in their thick clothes, heavy weapons in hand,
they howled and went back to playing their live-action
first-person shooter.

Like I said, ferals aren't much of a threat unless they
come at you in numbers, but you do have to be careful.
The dog-soldier who sniffed me out after I shot his
friend wasn't. Maybe it was his first night out with the
boys, or maybe he couldn't handle his liquor as well as
he thought. Who knows? Whatever the reason, he spent
a little too much time gunning his engine, raising his fist,
and whooping, and not enough time looking over his
shoulder.

Two moaners barreled into his back.

It may have looked like a coordinated attack, but he
was just whooping the loudest and had the shiniest bike.
Ferals love two things: shiny lights and liveblood screams.
Liveblood screams are different. They sound . . . *wet-
ter*.

When they hit, the dog-boy teetered. Probably
would've been a big nothing if the bike hadn't ridden
out from under him. It climbed the coffee table, tore up
the magazines, and fell sideways. I think the dog-boy
said, "Whoa!" Took him a second to realize his situation
wasn't so funny. Even when he did, his first cry for help
wasn't very loud. The fall must have winded him.

Ferals are fast. Before his friends realized they had a

man down, four swarmed him. Two bit into his shoulders, their teeth grinding through his leathers until they reached skin. A woman straddled him, eyes so wide I think the lids were gone. It didn't look like she could do much. Her arms were cut off above the elbows. But sometimes you just have to improvise. Fistless, she stabbed her pointy stubs at his head in quick staccato bursts.

Now the other hakkers heard him. They dropped whatever they were mutilating to help. With a sudden pause in the slaughter, I figured I might as well let go of Boyle so he could do his thing. The LBs busy, he herded as many chakz as he could into the hallway. Mostly I followed his lead, keeping one eye on the hakkers.

He must have noticed my divided attention, because he shouted, "Don't look; just move!"

We didn't have long. Quick as a gamer's fingers, they pulled the ferals off and chopped them into even smaller pieces. There wasn't much they could do for the dog-boy, what with his jugular slashed and his face looking like something a cat threw up.

Score one for the zombies.

A hairy ginger with more freckles than skin kept hakking even when there was nothing left but limbs. When the chak pieces didn't stop moving, he freaked.

"Stay dead!" he screamed. "Stay dead!"

Hey, pal, we would if we could.

The ginger wasn't the only rattled hakker. That was the second man they'd lost. No one goes on a chak attack without thinking he might cash it in, but *might* is a long walk from really believing it. They weren't just grieving their fallen comrades; they were grieving their own mortality.

Knowing how quickly that grieving could turn to
rage, I pulled at Boyle again.

"Come on! Now!"

Ignoring me, he steered a few more chakz down the
hall. I don't usually try reasoning with a chak, but I figured it was worth a shot.

"Boyle, do the math. Get cut up here, you'll *never*
build that sanctuary."

That did it. He turned and we ran. Between us and
the basement door were about seven uncoordinated
bodies, stumbling around as if they'd only recently dis-
covered they had legs. Ashby was beyond them. He had
the basement door open, but instead of going down, he
stood on the top step, waiting for Boyle with a wimpy
grin plastered on his face.

Despite the obstacle course, we moved fast. I thought
we'd all make it until a roar rattled the walls. It was an
engine, but not a wussy rice-grinder whine. This was gut-
tural, an all-American *putt-putt*.

Some buried masochistic streak made me turn for a
quick look, not that you could miss a hairy monster astride
a gleaming Harley Softail Fat Boy. No grungy thug, the
rider was nice and clean, a wash-and-werewolf decked
out in impeccable studded leather. He and his machine
were pointed down the hall, right at us. He flashed a grin,
gunned the engine, and my chest rattled like a space shut-
tle was taking off. Boyle summed things up nicely.

"Shit!"

We picked up speed, pushed the others hard. Still at
the door, poor Ashby found himself faced with a pack of
oncoming bodies. Looking as if he was about to say *heh*,
he fell backward and disappeared. Seeing his buddy van-
ish, for the first time Boyle shoved ahead of the others.

By the time I neared the doorway, I couldn't see Boyle or Ashby, only an Escher-like maze of heads, torsos, and limbs rolling down concrete steps into a musty, dark basement. Unlike the mess left behind, I assumed these body parts were all still attached.

I was about to dive into the pile when the wash-and-werewolf put the Harley in gear. The rear tire screeched against the linoleum. The bike flew forward.

If he kept his mean machine straight for about fifty yards, Lon Chaney Jr. would fly down the stairs, crushing everyone and everything, including me. Judging by all the flailing on the steps, nobody was thinking about getting out of the way.

I went into a lightning round of Trivial Pursuit: How many seconds does it take a Softail Fat Boy to go from zero to sixty? Five? How long was the hallway? Fifty yards? How fast could *I* go from zero to sixty? Fast enough to reach the knob and pull the door shut? And if I didn't get it exactly right, what would it feel like when that thing rammed into me?

After wasting a precious two seconds on that crap, I grabbed the silver knob and jumped, yanking the door with me. As I flew, still in midair, I swear Chaney got close enough for me to see his eye color. Dirt brown.

That, I remember.

The door was half-closed when his front wheel caught it. The fire-resistant slab of gray slammed into me so hard I not only stayed airborne, I played Superman, up, up, and away as the door crashed into the frame. When gravity caught up, I fell onto the pile of scrambling bodies at the base of the stairs. A Twister game of the dead. Patent pending.

Shaking off the vertigo, I extricated myself and

looked up. There was a big wheel-shaped dent in the middle of the door. The hinges were bent. The cement around the frame had cracked, but held. I doubted Mr. Chaney looked nearly as good.

We were safe, but not for long. It wouldn't take much for the Livebloods to pull the bike out of the way. Then they'd come for us.

I looked around for blunt, heavy objects, but it was too dark to see anything. I was trying to remember how many bullets I had left in my Walther when a flash of light got everyone's attention. Boyle was standing in the center of the wide, shapeless space, holding a cheap plastic lighter with a tiny flame. Ashby stood behind him, looking like an accessory, but none the worse for wear. Other than the half shapes of nervously shifting bodies that reminded me of cattle stuffed in a railcar, I couldn't make out much else.

A community organizer to the end, he spoke softly. "Everybody stay calm. We don't need anyone going feral."

But something else, even harder to ignore, competed for our attention, a loud . . .

Crunch.

All eyes shot to the door at the top of the stairs. They were already trying to move the bike.

Turned out Boyle wasn't the only one who could talk. Some genius announced, "They have to come down on foot, one at a time. We can take them."

Ashby repeated the last two words. "Take them. Heh-heh."

Creak.

A more resigned voice spoke up next. "Then what? If we make a pile of bodies, they'll burn this place to a cinder in the morning."

"I'm ready for it," another said. "It's better than going on like this."

That was it for intelligible speech. Hisses and grunts followed, most sounding like they agreed.

Boyle, for whatever ridiculous reason, turned to me. "Got any better ideas?" The equivalent of asking, "Excuse me, buddy, can you stop the rain?"

Crunk!

Back up at the door, cement drizzled from the cracks. It came down so freely, I looked around for an umbrella. We couldn't go out. We couldn't fight them if they got in. What was left?

"Barricade," I said. "We pile shit against the door. Hakkers don't have a big attention span. Keep them out long enough, maybe they'll get tired and go home."

I thought it wasn't a half-bad idea, but Mr. Last Stand chimed in. "Barricade it with what? Cardboard boxes? How do we brace them? They'd just push them down the stairs."

One of the smart ones. Asshole.

Clank!

That last one sounded like the whole doorframe was coming loose. Everyone shifted like a bunch of cows. I thought I heard a few low moans.

Boyle heard it, too. "Stay calm! We'll be fine!"

He didn't sound like he meant it.

Unlike having my back against the wall and a chain saw in my face, it was quiet enough here to pray. It was one of those desperate moments when you hope an angel appears and you don't particularly care if it's from heaven or hell.

That's exactly what happened, sort of.

From somewhere out in the dark, a wispy, boyish

voice nervously said, "Don't worry. I called the police ten minutes ago."

At least it broke the tension. Everyone with a mouth laughed.

I knew the voice. "Turgeon? You down here? Where are you?"

"I'm sitting on some sort of crate. I think I have a splinter."

That earned him another laugh. I couldn't tell if he was relaxed or in shock. If he was relaxed, I'd have the pleasure of telling him, *I told you so*. If he was in shock, what would be the point?

"If you're on a crate, better crawl inside it and kiss yourself good-bye, Mr. Turgeon. There's no way the cops would bother showing up to save a bunch of chakz."

Turned out he was the one who had to spell things out for me.

"You forget, Mann," he answered. "I'm not a chak."

And that was when I heard the sirens.

6

I suppose the hakkers thought the sirens had to be for someone else. They kept at the door, grunting and banging, but couldn't get it open. When the piercing wails grew louder and it was clear the police were getting closer, not farther away, they sounded confused. They whispered, told one another, *Nah, couldn't be*.

Then, like monkeys with their hands stuck in a jar, they went back to rattling the bike. When it was completely obvious the cops really were headed this way, I swear I could hear their brows furrowing. It was only when the brakes squealed right outside the building and the police tromped into the lobby that it finally occurred to them something was up and they stopped trying to move the bike.

Great entertainment, but Turgeon was the only one expecting an actual rescue. The rest of us figured the cops would end up on the hakkers' side, especially with two liveblood corpses upstairs, three, if the werewolf died in the crash.

Any minute now, we'd be facing guns along with the chain saws.

Loud and irritated the way only cops can be, their commanding voices filled the air, demanding to know what the fuck was going on. We all got quiet the way only dead things can. The silence is kind of a group thing. If one of us does it, everyone joins in. It's like yawning. We're great to be around in libraries, except for the smell. It also made it easier to hear what was going on above.

Not that it was tough. The boys in blue made as much noise as possible, like they wanted to give any LBs in earshot a chance to vacate and avoid trouble. That was a good sign. Another good sign was the sudden change in the hakkers' topics of conversation. Instead of macho whoops and gleeful academic questions like, "Who wants a piece of this next?" they were talking about packing up and getting the hell out.

But one idiot straggler—there's always one—drunk as a skunk, unable to believe his eyes, actually screamed at the cops, "What the fuck you doing here?"

I was almost thinking I'd pull through this mess in one piece until I heard the sandpaper-against-a-bass-drum voice that answered. Angry, full of bile. How do I put it? It was the kind of voice that even if you knew the owner was supposed to protect you, you'd rather take your chances with the crooks.

"You've got a *lawyer* stuck down there, dipshit! Get that twisted hunk of crap away from the door before I put you in lockup and introduce your fat ass to some real criminals."

Boyle blew out his lighter. A metal groan filled the dark.

"Hey, man, easy on my bike, okay?"

So the wash-and-werewolf had survived the impact. Only two bodies, then.

He was told to shut the fuck up. The mangled door-knob jiggled; the door shifted like a sarcophagus lid, then froze. It wouldn't give.

I heard that voice again: "There a Sturgeon down there?"

From the gloom, my client's shiny head rose like a miniature sun. He shifted past the quiet dead, a twitchy smile on his face, and stopped at the base of the stairs.

"Turgeon. William Turgeon. Yes. Could you . . . identify yourself?"

"You hurt?"

"I don't think so. I'm not bleeding. Could you identify yourself, please?"

"He won't answer," I whispered. "Not even with the magic word. It's Tom Booth, head of Fort Hammer homicide."

Turgeon gave me a quizzical look. "Isn't he . . . ?"

I nodded. "My old boss."

Also the man who diddled my wife and found me standing in a pool of her blood. Small world. Tiny world. So tiny, sometimes I wish I could put it between my thumb and forefinger and crush the damn thing. Booth must have caught a night shift, thanks to the budget cuts. Dragging his ass out here was the last thing either of us needed.

A stubborn son of a bitch, he went at the door again, pulling, yanking, kicking, growling. Much as he might be our savior, no one from our side helped. I could feel the dead stiffen around me, worried they'd fallen from the pan into the fire. They must have heard me say his name.

Booth hated me most, but after that, it was any other chak. He figured we were all RAR. Any overturned conviction was like someone tracking mud across his nice clean kitchen floor.

After a few full, long minutes, the yanking stopped.

"Could you ladies stop scratching your ball sacs and get some kind of wedge for this thing? A crowbar, something? Just give me one of those chak arms lying on the floor."

Big charmer, Booth.

The next crunch was loudest. With a sound like Bigfoot's fingernails against a blackboard, the door swung back into the hall and fell off its lower hinge. A flashlight beam danced down the steps, Booth right behind it. Lantern jaw and a curly red fuzz on his head, he looked as strong as I used to wish I could be. Good-looking, too, if it wasn't for the pug nose that said canine in a big way. A show dog, but a dog.

Turgeon motioned for Boyle to join him at the base of the stairs. Ashby gave off a nervous *heh-heh* and followed. Turgeon looked at me to do the same, but I shook my head. With Booth, I was better off hiding with the mob. Fortunately, Turgeon understood and didn't ask twice.

Spotting Turgeon's pinker flesh, Booth waved him up the stairs. "Let's move it."

Turgeon pulled at Boyle and Ashby. "These men are with me."

At the word *men* Booth twitched and turned away like he couldn't stand the smell.

All the while, I was backing up, hoping to disappear into the darkness. No such luck. After they were a few steps up, Boyle, thinking he was doing me a favor, pointed me out. Unlike the nosy Turgeon, he didn't know the history.

"You, too, Mann. You're with us."

Booth tensed up so fast I heard his bones crack. Hiding was no longer an option.

After a pregnant pause, Turgeon managed to speak up. "Yes. He's working for me," he said. Then he lowered his big head and flinched as if expecting to be hit.

Booth pivoted his flashlight into my face. I winced, not because I had to. My pupils don't work quite the same way anymore. I was hoping it'd made him feel better if it looked like I was squirming. It didn't.

"Hessius Mann." There was so much venom in his tone that even though the basement was packed, everyone around me stepped back.

Saying nothing seemed worse than saying something, so I shielded my eyes with my hand, and nodded. "Tom."

He turned to Turgeon like he was ready to push him back down the stairs. "Do you know what it did?"

I'll say this for Baby-head: He was frightened, but held his ground. "He was exonerated, no? Partly because you beat him during his arrest?"

Booth sneered. I could smell the wood burning. More than likely he was pondering the downside of caving in Turgeon's head with the flashlight. But Turgeon was a liveblood, and where the living were concerned, in the end, Booth followed the rules.

Besides, he still had his favorite chew toy to play with, me.

"Remember what I said I'd do if I ever saw you again, Mann?"

Crap. I didn't. I knew it was something colorful, earthy, involving body parts detached and being forced into various orifices, but the details escaped me. I tried to remember; I really did. I even had it recorded somewhere.

I kept my voice even. "It's not like I was expecting you."

Turgeon cleared his throat. "Detective, I'd like . . ."

The sentence ended with Booth's finger an inch from Turgeon's nose. "You know what I'd like? I'd like you to shut up. We've got two dead bodies, the real kind, upstairs. One with a mangled face, so I can guess what happened there, but the other has a nice neat bullet hole." He tapped Turgeon's forehead. "Right about there. I'm guessing, but the entry wound looks to me like a nine-millimeter reduced-velocity, maybe a Walther P99." Finger still on my client's forehead, Booth turned to me again. "That'd be a good gun for a chak. You wouldn't have one on you, would you, Mann?"

Matter of fact I did, tucked back in my waistband. "Why would I be carrying, Tom? It's illegal, last I heard."

He came down the steps and leaned his face in, daring me to twitch, but my body only does that at random. There was broiled chicken and barbecue sauce on his breath. Home-cooked, I think. He'd been pulled away from a meal.

"Because you're one of the 'smart' ones," he said. "And it'd be stupid to show up here tonight without a gun."

"Nice of you to say so, but I'm not feeling very smart right now." No shit. If he frisked me, it'd be all over. Even our cut-rate ballistics department would match the bullet to my piece in under an hour.

"I bet," he said. "What is it they do to killer chakz?" He held two fingers up and scissored them, imitating the clippers they use on our heads. "D-cap."

I knew Booth pretty well, and one of the things I remembered was that he always held his breath when he patted down a chak. First, though, he'd give himself a good breath. He never warned them; he just inhaled and started patting.

If he inhaled, I knew I was in trouble.

He turned away and sucked down some air. Oh, shit.

"I shot that man," Turgeon squeaked. "With a Walter . . . uh . . . that gun you said."

We both turned to him. Booth clenched the flashlight tighter. "You?"

"I had to. He was about to kill someone with a machete."

"A chak?"

"It was dark. But that wouldn't make any difference in court, would it? If you bring charges. And I do have witnesses."

"I saw it," I said.

"So did I," Boyle put in.

Booth laughed. "Chakz can't be sworn in. Let's see the gun."

Turgeon cleared his throat. He sounded dry. "I . . . must have dropped it."

Booth exhaled and looked around. I knew what he was thinking. If he pursued the shooting, he'd also have to pursue the technically illegal hakker attack. The livebloods had fled, chakz his only witnesses. He grunted.

"Get out. Take them with you."

He didn't have to say it twice. The four of us filed up the stairs, Ashby first, me last. As I passed Booth, I tried to ask him about Lenore. I don't know why—maybe because I used to admire the guy, maybe because I still had a thing for the truth, maybe because there were things he'd seen that might fill in the blanks for me.

"Tom, I didn't . . ."

"Don't. Don't even think about it. Keep shambling."

"My mistake."

Back in the hallway, a few uniforms blocked our path until Booth reluctantly said, "Let them the fuck through."

"Heh-heh," Ashby said. "We're going through. We're going the fuck through."

"Sh," Boyle said. "Sh."

I wished the night had been cooler, but it was thick with August heat, so the humidity held the smell of rotting meat high in the air. As we walked, Boyle put his hand on Ashby's head and tried to steer the kid's gaze down at the ground so he wouldn't see all the mangled bodies. But even the floor was littered with parts.

"Is that Mrs. Winter's arm? Heh-heh."

Boyle tried to keep him quiet, but Ashby kept naming limbs, recognizing who they belonged to from the torn clothing or the jewelry. Fortunately, when the kid spotted the Humvee, that grabbed all his attention.

"Nice car! Will we ride in the nice car?"

"Yes, Ashby."

"Heh-heh."

Once we were crunching along the road, the kid stopped using words altogether. He just made that little *heh-heh* noise. Turgeon looked like it was driving him crazy. Me, I was so relieved to be heading away from Bedland, it was as good as a song on the radio.

Turgeon didn't speak until the dull glow of the city was visible; then he half stammered, "That was . . . close."

He'd pulled my ass out of the fire with Booth, so I was feeling generous.

"Any landing you can walk away from, right, Mr. Turgeon?" I said. "And, hell, you were right about coming tonight. If you'd listened to me and waited until morning, we'd be trying to find Frank Boyle's pieces, no offense."

"None taken," Boyle said.

"I was . . . happy to thwart that Detective Booth," Turgeon said.

I shrugged. "He's not so bad. Good cop. Just has a blind spot."

"Are you joking?" he asked. When I didn't answer, he added, "You might want to leave that gun with me. I can . . . you know . . . make sure it disappears."

I pulled out the Walther, emptied the clip, and handed it over. "Not the kind of thing I'd expect from a live-blood attorney, sticking his neck out for a chak. Mind my asking if you do that sort of thing a lot?"

"No," he said. "Never."

He opened his glove compartment, tossed in the gun, and pulled out an envelope stuffed with cash.

"How many of those do you usually carry?"

"As many as I think I might need."

After he handed me the envelope, we all got quiet for a while, but it was a long ride. At some point I turned to the man of the hour, the guy we'd risked our necks for. "Boyle, you really going to use the money to build some kind of shelter for chakz?"

"That's the plan. What do you think, Ashby?"

"Sounds good. Good. Good. Heh-heh."

I believed him. So who knew? Maybe it was worth it. But every silver lining has a cloud. Something told me I just hadn't found this one yet.

As we passed through the edge of the Bones, I spotted a familiar silhouette by a vacant lot. It was Misty, rubbing a rag against her skirt like she was trying to set it on fire. The shadows farther back in the lot shifted, telling me she wasn't alone.

There was only one thing I could think of that would get her out at this hour: scoring meth. Damn.

"Turgeon, pull over here. Let me out."

When she saw the Humvee, Misty reared like a deer and looked ready to book. Worried I'd have to chase her down, I popped the door and unbuckled my belt. To my surprise, the minute she saw my kisser, she gave me a big smile. It wasn't drugs then, not with that grin.

Relief washed over me, uncomfortable as any emotion, but not unwelcome. Remembering my manners, I turned back to Turgeon. "Guess this concludes our contract."

"Uh-huh," he said.

"Thanks for helping me out with Booth."

"You're welcome."

I was going to tell him he wasn't so bad, but seeing as I hadn't said he was bad in the first place, it didn't seem appropriate. He was probably exhausted from all the excitement, eager to get to some comfy hotel bed, and I doubted I'd be contacting him for an effusive letter of reference anytime soon. So that was about it.

"Good-bye, Mr. Detective, heh-heh."

"Bye, Ashby. Hey, Boyle?"

"Yeah?"

"You have any trouble when you try to set up that home, you let me know, okay?"

"Will do, Mann."

I closed the door. The environmental terror headed down the road, a big, bright yellow toy in a junkyard. Case closed.

"What took you so long?" Misty said.

"Traffic," I said, pointing out at the barren streets. "But what're you doing out at this hour, young lady?"

She made a face, pulled off a flat, and rubbed the bottom of her foot. "That chak you sent me to clean up? He may have had trouble with his finger, but there was nothing wrong with his feet. Took me two hours to chase him down. I had to get Jonesey to help. Got damn bleach all over my skirt. It's ruined."

One of the shadows shifted into the light. It was Jonesey. The gang was all here.

"Hey, Hess." He was still looking a little out of it. Misty probably wanted to keep an eye on him after I mentioned the feral thing.

"Hey, yourself. Weren't you heading off to—" I stopped myself short. Last we spoke, he was going to try to get his crack back. If he'd forgotten that brilliantly suicidal idea, I wasn't going to remind him about it. ". . . Disney World, or some other happy place?"

"Funny. That guy you were talking to in the backseat, that was Frank Boyle, right? The one who inherited all the money?"

"Six points to you, Jonesey."

"I hear you say he was going to build a home for chakz?"

I nodded. "That's what he called it. Could be our first philanthropist, if Turgeon doesn't rob him blind."

After the nod, Jonesey only half listened. He was rolling the idea around in his head, hoping to get it stuck somewhere. "Safe place? Huh. Safe. Yeah. Y'know, that is such a good idea, a really good idea. I've been thinking about stuff like that, like maybe we could get a little organized, try to protect our rights more. I . . . I could help do that. I used to motivate people. I could put together a rally."

"Yeah, Jonesey. You could," I told him.

"I'm going to think about it."

"Well, don't hurt yourself."

"Funny. I'll see you, Mann."

He walked off, nodding to himself. Misty put her hand in the crook of my arm. We watched him for a bit, then headed in the opposite direction.

"So, it went well, huh?"

"I'm still here."

"Did you mean that, what you said to Jonesey about organizing chakz being a good idea?"

I laughed. "Hell, no. It'd be like getting cats to line up."

"Really? Because I bet he could do it."

I stopped and looked at her. "I hope the hell not. If he succeeded, even a little, it'd be worse than the mess I just left behind. Get more than five chakz together in the same place, the livebloods will think we've gone feral en masse and start D-capping like we were flowers and they needed a bouquet. Haven't you ever seen a zombie movie?"

She scrunched that pretty, pockmarked face of hers. "Then why'd you lie?"

I shrugged. "I wanted to keep his brain busy. After I snapped him out of that feral fit, he was planning a home invasion. An hour from now he'll be trying to assemble a moon rocket out of piss and cardboard. Why not let him hold on to something?"

She seemed a little deflated. "Same thing with Frank Boyle and that home?"

"I have to admit, that's a different case. He's smart. If Turgeon's honest . . . and Boyle plays it right, buys some property as far from what they call civilization as possible. Then maybe . . ."

Misty narrowed her eyes. "So you *do* believe in something?"

"Now, don't go talking crazy like that."

"Come on, Hess, new life comes out of the dead, right?"

"Sounds like you're expecting a tree to grow out of my chest."

She slapped my shoulder. "Shut up. I'm just saying maybe something's watching out for people like us. Maybe the universe has plans for Boyle, or Jonesey, or even you."

I didn't want to get into it. Like Jonesey and his PAC of the living dead, if it made Misty happy to believe in some spaghetti monster in the sky, if it kept her sober one more day, I didn't see the harm in it.

We found an all-night CVS. Feeling like a big man, I bought Misty a new coffee machine, and myself a new digital voice recorder with two gigs of flash memory and a couple of James Bond microphone attachments. I paid too much for both, but what the hell.

Our prizes wrapped in plastic, we headed home. After we made it up the stairs, she made for the mattress in the front room. I yanked off my tie and shambled toward the office recliner. I thought about the cash I had, how I could actually get some furniture for the place. I had to admit, right then and there, it looked like a happy ending. It was almost enough to make me think the universe *did* have plans for me.

Then again, I've seen too much of its other work to consider that a good thing.

7

Happy ending? Tell it to my dreams.

No sooner did Mr. Sandman whisk me out of my dried husk than I was in a nightmare. I still dream, but wish to hell I didn't. And this one I remembered. It was in a kind of Technicolor that makes your skin crawl. I was in the suburbs of Fort Hammer. Lenore was there, alive. We had two kids playing out back. I didn't know their names. I think it was a boy and a girl.

The bell rang. I got a bad feeling about it, but I opened the door anyway, because it's silly not to, right? There was a mattress-wide guy on the front step. He was hairless; his rounded shoulders matched the curve of his bald head. He had waxy skin, a thick brow, and dead eyes. *Dead* eyes. He didn't look at me. He looked off to the side and waited, like I was the one who was supposed to know what came next.

Telling myself I was crazy for being nervous, I asked, "Can I help you, buddy?"

Now, he looked at me, but I could tell he didn't like it.

Not me—he didn't like seeing anyone else's eyes. His thick lips parted. He struggled to make some sounds. It was a big effort, frustrating in the extreme. It made him angry to have to try.

I felt bad, but I couldn't make out any words. "Sorry, I don't understand."

He did it again, made the sounds, only slower and louder. His bare feet lifted a bit as he shifted from side to side. I could tell it was the same noises in the same sequence, but that was all. "Sorry?"

He gritted his teeth. His muscles tensed. I was creeped-out big-time and worried that if he smelled it on me, my fear would add to his frustration. He repeated himself a third time, but still no go.

I twisted my head to look past him, hoping there was a neighbor out, someone who might know what this was about, someone I could ask for help. Instead, all over the cul-de-sac, there were more like him, dozens, like a plague. They weren't exactly identical. One was a little shorter, another a little thinner, but they were all the same. There was at least one at the door of each house.

I turned back to mine and realized he'd been talking all along. Maybe he said it more clearly this last time and I hadn't paid attention. There was nothing I could do about it now, or about what came next. When I shook my head apologetically, his eyes flared. His thick lips curled into a bestial snarl. He screamed the sounds so loud it hurt my ears. I had to take a step back.

The others heard him. In unison, they turned toward my house, toward me. They walked toward me, slowly, like the shadow of a cloud.

Panting, he glared at me, waiting for my response. Our eyes met. He saw my fear.

"I don't understand!"

The nearest of the others reached my lawn. He looked angry, too. They all did. They were growling now. The one at my door stepped in. I tried to stop him, but couldn't. He was too big. I fell backward. He didn't hit me; I fell because I was so afraid. I lay on my back, helpless as they came.

The terror was so strong I wanted to curl into a ball and roll away forever. I tried to fight it, distract myself, but part of me knew that sooner or later, it was going to get me.

They were going to get me. And make me one of them.

"Hess, Hess! Wake up!"

Reality split like the pants on a fat man. I was in two places at once, no idea which one was real, which to believe in. I was standing in the living room surrounded by the idiot jackals. At the same time I was lying in the ratty recliner, looking up at Misty. If I had a choice, I knew which one I wanted, even if I was dead there. I lunged for my office.

"Hess, will you . . . ?"

The living room and the bald men flickered. There was a shiver or two, or three. As the dream let go, I threw myself out of the recliner, literally falling back into my office, the more palatable hell.

Sickly light dribbled through the holes in the yellowed shade behind Misty. It was morning. Misty, seeing my eyes open, stopped screaming and let go of me. Something was wrong. The more she came into focus, the more she seemed upset. About what? I wasn't moaning, was I? Not now. Things were looking up, right?

I sat and rubbed some splinters from the floor off my fingers.

"Sorry, Misty. Was I screaming in my sleep again? The drug dealers complaining?"

She shook her head. There were tears on her face. She looked like she had a dog I didn't know about, and it'd gotten hit by a car.

"What?"

"You have to see. . . ."

"What do I have to see?"

She could hardly talk. She turned her back, looking like she was going to run. Instead, she turned on the TV. A familiar talking head, the "litter-news" blonde. Over her shoulder a drone camera showed a stretch of the desert highway outside Fort Hammer. The scene looked familiar, like it was the same footage they used yesterday during Colin Wilson's story. Was it something new about him? Not bloody likely. Misty wouldn't shed tears over that. Still trying to orient myself, I caught a few snippets from the speaker:

". . . another chak body in pieces . . ."

". . . again, no head . . ."

". . . the mess never ends . . ."

Cut to garbage bag commercial. Nice placement.

The thought of another head out there gave me a shudder, but that still didn't explain Misty's reaction. While the set squawked about the bag's tight seal, I searched for her eyes in the dim room. What was I missing? She's bighearted, might be sympathetic about a D-cap, but it's a rough world and she knows it.

"You worried about me? Okay, so I was freaked out about Wilson, but do you really think a second D-cap story is going to put me over the edge? Hey . . . did I even tell you about Wilson?"

She didn't say.

The news came back on. Bust-shot blondie had up a picture of the victim's face. They always publicize the identity so they can charge surviving family for the cleanup. All at once I realized why Misty was upset.

It was a photo from better days. He was sporting one of the genuine smiles he had when with his loved ones, a grin that seemed to say, *Me? Lose my husband and child? End up convicted, then ripped? Cut into little pieces for the litter police to find? No way.*

They ID'd him off his fingerprints. Funny how fast. Maybe because he was tied up with the Bedtown hakker attack. Whatever.

It was Frank Boyle.

Less than twelve hours ago I'd risked my neck for him, and now he'd lost his. Another fantastic plan from the universe that brought you mankind.

A syrupy electric current, thick and deadly, rolled along my spine and into my gut, so strong it almost made me feel alive. But my body couldn't handle the overflow. The first thing I wanted to do was smash the wall with my fist, but before I could a wave of nausea swept over me. I looked around for a bucket until I remembered I couldn't throw up anymore. Out of some old reflex, I started panting.

"So one of the hakkers got him?" Misty asked.

I hadn't noticed, but she'd moved up alongside me and put a hand on my shoulder. We both stared at the set as it flashed a body-wash ad. She stroked the crumpled jacket I hadn't bothered taking off, trying to comfort herself more than me. When someone started yammering about the stock market, she turned the television off.

The hakkers. Not a bad guess, given the circumstances. But I doubted it. "Booth put the fear of the lord into them. They were heading in the opposite direction."

"Then who?"

I stated the obvious. "Cara and Marty Junior. His brother and sister. Turgeon said they wanted him out of the picture. But what the hell happened to Turgeon? Anything about him on the news?"

She shook her head no. "Do you think he's all right?"

I shrugged. "At best they'd paid him off; at worst the body just hasn't been found yet. Forty million is a lot of money. Enough to start a war in some parts of the world. Should be easy to get a few people offed for that much."

"But they're *family*...."

I tried not to laugh. "There's no enemy like a blood enemy."

Some species eat their young, but siblings can do even worse. I didn't have any myself, as far as I knew. Oh, my father liked to scare me by pretending I once had a brother who'd gotten out of line and had to be dealt with permanently, but I'm pretty sure he was kidding. Point being, while I didn't know if the Boyles were behind this, I knew they sure as hell could be. Hell, do you even call it murder when the victim's dead to begin with?

"We've got to call someone, tell them what we know."

"Yeah, if only we knew a detective."

"That's not what I meant."

"I'm not hurt. I haven't dealt with this kind of thing since I was alive." I struggled to my feet and started pacing. "The cops won't help. They wouldn't listen to me, wouldn't care about Boyle. But if Turgeon's in danger ... Misty, didn't he leave ... a ..."

"Phone number? Yeah, there was one on his card, I think."

I snatched it from my desk and struggled to punch the numbers on my cell. Chakz don't have the same dexterity in their fingertips. At least I didn't. It was like trying to dial with heavy work gloves. That's why I never text.

After a few awkward seconds, Misty looked like she wanted to grab the phone out of my hands. "Do you want me to ... ?"

"I got it," I snapped. Now I knew how Max, Lenore's grandfather, felt whenever I tried to help him up the stairs.

I somehow managed, but it was a worthless effort. Turgeon's phone number took me straight to voice mail. His recorded voice pronounced his name like nothing was wrong. I left a message saying something was, and he should get in touch ASAP.

The fact that he didn't answer meant nothing. The battery could be dead, he could be dead, or he could be on a flight to the Bahamas with his share of the take. I hoped it was the battery.

What next? Could I let Frank Boyle's killers go without doing something? As for Turgeon, I didn't particularly like him, but I owed him. The odds sucked royally. Liveblood millionaires and a chopped-up chak. It would be the hakkers all over again, only this time my opponents would be intelligent, so it wouldn't be a fair fight. I wouldn't hear them coming.

Tell that to my roiling guts. Even if I tried to let it go, I doubted it would let go of me. I'm not exactly a starry-eyed idiot, but I really thought Frank might build that home, and maybe I could get myself a room. That alone could drag me to feral city. I was going down one way or another, sitting or standing. So I grabbed my coat and headed for the door.

"Where are you going?"

"I've got some things to do."

She cut me off in the hallway, forced her face in front of mine. Brave girl, given my kisser.

"Hess, are you . . . okay?"

She knew I wasn't. That wasn't the real question. What she wanted to know was whether I was going to keep it together or do the wild thing. I was her lifeline as much as she was mine. If I went down, so did she.

It wasn't multiple choice. There was only one answer I could give. "Yes. I'll be fine."

"You sure?"

I looked around, trying to think of some proof. I stared at the paint peeling on the walls, watched a rat scurry off with a piece of hamburger bun in its teeth. Its hunger, at least, gave it something to do. That was my answer. It was something to do.

"I have to find whoever did this. I'm not going anywhere until I do. Ask me again when it's over."

She gave me a slow nod, like a nanny not quite buying the child's explanation, but not wanting to challenge it.

Before she said anything else, I handed her my cell. "Put Turgeon's number on the speed dial for me? I want to keep trying him."

It took her half a second, but by the time she handed my phone back, she was warming to the idea of working on this. "I'll keep an eye on the news and take notes for you."

"Use the pad, not the Post-its. Number everything," I

told her. Post-its are great for small stuff, but this would require more organized thinking.

"You got it. Hess, where are you going to start?"

"Where do you think? Scene of the crime."

"Don't forget your hat. You need the shade."

I grabbed it, and some of Turgeon's cash, and headed out alone, except for the day, and the day was never much company, especially during the summer. Moist heat makes it easier for bacteria to grow, for rotting to set in. The sunlight makes it easier to see the gray tinge to my skin, makes it harder for even a "lucky one" to blend in, unless there was a real early Halloween party. I wasn't wild about it, but if I really was going to do anything, I had to leave the Bones.

I kept the hat on at the Rent-A-Wreck, hoping I could get in and out before they realized I was among the dearly departed, but the agent grabbed my hand to shake and spotted the gray skin. With a grin he doubled the fees for the cheapest piece of shit on the lot. I didn't object so much as groan, but he still went into his song and dance. It wasn't enough he was screwing me; he had to yammer on about the extra insurance for chakz, and how he was within his rights to refuse to rent to me at all. I handed him the cash. My nice big wad of bills was already getting smaller.

I kept the windows up and the clunky AC on. The trip was uneventful, a straight shot, so I didn't have to worry about my driving much, and it was broad daylight, so no hakkers. My biggest concern was that the damn four-cylinder tin can I was driving would overheat and leave me to bake in the desert.

Once I recognized the spot from the news, I pulled over alongside the prominent No Dumping sign and got out of the car. Fucking desert. The heat from it rose right up through the bottom of my shoes. First thing I noticed was that someone had dumped a few garbage bags right next to the sign. Funny. They didn't mind the kitchen trash so much as the bodies. It didn't attract coyotes as much, or freak the families on their way in or out.

I scanned the dried weeds, the dust swirls, the sand that wanted to be dunes but couldn't get its act together because of the rocks. Beyond that, except for a few pieces of shriveled, dried plant, the ground was flat. A few marks could be tire tracks, or not. I followed and they petered out. A bit of police tape twisted in the wind.

I trudged around, kicked some sand, pretended some other marks might be more tire tracks, or a spot where an arm or a leg might have been. Wilson and Boyle were both dumped here. Were the heads out there, too, still . . . thinking?

That image wasn't helping. I had to focus, but there wasn't much to focus on here. Maybe I should head back to town, try to retrace their steps. But I had no idea where the Humvee headed after it dropped me off; I only knew where it came from. Big piss yellow thing like that would be easy to spot, though. Some druggie or low-level chak back in the Bones may have seen it and thought he was hallucinating.

I headed back toward the rental, absently calling Turgeon as I walked. One ring, nothing. Two rings . . .

I heard a chirping behind me. I whirled, tried to follow the sound. The ten rings passed and I got his message again. The second time I hit the number on the speed dial, I found it, facedown in the sand, a brownish streak along the plastic, a darker color than the silver or the sand. Blood.

I wished I had a plastic bag to put it in, so I wouldn't contaminate the evidence. Old instinct. I tore off a piece of shirt and picked it up as gingerly as I could.

It wasn't good news. Chakz don't bleed like that. If we bleed at all, it's more what that old horror writer Lovecraft called a "putrescent ooze." The red stuff on the phone belonged to a liveblood, and I had a sinking feeling I knew who.

Poor baby. He was as much out of his depth as I was out of mine. Had a gun, didn't he? Two, counting mine. I wonder if he went down fighting. I was sure Boyle did. He'd go crazy trying to protect . . .

Ashby. I'd forgotten all about him. Fucking memory. They hadn't found his body either. Whoever did this probably didn't expect a third party. The chances were slim to nothing, but maybe he'd survived. I had no idea where Turgeon lived or worked, but if the kid could walk, he'd likely head back to the only place he knew.

I hopped in the car and made for Bedland.

The radio told me what to expect. The place was still a mess. A bunch of the inhabitants *had* gone feral—wonder why. The national guard was all over the place. Ignoring the sanitation truck where they piled the bodies, I parked. If I'd been a liveblood, the guardsmen might have stopped me for my own protection. As it was, as long as I wasn't moaning, after casting a suspicious glance my way they didn't care.

They'd already cleared the buildings, but were still hunting the brush. As I walked along, every now and then I'd hear a rifle crack echo through the dry woods. Cripple 'em, D-cap 'em. Boyle and Wilson could have been anyone, really.

There but for fortune.

With all the decapitations, it wasn't easy finding a familiar face, but an hour later, as far away as you could get from everything, down in a basement rec room, I stumbled on Thornell. With the gunshots muffled to near nothing, he was shooting pool all by his lonesome. He looked up when I came in.

His arm was back on. Krazy Glue and thread. I didn't think the hand was working, but it made a nice bridge to lay the cue on. With a sound too much like a rifle crack, he sank an easy corner shot.

"Mann, you came back," he said.

I was going to ask how he could play games with the shantytown crumbling around him; then I realized he was just like me. He had to do *something* to keep busy. Solve a crime, play pool. To each his own. From what I saw outside, they'd lost at least thirty people.

I heard a howl from somewhere outside. Thornell rubbed his cue with chalk, loudly, trying to drown it out. I didn't know if he had heard about Boyle, or if it would make any difference. I had to be careful. Finding out he was chopped up could be the straw that broke Thornell's back. I decided to play it by ear.

"Pretty crazy seeing you. What do you want?" he said. "Got more good news for a chak? Better hurry while there's some left."

"I'm curious about Frank Boyle," I said. "He have any enemies?"

Another gunshot, then the crack of the cue ball against number eight. "Enemies? Are you fucking out of your mind? Sure, he had enemies. Almost seven billion."

"Good point." I waited a few shots, then asked the big question: "That kid Ashby find his way back here by any chance?"

Thornell stood up straight as an arrow. Pay dirt. "Who wants to know?"

I shrugged. "Me. Why? Anyone else looking?"

"The cops, maybe," Thornell said. "Didn't you used to be a cop?"

"Used to be," I told him. "Look, I just want to see if he's okay, that's all."

"He's not," Frankenstein said. He nodded toward what looked like a supply closet. I took a few steps toward it.

"So much for that haven, huh?" Thornell said. So he did know about Boyle.

Something popped into my head. I hesitated to mention it. Then, I don't know why, but I said, "You know Jonesey from the Bones? He's thinking about organizing a rally."

Thornell seemed amused. He snorted through his nose. "Really? A chak rally? That's bat-shit crazy."

I agreed, then opened the door.

The space on the other side was small, windowless, full of mops, cleaning supplies, and a big pile of rags on the floor.

Only the pile of rags had a nervous laugh. "Heh-heh."

I got closer, nudged the pile with my foot. It trembled.

I tried to remember how to sound gentle. "Ashby, you remember me?"

"Heh-heh."

I scanned his body, checked his limbs. He looked like he was in one piece.

I knelt so he could see my face. "I was in the car with you and Frank, remember? Big yellow car?"

He picked his head up a little. "Cool car. Heh-heh. Frank. Frank. Frank."

I spoke slowly. "Did you see what happened to Frank?"

He shook like his whole body remembered. "It was bad. Heh-heh. They thought I shot the cop, but he shot himself. Heh-heh. I ran and I ran. Frank knows I didn't do it. He has to tell them or I'll be executed."

Damn. He was half in the room, half back in the convenience store. "Right. Frank knows you were innocent. He was in the big yellow car with you and Mr. Turgeon. Do you remember that? You dropped me off and drove away?"

"Frank shoved me. I ran and ran. They thought I shot that cop. They jumped out and came after me."

They?

"Who came after you? Was it Boyle's brother and sister? Cara and Martin? Do you know what they look like?"

Stupid question. They'd have hired some local goons.

"Thought I shot the cop. Had a pair of clippers. Needed two hands, heh-heh," he said. Then he clamped his fists, slammed them together, and made a cutting noise.

"Did you see what happened to Mr. Turgeon? The driver? Guy who looked like an egg?"

He twisted his head. I thought he was nodding.

"Frank?" he said. "Heh-heh. Can you find him?"

This was getting nowhere fast. I patted him on the knees, rose to leave, and said exactly the wrong thing. "I'm going to try."

He got up, ready to follow.

"I'm coming with you," he said. "Heh-heh."

He was the only witness. I figured taking him would be safer than leaving him here. The place was falling apart at the seams, and the Boyles might decide to tie up loose ends. Maybe I could sort through all that gibberish and get some details. Besides, like Thornell, like me, he needed something to do, too.

"Heh-heh."

But the laugh was already getting to me.

8

Parrots. We sounded like a couple of parrots.

He'd say, "Heh-heh. We're going to find Frank."

And I'd tell him, "Sure, kid, sure."

It was a long drive back. Two or three times as long as it should have been, and I was speeding. All the while, I didn't have the heart to ask Ashby if he realized we were only looking for Frank's head. The rest had already been accounted for.

I've done stupider things than letting him tag along, but I couldn't think of any. The really stupid part was thinking I could make sense of him. He was like his own ghost, stuck in what paranormal investigators call a "residual haunting," a spirit replaying his trauma over and over. It's not intelligent, can't chat about the weather; it only plays it routine.

When he wasn't talking about finding Frank, he didn't even realize Frank was gone. Every now and then, for half a sentence he'd worry about his "upcoming" trial—

you know, the one where he was convicted and put to death? Then he'd spin back to Frank.

"Heh-heh."

The big thing I couldn't figure out was why he hadn't gone feral. Hell, I had enough trouble dealing with my own brain. How far a leap could it be from "heh-heh" to gnashing teeth? Did the brain damage work like a defense mechanism? If the gods watched out for drunks and madmen, God was his autopilot. Meaning, if he couldn't pay attention to anything long enough to get depressed about it, he'd never get depressed.

Ha. If I wanted to avoid doing the wild thing, maybe I should bash my head with a crowbar a few times. Listening to him, I certainly wanted to.

It wasn't until we cruised past the No Dumping sign, the land around it barren and lonely even in the daylight, that something different happened. Ashby spasmed like he'd been slapped, and spit out a jumble of words. He was talking so fast I was afraid to interrupt. I pulled over and listened, fishing as best I could in the babbling brook.

I thought about having him walk around, but it seemed cruel. The kid was sounding more and more upset, so I decided to get him back to town.

As the desert receded, Ashby calmed down. It was all, "Heh-heh. We're going to find Frank," again.

I had a few ideas about what to do next, but kept losing track of them. I didn't know if any of them were good, but, afraid I might lose the one that was, driving with one hand I unpacked the new recorder I'd bought with Turgeon's money. Nearly lost a finger on the titanium-plastic packaging. It was a pretty nice machine. Even came with a suction-cupped microphone, for recording phone calls, or conversations on the other side of a window. Once I got the batteries in and stuffed the microphone attachments into a pocket, I made a few notes, hoping I'd remember how to access the time stamp.

I was almost finished when the air conditioner stopped working. Aside from Ashby's being such a great conversationalist, now I had to worry about staying fresh. Fucking microbes. Any chak who isn't a germaphobe is kidding himself. I thought about getting some of that power body wash, but it might eat my skin away.

Did you know you could melt a chak with a can of Coke? There's a video up on YouTube. Takes a long, long time.

We reached Fort Hammer proper by the ugly midafternoon. The heat was making all sorts of smells rise off the pavement. I dropped off the car, paid the extra fees the manager slipped onto the bill, and headed to the local library, hoping to get a lead on Martin and Cara. Instead of the car, I had to steer Ashby. The guy couldn't even turn a corner by himself.

The library was a small stone building with two faux pillars out front. Since it was a public place, technically they couldn't kick us out unless we caused a disturbance, by, I dunno, eating one of the librarians. It was a step down from the Styx, our local cybercafé, one room about the size of a hotel lobby, with an Internet connection less reliable than a check in the mail, but I didn't think Ashby would go over well with the Bohemians.

Once I maneuvered the kid through the doors, I felt a blast of cool air. At least it was air conditioned. I wasn't cooking anymore. I was also relieved to see that, for a change, the Internet was up and running.

The only thing that made me worry was an old beanstalk standing guard at the head of the terminals. He was tall, withered, skin and bones except for the skin part, and his eyes were mostly white. I would've taken him for one of us, but a glob of spit on his lip pegged him as a liveblood. He was one of the homeless, trying to get out of the heat. Didn't blame him, but street folk tend to get territorial, especially around chakz, since we're the only ones they can push around; *this box is mine, that rag is mine,* and so on. But this poor old bastard looked less mobile than the book stack he was leaning against.

I found two terminals side by side and set up Ashby with some game that had bright shiny lights. My keyboard had the escape key missing, no metaphor intended, but some of the others looked worse, so I settled in and tried to do what I do worst—focus.

After checking my recorder to remind myself why I was there in the first place, I started with the *clickety-click*, seeing if I could come up with an address for the living Boyles. The only thing slower than my typing was the response time. I wanted to throw more coal into the damn thing's furnace to try to speed it up.

I'd like to say the answer popped up, but it was more like it dribbled in, an apartment in the center of town on, wait for it, Wealthy Street. We were never much for street names in Fort Hammer. It was a family home. Both siblings and Martin Senior were listed. I guess word of his death hadn't made it to the directories yet. In a way, it was better than a private estate, where they could have their security do all sorts of things to me in secluded splendor. I might be able to sneak in and out as part of the trash. If they were even still in the city.

Rather than wait for the full Google, I pulled out my recorder to get down the address. Almost had it, too, but the white-eyed string bean I spotted on the way in started screaming. I hoped he was doing a random schizophrenic thing, but the finger he jabbed in my direction said otherwise.

"'Son of man, can these bones live?' 'O Lord God, thou knowest!'"

Great. An evangelist. I knew the quote. Grandma was a churchgoer. Ezekiel in the Valley of Dry Bones. Famous passage, even has its own song—the leg bones connected to the hip bone, etc. But the old man wasn't singing. He came closer, finger first.

"Unclean bones!"

I'd have been offended if it wasn't so accurate. Ashby turned from his screen, looking worried. "Heh-heh."

"You reek of brimstone and death!" Now he was aiming at Ashby.

"Hey, take it easy," I said.

"Breathe!"

When I stood to block him, everyone in the small library stopped and stared. I guess we were more interesting than whatever they were reading.

The old man went into a fit, eyes rolling all over the place. If he'd been a chak I'd expect him to start moaning.

"Breathe on these dead!"

"Easy, easy! Could you give it to me in English, pal?"

He shook his finger at the kid. "There! There! Behold!"

His nostrils flared. His eyes rolled again, but this time he looked like he was really grossed out. I took a sniff and suddenly realized what his problem was. It was

Ashby. His face and arms looked okay, but the smell was unmistakable. The kid had some rot on him somewhere, probably made worse after the hot car ride.

The last thing I needed was a fight with a crazy live-blood with a good sense of smell. I had the address, so I'd done all I could for now anyway.

"Okay, got it. We're going! Come on, Ashby."

"Heh-heh."

"Back to the valley, back to the dust, unclean dead!" he croaked.

"Right. Exactly. We were headed there anyway." I pulled the kid toward the door, then back out into the sun.

The old man kept yelling, but didn't follow. Soon as we were clear, I yanked my hand back from Ashby. I should've been more careful about touching him. That stuff can spread fast. I'd been in a car with him last night and hadn't even noticed. I had to get him back to the office so Misty could have a good look at him.

Taxi was out of the question. Only a few would hit the Bones to begin with, and an odor like the kid had could ruin the comfy seats. Turned out the smell was so bad, I couldn't even get him on a bus. I walked him, fast as I could, nearly shoved him up the stairs and through the door.

Misty caught the smell before she even saw his face. I made some quick introductions.

"Can you take care of it?"

Her hands went to her hips, lingered, then covered up her nose. "You know I'm not a cleaning lady, right, Hess?"

"I know; I just have a lead I have to follow fast," I said; then I tried to look helpless.

She narrowed her eyes. "If there's any deep cutting, you'll be helping."

"Promise," I said. I felt bad about that. I had no idea when I'd be back.

"Heh-heh."

Ashby gave her what looked like a smile. Misty tried to smile back, but couldn't quite manage it.

9

I thought getting into the building would be the hard part. I don't know who I was kidding. Turned out reaching the damn thing was the challenge. Unless we're delivering something or picking something up, chakz do not belong on Wealthy Street—and I definitely didn't look like a cheery FedEx man. The second I got off the bus, heads turned. Wherever I walked, livebloods gawked. Heaven forbid I should ask for directions.

I pulled the hat down so far I nearly tore the brim, but my face was only half the problem. My crumpled clothes didn't even match the pavement. It was only a matter of time before someone called the cops and had me arrested for aesthetic reasons. With my luck, Booth would show up.

I stuck to the alleys as much as I could, but even those were so clean that I stood out. Then again, so did my destination. No gleaming tower, 128 Wealthy Street was its own kind of zombie. It was dark, and had a kind of foreboding nineteenth-century splendor, with high gables, deep roofs, terra-cotta spandrels, and the like. Almost like a big, finely decorated fortress. It was also one of the most desirable addresses in the city.

The Boyles were on the sixth floor, not quite the penthouse, but not too shabby, either. There was no way I'd be getting past the doorman, so I wandered along the side and manage to slip into a service entrance and make for the stairs. That much was on my side. No one uses stairs anymore. So there was nothing between me and their apartment.

The big question was, What was I going to do once I got there? There was a time when I could stare a suspect down and he'd confess. I didn't think I'd be that lucky, especially without a badge, but I did think that if I could talk to them, even for a little while, they'd let something slip. See, I doubted they'd knocked off a brother every day. Odds were this was a one-and-only event in their little lives. First-timers are always sloppy, especially emotionally. They'd give me something. Maybe it would just be a narrowing of their eyes if I mentioned Turgeon's name, or a twitchy lip when I talked about Frank's plans for his inheritance, but it'd be something. I only hoped I'd be on the ball enough to spot it.

After that, I had no idea what came next, but at least I'd know I had my perps.

The hall was wide, neat plaster with art deco sconces that looked original. The Boyle residence was one of three on the floor. I straightened my jacket and tie as best I could, took my hat off, and knocked on the heavy oak door.

A lock clicked; it swung inward. An old geezer, nicely dressed, in pretty good shape, still with some color in his hair, blocked my view of anything behind

him. Butler, I figured, judging from the stiff posture
and stone manner.

That gave me an advantage. He had no idea what to
make of me.

I put my foot in the frame and said, "Cara or Martin
Junior in?"

He took a step back, purely on instinct. Seems the
thing to do when a dead man comes to your door.

Recovering from his initial shock, he scowled pretty
fiercely. "How did you get in? Get out of here. Get out
of here at once."

I could tell he was used to having chakz obey him, so
I came on strong, just to keep him off guard. "No can
do, Jeeves. But the sooner I talk to them, the sooner I'll
be gone. Want to tell them I'm here? And maybe take
my hat?"

"I'll do no such thing!" he said.

His hand came out, fast and flat, to shove me in the
chest. He probably thought one quick push would send
me sprawling into the hallway, so he could slam the
door. If he'd been ten years younger, ten years faster, it
would've worked. As it was, before he connected I managed an uppercut to the solar plexus. For a second I was
afraid I'd hurt myself more than I'd hurt him. My wrist
felt like I'd nearly snapped it. But I caught him right
where I wanted. He keeled over, went fetal, and started
moaning.

I stepped over him into a huge living room tastefully
decorated with a few paintings. Chayce was the artist, I
think. He was a pretty big local talent that the beautiful
people oohed and ahhed over. Not to my tastes, but I
admit he has a nice use of negative space.

The art appreciation class didn't last long. No sooner

did my street-worn shoes settle on the plush carpet than a stately woman rushed in.

"Is someone at the . . . ?"

Her gaze went straight to the guy on the floor.

Cara, I presumed. Couldn't be sure yet. There was a photo on the computer, but I only saw it for a few seconds. She was very thin, but lovely, even in middle age, and had a finely carved face that showed just the right amount of cheekbone. It was only when I saw a bit of Frank's eyes in hers that I was sure it was his sister. For a second I felt like a garish intruder, until I remembered why I was there. If she was guilty, she deserved it; if not, she should be grateful someone cared.

"Your butler's fine," I said. "Just had the wind knocked out of him. I want to talk to you about your brother Frank Boyle. I was with him last night. I gotta wonder, do you know what he was going to do with all that money? Can you guess?"

She didn't guess. She just screamed.

"Hold on!" I said. "Relax! I'm not going to hurt you."

But she didn't relax, either. She kept screaming.

I took a step toward her, hands out, trying to calm her down, but that only made her scream louder. "Hey! I just want to talk to you! You know a man named Turgeon?"

No narrowed eyes. No sloppy giveaways. Just screaming, long and loud.

A glimpse at a gilded-frame oval mirror next to one of the Chayces gave me a picture worth a thousand words. There we were, she stately as a statue, me a monster, hovering over her servant, lumbering toward her.

Shit. I knew I wasn't alive anymore. I mean, it's a hard fact to miss, but inside, even when my brain didn't work,

I was still, deep down, acting and thinking like I was the same. I don't think I really realized until that moment exactly how much I wasn't.

I made for the stairs and ran down as fast as I was able. Even in the alley, I could still hear her screaming. I thought I could still hear her two blocks away, but that was probably my imagination.

Looking back, I probably could've played it better.

10

Fans were running, the shades were drawn, but the office was only a little cooler than a furnace. Worse, it stank like an indoor swimming pool at a morgue. Having gotten back home a lot sooner than expected, I was, as promised, helping Misty with the cutting. I couldn't hold the knife steady enough, so I held the flashlight. I was always the one holding the flashlight. It never stopped me from giving advice.

"Christ, Misty, careful; he needs that muscle to move the arm."

I was being a little rough on her, but I was antsy. Long day.

"Heh-heh."

She gave me a withering look. "I'm trying to be gentle, but you know I've got to get it all."

She was in a funny position, kneeling by Ashby, holding his arm up, going at the underside with a small X-Acto blade. After every scrape, she dipped the blade in an ashtray filled with bleach.

"Damn, it's in a weird spot, nearly in his armpit. Move the ashtray closer, will you?"

"Ashby, ashtray. Heh-heh."

"No wonder Boyle missed it," I said.

"Frank, heh-heh."

"Hold still, Ashby. Hess, can you tell him to hold still?"

I looked at him. "I can try, but it sounds better coming from you. I think he likes you."

That got me another look. After a few more scrapes and grimaces, I had to ask, "How bad?"

"Not terrible," she said, twisting her neck. "Not even an inch deep. I think I've almost got it all."

She flicked the blade. A dollop of rot fell into the ashtray. When she started scraping again, she must have hit clean muscle. Ashby twitched.

"Heh-heh-heh-heh-heh . . ."

"Where did you go, anyway, Hess?"

I made a face. "Anything on the news about a chak breaking into a ritzy apartment in the center of town?"

She stopped working to stare at me. "No."

"Then I don't want to talk about it."

She sighed and waved me closer. "That's it. Pretty sure I've got it all. Hold his arm, will you? And hand me the needle and thread."

I pulled them from the kit and forked them over. "Just don't ask me to thread the damn thing."

"Don't worry; I won't. But you have to keep him still."

I grabbed his elbow and shoulder and held tight. Needle between her lips, Misty pinched the skin together good as I've ever seen a doctor do, held it with thumb and forefinger, then grabbed the needle with her free hand and sewed.

As the point disappeared, then reappeared on the other side of the skin, the kid gawked at his arm like it didn't belong to him. It's not good for a chak to think that way. Makes you careless. I snapped my fingers to get his attention.

"Look at something else, Ashby."

He listened, shifting his attention to the stinky blobs of gray-green pus floating in the ashtray.

"That's how we all wind up, pal," I said. "Efficient fuckers, microbes."

"At least it wasn't maggots," Misty said.

"Hell, yeah."

We almost never get those, unless we try eating. We don't need to eat, but some of us like to go through the motions, like Jonesey with his espressos. Not enough protein in black coffee to do much damage, but a chak eats a burger, he's asking for an infestation. I've seen it happen. Think the living are stupid? I agree, but chakz make them look like geniuses.

"Heh-heh."

"Hess, he's twitching."

"Easy, kid, you're in good hands. The best. I've seen her reattach a foot with some Krazy Glue and a staple gun. Course, it didn't stay on long."

Ashby writhed, did his nervous laugh, and went back to watching his arm.

Misty tsked. "Did you have to tell him that last part?"

I wasn't kidding about him liking her. Since we'd started, every time she opened her mouth, he calmed down a little. It gave me an idea.

"Kid, instead of the arm, why don't you look at her? She's not so bad to look at, right?"

Ashby looked at me, puzzled, then turned to Misty. An intense expression came over him, a kind of fascination, almost the same way he stared at the lights on the computer game.

"Told you he likes you."

"Hess, you're making me blush. Not a good idea while I'm sewing."

"Frank never cut me."

We both stopped and looked at him. It was the first coherent sentence out of his mouth since I'd brought him back from Bedland, subject, object, verb, everything. Misty did have a knack for bringing the human side out in people, even the walking-corpse kind. Then again, most chakz are shocked when *any* LB is nice to them.

She gave him a slow smile. "I'm sorry, honey, but I had to use the knife. If I left any rot in there, it'd keep growing, infect you. You could lose a lot of muscle."

"And those boyish good looks," I added. But it was like I wasn't even in the room.

He kept staring at Misty, scrutinizing her as she made her last few stitches. I watched him watch her. Finally he turned his head nearly sideways and asked, "And then I'd die?"

Misty looked up at him. He waited to hear from her, but she didn't know how to put it. "Hess, you want to answer that?"

I shook my head. "I think you should. Probably doesn't matter what words you use. Maybe he's remembering puberty."

"Hess!"

"Well . . . maybe he's remembering *something*."

"Fine. No, Ashby, it won't kill you, but it can eat away at your flesh, make you mostly bone. You don't want that, do you?"

Her motherly tone made me wonder if she *had* a kid of her own out there. Misty wasn't much for talking about her past, and I wasn't much for asking.

He shook his head. "No, I don't want that."

She made a few more stitches and said, "There, all done."

I let go. He twisted his arm, looked at the line of plastic thread, and grinned. "All done, heh-heh. Do I look okay?"

"Of course you do," Misty said.

I nodded. "Like you're all set for your junior prom."

Halloween prom, maybe.

His eyes followed her movements as she stretched her arms and back, then returned the needle and thread to the little kit. I almost enjoyed watching her myself.

"Misty, you're a real Frankenstein Nightingale. And I mean that in the nicest way."

I pulled one of the envelopes out of the desk drawer and pulled out a few more bills.

"Wish you'd deposit that," Misty said, screwing the cap back on the bleach bottle. "I don't like having it around."

"You and me both."

"You should deposit it," Ashby said.

"That's right, Ashby," Misty said. "He should. You tell him."

She took the ashtray, dumped the contents in the small toilet off my office, and flushed. Ashby was riveted, like he was watching his favorite movie.

"You got a next move, Detective?" she asked.

I shoved the envelopes back in the drawer. "I was afraid you'd ask that. I still don't know what happened to Turgeon. Oh. Wait a minute. Maybe I do."

"What do you mean? You think he survived?"

With a stubby thumb and forefinger, I gingerly took out the bloody cell phone. "No."

"Oh, my God, Hess, is that . . . ?"

I nodded. "Evidence. And my pocket isn't exactly a sterile environment. We got a plastic bag around here somewhere?"

Exasperated, she said, "Sure, why don't I just pull one out of my butt?"

"Probably be cleaner than my pocket."

"Heh-heh. Heh-heh."

She shook her head at the kid. It was me she was annoyed with, but Ashby took it personally. Surprising us yet again, he looked sheepishly at Misty and said, "Sorry, can't help it."

"Oh, that's okay, honey. I know it's not your fault," she said. She stuck a thumb in my direction. "Him, though, I know he can keep his trap shut when he wants. I've seen it."

"Hah," he said. Just like that, a real laugh. Hah.

At first I thought of Misty only as a good way to keep him steady, but this was getting interesting. I pointed to the door. "Misty, a word in the reception area?"

The "reception area" was a gray piece of work; the only bits of color were what peeked out behind the peeling paint and looked sticky. It doubled as a storage space and Misty's bedroom. She sat on the edge of her cot and crossed her legs. As I sat next to her, some vague half memory told me I should be looking at them. It was just a twinge, and it left as soon as it came, but it made me realize Misty had been looking healthier lately.

I whispered, "I want you to try to ask him about last night. Whatever happened, he was there. When I talked to him about it, he kept flashing back to his arrest, but you . . ."

"You really think I can focus him?"

"Looks that way so far," I said. "I'll give you some privacy."

She nodded and stood. I hesitated, but then I figured, Why not? "It probably wouldn't hurt if you sat down close and crossed your legs."

"Hess!" she said. She slapped me playfully on the shoulder, then paused and frowned. "Really?"

I shrugged. "Worth a shot. If you don't remind him of his mother, maybe you remind him of some teacher he wanted to screw."

She rolled her eyes and went back in. I settled back and leaned my head against the wall. The rot smell wasn't so strong here, and I caught a whiff of the cheap perfume she used, buys it by the quart. Big heart, Misty. Works with the bleach so much, her hands are always dried out. I keep telling her to use those big yellow gloves, but she never listens.

I heard her talking, softly, Ashby doing the nervous laugh, but I couldn't make out any words. I put my ear against the plaster. Still no go. With no confession forthcoming from the Boyles, Turgeon was my only other link. Even if he was dead, it'd be a lot tougher to hide a liveblood body. His boss, at least, would be missing him. That was something I could follow up on.

After a while, there was more "heh-heh" than not.

When she opened the door I could hear Ashby running like a lawn mower—"Heh-heh-heh-heh-heh."

"Anything?"

"I think so. For some reason, they went back out of town. A black car cut them off and two men attacked them, one with a lot of muscle and a scar on his forehead, the other older, African-American, I think, with short white hair. They forced them to drive off the road, out into the desert. One of them pulled out a set of head clippers. Ashby says they tried to hold Frank down, but he put up enough of a fight to kick open the door and push Ashby out. Ashby thinks they chased him, but he wasn't sure."

I blew some dry air through pursed lips, but still couldn't whistle. "Maybe *you* should be the detective."

She sat down and rubbed her temples. "No, thanks. I don't have the stomach."

"I could give you mine."

"Cute."

I tried to picture the scene. "The goons were probably hired guns. If they were local, the descriptions might ring a bell with Jonesey. Anything about Turgeon?"

She shook her head. "Only that he and Frank had been talking about a man named Kendrick."

"Frank Boyle's husband. It might mean something, or maybe Turgeon was just being nosy again."

"Heh-heh-heh-heh-heh."

Misty shrugged. "Anyway, that's when he started making that sound over and over. Maybe if I had nicer legs."

"Your legs are fine. You could stand to eat more. But the name shouldn't upset the kid. Kendrick wasn't Ashby's dad."

"Heh-heh-heh-heh-heh." It was coming out nonstop now, like a machine gun.

"Maybe it upset Frank and *that* upset Ashby?"

"Heh-heh-heh-heh-heh."

It made sense, but it felt like it should make more sense, like I'd understand if I could only focus. The laugh was getting to me, though.

"Heh-heh-heh-heh-heh."

I rapped my forehead. "Okay. It doesn't look good for Turgeon, but if Ashby survived, maybe he did, too. Misty, can you call around to the hospitals, see if he checked in?"

"Sure. What about you?"

"I'll go check out the other possibility."

"Meaning?"

"Do I have to spell it out? No one gives a shit about Frank Boyle, but if a liveblood turns up dead under suspicious circumstances, they take the body to the police coroner."

11

Fort Hammer's police station was an old building in a city full of them. It'd been renovated a few times, when the economy was good. Built in the 1920s, it had an art deco look, the craze that swept the nation when archaeologists found Tut's tomb. Everything looked like ancient Egypt for a while—worshipers of the dead. In the 1980s they added a new wing devoted to holding cells, designed to match.

To me, it was different things: office, library, dungeon. When my photographic memory went, it took a lot of the picture albums with it. I could no longer recognize the exact spot on the wall where I'd rammed a perp's head into the fine stonework, or exactly where I'd leaned back for a smoke while the rest of the department was laughing over a job well-done or hooting over some woman's rack. I got tingles, though, feelings like I *should* remember.

I did know where the rear entrance was, and I was smart enough to head there fast. If any of my former coworkers saw me, I didn't doubt I'd be buried so deep I could crawl down into China. Funny. Boyle wouldn't even get that burial. Then again, Booth wouldn't bother to D-cap me first.

The morgue was in the basement, open until three—I didn't even have to worry about running into the coroner, Anthony Philbrick. A round guy with a vague goatee, he had a pretty good sense of humor. He was one of the few I used to clown around with. Not someone I wanted to see, and not because I didn't like him. While I was in jail, I heard that ever since he saw Lenore's body, he hadn't cracked a grin.

The after-hours guy was a chak. I could picture him easily, but I was damned if I could remember his name. Half his abdomen was gone, but that was always covered by his clothes, so you wouldn't notice unless he bent in a weird way. His face was intact except for a missing chunk of his chin. Nothing unusual. Maybe I remembered because he didn't wear the typical chak deadpan. There was a slight look of shock haunting his face, as if all his worldly concerns had been blown away all at once, and part of him was still going, "Oh."

Not surprising. He got the job because he was a vet. He did four tours before an IED caught him, got brought back in the early days, when people thought ripping was a good idea. His folks did it. Unlike a lot of others who tried it and ran, they stuck by him. Even Booth didn't dare stop that hire. And I couldn't remember his name.

I knelt by the basement window. There he was, running a hose on the tiled floor, steering some gunk or other toward one of the drains. I'd been hoping to play on his sympathy as a fellow chak, but that wouldn't go over big if I didn't even know what to call him. Still, nothing ventured, nothing gained. Maybe it would come to me.

I rapped on the window, half expecting him not to remember me, half hoping he wouldn't. But when he saw me he waved. Not knowing if that was a good thing or a bad thing, I motioned with my hands for him to open the door.

A few seconds later, his ghostly face greeted me.

"Mann," he said. Given his natural look, I didn't know whether he was surprised to see me or not.

"Hey," I answered.

He studied my face, avoided eye contact. "You been on leave, Detective? Haven't seen you around here in a while."

Wow. Not only did he not realize I was dead, but either he didn't remember or no one told him I'd been arrested for killing my wife. I wasn't about to tell him.

"Something like that," I said. "Listen . . . can you help me out? Any bodies come in last night or today? Big guy named Turgeon?"

"You mean liveblood?"

"Yeah."

He shook his head. "Got a John Doe, but that's it."

"Can I see him?"

He shrugged and pointed. There were three silver tables along one of the tiled walls. One had a sheet over it. The tiles were the ugliest damn yellow I'd ever seen in my life. Reflected the fluorescents and made everything look sickly.

I stepped up and pulled the sheet back. It definitely wasn't Turgeon.

"I think you meant *Jane* Doe."

"Right," he said. "Jane. I should change the tag."

He spun, put the mop down, and started looking for a marker. I took another look at the body. "Looks like a car accident, if anyone wants to know. Hit and run."

"Uh-huh."

I covered Jane up with the sheet and looked around. "That's it?"

"Yep. Quiet week."

The rest of the tables were empty. The log only had one entry. Then I noticed a couple of plastic bins under the dissecting table.

"What're those?"

"Chakz," he said absently. "From the desert."

"From the . . ." I pulled one out. There was a label on top: *Wilson*.

"Colin Wilson, like on the television?" I felt a wave of déjà vu as I said the name, like I'd been here before and didn't like it the first time.

"I guess."

"The other one. Frank Boyle?"

"Maybe. Sounds familiar."

I pulled the second bin out just to make sure. Yeah, it was Frank. A little shudder ran through me, my body warning me to watch it with the emotional reactions.

"Mind if I take a look?"

He stopped looking for the marker to eyeball me. "Why? What's a liveblood care?"

"I . . . I'm curious."

"Go ahead."

I opened the lid. Frank Boyle's arms were stacked on top, the legs below that, the torso on the bottom. I checked his pockets, but they were already emptied.

Out of a sick curiosity, I looked at Colin Wilson, too. Not what I expected, though, really, how could I expect anything? His clothes weren't as neat. He had a tattoo on his right arm, which was beefier than I'd pictured it being.

I looked from one to the other. Pieces of a man I barely knew, pieces of another I didn't know at all, but both of them haunted me.

I hadn't noticed, but the vet had walked up beside me. "Notice anything?" he said.

I snapped my head around. "No. Why? Do you?"

He shrugged. "Yeah. I told Mr. Philbrick about it, but it's just a couple of chakz, right?"

"What did you notice?"

"You're the detective; can't you see?"

I shook my head. "Sorry."

Kind of like a mechanic showing me something obviously wrong with my car, he knelt beside me and rummaged through the parts until he had both torsos standing in their bins side by side. He nodded at the necks.

"There."

I stared. I'd figured they'd used a hacksaw or something, but the cuts were both razor clean. "So they used choppers."

"Yeah, but what else?"

I looked again and shrugged. "You going to tell me?"

"Spring assist makes it too easy. Street gangs started using them on one another, so choppers were made illegal, right?"

"Right, but so're a lot of guns."

"Guns are different. I'll show you." He stood up, opened a tall closet, and withdrew a set of choppers. Unhinging the blades, he stepped toward me.

When he got a little too close, an image of Colin Wilson's head flashed in front of me, and I fell backward to get out of the way.

"Easy!" I said.

"Sorry," he answered. He knelt by me and pointed to the edge of the blade. "I just wanted to show you this. See? They make all the blades a little different, like a signature, so they can track them if they're ever used on livebloods."

His gray finger graced a part of the blade. At first I thought it was jagged, but then I realized it was a pattern. "I get the idea."

He put the blade away, then pointed at the necks again. "Those chakz were D-capped by the same set of choppers."

What the hell?

I stared at the marks on the necks long enough to realize he knew what he was talking about. The cuts were smooth except for some very small notches grouped right next to one another, two half-circles, a triangle, a square, and another half-circle. Same on each.

Whoever killed Frank Boyle also killed Colin Wilson, or at least had access to the same clippers. What did that mean? Maybe nothing. Ashby described two goons. If they were for rent, like rat catchers bumping off pesky chakz so you don't have to, they wouldn't think twice about leaving the same calling card. Someone else might have hired them to get rid of Colin Wilson, maybe because he was hanging out on their lawn. The Boyles hired them of get rid of their inheritance problems. The rat catchers might not even have known how much money was involved.

That fit, except for one detail: the heads. Both were missing. Why? That electric syrup hit me again, flashes of disembodied heads chatting in the desert while the coyotes gnawed at them. Hard enough to keep my obsessions and the world separate; now it felt like they were crashing into each other. I groaned and twitched my own head, trying to clear it.

The vet looked at me but didn't say anything.

Proof they'd done the job? *Here's the head; where's my cash?* Maybe in the Middle Ages. A photo or fingerprints could do that just as easily, without the gore or the bother. I couldn't see Cara Boyle going for a deal that involved eyeballing her brother's body parts unless she really hated him for some reason—and nothing Frank said about them suggested that kind of rift. If anything, he seemed confused and a little hurt that they'd been left out of the will. It didn't make any sense, but in a way that made you wonder if making sense was worth it.

"Funny, huh?" the vet said; then he started packing the pieces back into the plastic bins.

"Yeah," I said. I pulled out a twenty and stuffed it in his pocket. "For your trouble."

He pulled it out and handed it back. "This is my job, Detective. I'm supposed to help you guys. Glad to do it when I can. Not like I'm ever going to be a cop myself, right?"

"Yeah, but neither am . . ." I hesitated. "Look, buddy, I'm sorry, but for the life of me I can't remember your name."

"Really?" He scrunched his face and looked around. "Tommy. I think it's Tommy."

12

At this point, it was an equation. Two and two equals four. If Boyle's attacker and Wilson's attacker were the same, who were they, and why? For the first time I was thinking maybe Boyle's siblings *weren't* responsible. If that was the case, the victims had to have something in common, other than being headless. I had to find out what it was. Given that I didn't know squat about Wilson, and Cara wasn't about to give me an interview, I figured I'd try the Internet.

The library was a hike from police HQ, their Wi-Fi iffy to begin with. My best bet was the River Styx, a coffee/cybershop. It was on the way home, about six blocks west, right on the border of the Bones, where the Bohemian LBs were trying to gentrify. Cute name, Styx, the river separating the living and the dead. Here they pretty much meant it. Chakz were expected to stay on our side of the street, out of the Styx.

By the time I got there, it wasn't getting any cooler, but night was showing up just the same. The dress code here was more my style than the center of town. In the dark, it'd be easier for me to pass, as long as I didn't stay long enough for someone to strike up a conversation or get a good whiff of me. Not that I had any rot, but we do smell dead.

I got there just in time to see a familiar chak being shoved out the dark brown door. It was Jonesey, espresso in hand, heat sleeve and travel lid in place. They didn't throw him out without serving him, which meant Jorelle was on duty as barista. Not Superman's dad—Jorelle was an acne-faced Frenchman working his way through college. He didn't mind where his tips came from as long as the little jar got filled.

There was a bit of a bounce to Jonesey's shamble, so I figured he hadn't heard about Boyle yet. Then I noticed his other hand was full of flyers. Was he advertising for a new strip joint? I thought about asking, but the living were around. If I was going to get a seat with a computer, I had to act like I didn't know him.

He knew the score. As we passed, he whispered, "Keep to the back, near the AC vents."

I slipped among the grain-stained browns that made up the furniture, posts, and walls, got myself a cup of joe from Jorelle, and made sure to tip too much. I almost forgot to take the coffee. I don't drink it. It was a decent crowd, easy to hide in, so I made my way toward the dark corner where they kept the older rigs. Might as well have been state-of-the-art to me.

Right before I sat, I noticed that one of those flyers Jonesey was carrying had been pasted up on the wall, next to all the ads for local bands, massages, and house sitters. It stood out because of the sloppy handwriting. I stopped in my tracks as I read it.

Join the Dead Man Walk!
Rise and keep rising! Peaceful Chak Rally in
Town Square
Listen to the dead; we are your brothers, your
sisters, your mothers, your fathers!

A rally. So the crazy bastard was running with it. I
should find him, talk some sense into him. I looked toward the door, but he was gone. By the time I turned
back, someone had already torn down the poster. Maybe
that problem, at least, would take care of itself, and I had
other worries.

The screen on the ancient computer flickered like the
lights in a horror-film hallway. I was never much for bells
and whistles, but a mouse would have been nice. A touch
pad is tough if you don't have proper hand-eye coordi-
nation. But the connection was clean. I logged in with
my debit card fast as you please, and winced at the balance. I hadn't deposited any of Turgeon's cash yet, and
only had enough in my account to pay for fifteen minutes.

I was about to do a search on Wilson when I got a
twinge. Not the muscle kind, but the what-am-I-missing
kind. Aside from the usual tingles and shakes, every now
and then I get this particularly annoying sensation, like
an itchy spot in the flow of consciousness that I can't
scratch because my hands are outside my skull.

I was forgetting something. I *knew* I was forgetting
something, something I should check on besides Wilson
and Boyle. It was something else. Someone from Bedtown, the hakker attack? No. I kept getting an image of
a baby covered in scrambled eggs. Great.

I checked the news pages, hoping to jog my memory.

Everyone had an article on the poor dead hakkers. An editorial suggested it should be legalized as a sport, so safety regulations could be standardized.

Nothing rang a bell, so I tried Frank Boyle. Other than today's reports on the body, there wasn't much about his afterlife. Never is. Even the Web, for all its porn and piano-playing cats, doesn't care much about chakz. It wasn't until I dug deeper, moved back a few years to when he was among the living, that I got some decent hits.

Frank Fulton-Boyle had been an architect, and pretty involved in the community. No shocker, given what I saw at Bedland. Even zombies are creatures of habit. The tall guy I'd seen next to him in the photo was Kendrick Boyle-Fulton. I guess they did the name-swap thing, like John Lennon Ono and Yoko Ono Lennon. I didn't find anything about the marital disputes Boyle mentioned, but I'd need a police database for that. Not likely, given my loving relationship with Booth.

Kendrick's murder made a big splash, though. There was even some national coverage. Domestic abuse among gay couples was a curiosity at the time, so the mass media, like a god with ADD, trained its eye on it until the next bleeding lead came along.

I also found a memorial Facebook page. Judging from the date, it was set up shortly after Boyle's conviction. Funny thing: It was dedicated to Kendrick *and* Frank. An awful lot of their close friends would not accept that Frank could beat anyone to death.

One of the FB albums had a shot of their adopted son, Duncan, at the funeral, in black suit and tie. Gray faced with mourning, he looked even more like Ashby. A comment from a neighbor said he was to return to

Russia, to live with an aunt in Kaliningrad. I thought about shooting him an e-mail, but I could always do that later, if I had a good reason. Until then, why ruin his day?

Couldn't find a thing about Boyle's postmortem exoneration, but that wasn't unusual. No surprise his loving pals didn't get back in touch, either. Chakz don't fit back into their former neighborhoods.

I don't know what I was looking for, but reading about the murder made me antsy. Different sexual preference, different job, and Lenore and I hadn't had any children, but the beating death, the wrongful conviction cut close to home. Electric-syrup time. Nice and sticky.

I slapped my brain around until it worked its way back to Colin Wilson. A few nanoseconds after I typed his name, I had what we called back in homicide a son-of-a-bitch moment. The first record that popped up was an article from the *Fort Hammer Ledger*, December 13, 2008, detailing Colin Wilson's conviction for the "bludgeoning death" of his wife, Cathy.

Golf club. History of domestic violence.

Like I said, son of a bitch.

I could hear Misty saying that the fact that I'd gotten all freaked out about Wilson in the first place could be part of the universe's plan. Me, I knew my brain just gets stuck on things. I still wasn't convinced the fact that the same choppers were used meant anything more than a freelance cleanup service. I had to back up a little before I laid one coincidence on top of another.

Could there be more?

Despite the ferals and the hakkers, there are *lots* of chakz. No one's counted, probably out of embarrassment, but a big chunk are from the early days, when everyone and his uncle was giddily yanking some favorite relative back from beyond the veil, like Tommy at the morgue. So we weren't all criminals.

Even so, take any two chakz and the odds aren't crazy that they were both exonerated for *some* kind of murder, since murder is usually what gets you executed in the first place. Figuring that eighty percent of victims know their killer, pick any two murder convictions at random, and how hard would it be to draw two who'd offed their significant others?

It's not fifty-fifty, more like getting a full house—unlikely, but not impossible.

I typed in a search string for "murder AND beating AND spouse AND executed" and got 4.8 million hits. Figured.

But that's *convictions*. I had a combo here—two people *exonerated* for killing their spouses. Adding "exonerated" brought it down to under a million. I tried adding "brought back from dead" and "ripped" and "RAR" but got zilch. Again, for that kind of info, I'd need a police database.

Still, it had to be rare. Hiring an attorney, getting a retrial, finding someone to pay for additional DNA testing cost time and money. If the person closest to you in the world is dead, and everyone else is convinced you did it, who exactly is going to spend that time and money?

Oh, it happens. I don't know how it worked for Wilson, but Boyle said his father paid for retesting the DNA. For me it was dumb luck, some police brutality, and a DA just starting out. I hear he was fired right after they brought me back.

Wait a minute. There weren't two; there were three,

and only one of us still had his head bone connected to his neck bone: me. What were the odds of that? Could it mean I was next on the hit parade?

Son of a bitch.

I sat there cursing like a bagman until the clock wound down and the computer disconnected. Just as well—people were starting to stare. I shoved my hat on and made for the door, rubbing my neck and wincing the whole way.

13

I was still rubbing my neck when I got back to the office, trying my damnedest to think things through without dwelling on the obvious.

"Cathy, Kendrick, Lenore. Why spouse killers? Why the head?"

Ashby kept quiet the whole time I was giving Misty the short version, but the second I mentioned Kendrick, he started in with that laugh and wouldn't stop.

"Heh-heh-heh."

I glared at him a second, then went back to pacing. "What do they do with them? Do they need them for something?"

"Heh-heh-heh."

Great. I was making him nervous; he was making me nervous. What a wacky pair.

"Quiet, Ashby! Are they making fucking lamps out of them?"

Misty stood between us. Apparently I looked pretty

angry. "Hess, maybe you shouldn't talk about this in front of . . ."

"Heh-heh-heh-heh."

I was in no shape to listen to reason. I wasn't even interested in trying. "I know, I know! But I have to. I've got to figure this out. Do they collect them? Is it a cult?"

"Heh-heh-heh."

"Kid, could you keep it down? Please? It's my neck we're talking about."

"Can't help it, can't help it. Heh-heh-heh-heh-heh."

"Could you please just shut the fuck . . ."

Before I realized it, I'd raised my fist, ready to punch the wall. Misty grabbed my hand and repeated, "He can't help it."

I shrugged off her hand. "Shut up," I said. But I said it slowly, deliberately. "Shut up. Shut up."

"Calm down!"

"I am calm!" I shouted. I shivered and gave her a smile. "Sorry, Mist. I'm not talking to you or the kid. I'm talking *shut up* in general. As in, what if they're taking the heads as a way to shut them up?"

"Heads can't talk by themselves, Hess. They . . . die."

"We don't *know* that. ChemBet and the government have too many reasons to lie about it. D-capping sounds quick and humane. What if it just makes the ferals less dangerous for shipping? The masses wouldn't want to hear that crushing or roasting was the only way to really end it."

Misty gave me a look, walked Ashby into the other room, and shut the door, muffling his voice. Now it almost sounded like a dance beat from a distant party. She came back in and shook her head. "Even if the . . .

heads . . . could somehow talk, what would the killers be shutting them up about?"

"You got me there. It's got to be simple, whatever it is. I know it. Why can't I get *my* stupid fucking head to work?" I stormed around, probably looking like I was going to punch something again.

"Hess, Ashby's gone. You want me to go in the other room, too? Please take a breath."

I stopped in my tracks and practically smiled. "You want to rephrase that?"

She rolled her eyes. "You know what I mean. Calm down."

I sat down. "I'll do what I can. The only obvious thing would be so they couldn't identify the killers. But so what if they did? No one listens to chakz. Their last words would be to some cop on trash duty before they were carted off to be burned or crushed."

"Even *some* garbagemen believe in chak rights."

"One or two at last count. Anyone who doesn't live in a shantytown or the Bones thinks the laws on the books are enough to protect us. Maybe they suspect the laws aren't upheld, but no one's really asking. If you were the killer, it wouldn't matter, unless you were . . ." I let the sentence trail off and left my mouth half-open. Maybe if I didn't say it, it wouldn't be true.

"What? Unless you were what?"

"Unless you were someone paid to uphold those laws. If word got out, you wouldn't do time, but you might lose your job."

"You mean a cop?"

"I'm thinking worse than that. What if it's Tom Booth?"

"No. Hess, you always said he was a good guy."

"When it comes to the living. I've never seen anyone hate chakz as much as he does. Never met anyone who took an overturned conviction more personally. What if he decided to correct what he thought of as injustices? He started with Colin Wilson; then the hakker attack pretty much handed him Boyle." I grabbed my neck again. "Funny, you'd think he'd start with me. Maybe he's saving me for last. What if there are more out there and he's planning on going after them, too?"

Misty rushed up and buried her head in my shoulder. "Hess, if it is him, what are we going to do?"

I shrugged, absently patting her back. "Move out of the state."

14

Misty was already packing, but I couldn't let go just yet. I was too involved. See, if Booth really loved Lenore, this could be his way of working things out. Wish he'd tried talk therapy or medication. But that made the loose ends my responsibility in more ways than one. Not only was I the one who figured it out; I was his motive.

I couldn't see getting any justice for Boyle and Wilson. As for Turgeon, my best guess was that he was alive, but the hired goons had put the fear of Booth into him. Sure, a fancy lawyer could tackle a chief detective in the courts, but not without the leads I'd gathered. Unless I somehow stumbled on my client as he was walking down the street, trying to find Turgeon was a dead end. Mostly I was thinking that if there were others on the hit list, I had to find and warn them. And since the only way to figure out who else was at risk meant using a police database, that meant one more trip into the lion's den.

I thought it best not to mention that to Misty, so while she and Ashby were busy sorting what to bring and what to leave behind, I stepped into the hall and made a call to my old partner, Jimmy Hazen. He was with Booth when they followed me back home that day. Last time I saw him, I was covered in my wife's blood. He didn't appear in court, but he signed a deposition describing in detail what an asshole I was.

I had to talk fast, real fast.

"Haze? It's Mann. Don't hang up."

He hung up. I dialed again.

"Look, we both know what you think of me, so before you hang up again, just think for a second that it must be something pretty important. I'd need a damn good reason, right?"

The silence that followed was achingly long, a void in the air like the gaps in my memory. Finally he answered, voice deader than any chak's. Two words: "Go on."

I told him some of what I knew, leaving out any mention of Booth. I tried to make it sound like a psycho was involved, that maybe Turgeon, a liveblood, was in danger. When he didn't cut me off immediately, I slowed down, let him fill in the blanks, but in the end he just said, "So what?"

"Haze, let me have a terminal for an hour, anytime, day or night. One hour. I swear if it doesn't pan out I'll lie down and let you kick the shit out of me all day long."

"I wouldn't want to get my shoes dirty, you son of a bitch."

"Is there anything I can do?"

Another pause, then: "Sign a confession. Gimme a statement *saying* you killed her."

I clamped my mouth so tightly I nearly crushed a molar. One wrong word and I'd lose him. I wanted to tell him I didn't do it, but between the two of us, how many times had we heard that from a perp? And I didn't even really remember. I took a different tack.

"A statement from a chak isn't admissible in court."

"I know. Call it a souvenir."

"What about the liveblood? What about Turgeon?"

"That's why I'm making the offer, on the off chance you didn't imagine the whole thing. Find something real on him, you can let me know. Right now I've gotta take a piss, then have a drink so I can forget we had this conversation. Do we have a deal?"

"Fine."

"Back entrance, midnight. You get half an hour." He hung up.

Never has any idiot, alive or dead, been happier to have successfully invited himself into hell.

15

Unfortunately, Ashby insisted on tagging along. He'd gathered from the conversation with Misty that all the excitement had something to do with Frank, and his loyalty to Boyle trumped whatever he saw in Misty. It was as if there was a whole amusement park in his head, and all day long, all the rides were free.

I couldn't see Booth pulling two late nights in the same week, and I'd just been in and out of the morgue, so I figured it was as safe as it was going to get. I thought about bringing Misty, too, but she was into the packing. Besides, for all I knew there might be outstanding charges against her, and I never knew when the fact that the police didn't connect us might come in handy. She wasn't eager to come with, in any case.

With so much business in Fort Hammer conducted long after dark, the buses run late. I used to think the city looked better at night because you can see less of it, but in some places what you don't see makes it worse. There are spots along those streets where the shadows vibrate like they're hungry, others where the inky nothing is plain sad.

Around about Eastman Avenue, it gets even darker than that. No one's bothered to fix the streetlights for years. Block after block, the only light came from the headlights on our bus. What didn't shine on potholes caught the husks of empty stores and apartment buildings, the spaces between the structural supports all holding a blackness thick as tar.

I was keeping it together pretty well until then. Now I was getting tense, imagining Booth leaping from the dark, clippers in hand. Adding to my sense of vulnerability, the windowpane by our seat was missing. If my nightmare decided to come through, the only thing to stop the blade would be the air.

At last the fluorescents in an all-night gas station appeared, a rectangular moon in a parking-lot sky. My threat level dropped a bit, but when the bus stopped across the street from the gas station, it was Ashby's turn to get antsy. Apparently he didn't like it when the bus stopped.

I nudged his shoulder and pointed at the lights, thinking they'd distract him.

Big mistake. He zeroed in on the station's one customer, so I started watching, too.

"Big boned" is a nice way of saying *fat*, but there are no fat chakz, and some really do have big bones. This guy's shoulders were door-wide, so he had to wear oversize clothes. With no meat below the rib cage, though, the T-shirt and denim jacket may as well have been on a hanger. His ride, an old pickup, was full of cans and bottles, stuff he could get a nickel a pop for, if the street people let him near a recycling machine.

He was at the pump, had the nozzle in his hand, but for whatever reason he couldn't seem to get it into the gas tank. Weirder still, each try was lazier than the last. He didn't stop trying; he just got slower and slower. I was as fascinated as Ashby, watching him push the nozzle against the side of the truck again and again, wondering if it would ever go in. After a while, it looked like he was missing on purpose.

Clunk. He tried. *Clunk*. Again.

Then he started talking. No window, so it was easier to hear what he had to say.

"Who gives a fuck?" he said loudly. "Who gives a fuck?"

"A fuck . . . heh-heh," Ashby parroted.

I had a bad feeling. "Maybe you shouldn't be looking out there, Ashby."

I fished in my pockets, hoping to find something shiny he could play with. The only thing I had was my recorder and the bills, and I wasn't about to hand either over.

The light changed, so I figured we'd be spared the rest of the scene. Only the bus driver didn't move. He was busy staring at the chak, too.

"Who gives a fuck?" the chak said again.

He stretched the last word. It melted into a familiar tone that matched the rumble of the bus. I knew that tone. One feral coming up. That chak was going down hard. Any minute, he'd be moaning. I had no idea why, but I doubted it was the nozzle. Maybe he'd had the worst day in his unlife, or maybe he'd just had enough.

No reason we had to watch, though.

I called to the driver, "Buddy, light's green!"

He gave me a dirty look, then went back to staring.

"Light's green, heh-heh."

I tried again. "Maybe you want to get out of here?"

"Who gives a . . ." the chak said one last time.

His moaning started in midsentence, low and long, a nice, deep, vibrating bass. Some lesser blues bands, looking for a gimmick, experimented with working moaners into their music, until they realized that the sound could make other chakz go.

The chak had a look on his face. He knew it; he knew he was going. That's the worst, to feel yourself slipping away. I guess he could have let go gracefully, but instead he pulled the safety back on the nozzle, squeezed, and squirted a stream of pinkish liquid at the gas cap, like he hoped some would seep into the tank.

It splashed on the truck, on the chak, on the ground. The warm air quickly carried the stink to the bus.

"Will you go?" I called again. The bus driver was riveted worse than Ashby.

Still moaning, but not quite gone yet, the chak leaned against the car and fished in his pocket for a cigarette. Once the coffin nail was in his mouth he pulled out a lighter.

After that, it all happened fast. A stringy-haired attendant in the cashier booth, who looked like he belonged in high school, grabbed a double-barreled shotgun and rushed out. The bus driver, suddenly awake, pulled a gun from under his seat and, despite my warnings about how firing a gun with all that gas was just as bad as striking a match, popped open the door and rushed out.

They kept a good distance as they pointed their guns and screamed, "Stop!" at him. Maybe they were thinking they could scare him into dropping the lighter, but they couldn't. He opened his mouth, teeth cracked and yellow. He didn't moan. He howled an animal threat, loud enough to make them back off another five feet.

Good thing, too. The extra space probably kept them alive.

Out of reflex, or a final conscious act, the chak's thumb raked the lighter wheel. Then, like all lost souls, he disappeared into the light.

The blast quickly changed color from a bluish white to a more organic yellow-orange. It didn't blow the driver and the attendant up so much as off their feet. The shock wave rattled the bus. Intense heat washed in from the missing window.

If it'd been moister, I'd have worried about rot all over again.

I'm pretty sure he meant it, that it was suicide. A quick decision under strange circumstances. He probably didn't like the idea of rushing around chewing on things like an extra in a grade-B horror movie. That's a real gut fear for chakz, you know, having your existence end like a scene from a lousy movie. It's not even the fact that it's a lousy movie so much as that you already know how it ends—no mystery. No meat.

As chak suicides go, it may have even been successful. I didn't see anything moving in the flames. Not that I'd ever try it myself. Though I remained unconvinced there was any other way we could be completely destroyed, burning looked real painful.

Ashby tugged on the cuff of my shirt like a sleepy kid who wanted to go home. "Too hot, heh-heh," he said, the side of his face lit orange by the flames.

"You said it." I pulled him up. "Let's walk. It's only about six more blocks."

At the front of the bus, I grabbed the radio and called

in the explosion, asking for fire trucks. The dispatcher wanted to know if we needed an ambulance. The driver and the attendant were both up, standing back, staring as the truck and the chak burned. They looked okay, but it wasn't my call, so I said, "Yeah."

We were a block away when I heard the sirens. Quick response. Why not? After all, our two great loves, gasoline and livebloods, were involved. Lots of cop cars followed. Must have been a slow night. At least it meant things would be quieter at the station.

They were. No one was outside the old building. There were some lights on in the windows, but no movement behind them. There should be night staff, but a lot of them could be off watching the gas station burn, which was fine by me. We headed around back. In the dark, the rear entrance looked a little like an alley framed by the building's two wings.

"Cool," Ashby said.

I think he was talking about the lower temperature. It was always cooler here, like the stone kept things naturally frigid. It tamped down the stench of abandoned fast food. Fewer rats, too. The basement windows were dark. Even Tommy had gone home.

I checked the door. Locked. I knew how to open it. Years back, a gang-banger got out of holding and nearly smashed his way out here. No one ever fixed the door, and it hasn't been quite the same since. But Haze said to wait outside, so I did.

Only, no one came to let us in. I looked at my watch: twelve ten. He could be busy with the fire, might keep me waiting out of spite, or he might not show at all. After twenty minutes even Ashby figured out things weren't happening the way they were supposed to.

"When are we going to find Frank?" he said.

I thought about telling him the truth. Now was as good a time as any.

"We're not really going to find him, kid. . . ."

There was more to the sentence, but after the first half his expression sank like a stoolie with cement shoes.

I dived into a sin of omission. "Hey, no, no. Simmer down. We're here to find someone who knows where he is, okay?"

Truth would have to wait. It always did anyway. Patient sucker, truth. I rationalized the lie by telling myself that sure, sooner or later he'd to have to deal with the fact that Frank wasn't coming back, most of him, anyway, but in the meantime I needed him at his best. Ashby might recognize a mug shot, or twitch at the sound of a name. Besides, if I strung him along long enough, he might even forget about Frank.

Would that be a cruelty or a kindness? I keep confusing the two.

Didn't matter. My backpedaling didn't wash. Ashby started making all these jerky movements, doing his laugh real loud, each *heh* ping-ponging wall to wall. Anyone inside, they'd hear. Chances were good they'd be unfriendly. So much for waiting.

"Come on," I told him. "Let's look for Frank."

I held the knob, pressed my shoulder to the door, and pushed up and in. I think there are special charges for breaking and entering a police station, but I didn't remember what they were. As we entered the stairwell, I spoke in as soft a voice as I could manage.

"If anyone's sleeping we don't want to wake them up and make them cranky, right? So it's really important that we be quiet; got it?"

"Heh-heh," he whispered.

Well, it was something.

It was a quick walk up to the second floor, then down the hall to homicide. The floor plan was open, desks and computers all the way up to the glass door to Booth's office. It was also completely empty.

My old desk was against the left wall, third up. At least, I thought it was my old desk. Looked awfully clean, compared to the others, and the hole in the wall must've been repaired. I doubted they kept it as a memorial to me. More likely they couldn't afford to hire a replacement.

The computer was on and logged in. Had Haze set it up for me? If I worked fast, we'd be gone long before they extinguished the gas station fire.

Rather than bother with the printer, I handed Ashby my recorder and told him to press the red button whenever I said *go*. He seemed to warm to the idea of doing something important, so two birds with one stone.

I hit the keys. With a missing liveblood the best bet for getting some official attention, I started with my client. The name Turgeon turned up nothing, but it wouldn't unless he had a record. There were always a couple of murders, knife and gunshot wounds, but none matched the baby-egghead description. I thought maybe I could get a license plate for the Humvee, but couldn't access the traffic cams.

Time to move on. I checked on any chopped chakz found sans head over the last five years. Chak files were originally kept under animal control, along with citizen requests to remove dead dogs and other roadkill. The more conservative types insisted that since we were soulless, godless, and otherwise suspect, that was where we belonged. The bleeding-heart liberals objected. Anything with a face had to have feelings, even garden gnomes. So eventually they compromised and put us under sanitation. That's politics for you.

A couple of hits came up quick. Nothing as spectacular as the desert cases, no effort made to identify the bodies, and it wasn't just the heads missing. Could have been Booth's handiwork, or maybe it just gave him the idea. Still, with Ashby dutifully recording my dulcet croak, I cataloged them all, times and places.

Next I hit the Justice Department records, looking for supposed spouse killers ripped under an RAR after having been exonerated. In the last five years, there were five: me, Frank Boyle, Colin Wilson, and two others: a woman named Nell Parker, who used to be some kinda women's advocate, and Odell Jenkins, who was, I kid you not, a brain surgeon.

Brain surgeon. That was worth a chuckle. I didn't expect more than that, but unlike Nell Parker, Jenkins actually had some newer entries. He wasn't a surgeon anymore, but he was a real rarity, a chak in good enough shape to get a job. He had a regular gig with Hammer Rejuvenations, LLC, a remediation company that did toxic-site cleanup. Made sense. If Jenkins was smart enough to tell asbestos from drywall, they could send him in without so much as a hazmat suit. Save on insurance, too. Lots of toxic sites in Fort Hammer to keep him busy.

At least it was something. If Jonesey could help me find Parker, I'd be able to warn them both. Not bad for a half hour's work. I had nowhere near enough information to convince Hazen of anything, but I figured I could e-mail him the details along with my "confession." At least he might follow up on Turgeon. There'd be a record of his 911 call during the hakker attack to back me up on that much.

"Okay, Ashby, let's get out of here."

"Did you find Frank? Heh-heh."

I was wondering how to answer that one when I noticed the light in the hallway shift. The shadows on the linoleum floor wobbled and grew. Jim Hazen? No. Of course not. Not in this life.

Next thing I knew, Tom Booth was blocking the only exit, and while he wasn't surprised to see us, he wasn't happy about it either. And he had company, a pair of toughs in black tees and jeans. Their pretty faces made mine look like it belonged to a cover model. They looked like they'd been in a thousand fights, losing more often than winning. One had dark skin, crew-cut white hair, bushy eyebrows, and enough wrinkles to be a grandpa. The other was younger, light skinned, thicker, stronger. He didn't look so bright, a forty-watt bulb at best. The scar across his forehead was big enough for his brains to have seeped out.

The kid started shivering and doing his *heh-heh, heh-heh* thing. He wasn't staring at Booth, though. He was staring at his friends. He was terrified of them.

"Ashby," I whispered, "these the two guys who attacked you and Frank?"

"Heh-heh," he said. From the way he said it, I could tell he meant yes.

I didn't need any more proof, but my opinion wasn't worth much. The livebloods who could give Booth grief would need something more, like a confession, something recorded that would play nice in the papers. Hand in my pocket, I slipped my fingers around my recorder and pressed a button, hoping it was the right one. All I had to do, aside from getting out of this in one piece, was try to look natural.

I nodded at Booth's new friends. "They accepting Orcs on the force lately? I knew things were bad, but . . ."

He shook his square head. "They're not on payroll. I hired them special, just for you. Professionals."

"So why aren't they jumping out of a cake?"

"Not that kind of pro. More a cleanup crew."

"I guess old Hazen told you I'd be here, huh?" I said. Booth nodded. "Good cop."

"Matter of perspective," I said. "That mean he does or doesn't know about Wilson and Boyle?"

Booth's lips curled like he was getting pissed, but instead he looked confused. "Who?"

"I'm dead, but I'm not that stupid. The chakz your buddies here D-capped for you because they had the gall to be innocent. I know you blame me for Lenore, but why not just come after me?"

At the mention of her name, a sound like a cracking walnut came from his clenching jaws. "That the shit-ass theory you told Hazen? You think I'm the man? Maybe I killed Kennedy, too, or brought down the towers. I take shits I'm more worried about than a couple of chakz."

He sounded for real. "But . . ." I said. That was as far as I got.

He tensed like he was going to charge. "If I thought you were still the man who killed her, even half that, I'd not only start with you, I'd do it myself. Cut your head off? Too good. Garlic press, maybe. But you're not; you're all just a set of recordings with a stench."

Crap. Was I wrong? I stared at the help. "Tom, you ever work with these guys before?"

He didn't answer me. He grunted a few words at them. "Break some bones and leave him close enough to the border so he can crawl out of town." Then he walked away.

16

If I hadn't ever been a decent detective I wouldn't mind being such a shitty one now. Don't know what made me think I could handle this one. Instead of getting involved, I should've just wandered into a cemetery and asked someone to bury me.

If it wasn't Booth, it'd be a pretty big coincidence he'd hire the D-cappers. That didn't quite fit either. The older one, Grandpa, didn't seem to have anything against chakz. He asked if the cuffs were too tight, and even lowered Ashby's head as he pushed him into the backseat of their sedan. He came across like a good limo driver, doing a lousy job he'd done a dozen times, intent on doing it well.

Mastermind or hired hand, if we were going to get away, Gramps was the one I'd have to take out. Knock him down and Forty-watt would wander around like a windup toy not knowing what to hit. I was surprised the old man let him drive. Despite the GPS, Grandpa had to keep giving Watt directions. They were kind of like Lennie and George from *Of Mice and Men*. Couldn't imagine why they were working together, but the third time Grandpa reminded him to turn right, I ventured a guess.

"He your son?"

I don't think he liked the question very much, because in response, he pulled out a piece and aimed it at me with one hand. He fished something out of his pocket with the other and held it up in front of me. It was a bullet.

"Know what this is?" he asked. "Know what it does?"

Recognizing the aluminum tip, I nodded. "It's a devastator. Like Hinckley used on President Reagan and Brady, back in 'eighty-one."

Random memory, quick lesson on bullets. Dumdum and hollow points are what they call *expanding* bullets. They shatter on impact so the pieces can do more internal damage. For a liveblood, that's life and death. For a chak, it may just be an inconvenience. The devastator is an honest-to-gosh *exploding* bullet. Behind that aluminum tip it had a lead azide center that blew up on impact. It could cost you bones, a limb. They say President Reagan only survived because the bullet that hit his rib and entered his lung failed to explode.

"Those're illegal, you know."

"So's my cleaning lady. I don't want you to get any ideas about being able to take a few slugs before rushing me."

"Well, not *now*."

"Good. Tell your friend the same thing."

Ashby was looking out the window, watching the streetlights. "Don't sweat it, Gramps. He doesn't have any ideas of his own. A little like our handsome chauffeur."

The old man winced. "Tell him anyway."

I nudged his shoulder. "Ashby, don't get any ideas, okay?"

"Ideas. Heh-heh."

"See?"

Grandpa's move with the devastator made me realize something that made me think D-capping Boyle was not their idea. "You don't have a lot of experience with chakz, do you?"

He got a little defensive. "You've got bodies, don't you? Made of the same stuff as everyone else. It's all meat, dried or not."

"Sort of. Blow an arm off somebody else, it's not going to come crawling after you, is it?"

Forty-watt opened his mouth for the first time. "Can they do that?"

"No," Grandpa said. "He's shitting you."

Of course I was, but Watt didn't know that. Grandpa shook the gun in my face. "Tell him you're shitting him."

"I am shitting you," I said. I gave Forty-watt an exaggerated shrug, so he'd still wonder if it was true.

Had to make sure, so I figured I'd ask. "Either of you have anything against someone exonerated for the killing of their spouse?"

"What? No."

So Booth and the chak chopper somehow hired the same team. Maybe Grandpa and Forty-watt had flyers up in the grocery stores, little chits at the end with the number to call. Somehow I didn't think so. Was it someone Booth knew? Another cop? Hazen? No, he'd open the car window to let a fly out rather than kill it.

It worked once, so I figured I'd just ask again. "Booth know who else you work for?"

"We get lots of work. Who do you mean?"

I made a scissor motion with my fingers.

"Oh, him. You figure it out."

"Do I get a hint?"

"No."

"Given his reaction to my questions, I'd say no."

"Well, you've got a fifty-fifty chance of being right, then, don't you?"

Grandpa didn't even blink. At least I knew it was a *he*.

"Did the chak chopper hire you *because* he knew you worked for Booth? Asked you to keep tabs on him in case I showed up?"

The old man snickered. "You don't give up, do you?"

"It's not like I've got a magazine back here to read."

"Want to play twenty questions?" He put the barrel to my neck. "Okay. Guess what I'm going to do if you open your mouth again?"

Hell, I'd probably have my answer at the end of the ride, which, as it turned out, was in the warehouse district. Cue gloomy jazz riff.

Every town has one, but not every town built them as huge, thin, and rickety as Fort Hammer. One good hurricane should've wiped them all out, but even physics doesn't work much in this town. Fifty years they'd been standing, and of course now, times being what they are, they mostly stood empty.

Watt maneuvered the sedan down narrow spaces tight as a behemoth's butt crack. He kept getting lost, but I couldn't blame him. One mass of tin wall and steel support is a lot like any other. It was like looking for a particular piece of hay in a haystack. After a lot of eye rolling from Grandpa, we made it. Hip-hip-hooray.

Watt got out, opened the door, and yanked at Ashby.

The kid struggled, if you can call it that. His thin bony hands swatted Watt's arms like wet noodles slapping brick. Just the same, Watt didn't like it. It looked like he might get rough with the kid.

"Hey! Easy!" I barked.

Grandpa tensed, but agreed. "Don't damage him yet."

"Listen to your father," I said as I climbed out of the car.

Watt looked at me like I was a wizard. "How'd you know?"

"I didn't. I guessed, but I wasn't sure until you told me just now."

"When did I tell . . . ?"

"Shut up." Grandpa grunted. "You want to give him our address, too?"

I grinned. "Does he take after Mom?"

He shoved me real hard for that. Made me wonder how far I could push him. A little chaos might break our way.

I laid into the mom. "She still on crack? Their kids usually have brain damage. Not that I have anything against crack addicts or brain damage. You've met Ashby, and my secretary used to be—"

Grandpa clocked me on the chin. I'd expected it, seen it coming, and moved back fast enough to avoid a broken jaw, but it still sent me to the ground.

"Anything else?" he said.

Watt was holding Ashby tight, and even if I wanted to abandon him, it wasn't like I could get up quick and run with my hands cuffed. I shook my head. Grandpa pulled me to standing.

Ashby was horrified. Or maybe he was crying.

"I'm okay, kid; I'm fine. We're just playing a little rough," I said.

"These are the men who took Frank. Is Frank . . . inside? Heh-heh."

Grandpa and I looked at each other. Neither of us answered. The old man may not have liked me very much, but I think Ashby reminded him of Watt. Maybe that's why Ashby got away from them the first time. Gramps may have "accidentally" let him go.

"I wish you hadn't brought him," he said.

"Me, too. You could let him go."

"These are the men who took Frank," the kid said again.

Grandpa shook his head. "I don't think so."

Watt slid the door open on a brand-new darkness. Inside, it was more like a cave than a building, the ceiling too far up to see. High up, the shadows of thick, dangling chains loomed, hooks at the end big enough to snare Moby Dick. Down below, with us, there was plenty of empty shelving, an oil-stained floor, and tracks where forklifts used to roll cargo. All mixed with dead leaves and dirt, it smelled like an oily cemetery.

Watt and Grandpa shoved; we stumbled along, tripping on whatever we couldn't see. Takes longer for a chak to adjust to the dark. As we went farther in, my eyes could barely sort one shadow from another.

Suddenly, though, my nose grabbed all the attention. A sharp chemical odor was piggybacking on the breeze. I thought it was cleaning fluid, but that'd be pointless in this place. It was too strong, anyway, and lacked the perfumes Mr. Clean likes to wear.

Then I saw the source—a circular tub, four feet tall and just as wide. In its youth, it may have been a Jacuzzi or a hot tub. Now it was more a cauldron, the kind cannibals used in those old cartoons for the missionaries they were having for dinner. It was filled nearly to the brim with a gross, slick liquid that gave the color green a bad name.

The man I'd been looking for stood to the side, head covered in a hood, the rest decked out in overalls, a gas mask, and protective gloves. Whoever he was, he hummed and swayed, looking like a toddler dressed in a costume. *Mom! Look at me! I'm a hazmat worker!* For lack of a better word, he *played* with the silvery tools laid out on a narrow table in front of him. He'd turn one sharp instrument over, pick up another, then put it back down someplace else. One, a leather strap at the end of a long pole, looked like a bondage sex toy. Another looked like a garden tool, something you'd use to snap off thick branches—say, an arm or a leg. Yeah, the head clippers were there, center place, sharper and shinier than all the others put together.

I could see where this was going.

Getting a head start on that electric-syrup feeling I knew was coming, I looked down and tried not to think. My bad. A duffel bag sat below the table. I thought it was for the tools, but it was still full, the string at the top tied. It was stuffed with roundish things, basketballs, bowling balls, or . . .

No. Couldn't be. Not just lying there like that.

I shuddered as the syrup roiled inside me.

As if he'd heard what I was thinking, the killer looked up and found my eyes.

"Where do you want them?" Grandpa asked.

The masked man looked as if he hadn't even thought about that part. He'd been too busy pouring all those cool-colored chemicals into the tub, making sure his nifty tools were nice and clean.

"How'd you work it with Booth?" I said. "I've got my guesses, but it'd be nice to know for sure. You plant them there ahead of me or did they work with him before? Odd jobs on the far side of the law? He still thinks they're going to beat me up, break an arm at most, right?"

He gave a little shrug that ruined the neat line of his hazmat suit.

I was actually doing okay until the moment he hefted the head clippers. Then it was like he'd stuck a chubby finger down my throat and touched the bottom of my stomach. A coward dies a thousand deaths, a brave man but one. Call me a coward, then. I could already feel the silver blades against my neck. I was ready to go to my knees and beg, offer to let him take the kid instead of me. But I knew it wouldn't have worked, and I already had crap enough to live with.

Instead I straightened and tried to pretend I was somebody else, role-playing my pathetic excuse for an existence. "Let the kid go. He's a babbler. Doesn't know what's going on from one minute to the next."

He shook his head no.

"Why? This how you get your jollies?"

He stiffened and shook his head no again.

"What, then? It's going to hurt you more than it will me? Little hard to believe, don't you think?"

Grandpa pointed at the vat. "That's what the acid's for, to make it easier."

"What do you mean, easier?"

"You'll see," the old man said. He and Watt put some thick gloves on; then, with a nod from the high priest, Grandpa put his hands on Ashby's shoulders.

"No!" I shouted.

I tried to move. Watt grabbed me from behind, but I managed a quick kick to his groin. I prayed it'd put him down, but he mumbled something about chemical sterilization and got me in a bear hug. My arms were pinned, and seconds later my feet were dangling off the ground. I grunted and kicked, but any strength I had was useless.

Ashby looked very worried. "Heh-heh."

Mr. Mask put a yellow-gloved finger to his lips and said, "Shhh! Shh!"

Ashby stared at him like he was watching a cartoon. I could see how he'd make the mistake. Watt tightened his bear hug until my ribs felt ready to crack.

Grandpa turned and whispered to me, "Don't tell him. It won't change anything. You'll only scare him."

"Sweet of you to be so concerned," I said, croaking more than talking. "What's he going to do with the kid's head? Keep it as another souvenir?"

His eyes flitted to the duffel bag, then back to me.

Grandpa gritted his teeth. "He doesn't want *his* head. He's an experiment. The acid should destroy him faster than fire. *Completely*. You tell him what's going to happen, he'll spend his last moments thinking about it. What do you think would be best for him?"

"Killing all three of you and getting out of here. But I guess I shouldn't let the perfect be the enemy of the good."

Ashby's head twitched from me to Grandpa to Watt to the mystery man.

"Are we going to find Frank? Heh-heh."

It may have been my imagination, but when the kid said *Frank*, it looked like one of the bowling balls in the duffel bag twitched.

Christ, I didn't want to think about it.

Gramps gave Ashby a paternal smile. "You'll see Frank in a second. First you gotta take a little bath."

"I don't like baths. Heh-heh."

"Even for Frank?"

"Frank didn't say take a bath. Frank said to run."

"That was a game," Grandpa said. "Game time's over. Now it's bath time."

He hooked him by the arm and walked him toward the vat. Ashby looked back at me with a grin that deserved to be a picture in the dictionary, next to the word *insipid*.

"A bath. A bath for Frank, heh-heh."

Death, real death. I knew there was worse than that, and hell, maybe it would be better if he didn't know it was coming. What did he have to look forward to, anyway? Fuck. Moral questions are easy when the situation's black and white. The tough shit is figuring out the lesser of two evils. You can't win, but you have to choose anyway. I decided that the bigger evil would be satisfying the son of a bitch with the headgear. If he was for it, I was against it.

"Ashby, for fuck's sake, fight!" I screamed. "Poke his fucking eyes out! Kick! Scratch! They *killed* Frank and they're going to kill you!"

"Killed Frank? Killed Frank? Heh-heh?"

Moving fast for his age, Grandpa snapped off a glove, yanked my head back by the hair, and stuffed it down my throat. But I'd made my point.

Ashby screamed, writhed, whirled, twisted, and kicked. Good for you, Ashby.

I tried to help, if only by fighting Watt. I pulled and kicked, but my best didn't impress him at all. As for Ashby, well, for a second it looked like he was actually getting away from the old geezer. Instead he flew side-ways into the concrete. Grandpa had thrown him to the ground to avoid the kicks. Then the old man plopped himself down on Ashby like a cowboy roping a calf, slapped another set of cuffs around his ankles, and tied his knees together.

As Ashby writhed, the masked man shook his head at me like it was my fault. I would have said if he didn't like it he should take his vat and go home, but there was this rubber glove in my throat. It filled my mouth and throat with an acrid taste that I was sure wasn't healthy even for dead things. I only hoped it wasn't burning anything important.

I wanted to scream. I tried. I tried to scream as Watt chained me to a support beam, tried again when the two of them hefted Ashby into the air. I kept trying as I pulled against the chains so hard it felt like I was break-ing my own bones. When I heard Grandpa caution Watt to be gentle in order to avoid spills, yeah, I tried scream-ing then, too.

As they hoisted him up and over, the kid's eyes looked like they were trying to pop out of his skull and run away without him. I froze. Watt and Grandpa, as if they were dumping fresh-cut potatoes into a deep-fryer, let go and hopped back.

With a final, "Heh-heh," Ashby disappeared. The vis-cous green crap didn't even splash as it swallowed him. It was so thick, it just made a sickening plop, like radio-active pea soup.

The liquid churned like water not quite willing to boil. Maybe Ashby was struggling as the acid ate him. I thought I saw a bone-white elbow rise above the sur-face, but it was gone before I could be sure. After a minute or so, the churning slowed. Swampy vapors, a lighter green, hovered on the surface. The chemical odor was joined with a smell like burning meat.

"Most of it's gone now," Grandpa said. "I think the bones take a little longer."

Even he looked a little grossed out, but our host was absolutely fascinated, intent as Ashby had been on Misty. To him, this was the equivalent of something shiny.

After another minute, the liquid, slightly darker, stopped moving altogether. For the first time, I believed something other than fire, or being ground by a millstone, could kill a chak.

The killer gave off a victory laugh, as if to say, *Wow!*

Grandpa wiped some sweat from his brow. "It's sure as hell better than chasing someone all over the desert. That Boyle fellow took hours."

Something in the bag twitched again.

Before I could think about what that meant, Watt undid the chain connecting me to the column. My turn.

The masked man stepped over to the table and regarded his pretty tools. He lifted the metal pole with the leather harness and stepped toward me. I think I made out a wide smile beneath the mask.

Then he said three words, drew each one out in a ridiculously singsong way. The voice was boyish, hauntingly familiar, but that could have been a put-on.

"We'll talk later."

17

I expected I'd be D-capped, my head harvested, my body tossed into the acid. The idea of losing my head always got to me, but I'd been picturing it clearer and clearer ever since I'd first heard about Wilson: blades pressing my neck, cold metal so razor-sharp I wouldn't have the slightest idea when they first sliced my skin. There'd be pinching as the muscles and veins snapped, more pressure, and one final crunch as my spine was severed.

Little happens the way I expect. With Grandpa and Watt flanking me, everyone's favorite mystery date came closer holding not the choppers, but the leather strap I'd seen among his toys. In a flash, I caught onto the plan. He'd use the strap to keep my head above the acid as they lowered the rest of me in. As my body melted into human stew, if the liquid was clear enough, I'd get to watch. I didn't figure I'd be able to talk after that, what with no lungs, but I did think I'd see, and keep seeing, unless someone buried me . . . or shoved me in a duffel bag.

Why? Maybe it was some kind of experiment, or maybe he got off on seeing pain, the way boys take a magnifying glass to a bug and watch it burn. Maybe there was no malice at all, just a gross curiosity.

Watt moved in to get me in another hug. I slammed the top of my skull into his nose, wishing I'd fought as hard for Ashby. The human skull is thinnest right above the nose. Hit it at the right angle, with the right amount of force, and you can send a shard up into the brain, killing the target instantly.

It didn't work. I heard a pleasant crack, but he didn't die. I'd staggered Watt, drawn some blood, seemed to confuse him, but, like Curly from the Three Stooges, he slapped it off and came at me again. He didn't even look as mad as Grandpa, who cursed me out in some language I couldn't identify.

When Watt got close enough again, I stomped both of his feet. No reaction. He grabbed me. I twisted my shoulders, but his arms were too thick, and the cuffs on my wrists didn't help. I yanked at the metal rings, hoping I could break my own hand and get a limb free. I couldn't manage it, and not for lack of trying.

The masked maniac moved in with the strap.

I moved the only part of me I could, my head, snapping it back and forth. Grandpa, still pissed, grabbed my skull and jaw and held them so tightly, I thought I'd swallow the fucking glove. "Hurt my boy, will you?"

His weathered palm covered my field of vision. I felt the strap slip around my neck, as cool and about the same texture as my skin.

Satisfied I was helpless, the figure came nearer. Grandpa repositioned his hand so we could see each other. I couldn't even bite the bastard's gas mask. The best I could manage was to exhale on him angrily through my nose. He clicked some sort of padlock on the strap, then stepped back, humming, until he glanced at Grandpa's hands. One was a rubbery yellow, the other pale pink.

"*Tsk,*" he said.

Grandpa opened my mouth and yanked the glove out. He flicked it in the air as if trying to get the zombie cooties off it and put it back on his hand.

Meanwhile, I could talk again, for all it was worth.

"Could you at least tell me why?"

Stupid question, the sort of thing you ask God on your deathbed. I got the answer I expected: stone silence. I wanted to come up with some clever, compelling last words, but all I managed to do was turn to Grandpa and splutter, "How can you do this?"

The old man didn't skip a beat. "With this pole, that acid, and those clippers."

I was spending my last moments playing straight man, lobbing them over the plate so he could whack them out of the park. With *my* baseball bat.

Tugging the pole, the Mask led me like a dog. Watt and Grandpa marched on either side of me. If I tried to head the other way, they pushed me toward the vat. When I buckled to my knees, they pulled me back up. When I collapsed again, they helped the Mask drag me by the neck.

Less than a yard to go and nothing I could do about it. Anything else I could say? I was pretty good at pissing people off, like with Grandpa, getting under their skin, but you never could tell how that might work out. If I insulted Watt, by the time he figured it out, I'd be long gone. Gramps wasn't stupid. He'd be on his best behavior with a vat of acid so close.

"You gotta realize your boss here is a psychopath, right, Gramps? You and your kid are connected to Booth, the cops. That means sooner or later, he'll have to kill you to cover his tracks."

The Mask kept humming. Grandpa gave me a shrug. "I got a rule about not discussing clients with corpses that break my son's nose."

"I can see that. But maybe you could make an exception?"

At the edge of the vat, they turned me sideways.

"For what it's worth," Grandpa said, "and I know that ain't much, I am sorry about this. About the kid, anyway."

That was it, then. Watt and Grandpa grabbed a leg each and lifted. I rose and saw the surface of the acid, smooth and quiet. The smell, though still thick, had changed. I couldn't say how. I guess I was looking in the wrong direction, because the Mask yanked my hair and held my head straighter.

No reason not to give it one last shot; I squirmed and flailed for all I was worth. I got lucky, caught Watt off balance. He slipped, but his hand shot out and grabbed the edge of the vat. The liquid inside sloshed, nearly touching his fingers.

Grandpa gasped. "Tony!"

"I'll yank him in with me; I swear I will!" I screamed. "I'll kick and splash and get it all over you fuckers!"

Grandpa twisted my leg so hard it felt like my hip would break.

I stared at the Mask. "I'll dunk myself, you son of bitch! I'll pull myself down, head and all. You won't get a single piece of me!"

He looked as if he was thinking about it for a second,

but then shook his head as if to say, *Nah. You won't do that.*

They lifted again.

I'd like to say my life flashed before my eyes, or that I had some profound insight, even that I was imagining what it'd feel like when I hit the acid. But there was none of that, no inner existence at all. I was totally focused on the here and now: the vat, its size and shape, the liquid, its different shades of green, a single red thread sticking out of Grandpa's shirt, how much it looked like a hair. I've never been more in touch with hard reality.

But as I got closer, the sensations dimmed. Something inside broke, let go, detached. It was like I was in a space capsule and the hull had been breached. I felt myself drift away. Thoughts slowed. Consciousness ran down. I wasn't in the scene at all; I was a million miles away, watching it, getting ready to weep for the poor sucker being tossed in the vat. If I'd been a liveblood, I might've thought I was achieving some other incredible spiritual state, like satori, dancing on the edge of eternal bliss.

But I was a chak, and it meant I was going feral.

A sadness in the pit of my gut rumbled and grew, filling me until it wanted to explode in a moan. What difference would it make? Even if the sudden savagery gave me a burst of energy, it wouldn't be enough to snap the handcuffs or the leather strap.

Funny. Ashby didn't lose what was left of his mind when he went in. Maybe I was right: He'd been damaged in a way that kept him static. Not me, though. Not damaged nearly enough.

Oh, well. I'd never been very good at the whole consciousness thing anyway.

But like I said, things usually don't work out the way I expect. This time it didn't work out the way any of us expected. So I wasn't in control, but it turned out neither were they. Something else was, and right before they got me over the rim, it came up to meet them.

A hand, pure, clean bone with a green liquid sheen, rose from the acid. It was followed by an arm. Together, they were more than long enough to grab Watt's meaty shoulder. A fleshless skull broke the surface next, acid rolling off the top. Chemicals oozed from its hollows as it lifted. The jaw lowered and made an impossible sound:

"Heh-heh."

They'd miscalculated. The acid bath, whatever was in it, didn't work on bone. Maybe the Mask had read the recipe wrong, or maybe it was some crappy brand of acid made in China. Who knew? As for the thing that came out, Ashby's unearthly remains, the sight of it bitch-slapped me back into my body.

What the fuck? I don't believe in ghosts. Sometimes I don't even believe what my eyes tell me. Whatever energized our molecular structure may work on the bones, too, but that didn't come near to explaining how a thing without muscle was moving or making noises.

The second hand came up and also grabbed onto Watt.

"Heh-heh."

Both hands pulled. Watt screamed.

Grandpa let go of me. Bad move. It gave me a chance to help the skeleton. I kicked with both feet, ramming Watt's chest. He tumbled toward the vat and that was all it took. The skeleton flipped him and dragged him into the acid.

As I fell to the floor, I heard his screams swallowed by a thick, horrible splash.

No longer held, I rolled away. Drops of splashing liquid hit my jacket and started steaming. Grandpa wasn't so lucky. He caught some on the side of his face. It started steaming, too. Ignoring the physical pain, the old man moved closer to the vat. Planning what? To pull Watt out with his hands?

Didn't matter. The skeleton, standing now, dug its hands into Grandpa's face, right where the acid was burning, and yanked him in, too.

As Grandpa bubbled away, I realized the pole attached to my neck strap was dangling. I looked around for the Mask, but all I could see was a slightly swinging chain near a door marked EXIT. Hands and ankles cuffed, I was in no position to chase him, but I tried. I got up, tripped, and fell after two yards.

"Heh-heh."

I looked back as the meatless skeleton clambered out of the vat, acid dripping in a small puddle at its feet. It didn't look like it had any more idea what it was than I did.

When it was happening, I thought Ashby had attacked Watt and Grandpa on purpose, for vengeance, or whatever. From the way it moved now, bumping and crashing into everything, I started thinking it was just trying to get out of the tank, grabbing whatever happened to be around. It was blind. It had to be. It had no eyes.

"Heh-heh."

Or throat. So how did it make that sound? Was it really his laugh, or just the way the bones creaked against one another? Was I only hearing it in my head?

It neared me, dripping, so I squirmed out of the way. I didn't know if it could hear, but I wasn't going to call. For all I knew it would run over to me like a wet dog and shake that crap all over me. So I stayed quiet and watched as it stumbled into the table, knocking over all those pretty tools.

I noticed that the duffel bag and the clippers were gone.

"Heh-heh."

By the time I squirmed up to sitting, it was farther away from me, banging among some crates. It was no longer dripping so much, so I called out, softly, "Ashby?"

It didn't react.

"Ashby," I managed again. "You in there?"

It hesitated. I don't think it'd heard me. It stood in front of an open door, the one the Mask must have fled through. Maybe it sensed the breeze.

And then the body, the moving bones, the thing that used to be a chak, that was someone named Ashby before that, threw itself through the door and creaked off into the night. I heard the acid bubble in the vat, the scrape of foot bone against concrete, and the fading sound of that crazy laugh: "Heh-heh, heh-heh, heh-heh."

18

Though my immediate prospects had much improved, my hands and ankles were still cuffed, and there was a leather strap around my neck. Reaching my cell phone was out, but I was sort of mobile. I hopped when I stood, dragged myself when I fell. After about an hour, I made it to a pay phone and punched the keys with my nose.

Though it was free and only three numbers, I sure as hell wasn't going to try 911. They'd probably send Booth. Maybe he wasn't out to D-cap me, but that didn't make us friends. I could tell him about Mr. Gas Mask until I was even bluer in the face than usual, and Booth would only wonder why my legs hadn't been broken.

To pay for a call, I had to punch in my debit card. Took six tries before I got the number right. Then I did like E.T. and phoned home. When I was finished, I leaned against a streetlamp and scanned the dark, straight line of road between the warehouses. The sedan was gone, so I didn't expect the Mask to leap out at me, and there was no sign of Ashby. Just the same, I kept my eyes open.

It wasn't only outside threats I had to watch for. My rich inner world had gotten pretty bad, too. In the warehouse, I'd started moaning. Street wisdom said it was only a matter of time before I went feral. Then again, if the street was so damn smart, why would it be on the street to begin with?

Half an hour later, a cab showed. The door opened. Misty's legs slid onto the pavement, followed by the rest of her. She was so shocked when she saw me, she tripped twice running over, then wrapped her arms around me. The cabbie, who had two grisly beards, one on each chin, took one look at us, muttered something about not being into that kinky shit, and drove off.

Misty picked the handcuffs with a safety pin. Able to move my arms and legs, I checked my body, satisfied that everything was still working. She got the pole off easily enough. It just unscrewed. The padlock on the leather strap was a problem.

"It's too narrow for the pin. I need to cut it off with some clippers or something," she said.

I rubbed my wrists. "Could you please not use that word right now?"

I told her a little about what happened, enough for her to ask if I was okay, enough for me to say sure. I wasn't. Yes, I was back in my body and didn't feel a need to moan right then and there, but it'd been a real long couple of days. I didn't know it, but it was about to get worse.

The second cab we called wouldn't take chakz. When a third showed, Misty offered the driver an extra twenty. He was hungry enough to take it. Thank the stars for the desperate among us, for they can still be hired.

Back at the office, while Misty worked at the strap with a file and a pair of scissors, I collapsed into my desk chair. She wanted to talk. I didn't. While she sawed away, I flicked on the set, hungry for anything except reality. I found what I was looking for. *Tea with the Dead* was on, one of a dozen zombie-themed shows. Most were comedies that portrayed chakz as a really lame, laughable threat, sort of like the Nazis on *Hogan's Heroes*.

After a while, I heard Misty's nails scratching, then felt the soft pads of her fingers on the back of my neck. She'd cut most of the way through the leather and was trying to tear the last inch. She grunted, strained, and I heard a sound disturbingly similar to ripping flesh. The collar came free.

"I keep thinking about poor Ashby," she said.

"You and me both," I told her.

"It's so crazy. Why would anyone collect chak heads?"

I shrugged as I rubbed my neck. "Because someone's a sick fuck, and sick fucks do fucking sick things." After a pause and a look at her face, I got a little more introspective. "Could be a ritual thing. Psychos like to collect souvenirs, body parts. Y'know, in some primitive tribes warriors collected the heads of their enemies; gave them someone to talk to."

Takes a lot to freak someone out when they spend all day with the dead, but she started rubbing her neck, too. "You joking?"

"I wish. I took some psych classes once, learned just enough to hurt myself. Freud wrote about some old chief who used to pull out the skull of his greatest foe, put a cigar in it, light it up for him, and have a good, long, one-sided chat—y'know, 'Buddy, you're the only one who understands me' . . . that sort of thing."

I must have shivered or something, because she started rubbing my neck and shoulders.

"Try not to break anything back there, okay?"

She slapped at my back. "You're tougher than you think. Lucky, too."

"Oh, yeah. My luck's been amazing. Got one chak D-capped and another melted to the bone. Think I should buy a lottery ticket today?"

"You blame yourself for Ashby?"

"It's not rocket science. I didn't have to let him come with me. Could've forced him to stay with you. I didn't, and he lost a lot of weight because of it."

She shook her head, but I wasn't sure who she was trying to convince. "He'd have tried to follow, and it could've wound up worse for him."

I had to laugh at that one. "You're the best, Misty, but get a bigger shovel, will you? *What* could be worse?"

"I don't know." She stepped away, looked out the window at the beautiful alley view. A cop car rolled down the main street, flashing lights that glanced on her face through the slats in the blinds. "The police are out in force. It's because of the riot at Bedland and the . . . gas station explosion last night. When you called I was watching TV. Some talk-show guy was going on about how they should just get it over with, round up all the chakz, put them in a pit, and take a flamethrower to the pile."

It figured. It was the same every time chak trouble made the news. Everyone would start talking bonfires. Good for ratings. It'd always blown over before, but I winced just the same. "That doesn't mean I did the kid a favor."

She turned back to me. "No, I'm just saying . . . you didn't know. We never know what'll happen. It *could* have been worse for him, even if we can't imagine it. Did you . . . did you ever, ever see anything like that before, just a skeleton walking around?"

I shook my head. "If that's what I saw. It was dark; maybe there was more of him left than I thought. Otherwise, how could the bones move? How could he talk?"

She came over and put her hand on my shoulder again. "Hess, maybe it's his *soul*."

Ah, the spaghetti monster in the sky again. I didn't know how to answer. Fortunately, I didn't have to. The sitcom was over and the news came on. They were leading with a story about a chak break-in on Wealthy Street. Cara Boyle was being interviewed. She was too upset to offer a decent description of what happened. I wasn't, not yet anyway.

I shot Misty a glance. "The riot and the fire, huh? Didn't mention my little part in the crackdown."

"I didn't want to . . ."

I waved her off. "Never mind. I know what you didn't want," I said. "Come to think of it, shooting that live-blood at the hakker attack probably helped a lot, too. I'm a one-man excuse for . . . what would you call it? Genocide seems redundant in this case."

"Hess, you're just making it worse. Thinking like that won't help you keep it together."

She was right about that much. I grabbed the remote, thinking I'd turn off the set. Given what happened next, it was the right instinct, but before I could hit the power button, the scene switched. A new face flashed up on the screen: the butler I'd socked in the gut. Only, according to the name on the screen, he wasn't a butler; he was the main man himself, Martin Boyle Sr., Frank's father. The guy who'd supposedly died from cancer.

What the . . . ?

For all my mistakes, the truth rushed me like a line-backer. "Turgeon!"

He'd lied. And I believed him.

I clenched my hands so hard it felt like I was driving my fingernails into my palms. No blood, of course. I stood and looked for something to smash.

"Fucking baby-headed Turgeon. He's the psycho. The son of a bitch played me. I led him straight to Boyle. I killed them both. I killed Frank, too."

We'll talk soon. It was his voice, muffled by the mask.

With nothing handy to throw, I punched myself in the head. When that proved too hard, I kicked the recliner. A loud crack filled the room. I didn't know whether it was the chair or my leg.

"Stop it!" Misty said. She pulled me back. "You'll break your leg!"

Electric syrup bubbled inside me. Frank Boyle and Ashby were perfectly safe until I'd led the son of a bitch psycho straight to them.

I planted myself in the recliner. From the way it bent under my weight, it was the thing that was broken. Misty looked relieved. I suppose I should've been, too.

"Hess . . . you couldn't have . . ."

I held up my hand to stop her. "Don't. I'm supposed to be a detective. I should've at least checked Turgeon's story before I did anything."

She stood there not knowing what to say, the concern making her face vibrate. Looking at her was only making it worse. I clicked the set off. "Misty, don't take it personally, but right now I need some me-time."

"Hess?"

"Misty."

She bobbed her head. "Fine. Sure."

"Shut off the lights on your way out?"

"Okay."

She scooped up the remains of the collar and headed out, pausing at the door. The curves of the peeling paint almost matched the shape of her unkempt hair. It'd been a long day for her, too. She looked drained, ready to collapse. She narrowed her tired eyes at me.

"You didn't kill anyone."

"Semantics."

"Are you going to be okay? You're not going to be in here for more than, like, a half a day, right?"

Chakz, she knew, could get so depressed they'd go into a torpor for a week or so before finally going feral. I waved my fingers at her and pushed the recliner back.

"I've just got to think it through. At least I know who to look for, right?"

She didn't believe me, but she knew me well enough to realize I had to be alone. She closed the door.

It was one of those times I wished I could still use alcohol for something other than killing germs. I lay down, leaned back, and tried to think of something that didn't hurt. It didn't work. It was no coincidence Turgeon had hired me to find Boyle. I was on his list. It was a way to set me up, too. I told myself that if I didn't pull out of the funk, he'd get me, but I couldn't bring myself to care.

I tried to sleep but couldn't, not really. I drifted in and out, but my head continued to buzz. The blood on the phone probably belonged to Grandpa or Watt. Maybe it was cherry syrup.

I went through some motions. The heads, what did they mean to Turgeon? There are all kinds of people, but four kinds of serial killer. There's the visionary, where the killer has psychotic breaks and imagines himself on a mission from God or the devil. Mission-oriented, where they believe they're cleansing the world of some evil, like children or women. Hedonistic, which doesn't necessarily mean they kill for the pure sicko pleasure, though it includes that, but their motive could also be money or comfort, like your Bluebeards or Black Widows. And number four, power, where the killer wants control over something. Most number fours were abused as children. They play the same game from the other side, thinking they've won something.

I didn't know enough to guess which Turgeon fit. It wasn't a chak thing. The victims were all spouse killers. Was he avenging a parent, or trying to kill the other one? Did he want to rid the world of them because they were evil, because it was fun, because he wanted control, or just because? Spinning wheels got to go 'round.

Useless, fucking useless.

I let it go, but that was a mistake. When I did, I had that drifting feeling again, like I wasn't holding on to anything, floating away from my body and up into space. It sneaks up on you like that. I grabbed at the train of thought but couldn't hold it. The old noggin only worked in spurts at best. Now, as it sputtered, something insectlike crawled into the gaps—bikers with chain saws, Boyle talking about the future, Ashby's hand rising from the vat.

Lenore.

Back when I was alive and had trouble sleeping, there was a trick I used. I'd stop trying to think in words and let the pictures take over. One image leads to another, and the next thing you know you're snoozing. This was the opposite. I tried to cling to the words, the things that worked in straight lines, but pictures kept poking in—bony hands, talking heads, laughing skulls.

Lenore again.

So much time passed I wondered why Turgeon hadn't come for me. Misty checked in now and again, but couldn't shake me out of it. She'd come back I don't know how often, hour after hour, talking, yelling, but no change.

I thought I heard howls and gunshots. I didn't know if it was from the Bones, or my ears were remembering Bedland. At some point, I wanted to get up, but the office had vanished and the floor was opening up. Below, there was a sickly green liquid. I struggled, but then gave up. They say once you've already said *fuck it*, it gets easier the second time. It certainly felt easier.

I was more than halfway gone, and nothing was pulling me back.

19

I didn't know how long I'd been there when the door clicked open and the rotten, stinking world rushed back into place. Misty stepped in, face wrapped in worry.

"Hess? Can you talk? You've got to get up. You have to."

It was dark out, so I pretended I'd been asleep. "Huh? Whazzat?"

"Jonesey's here. He's pretty upset."

Before I could say a word, Jonesey was halfway inside, pushing past Misty like she was a set of drapes. Things still felt arm's-length distant, but some habit told me I should keep up appearances in front of a guest. I managed to turn on the lamp. The light hit him under the chin. His head was bouncing like a doggy decorating the back of somebody's car.

"You look natural," he said. I think it was a compliment.

"And you look like you've seen a . . ." I caught myself. "Never mind. What's up?"

"Everything." He took to pacing, and talking too fast for me to follow. "It's gotten bad out there, right? Big cop presence? But I keep working on the rally, one pamphlet at a time, one chak at a time. It's happening, too. Really, really happening. I've got commitments. One chak talks to another, and those chakz talk to more. It's like a virus of positive energy . . . and then . . . and then . . ."

I was grateful for the pause. "Is there a point in there somewhere?"

"I managed to get the police to back off a little. The *police*. To. Back. Off. It was a miracle, a light from the sky, the dove from above. When they saw me in action, defusing tension, getting chakz to cooperate peacefully, I earned their *respect*."

I tried not to roll my eyes. "Yeah. And now you'll be the first chak elected president."

Making fun made me feel better, but Jonesey wasn't in the mood.

"Shut up. Don't talk like that, Hessius. I don't think I could take it right now."

"Since when do you call me Hessius? What the hell *is* going on? Sit down and take it slow, for Pete's sake."

He sat down. The change in the angle of the lamp did nothing for his looks.

"Boom, everything goes to confusion. Boom. Out of nowhere, fucking nowhere, like out of the darkness before the world began, this . . . this . . . *skeleton* shows up and starts tearing things apart."

At long last, something got my attention. I clenched my jaw. "Tearing things, or people?"

"Both, if he gets the chance. He's worse than feral, and he's strong. He puts his fist through a windshield, tries to grab the driver. The cops freak, the chakz freak, and everybody's running like crazy back to square one."

"Enough about the political climate. Focus. The skeleton, where is it now?"

Jonesey couldn't sit still. He jumped up and started acting the story out. I have to admit, it helped. "The cops go after him, guns blazing, but they miss, miss, miss, and he ducks into an alley. Then they lose him, ten of them, probably because they're so weirded out. So am I; so's everybody. Two chakz moan just because they were watching. But I don't panic. I stay in control, Mann, and I look, look, look and spot his freaky ass. I follow, figuring I can, you know, try to talk him down or something, but it's like he can't see or hear me, like I'm the same as any other thing in his way. I stand in front of him and he nearly tears *me* apart. And all the while keeps making this sound, like . . . like . . ."

"Heh-heh?"

Jonesey snapped his fingers. "That's the one." He twisted his head and stared. "You know him. You *know* him?"

"I know who it *was*."

He shook his head. "He, Mann. *He*."

That was Jonesey. He'd call a lamppost *he* or *she*. Part of his philosophy. Treat something as if it's a person and it's more likely to act like one. I somehow didn't think it applied to a bunch of bones—me, either, for that matter. I was barely back from the brink, and the only thing holding me there was the thought that I could prevent some damage if I put a stop to *it*.

But hope springs eternal. Jonesey even thought I might have some answers. "How does he even talk? How does he walk? There's no muscle."

I shook my head. "I said I knew *who* it was, not that I know *what* it is. All I can tell you is that it's what's left of a chak after an acid bath, and its name used to be Ashby."

He blinked. "Acid bath? You mean like a bath with acid in it?"

"Yeah. Long story. Right now we've got to find it before the police do, or before it gets its hands on another liveblood."

Jonesey's mouth opened so quick his jawbone cracked. "No, no, no. Another?"

I nodded. "Already killed two. Arguably self-defense . . . after the fact. Where'd you see it last?"

"Collin Hills."

He might as well have said Disneyland. Collin Hills was a McMansion neighborhood separated from the Bones by General Buell Park. A definite no-no for any chak.

"Collin Hills? Fuck . . . how . . . ?"

Jonesey went back into his pantomime thing, swooping his arms to imitate the skeleton's movements. "He headed into the park, over the fence, then over the freaking electrified wall!" Finished, he slapped himself in the head. "If he gets into one of those houses you know what that'll mean. . . ."

I did. The LBs were already on pins and needles. If it so much as tromped on the landscaping in a gated community, it'd be like what they did with the Japanese-Americans during WWII, without the food and water. I already had enough to feel guilty about.

For the first time in ages, I got to my feet. "What day is it?"

Jonesey gave me a look like he remembered having

this conversation from the other side. "Check your watch," he said.

"Right."

Three days. Good enough for Jesus and vampires, good enough for me.

I'd need something serious to deal with this. Ashby'd saved my ass twice—first by coming out of the vat, now by giving me a reason to get up. In exchange, I'd have to put him out of his misery.

It. I'd have to put *it* out of its misery.

I'd given my gun to that freak Turgeon, but I doubted it'd do any good here. I reached for a crowbar I kept at the side of the desk.

Jonesey looked at the iron the same way he'd just looked at me. "You said you knew him. Can't you talk to him?"

I tapped the bar into my palm. "Already tried. And don't ask me about *it* again until later. Much later."

I thought I'd have to talk Misty out of coming with us, but as we headed for the door she didn't say a word. And she looked as bad as I felt.

"You been eating?" I asked her.

No answer. She didn't look high, so I guessed she'd been worried about me, keeping vigil. I told Jonesey to wait outside a minute.

I said, "Three days, Misty. I'm lucky Turgeon didn't come for me. Uh . . . he didn't, did he?"

"No," she said. "Maybe he was just as freaked out as you were by . . . you know. . . ."

Ashby. I shivered. There but for fortune.

"How long would you have waited on me, Mist?"

"Until the end, until you changed."

"Then what? Would you have done like I asked?"

She sighed and nodded. "I've got a sledgehammer under my cot."

I gave her a hug. "Thanks."

She grimaced. "Fuck you, Hess."

I headed out.

Putting a bunch of McMansions on the far side of General Buell Park, so close to the Bones, sounded like real bad planning, but they were here before we were. Not before the street people, but Collin Hills was intended to reclaim the area from them. When chakz started stumbling around in the abandoned buildings here, sales dropped to nothing. To keep the current homeowners from bolting, the developer installed a big stone wall, topped with an electric fence and a twenty-four/seven security system.

In practice, up until now, it worked. Chakz never went past the park. We're not interested in making that kind of trouble anyway, and the police made it real clear what the consequences would be if we did.

So of course that's where Jonesey and I were headed.

We passed a few patrol cars cruising the neighborhood. They used to be as rare as UFOs. Things had changed. Otherwise, the Bones looked empty as usual. Not Buell Park. Flashlight beams flitted along the overgrown bushes like morbidly obese fireflies. The police were looking for the thing.

As we neared the park entrance, I caught a thick whiff of kerosene. Roundabout the knees of the bronze statue of Buell that stood in the center of the park, I caught a fiery flash. It wasn't a flashlight. The boys in blue had a new toy, a flamethrower. Great. It might not work on the skeleton, but it sure would work on me and Jonesey.

Back when I was alive, I sucked so badly at staying hidden it was a joke in the neighborhood. It was one of the few parts of my skill set that being dead had improved. If I wasn't stupid about it, and no one was staring right at me, I could get around pretty well without being seen. Jonesey would consider it politically incorrect to say so, but it had to do with being more a *thing* than a person. LBs don't realize it, but they're wired to sense other living things. Unless you had a dog's nose, or we had some rot, there's nothing to sense here. It's one of the reasons it's so easy for a chak to sneak up on a livedblood.

Some moans to the south got the cops all excited. When they raced off to follow, it gave us a break. We crouched like crazy just the same, avoiding the paths, plodding through a rat's nest of hedge and tree.

"There been a lot of moaners lately?" I asked.

Jonesey gave me that look again. "A couple every day now. Like I said, I got most of the cops to go home before your friend showed up; now it's . . . Where *have* you been?"

"I said we'd talk later."

Another moan, forlorn as a lonely loon crying in the middle of nowhere. I saw a powerful blast of flame, heard the creaking rush of burning wood, and a few seconds later felt some heat in the air.

Jonesey shook his head. "At least they could've *made sure* whoever it was had gone feral first."

"Come on; we've got business."

The twisted mass of branch and leaf ended in an eight-foot black iron fence. As we sneaked up, I could see lights on in a few of the Collin Hills houses. There was a second blast from the flamethrower, more distant.

Another moaner gone. Before the glow vanished, we were over the park fence and across the well-lit street.

We hit our knees behind a row of parked cars. I didn't like it here, not at all. Unlike the Bones, everything worked, especially the streetlamps. It was so bright I felt naked as a dead jaybird.

The Collin Hills wall was behind us, a big stucco sucker tipped with barbed wire. The wire was the good stuff, thin black strips that fit right in with the decor of the terra-cotta rooftops beyond. To add insult to injury, it was electrified. A small sign warned about the voltage. That level of electricity wouldn't destroy a chak, but our flesh would sear and stick to the wire. We'd end up doing major damage trying to pull free.

"Where'd it climb over? You see it happen?" I asked.

Jonesey muttered some mnemonic to himself, then pointed to a spot down the block half-hidden by an oak. "There."

We crept closer. Thanks to the great lighting it was easy to see that the stucco covering had been chipped, revealing the less dainty color of the concrete beneath. The broken patches made a line, more or less, that headed up to a spot where the wire looked slightly bent.

"So it climbed? I didn't think it could *see*."

"He didn't. Not exactly." Jonesey went into another weird little pantomime. "He runs up like this, hits the wall like he doesn't see it, then feels it with his hands. He reaches up, but the wall's too high. So he gets angry. He punches. He scratches. When he stops, he fingers the holes he made; then he uses them to pull himself up a little. He still can't reach the top, so he does it again and again, until he lobs himself over, nothing but a spark and a *gzt* from the wire. I expected alarms, but there was nothing. I've seen some freaky shit, but I'm telling you, *that* was freaky."

"Chakz never come here. Maybe the alarm broke and the owner didn't bother to repair it." I eyed the wall and the tree. "Bottom line, it can do it; we can do it."

Jonesey gave the handholds a shot while I shimmied up the oak. By the time I'd made my way across an over-hanging branch, he'd gone up as far as he could without touching the wire. Flat against the branch, I reached down, grabbed his hands, and swung him over.

It was close. The soles of his shoes cleared by an inch. Once he landed, I squirmed along the branch as far as I could, then jumped. I hit the ground on a patch of wood chips. Some splinters, but no big damage so far.

The lights of the security gate glowed beyond the neatly trimmed hedges. I could see the rent-a-cop in his little house, guarding the main entrance. He was awake, listening to some iThing. Good. The skeleton hadn't at-tracted attention here yet.

With no trail to follow, we skirted the edges of the properties. I was hoping it might still stink of acid, but the whole place was thick with the smell of chemicals, fertilizer and chlorine from the pools.

On the one hand, we hoped we'd bump into it; on the other, we were so terrified we would that we were star-tled by every cricket chirp. We really jumped when we heard the dog. A big one, it barked three times, then let loose with a final, pained yelp.

Not good for us or the doggy. It sounded like it was nearby, right in the next yard. With a quick glance at each other, we gave up on crouching and ran toward the sound.

When I saw how the pretty little picket gate was mangled, I half knew what to expect. I didn't expect something heavy to fly through the air and land at my feet with a warm, wet thud. Jonesey clamped his hand over his mouth. I had to bend down to make sure. It was a rottweiler, head twisted around so it had a nice view of its own tail. The heart-shaped collar said the dog's name was Annie.

"Heh-heh."

Beyond the gate, I saw it. The moonlight and streetlamps gave it a kind of perfect, white metal sheen. The color fit. It was bouncing around the fenced yard like a silver pinball: hitting a wall, changing direction, hitting a fence, changing direction again. Sometimes, out of frustration, I think, it lashed out at whatever was nearest, like a lawn mower. Something like that must've happened to the dog. Either Annie had been stepped on, or she got wide-eyed at all those yummy bones and attacked.

"Heh-heh."

As for the skeleton, left on its own, eventually it'd either fall into the pool or find the exit and wander out. We didn't have time to see which, because the house lights came on. We didn't have time at all.

Moving fast, I grabbed the longest thing lying around, a pool net, and whacked the skull with it to get its attention. Jaw slack, it turned, laughed, and headed toward me.

Careful to stay out of its reach, with a few more well-placed whacks I managed to steer it out the gate, all the way across the next yard, and then into a little patch of trees near the security wall.

So far so good, and I knew what had to happen next. But with all of Misty's soul talk and Jonesey insisting on calling it *he*, I was having trouble. I had to wonder if Ashby might still be in there. It was the fucking heads all over again, theme and variation.

Was he still thinking, still *feeling*?

If I played it long enough, the guessing game would drive me feral all by itself. I had to tell myself it didn't matter. It just didn't matter. It couldn't. It, it, *it*.

I gave Jonesey the pole, told him to keep whacking the skull and backing up. I took out the crowbar. The skeleton moved past me, blind, oblivious. I came up behind it.

In case it was an issue, I wanted it to be quick, merciful. There was survival involved, too. I had to make sure the first blow immobilized it, so I wouldn't wind up clawed to pieces. So did I hit the neck or the hips first?

I swallowed hard and swung at the neck for all I was worth. The bones were strong. The first blow only staggered it. It took another swing, so strong it nearly yanked my arm out of the socket. It sent the skull flying. The body crumpled. The skull careened into the stucco, bounced off, and fell where I couldn't see. It was only quiet for a beat.

"Heh-heh."

Damn. It was still talking. I didn't want to think about it. Fortunately, I didn't have to. Behind us, a door was opening.

"Annie? Where are you, girl?"

They'd find the dog. Even if the alarms didn't work, there'd be lots of screaming.

I stepped toward the bushes where the skull had landed.

"Jonesey, grab those bones," I whispered.

"What're you going to do?"

"Finish it."

I saw a clump of white and poked it with the crowbar. A stone. A big white stone. I had to wait until I heard the laugh again. It only took seconds.

"Heh-heh."

The sound was waist-level. It hadn't hit the ground. There it was, held by a web of branches, wedged in the bush. I stuck the crowbar in and lifted it by the eye socket. The jaws kept moving. Alas, poor Ashby.

"Heh-heh."

Trying to act dead, like an *it* myself, I laid it sideways on the stone, pulled back, aimed, and swung. I didn't just swing once; I did it again and again. I cracked the skull, snapped the jaws, and kept swinging. It—fine, maybe *he*—had saved my neck, or to be accurate, everything *below* my neck, and here I was pummeling his remains.

Misty's words echoed in my ears: *It could have been worse.*

When I was finished, the stone was covered with white dust and a few pieces no bigger than a marble. But I swear—I'm telling you, I *swear*—that even the white flakes looked like they were still moving, curling, twitching.

I backed away, scaring the shit out of myself when I bumped into Jonesey.

We both stared at the shivering pieces a while before they finally stopped.

"How the hell was he moving at all?" I whispered. "No muscle, no ligature. Nothing."

I was thinking out loud, but Jonesey answered. "A luz."

"A what?"

He shook his head apologetically, like he was sorry he hadn't thought of it sooner. "It popped into my head just now. It's from the midrash. A luz is a bone in the human body that's completely indestructible. They believed it contained the soul. Maybe after everything else was burned away, your friend was one big luz."

"The midrash? You Jewish, Jonesey?"

"I . . . I don't remember."

20

The same oak tree got us back over the fence. We dumped the bones, luz and all, into the sewer. It hadn't rained in a while, so they landed with a low, distant clatter.

Ashby, ripped and RIP.

Alarms were beeping and clanging everywhere. Police, with their flashlights and flamethrower, rushed into the front entrance of Collin Hills. We waited, then made it back into the park.

Soon all the screams were behind us. Annie's owners might be bereft, but for the cops it'd just be a dead dog. There'd be a few chakz dragged out of bed, more tension, more patrols, but nothing as bad as if that thing had stumbled in on some family curled around the TV laughing over *Tea with the Dead*.

The deeper into the park we went, the fewer working lights, leaving us to rely on what there was of the moon. We tramped through the grass, silent as zombie church mice. I kept rubbing my hands, thinking little pieces of

Ashby were still on my fingers. I didn't want to say anything to Jonesey. I especially didn't want to tell him how I'd nearly moaned before he walked in on me, or how I wasn't sure what was holding me together now.

But as the shapeless bushes and half-dead trees gave way to the broken-box rectangles of our beloved neighborhood, Jonesey decided to tell me what I was feeling.

"You must be pissed."

Pissed? More like if there was a button on the wall that said, PUSH TO END WORLD, I was ready to press it. I wiped my hands on my pants and looked at him.

"I know *I'm* pissed," he said. "Now, more than ever, I'm ready to pull myself up by my bootstraps and get out there and organize." To punctuate his clichéd imagery, he slammed his fist into his hand. "And you're going after whoever did this, right?"

Me? I said, "Yeah."

He shook his head. "You don't sound so sure of yourself, Hess. You have to sound sure of yourself."

"Oh, for the love of . . ."

He stepped in front of me, stopped me in my tracks. "Say it again, Hess, but this time like you mean it."

My sympathy only goes so far. I growled at him. "I swear, you tell me to turn my frown upside down, I'm going to rip off what's left of your lips and feed them to the rats."

"Good. At least now you look pissed," he said. He grinned as if he'd accomplished something.

By the time we hit the sidewalk I figured I'd grunt something more. "I said yeah; I meant yeah. Of course I want to find him. I'm just not sure I can. I've been going from one horror show to another for days, and more often than not, I'm the star. This guy's a major screwball. I don't know why he's doing it. I don't even know if he knows. I'm not sure I could have found him in my best days, and those are long gone."

He nodded sympathetically. "I hear you. But you know what I'm going to say. You gotta act as if."

If I'd met Jonesey when he was alive, I would've hated him, thought him a parasite for shoveling a crappy line of shit at people, living off their hopes and dreams. But seeing that ridiculous Pollyanna expression plastered on his grayish skin was, if nothing else, funny.

I threw my hands up. "Fine. You can act like an asshole, no reason I can't act like a detective."

"That's the spirit!" He slapped me on the back.

Whatever. As if. As if what? Turgeon was probably an alias, and I didn't even have fake names for Grandpa or Watt. My only leads were the two chakz I'd found on the police database. A quick check on the recorder gave me their names—Nell Parker and Odell Jenkins.

Two chakz. Right. And here I was standing next to my own personal chak database.

"Jonesey, you know a Nell Parker?"

He went into his little mnemonic dance. "Bell ... toll ... death ... Nell Parker. Oh, man, oh, man."

"What? Believe me, at this point I'm pretty sure I can take it."

"She's hooked up with Colby Green. *Colby Green*. You don't want to go down that route. Forget it."

I made a face at him. "Geez, you run hot and cold. I thought you wanted me to act as if."

"Yeah, but you should act as if you've still got a brain. I mean ... Colby Green? I home-delivered some ketamine to his estate once. He has these special bug zappers set up out front. Bug gets fried, falls into a small reanimator at the bottom, then comes back, only to get fried again. And that's what he does to *bugs*."

I knew the stories. "So I take it you don't buy the press about how he fights for chak rights?"

"Sure, he fights for our rights, but that's just to keep his *access*, Mann. He runs *the* biggest chak-up palace in the country, as a hobby. In his basement, he's got chakz in pens, like cattle. Some of his friends are into dead *kids*, you know what I'm saying? Cancer victims or whatnot whose parents brought them back in the early days, then abandoned them when they decided they were freaks. Anyone tries to press child-rape charges, Green's lawyers argue that since they died six years ago, even though they were ten at the time, *now* they're sixteen, the age of consent, so it's *legal*. It doesn't get more perverted. And Nell Parker? She's his favorite stripper."

"That's a long walk. Her file said she used to be a women's advocate."

"Yeah, well, she walked the walk. Right now she'd be better off if your psycho got her."

"That's sort of what Misty said about Ashby, but I don't see it. It's not as though she can quit when she's a head."

"Funny. Stay away. You need someone to help? Fuck, help *me*. I've got maybe thirty chakz lined up for the rally, but, honestly, most can't march in a straight line, let alone hold up a sign. I could use you. What do you say?"

He pulled out one of his flyers and handed it to me.

"Come on, at least read it."

Crazy as life was, the rally struck me as crazier. I crumpled the flyer and stuffed it in my pocket. "Sorry, Jonesey, wrong *as if*. I liked your first speech better."

Two blocks north there was a train station on a line that'd take me north to the Colby estate. It practically had its own stop. I'd missed the last one for the day, but there'd be another in the morning.

"Hess, you do this and I'll . . . I'll tell Misty."

With a bit of effort, I managed to glower. "Tell her or not, I'm going. But do us all a favor and don't. She's got her own problems. After I'm gone, I'm sure she'll be happy to help you paint some signs, though." I pulled some bills out of my pocket. "For supplies, and a couple of hot meals for Misty. She likes breakfast, home fries, but make sure she eats the eggs, too."

By the time he stopped looking at the money, I was half a block away.

"You're nuts!" he called out.

Depends on how you kept score. Colby Green was the shit you find on the bottom of a shit pile. I could easily, real easily, wind up stuck there as one of his playthings. But I had this weird idea that someone as fascinated with chakz as he was might believe what I had to say about Turgeon. Whatever his reasons, he might even help try to stop him.

And that was worth the risk.

Back at the office, Misty looked like she was asleep, so I stepped over her. She wasn't.

"You find Ashby?" she said in a half mumble.

"Yeah, it's all fine now."

Her eyes popped open. She propped herself up. "Meaning you put him down."

"Had to, Misty. You know that."

She slumped. "I do. You've got to pull yourself together and get the guy who did this, Hess; you have to."

As if. "That's what I'm trying to do."

She went on. "No more lying around watching the inside of your eyeballs."

"Did you hear what I just said?"

I headed for my office, but she grabbed my arm. "Don't act like we both don't know how close you were. You were into that, that . . . *torpor* shit. And then I'm supposed to smash your head in? I can barely lift that sledgehammer. You scared me, you son of a bitch; you really scared me."

I looked at her. "I'm back now, okay? I'm back and I'm going to try to find Turgeon, at least warn his victims."

She let go.

It was only when I stepped into my office that I realized how tired I was. I didn't want to sleep, but my brain insisted. I threw myself down and closed my eyes. It was the real deal. If I dreamed anything, I didn't remember.

Judging from the shadows through the blinds, I slept the morning away. It looked like noon. If I was going to do this thing, I'd better be on my way. I took a few hundred for expenses and thought about how nice it was for Turgeon to provide the funds for his own investigation. Then I had a funny feeling.

I decided to check all the bills. I'd looked over the first wad when he handed it to me—that was legit, but not the other two. At least half were phonies, unless they elected Dumbledore president of the United States and nobody told me. Shit. By the time I finished counting, I had about a third of what I thought. So much for redecorating.

Cursing, I grabbed it all and headed out.

Misty was still lying down. "Where you going now?" she said, still half-asleep.

"To deposit the cash at an ATM, so the debit card will be good. Then I've got to catch a train."

"To where?"

"A lead. For real. I don't know how long I'll be gone. Go find Jonesey. He's got some work for you, and some money for food."

"You couldn't tell me that last night? I'm starving," she said drowsily. "You sound better, like . . ."

Her eyelids fluttered. She mumbled something I couldn't make out. Poor thing had probably been awake the whole time I was losing it. Now she was catching up. A little bit of drool slid from her half-open mouth, down to the rumpled pillowcase.

I pressed my dry tongue to the roof of my dry mouth and tried to remember what it was like to drool.

21

Turned out I'd slept through more than just morning. By the time I was on my way, it was late afternoon. The ride was nothing to speak of. My car was empty. There were flashes through the filthy windows whenever the power lines sparked. The train passed ticky-tack suburbs, trash-strewn woods where teens ran wild, before it squeaked and shuddered into Cherry's End.

The only thing visible from the station was the forest. I got off the platform and still didn't see much of anything. Why? Because that's how Colby Green planned it. A few years ago, there was a court case over whether or not Cherry's End was even part of Fort Hammer. Green was rich enough to muddy the jurisdiction. Even got his own area code.

The huge stone wall surrounding his property sneaked up on me. That's hard to manage with something so big, but this was no Collin Hills, protected by cinder block made pretty with a trowel swish. Consumerism is a superficial sin for superficial people. Ninety-nine percent of the folks living at Collin Hills couldn't tell you what cinder block was made of. Green knew exactly where his Italian marble came from, the city, the quarry, the name of the foreman. Not that he cared about architecture. From what I understood, he was like that with everything. He knew the world inside and out and now wanted to play with it the way a cat likes to toy with a mouse, amused at the way it hovers between life and death.

Which is probably why he likes chakz so much.

I followed the wall maybe ten minutes until I spotted the front gates, iron monsters buttressed by Italian marble columns. Sneaking around a lion's den seems disrespectful as well as pointless, so I figured I might as well walk up and knock. It is, after all, one of the few places open to chakz.

Adjusting my jacket and tie, I told myself that if I presented the case just so, and he really liked this Nell Parker, at the very least he'd want to take steps to protect his property. Made sense to me. But making sense just made me uncomfortable, the world being fucking crazy.

The gate didn't get closer as I walked so much as bigger and bigger. When I finally got to the iron, I heard some weird sounds—a *bzt* followed by a g*zt*. Peering between the bars, I looked up and saw those bug zappers Jonesey was talking about, bugs swarming, dying, being "reborn." No rumor, then.

Bzt! You're dead! *Gzt!* You're back!

I hoped to hell he didn't have any puppies.

"Can I help you?"

I was so busy being horrified I hadn't noticed the camera and monitor. A round face with a lascivious grin that reminded me of the master of ceremonies from *Cabaret* eyeballed me from some unknown location.

"My name is Hessius Mann," I said. "I'm a detective. I have reason to believe someone may try to break into the estate."

His lipstick smile turned upside down. "Detective? No, no. That's next week. You must have gotten the wrong schedule! Today it's Voyage to the Bottom of the Chak! A *nautical* theme. Oh, well, come on in! The party is just getting started!"

"Wait, I'm not . . ."

The screen went dead; the gates swung open. Dogs barked in the distance. Looked like I'd be entering under false pretenses.

There was a wide, white gravel driveway, but I took a gray stone footpath instead, passing bubbling fountains and major landscaping. I don't know the names of many plants, but there were lots, different leaves, different flowers, different smells, all neatly arranged.

It wasn't until I passed some rows of tall hemlocks that the main building punched me in the face, and it wasn't interested in leaving much space for clouds or sky. I didn't recognize the architectural style, or even if it had one; I only knew there was a lot of it. So this was Xanadu, or the Best Little Whorehouse in Texas, on steroids, if you prefer. I'd seen pictures, but they didn't do the place justice. The only camera that could take the whole thing in was up in orbit and available on Google Earth.

"In my father's house are many rooms," it says in the Bible. Judging from the number of windows, Colby Green was in competition with God.

A few seconds later, I was facing a twenty-foot black

slab with a knob. I felt like I should sacrifice a goat to it, but then realized it was a door. It swung open, the clown from the security monitor behind it, wearing an open magenta silk robe. It definitely wasn't his color.

He winced at the sunlight and gave my arm an old-man grab, the kind that's stronger than you expect, like it's holding on for dear life. Then he dragged me into a foyer that could have comfortably held a 747, and twisted me around for a look.

He didn't like what he saw, but that made two of us. In the quieter light, his grin looked more like a side effect of too many Botox injections. His eyes were still expressive, so I could sort of tell what he was thinking as long as I didn't pay too much attention to that smile.

"Nice try," he said, "but we have much, much better outfits in the dressing room. How are you with pole dancing?"

"Hold it. This isn't a costume. I'm here on business."

His eyes joined in with the grin. "But you're a chak."

"Gee, and they told me at the funeral that I looked so natural."

"Forgive me!" he said with a chuckle. "Chakz generally only arrive here for one reason."

"I know, but I'm here for another."

"A chak. Here for another reason."

"Someone tells you two and two is four, does it matter who says it?"

"I was never very good at math."

"I'm hoping your boss is."

"Ah, well, I'm sure you won't be disappointed. Mr. Green is good at everything."

He let go of my shoulder and wiped his hand on his robe, like I was the one who'd have cooties. "He's in the playground, watching some entertainment with his guests. You're welcome to try to speak to him. I can't promise anything. I can't promise anything at all." He lowered his voice to a giggly whisper. "I can't even promise you'll be permitted to leave."

"Thanks. I'll keep that in mind. Which way? Do I need a map?"

"A guide to fashion, perhaps. You're sure you don't want to freshen up just a bit?"

"Nah. Under the circumstances, I think I'm better off sticking out, don't you?"

He flared his nostrils. "I get your point. And believe me, you do. I'll take you there, but I'd wait until Nell finishes dancing. She's his favorite."

"Oddly enough," I said. "That's what I'm hoping."

He gave me a shrug that said he didn't understand and couldn't care less, then led me down an arched hallway three times wider than my office. It was lined with life-size statues, all with an erotic bent. Some involved men and women, others animals, some both. When the hand on one statue moved to stroke itself, I nearly jumped out of my wrinkly skin. They were animated, like those figures in Disneyland's Hall of Presidents. Did Green think it funny?

When I started, the gnomish doorman sneaked a peek to see if I had any further reaction to the decor. When I didn't supply any, he trotted along, a little disappointed, then opened another set of doors into what had to be the "playground."

It was big, of course. The lighting was intentionally soft, almost dim. The arched ceiling, a floor or two up, was covered with twinkling lights in the shape of constellations, only, like the statues, they were animated, so that, you guessed it, it looked like the stars were screwing. The rest of the space was part stage, part pool, part recreation area. There were jungle gyms, swings, all sorts of toys, but no one under thirty was playing with them. No one living, anyway. The stage area, aside from three silver poles and a black velvet curtain, was empty at the moment. There was plenty going on everywhere else.

The smell of chlorine from the pool was strong, but not nearly strong enough. For the first time since I died, I felt like I needed a shower. Like the emcee man said, there was a nautical theme. Chakz were dressed as everything from pirates to cephalopods. Some of the LBs were playing dress-up, too, fish masks and all; others didn't bother. Among them I spotted some of Fort Hammer's rich and famous. The only one I could put a name to was the DA, and frankly it would've been safer for me if I hadn't.

My fellow reanimates didn't look happy. Then again, they didn't look unhappy, either. Surprising, considering the uses to which their orifices were being put. Mostly, they looked uninterested, even bored. A few glanced my way and gave me a look that seemed to say, *What's the big deal? We're stone dead already.*

That's why no one ever bothered to make chakking-up illegal. Victimless crime.

Trying hard not to recognize anyone else important, I searched for Green among the mass of entangled flesh. Funny, I hadn't figured on Fort Hammer's own Caligula being all by his lonesome, but he was. He was in the shallow end of the pool sitting in a half-submerged lounge chair. His open robe floated around his fiftysomething gut, chlorinated water lapping at the matted hairs on his belly.

Aside from an obvious penchant for eating, he was in good shape. Even if sex was his only vice, you'd think he'd have caught *something* by now, but he didn't look ravaged by drugs or illness. The hair seemed real, and he looked younger than Misty. Not young at heart, though. I expected giddiness, like the emcee, but Green had a predatory stillness. He wasn't quite as motionless as a chak could get, but close enough.

I made my way toward him, dodging couples, triples, and quadruples, trying not to step on anyone, ignoring invitations to join in. Other than Green, the only other people in the room "uninvolved" were two thugs leaning against one of the columns that lined the room and held up the faux heavens. They were dressed in black, wore sunglasses, had black hair, square jaws, the whole *Reservoir Dogs* look.

As I neared Green, one came forward and patted his jacket pocket to let me know he was there. I gave him a nod, then knelt by the edge of the pool near the main man.

"Mr. Green," I said.

There was lots of noise in the room, grinding, heaving breathing, gasps, but when Colby Green turned toward me, a few drops of water fell from his hair and I could hear them hit the pool. The bat-black of his eyes sized me up like an hors d'oeuvre, something interesting enough to taste even if he was full. I think it gave me a small sense of how Misty felt out on the streets.

Before he could decide on his own what to do about me, I started talking, fast. "My name's Hessius Mann. I know it's unusual, but I'm a detective. I've got good reason to think—"

A piano song interrupted, playing over hidden speak-

ers. The music was electronic, intentionally tinny, and
vaguely familiar. Green put a finger to his lips and nodded toward the stage as the recorded lyrics began.

*Got a feelin' it's all over now—all over now, we're
through.*

Took me a second, but I placed the tune. It was the
closing theme from *All in the Family*, an ancient sitcom.
That's the kind of crap I have no trouble remembering.
If that weren't strange enough, a female chak, pale as
paper or maybe a blue-tinged moon, emerged from the
side of the black velvet curtain and strutted to the center pole.

Nell Parker, I presumed.

And tomorrow I'll be lonesome, remembering you.

Unless it was a ton of makeup, or the lighting, she was
in great shape. The only thing that looked fake was the
bowl-cut hair, bleached beyond platinum to match the
alabaster outfit. The lighting gave her face some grayer
patches, even a swipe or two of charcoal black, but the
only real color on the stage was the green in her eyes.
The color had to be fake, contacts, but they looked great,
stuck out like emeralds on a sandy stretch of beach.

She spun and gyrated. The line between the folds in
her dress and the curves of her body disappeared into
the pattern of her movement. Women's advocate? Sure,
but she must've been a dancer, too. Strong hips, small
breasts. Not boyish in any way, and there wasn't anything missing. Not a bit of rot. One of the lucky ones.
Oh, there were signs that she was a chak, but only two.
Her eyes were a bit too sunken, and her expression was
dull, detached, absent, echoing the ennui all the chakz
here had.

A pole dance is about voyeurism. Look but don't

touch. You watch the dancer enjoy her own sexuality. Toss a chak into the mix and it's something different. She swooped, flipped, and tumbled at an easy, erotic tempo. One moment her body rippled in a perfect imitation of hunger and longing; the next she spun away with a quick flash of disdain. I thought for a second she was looking at me. But, like a pro, she'd made eye contact with everyone.

I think I could guess what she meant to Green. It was echoes, all echoes, but so perfect she blurred the line with the real thing. That was his fascination, the line between the living and the dead. He wasn't the only one. I barely noticed when the song ended. Barely heard it when a voice came over the loudspeaker.

"Ms. Parker will be back shortly to join in the fun."

She flitted away, her eyes' green sparkle lost in gray as she passed through the black velvet curtain. Before it floated closed, I noticed a circular staircase behind it.

Booth used to tell me that detective work should never, ever be personal. The cold formula's the important part: two and two equals four. It doesn't matter if it's two apples or two oranges, two drug addicts or two helpless infants. Best not to pay attention to anything else. The moment you *think* you can have feelings and do the work is the moment you're about to make your worst mistake.

Colby turned toward me. "Now, what was it you had to say?"

I didn't answer. I was too busy watching the air she'd left behind.

22

Until I became a chak, I never realized death could be, on the one hand, so . . . active, on the other how much *desire* would be gone. I'm not talking erectile dysfunction. I mean the taste of food, the feel of fresh air, the peaceful tingle from the sound of an ocean surf. Now it was all through a glass darkly, to coin a phrase.

So what was with my reaction to this dancer, this Nell Parker? I had no idea. I was worried, really worried, that it meant my undead nervous system was completely fried, taking another step toward the big F. But I also couldn't let go of the possibility that it was all her, the fact that she managed to *remind* me of being alive, the way it ached but didn't hurt.

I assumed I was free to stare, that Green would think I was a typical chak, slow on the uptake, but when I finally turned to him, his eyes were narrowed. I pointed toward the stage.

"I've got good reason, real good reason, to believe someone's out to hurt Nell Parker."

His eyes stayed narrow. "You're worried about her? Did you like watching her dance? She can take a lot without getting hurt."

"I don't mean that kind of hurt. I'm talking about something more permanent."

The black in his eyes twinkled. "Nothing's permanent."

"They say a D-cap is."

The amused twinkle vanished. He stood, leaving the chair bobbing behind him in the water. "Let's talk privately."

He closed his robes and climbed out of the pool. Dripping on his guests as he went, he strode back into the giant hallway, myself and the two gunsels following. From there, he took a left into a smaller hall, where, not so different from the dim lighting behind us, late-afternoon sun streamed in from a glass roof.

Wordless the whole while, he stopped at the only plain thing I'd seen in this massive place: a brown door. The office on the other side of it almost looked normal: dark paneling, bookshelves, and few paintings that actually didn't involve fornication. There were plenty of comfortable chairs, but all four of us remained standing.

There was only one visible sign of his proclivities. On the desk, next to a laptop, sat a candy bowl full of Viagra. I tapped the rim. "Surprised you use the stuff, Mr. Green."

"It's for the guests. I'd offer you one, but they only make chakz tense. I have people working on that, though." He pulled a bronze bowl from a shelf and held it toward me. It was filled with pills, too. They were the same oblong shape as the Viagra but bigger, and with more of a neon tinge.

I made a face.

"Can't happen, right? Impossible? But I like a challenge. Chakz don't have eye color, either, but Nell does, and they're not contacts. She's the first. That's what makes things worth trying. Over and over and over, if need be."

I waved off the bowl. "No offense, Mr. Green, but some people think doing the same thing over and over and expecting a different result is the definition of insanity."

He laughed. "Unless it's something you *like* doing over and over." He shook the bowl. "Think about what you and Nell could do over and over if they worked." He took one of the pills, licked it, then held it out to me. "No?"

When I didn't budge, with a shrug he tossed it back in the bowl. "They're experimental anyway. Lots of side effects."

"Headaches and nausea or erections that last more than three days?"

"Something like that. But I'm being rude. You were saying something about Nell's head. It is one of her more interesting parts."

This was my shot, so I gave it to him as simply as I could. "There's a psycho in town calling himself Turgeon. He's D-capping chakz accused of killing their spouses and, near as I can tell, keeping the heads. He's already got two, Colin Wilson and Frank Boyle. Nell was executed for beating her husband to death, only she didn't. That makes her one of three chakz left in Fort Hammer who fit this guy's MO."

He smiled. "And you're another. Your wife, Lenore."

That surprised me, until he pointed at a video camera

near the ceiling. "They do amazing things with real-time facial recognition these days. You didn't think you'd get in here without my knowing exactly who you were?"

"I try not to think at all when I don't have to."

He laid his long fingers on the desk, leaned toward me, and inhaled, like he was enjoying my smell. "I love chakz, Mann. You utterly fascinate me. I think you might even hold the answer to the biggest question ever asked."

"Why is there always one sock missing after the wash?"

He snorted. "Whether the eternal soul exists. Are we just our bodies, turned on or off at will? Figure out whether a chak *is* still somehow the person they were and you have the answer. If they're not, it's the soul that's missing. Is Nell Parker's revived corpse still Nell Parker? Are you Hessius Mann, a detective? Or do you just go through the motions?"

"I can't answer that, Mr. Green, except to say that you left out a possibility."

He blinked. "What's that?"

"That livebloods just go through the motions, too."

He laughed in a way that didn't make me feel like bonding. "That's the other possibility, isn't it? That *none* of us have souls. I admit the comment shows some intelligence. I've met higher-functioning chakz, but not many. Nell is one. Hell, I'd have to say she's one of a kind. She'd wrap me around her finger if I didn't keep her under lock and key. Yet I don't even know if she's real."

I think that lock-and-key thing was a relief. "You keep her protected, then?"

He tilted his head. "Of course. I always protect what's mine. But tell me about the decapitations, *Detective*.

Any idea why your Mr. Turgeon would do something so extreme?"

Talking about Nell, calling me *detective*. He was playing me, testing me, poking around for an answer to his big question. I didn't mind. For one, maybe he could tell me if I was for real. For another, I still had the crazy idea in the back of my head that if I could convince him Turgeon was real, he might help.

I went into my song and dance. "I don't know. Maybe he's a cross between Dexter and Batman; his daddy killed his mommy and now he's getting revenge over and over."

Green leaned back, looking professorial. "Interesting, but you said he kept the heads. Why would he do that instead of destroying them?"

"Not sure. Keep them quiet so they can't identify him." I flashed on what Turgeon said to me. *We'll talk later.* "Or maybe he keeps them for . . . company."

"So you think the heads can still talk? That's not what the papers tell us, Detective."

"It's a big world. I saw a set of bones the other day that shouldn't be moving, but did. And like you said, chakz aren't supposed to have eye color, either."

"The commissioner shared the story about the bones in the Bones," he said. "Sounded like the Loch Ness monster to me, but your point is taken. None of that really gets to the heart of Mr. Turgeon, though, does it?"

"Past that, the best I have is that he's a sick fuck, no offense."

"None taken." He picked up the bowl of Viagra. "Sociopaths and serial killers beg the same sort of question, don't they?"

"Sorry, what was the question?"

"Souls. Do they have them?" He swirled the pills. "They say eroticism reveals our inner self, our true self. Serial killers are anything *but* erotic. If you're right about acting out something involving his parents, maybe he keeps the heads around because he needs their approval?"

I furrowed my brow so fast, a flap of skin on my forehead cracked. "You mean like he can't *bring himself* to destroy them?"

Green ran his finger through the pills. "It's a thought."

It occurred to me he was thinking *a lot* about Turgeon. They say that's how he is about everything, like knowing where the walls' marble came from, but I wasn't sure. Either way it sure as hell sounded like he was taking me seriously.

"Mr. Green, do you think you could get the police to take a look? It'd be in your interests, right?"

He nodded. "It would, and I could. The commissioner is in one of the back rooms right now. Shall I tell you what he's doing with who? It'd give you quite a bit of leverage. Married, you know."

I shook my head. "Thanks, but I don't need anyone else after my head. Will you talk to him?"

He leaned in as if to pat me on the shoulder. Instead, his hand lingered and squeezed. "Could you write it all down for me, Detective? Everything? In your own words?"

The conversation had taken a weird turn, but I wasn't sure in which direction. Did he want the details for the commissioner, or was I being poked and prodded without benefit of dinner and a movie?

But what choice did have? I shrugged. "Yeah. I could do that."

His eyes lit up, making him look a little too happy. "Excellent! Use my laptop."

He rose, headed toward the door. The Reservoir Dogs fell in behind him. I didn't care for how quickly they were moving.

"Mr. Green," I called. I pointed to my head. "Not sure how much detail I can give you."

He gave me a smile, practiced, deliberate, the way a snake would smile if it could. "Hessius Mann, do what you can. I'll do as I like."

Before I could so much as grunt, the door closed and the lock clicked.

What the fuck?

Maybe he just didn't want me wandering around. Or maybe the whole chat had been a new way for him to jerk off over his big life question, and he liked it so much he might want to try it again. Or maybe something worse was going on.

If I was imagining things and I did anything about it, I could piss away my big chance for some help. I sat at the desk. There was some kind of form on the screen. Half of it was already filled out, including my name, address, and photo. It looked like he was collecting info for some kind of database, not a good sign. But I played along, adding what I could, doing my best to describe Turgeon without using the words *baby* or *egg*. As I hunted and pecked at the keys, though, I kept thinking about the door, getting more and more antsy.

After about fifteen minutes, I remembered what the emcee said:

I can't even promise you'll be permitted to leave.

That did it. Crap. I'd just been a prisoner at the warehouse. Friend or foe, good, bad, or ugly, I wanted out, now, and I wasn't going to ask to be shown the way. I found the wire leading up to the surveillance camera and yanked it. Then I picked up one of the nice, comfy chairs and threw it through the nearest window. Shielding my face with my arms, I jumped through the shattered frame. Was it the wrong move? Wouldn't be the first time.

I landed on a slate floor. I was on some kind of porch ringed with bushes thick with red berries. Late afternoon having given way to evening, I stumbled into the wicker furniture, trying to get my bearings.

And then I heard a sound like chimes. Three rings, pause, three rings again. It took me a while to realize it was an alarm, set off, no doubt, when I smashed the window. Footsteps tromped nearby, getting louder. Yep, an alarm.

I jumped over the bushes and scurried like a rat along the edge of the house, doing the quiet-dead-man thing. It didn't mean I was safe, not by a long shot. You'd need an army to keep this place secure, and Green could afford one. Given his hobby, they were probably trained to spot chakz, too. I slipped by at least ten of his men before reaching the delivery entrance at the rear of the house. I guessed it'd be a quick run to the hemlocks and the way I came in. The gate would be locked, so I'd have to figure some other way over the wall.

Only, I didn't go. Something held me back.

It wasn't torpor, it wasn't the guards, wasn't a Nancy Drew hunch, or a weird schoolboy pang about Nell Parker. It was a sound. It came from behind me, from the other side of the thick glass of a low basement window—moaning. Not just one voice, five or six.

I knelt and rubbed the glass to get a decent view. Inside it was like the chak pens Jonesey had warned me about. He was half-right. They weren't exactly pens, more like jail cells, solid metal bars, floor to ceiling. Straw covered the ground—to catch any gleet ooze, I suppose.

There were only two cells, a seven-foot space between them, one along each side of a deep room. The chakz on the left, some still dressed in party costumes, looked sullen, but functional. There was a cowboy, the hole where an eye used to be visible through his mask, a noseless robot, and two mermen danglers. They were all pretty quiet.

The moaning was coming from the second pen. It was standing room only in there, so many chakz I could barely distinguish one set of limbs from another. A gleet whose skull was half exposed chewed at the rubber gills covering his chest as if they were macaroni. An eye dangler in a scuba outfit started wailing as I watched. Four others looked as if they'd been at it a while, and were ready to blow. Shoved into tight quarters like that, it was only a question of time before they all went. Charred bones and burn marks told me what happened to them when they did.

With most of the guards outside looking for me, only one was here, a goofy-looking guy with a huge Adam's apple and a tense face. He had a gun in his hand, a magnum, and a key ring clipped to his belt. He was nervous, eyeing the moaners, trying to keep his distance. That meant putting his back to the other cell, where the "safe" chakz were. You know, the ones who were still smart enough to grab you from behind and try to get those keys.

I felt bad for him, wondered which chak would figure it out first.

The cowboy won. While Goofy watched the moaners, he watched him. When Goofy took a step back from the moaners, the cowboy took a step forward.

Goofy was just about to bring himself within reach of the eager cowboy when his Adam's apple rose like a radar antenna. His expression changed. He was about to turn around, catch the cowboy, and ruin it all. So . . .

I rapped at the glass.

That's all it took. The second Goofy looked up at me, the one-eyed cowboy reached through the bars and wrapped his arm tight around the man's neck. The other chakz joined in. In seconds, six arms held him against the bars. Two hands were clamped over his mouth, a third over his nose, and they held on tight until he passed out. The cowboy was smart enough to snag the keys before the body fell out of reach.

Next thing I knew the cell door was unlocked and the cowboy was opening the window. It made me wonder if Green was wrong. Maybe the smart ones aren't so rare. Maybe some of us are just smart *enough* to act dumb.

When I didn't climb in right off, the cowboy looked annoyed. "Can you talk? In or out?"

With his fellow escapees stumbling out into the hallway, I was blocking his path to the window. In or out? I wasn't sure. If I had half a brain I'd use the distraction of the escaping chakz to make for the hemlocks and catch the next train home.

I knew Green wasn't being straight with me, but I had a feeling it wasn't only so he could experiment with me. There was too much talk about Turgeon. There had to be something else going on, something with Nell Parker.

If I could find her, she might tell me. And at least I could warn her personally. I can't say I didn't like the idea.

A group of guards storming along near my hiding spot decided things. I leaped in.

Seeing the guards, the cowboy shut the window. As he watched them rush by, he looked even more annoyed. "Shit, if you'd been faster, I'd be at the wall by now."

"Hey, if I hadn't set off the alarms and tapped that glass, you'd still be locked up. Besides, how could you even reach the wall? He's got at least twenty men on the grounds, and you've got no depth perception."

"A smart one, eh? Here. Got something for you." He reached his hand into his pocket and pulled it back out, giving me the finger. Not the actual finger, just the FU sign. "I've got the layout memorized. Forty-seven seconds to the wall, twenty to reach the woods."

"Show-off. If you're so damn smart, why come here in the first place?"

He made a face. "Same as everyone. Money. They let me in for the party. I was planning to pick a few pockets and blow. Didn't know about the chak checks. Every fucking hour. You don't react fast enough, ask how high when they tell you to jump on something, they think you're about to go feral and throw you down here. And once you're here long enough . . ." He nodded toward the moaners. "Green leaves them in there until they tear each other to pieces. Then he burns whatever's left. Watching that shit, I don't know how I kept it together."

Another lost soul, or whatever. I wanted to give him a few bucks for his troubles. Instead, I don't know why, I pulled out Jonesey's crumpled flyer and handed it over.

He glanced at it. "A rally? You kidding me?"

"It's stupid. It's dangerous. It's something to do."

I headed for the hall.

"Wait a minute! What about *them*?" He pointed toward the moaners.

"Up to you, cowboy," I said.

"Oh, thanks. Exit's to the right, by the way," he said.

"Thanks," I answered. Then I headed left.

23

The escapees pooled in the hall, blocking the way. I had to push through them. Once I made it out of the pile, like a bunch of zombies they followed me. I tried explaining that the exit was the other way, but they either didn't believe me or, in the case of one earless guy, didn't hear me at all. With a nod to Frank Boyle's efforts during the Bedland hakker attack, I tried turning them toward the exit, but some slipped by and toddled deeper into the basement.

My Boy Scout efforts ended when a howl and a thud snapped all our heads back toward the door to the jail cells. There, the one-eyed cowboy flew into the hall and headed for the exit faster than if he'd been riding a horse. The moaning inside had turned into growls.

Son of a bitch, he'd opened the cage.

Far down the hall, I could see a staircase, but there was a lot going on between me and it. The chakz that'd slipped by me were already meeting up with some seriously armed LBs on their way down. I started running the other way, thinking I'd follow the cowboy. But once I took some turns, raced up and down some carved stone hallways, I was totally lost. The place was a fucking labyrinth. If the ferals didn't get me, I was afraid I'd run into a Minotaur or a giant piece of cheese.

A fancy wooden-slat-and-banded-iron door took me into a huge room, a cross between a wine cellar and some kind of freaky herb garden. I was thinking it was a dead end until I saw a bit of luck. A fire ax and hose were mounted behind one of those glass doors marked IN CASE OF EMERGENCY. The ax was only half the fun. Sitting next to it was a great big, juicy series of circuit breakers. A little chaos could go a long way in helping the chakz escape, and me get around.

So, ax, meet circuit breakers. Circuit breakers, ax.

My first swing didn't do much. The second earned a major spark shower and plunged the place into darkness. The emergency lights kicked in, but they were few and far between, leaving the basement dim enough to make it hard to tell the living from the dead. Plus, I still had the ax.

Screams came from all directions, wet and dry. Guards barked to one another, trying to organize themselves enough to cut off the exits, keep us down here.

"Herd them south! Nets up!"

"Twenty-one, where are you?"

From what I overheard they'd already screwed up. A couple of ferals had reached the grounds, forcing the guards to split up. I crept along, trying to stay away from everything, until I kicked into something on the floor. It spun and sloshed. A water bottle, half-full. Nice that Green kept his employees hydrated. I scooped it up.

About a minute later, I found another staircase. Unfortunately, there was a guard in front of it, and, unlike the others, he was decked out in thick body armor, like he was training German shepherds to attack fat, ugly people. He also had a flamethrower.

I got as close as I dared, then made it to a small, windowless room off the hall without being spotted. It could've been knocking the lights out, or maybe it was Nell's hoochie-coo dance, but I was starting to think I might be able to pull some shit off.

Water bottle in hand, I got ready to try an old trick. It didn't always work, but with all the yelling going on it might. I took a mouthful, let it soak my leathery throat. Then I shouted, nice and LB-wet: "This is twenty-one! They got my radio. I think my leg's broke."

I hoped the guard wouldn't hear the water spitting out as I spoke.

"Hang on, Mike!" the man at the stairs said. It worked.

Through a crack in the door, I saw him lumber toward the room, his outfit making him look like the Stay Puft marshmallow man. I pulled away, pushed my back to the wall, and waited. When he came in, I jumped out, then used the ax to wedge the door shut.

"Hey!" he said.

He slammed into the door, but his protective gear acted like padding, making it tough for him to really pound. I doubted he'd use the flamethrower. Even so, it wouldn't hold forever, but it didn't have to.

I scooted up the stairs, moving on all fours, keeping low and lower as I reached the top. I stuck my head out near the floor. The stairs opened on a white-tiled corridor, silver cabinets lining the wall. Best guess was that it was a storage space for the kitchen. With all the action downstairs and outside, it was empty.

There was a second staircase right across from me, heading farther up. Up was probably a good bet if I wanted to find Nell Parker. Green's "playground" had been at least two stories tall, and she'd slipped up some stairs after leaving the stage.

After listening carefully for any possible company, I went for it. At the top of the second staircase, I stopped short at the sound of running. Green's personal guard, the two dog-gunsels, were pounding down the hall. With the glasses and the hair, these guys really could be twins. One had a slightly fatter jowl, maybe.

The other had his hand cupped over his ear. "*More* ferals inside? Bullshit!"

He slapped his pal on the shoulder, bringing him to a stop. "This is fucked-up. Nobody knows what's coming or going. They want me to seal the basement manually. You check on the girl. Green still wants her ready."

I assumed Nell was "the girl," but ready for what? Was Green going on with the show?

Dog One headed back where they came from. Once he was out of sight, I followed Dog Two nice and easy, sticking to the walls when I could and hoping the cameras were out thanks to the blackout.

A few rights, a few lefts, I didn't count. Instead of quieting down, like they would if things were getting under control, the shouts and gunfire were getting louder, which meant things were getting worse.

The current hallway ended in a glass wall with a nice view of the playground. I guess it was like a TV for the servants, in case they got bored. Dog Two stopped at the last door and rapped. As he stood sideways, I ducked to the side of a pedestal holding a headless Roman bust. No accounting for taste.

"You almost ready, Nell?"

"What the fuck's going on, Charlie? Where's the lights? What's with all the noise?"

Her voice was rough, typical for a chak, but it surprised me just the same. It wasn't what I expected from her.

"Don't worry about it; just get ready."

"Why? He really still wants me to go on?"

The dog started barking. "Do I look like him? Do I sound like him? Just get the fuck ready!"

"Be nice, Charlie! I'm doing it. Takes a while, is all, especially without the electricity. I'll be out in fifteen."

"Make it ten," Charlie said. He stomped off, right past me.

Ten minutes. If I was going to talk to her, it'd have to be quick. I didn't think knocking would work and I figured the door was locked, so I raced up and shoved my shoulder into it. Either the door wasn't locked, or I was a lot stronger than I thought. It flew open, slammed against the wall.

And there she was, stark naked, standing on a plush white carpet, surrounded by mirrors and racks of outfits. All the clothes were in shades of black or white, except for one gown that was as green as her eyes.

She snatched a towel and covered up. That was bizarre. Modesty in a chak was unheard-of. She looked pissed, too.

"Who the fuck . . . ?"

Green said she was smart. All those dance moves meant she had a lot on the ball above the brain stem. That shit requires neurons. Of course, I was the one whose tongue started acting like a dead piece of pigskin.

"You're in danger. Someone's going to try to kill you."

She glared. I looked away as she grabbed a robe. All of a sudden I felt like I was in one of Green's weird little experiments, as if someone was watching from somewhere, trying to figure out if we were real or not.

"Kill me?" she said once she covered up. "Little late for that, don't you think?"

I took a step closer. "I don't mean kill. I mean cut up, at the neckline. D-cap."

She stopped at that. "Like those chakz on the news? The litter?"

She *was* smart. "Exactly. They were executed twice for killing their spouses. First by the prison, then by decapitation. Sound familiar?"

Her face flipped through a dozen expressions like it was searching for the right one. "Wait. What? Hold it. Who the hell are you? What are you playing at? You'd better get out of here before they catch you. They've got a nice little spot in the basement for troublemakers."

"I know; I've seen it. I'm Hessius Mann. I'm a...." Calling myself a detective sounded silly in this place, like I might just as well say *cowboy* or *spaceman*. "Never mind. What matters is I'm telling the truth. Just give me a minute and listen to me, please."

I told her what I knew. I think I spoke in English sentences, but I was talking fast.

By the time I finished, I could tell she hadn't bought into me or the story. She was glaring again.

"Nice story, but I've got two big problems with it. First, no one's *ever* tried to help me, not when I was alive, not since I died. My husband? I didn't kill him, but I *would* have. The bastard deserved worse than he got.

The second? Even if it is true, *this* is the safest place I've ever been. I'm his favorite. He watches after me."

"I hate to burst your bubble, but I'm afraid there's more to it. There's something going on here, and Green's not saying what it is. There are ferals loose out there. The estate is practically empty, and he still wants you ready for a show? You call that watching after you?"

"Okay, so maybe I'm not always treated perfectly, but I've got it better than any chak I know! See this room? It's mine! See this stuff? Mine!"

She pointed, and every time she did, her robe flopped open and I couldn't see anything else. I don't know why—I didn't know her at all—but I stepped closer still and grabbed her shoulders.

"Okay, forget the ferals; forget my stupid theories. You think you'll always be up here? You don't think he'll run out of variations and you'll wake up in that basement sooner or later?"

She twisted away. "What have you got, some kind of noir audiobook hooked into your brainpan? Why am I even talking to you?"

I had no answer for that one, but I couldn't leave. There was something about her that pushed all my buttons, even the ones I thought were broken. I was scared for her, and at the same time she was pissing me off.

I grabbed her arm and pulled. "Listen to me! I've got to get you out of here!"

I'd never had a fight like this with a chak. Even our arguments were tepid at best. This was so . . . so different.

She started screaming. I was so crazy, I actually tried to drag her out. But she was a dancer, strong legs, arms, and hips. She knocked me off easily, then reached for a lamp to bash my skull in.

I heard the Reservoir Dogs thundering down the hall. How'd they find me? Cameras? Of course—some of that emergency power would be tapped to keep tabs on Green's favorite.

That was it, then. She was staying.

There was one window, so I went for it. Before I tried to open it, I turned back to look at her. "You win; I'm out of here. Just remember what I said. Keep your eyes open. Just do that, okay?"

She lowered the lamp and laid those real-green emerald eyes on me. "Who the fuck are you?"

"My name is Hessius Mann. I'm a detective."

It had never sounded more stupid. And, for a dead man, I'd never felt more alive.

24

I was better off when I was depressed. Hessius Mann, detective, didn't last.

First, the window was stuck. By the time I'd opened it half an inch, the Reservoir Dogs were through the door. I was off my feet before I knew what was happening. The one with the slightly bigger jowl smashed my head into the floor. If the rug hadn't been plush, I'm sure my skull would've cracked.

His twin wrapped some plastic cuffs around my wrists, tying me like a garbage sack. The skin tore. I'd have rips for Misty to patch—if I ever saw her again.

But as they yanked me toward the door, I gave Nell Parker a wink.

The muscles on her face moved like the feathers on a startled bird. I wondered if that meant I was getting to her. Once I was in the hall, though, she stepped up to close the door. As the line of light narrowed, before she vanished, I caught another expression on her face, like she was thinking. It was something, I guess. Better than nothing?

I don't know. I was never one for whistling in the dark. I could never carry the tune.

I tried to keep pace with the dogs, but they kept speeding up. They'd pull me off my feet, half carry, half drag me. We headed back down the stairs I took to get up here, through the tiled hall, and into a kitchen big enough to service a hotel.

There, they plopped me right next to the recycling. Nice smell.

Except for flashlight beams skittering across the windows, it was dark inside, and quiet, except for muffled gunfire. The slightly smaller gunsel lit a ciggie. The other stared at me like I was the Loch Ness monster.

"Something on my cheek?"

"I don't get you," he said.

"That a question?"

The smoker took a drag and wagged a finger. "Green said to keep him here. Didn't say to talk to him."

"Didn't say anything about smoking in the house, either."

The smoker shrugged. "The detectors are hardwired. No one will ever smell it over the rest of the stink." His pal kept glaring until the smoker raised his hands in surrender. "But I take your point. So talk to him."

Mr. Curious turned back to me. "The runners I understand; they want out. Ferals everybody understands; they're animals. You, we let in, you break out, and then instead of leaving, you sneak back in to talk to a dead stripper. You working for someone?"

"Nobody living," I told him.

"Maybe he just likes her," the smoker said with a puff.

"He's a chak. They can't like anyone."

"You sure?"

He brought his face closer, genuinely puzzled. "That it? You planning to run off with her and start a new life in the suburbs? Get a nice morgue? Adopt two-point-five chak kids?"

"No, thanks. I'm more the beach-house-and-dead-dog type."

As he pulled on the filter, the red tip of the cigarette lit the smoker's face. "Hey, in his case, it really could be two-point-five kids."

A burst of gunfire startled him, knocking the ash from the end. We all froze until it stopped; then I heard something else: car wheels on gravel. I thought maybe the cops were arriving, but there were no sirens, and the sound got quieter instead of louder. Someone was driving away, fast.

"Mr. Green's guests leaving?" I asked.

They eyed each other in a way that said I was right.

"Did anyone even call the police?"

Again, they eyed each other. This was too easy.

"But you've got ferals out there."

The closer dog kicked me. "Shut it. You'll be moaning soon enough yourself."

"I'm just asking. Hate to run into one with my hands tied, you know? Hate to run into a bunch of them with my hands *free*. I saw that cell before it was opened. There were maybe thirty in there. You boys know what you're dealing with, right? Numbers that big, pack instinct kicks in. You can't just pick them off. They start hunting."

I was lying. It was an urban legend, but as far as I knew, a bunch of ferals have as little idea what they're doing as one. But I wanted to see if they knew that.

The smoker eyed his jowly twin. "Nothing to worry about. It's covered."

I pretended he was talking to me. "Thanks. You wanted to know what I was doing up there, right? Seeing as how we're all friends now, I'll tell you. I was trying to warn Nell, same way I tried to warn Green. There's a psycho out to nab her, maybe the same guy who knocked out your power. . . ."

I stopped in midsentence. They were looking at each other again, like it was all old news. "Wait a minute. Did Green *know* someone was after her before I got here?"

I fell into that one, but it fit. It would certainly explain all his clever observations about Turgeon's motives if he'd already been thinking about it. Crap. I didn't see that coming at all; then again, I didn't expect what happened next, either.

The jowly dog cupped his ear. "Didn't catch that. Changing her mind? Who told her she had one?"

So I had gotten to her, a little at least.

"Okay, we'll put this one downstairs, then deal with her."

"The basement?" I said. "Ah, come on, boys! Can't you just lock me in a cabinet? I promise I'll be good."

"No."

Getting ready to leave, the smoker looked around for a place to crush his coffin nail, only everything was clean white tile and polished metal. He looked at me for a second, like maybe he could get me to swallow the damn thing, but then he walked to the sink and opened the window behind it.

When he leaned forward to toss the cigarette, two gray hands, torn flesh dangling from the fingers, reached up and grabbed his arm. The feral had probably been crouching out there for an hour, an unseen thing. Sure could see him now, though.

As I said, once a chak grabs on to something, feral or not, we don't ever have to let go. The feral's fingers had pierced the smoker's black suit sleeves. The fabric glistened with fresh blood. By the time the jowly dog got there to help his pal, the smoker was across the sink and halfway through the window.

He started screaming. Oh, I understood why, but it was definitely the wrong thing to do. One of the reasons we have such bad press is that pained, wet liveblood screams attract ferals. Jowly Dog knew that much wasn't an urban legend. As he tried to drag his buddy back inside, he kept saying, "Shut up! Shut up!"

Man, did I hear moaning then. Lots, like it wasn't just one, but a mob hiding right below that kitchen window. Maybe I was wrong about the whole pack-instinct thing.

If the idiots hadn't cuffed me, I might've helped the dogs out. I'm not one to hold a grudge against the hired hands. Thinking the ferals'd be in soon, I realized I might not get to my feet fast enough, so I squirmed across the floor and through a swinging door. Last I looked there was a real tug-of-war going on at the window. Five feral hands pulled at the smoker.

Bet he wished he'd quit.

The kitchen sounds grew more violent. There was a tearing, deeper, more heartfelt screaming, and then one gunshot. I was in a short access hall, another swinging door about five feet away. I rolled through it onto to the wooden floor of a huge dining hall, accent on the "hall."

The table had fine china and silverware set for fifty. There was still food on the plates. Everyone had left in a hurry. Tall windows lined the wall; wild shadows from them rolled across the table like waves.

After I kicked a few chairs in front of the door, thinking they'd at least slow the ferals if they came in from the kitchen, I tried to stand. I backed into a steak knife, grabbed it with my fingers, and sawed at the plastic cuffs.

I couldn't see what my hands were doing, but I could see out the windows. Ferals, *real* ferals, much farther gone than Jonesey in the alley, or me in my office, swarmed over a statue garden. Right now, at least, they had the guards outnumbered. The LBs were shooting and backing up, but the ferals didn't give a shit. One used what looked like the smoker's arm to whack a gun out of a guard's hand.

I didn't see any point in trying to talk to Nell again. I also didn't see any point in trying to leave in the middle of a war where either side wouldn't think twice about going after me. I spent the next half hour slipping from room to room, looking and listening. I wasn't trying to find anything in particular, but whenever I heard talking, I didn't shy away.

Inside, over time, things quieted. Outside, not so much. The little firefight I saw through the dining room window was over, but the guards complained that they'd won too easily. They were worried there were more out there, waiting.

At the end of one long hall I found a huge stained-glass window depicting Epicurus the sage. Another bit of dead-mind trivia—he was a Greek philosopher who believed that pleasure was the sole intrinsic form of good. Had to be Green's hero. Figured.

No sooner did I smirk over it than some bluish lights reflected off the glass. Then they started getting bigger, as in closer. I kept low and slipped into a closet. Inside, I left the door half-open and acted like one of the coats.

Seconds later, the satyr himself, Colby Green, appeared. He was flanked by four men with AK-47s and high-intensity flashlights. The flashlights were the source of the blue glow.

Green was talking a mile a minute, not to himself but to someone on his Bluetooth. His voice had this weird tone. It sounded angry, but fatherly, like he was talking to a petulant child. It was definitely an act for the benefit of whoever was on the other end of the line.

"I've warned you once. I will not warn you again," Green said. "Stop babbling. Listen. As my people have been trying to tell you, we've had an incident. Yes, ferals. No, I did not contact the police. My men have them surrounded outside. Yes, I thought you'd like that. The situation will be under control soon enough, but the swap has to be delayed."

He stopped short, listened for a while, and rolled his eyes. "Well, you'll *have* to wait. Do *not* get any foolish ideas. You've already had one, but if you calm down and cooperate, you might survive it. Do you understand that? Calm down. Cooperate. I'll contact you when it's safe. Yes, she'll be ready. Things will occur exactly as we discussed, just not exactly *when*. Twelve hours. Are we clear, *Mr. Turgeon*?"

He hissed the name in a way that made me sorry we hadn't compared more notes on our favorite psycho, but now was not the time. My feelings on the matter were mixed at best anyway. As they passed the closet, I had one of those moments where the emotions rushed me so strongly, my body shook from the overload.

It was clear. Green *knew* Turgeon and he was planning to hand Nell over to him. Why? What kind of hold could that sick bastard possibly have on a man like Colby Green?

I was so busy trying to wrap my head around that one that I almost didn't hear the crash and tinkle of breaking glass. I peered out of the closet to see that Epicurus was gone, and a horde of semihuman silhouettes clambered in through the remains of the stained glass.

I think I knew what was happening. Just like Green said, his men had surrounded the ferals outside. They probably thought that from there it'd be easy to steer them into a corner and open fire. Instead they'd only managed to force them inside.

Colby and Co. broke into a run. Their blue-tinged flashlight beams vanished around a corner. I stepped out, planning to do likewise, but there were so many, I wound up standing there and staring like an idiot, long enough for the ferals to race up . . . and ignore me.

Huh. Maybe in the dark they'd taken me for one of their own, especially since I wasn't screaming. More likely they found the pretty blue lights more interesting.

Hoping they'd keep ignoring me long enough for me to get the fuck out of there, I started moaning and gnashing my teeth. That was when Green's men doubled back and opened fire. Even with bullets tearing through their bodies, the raging ferals hurled themselves forward.

Me, I headed for the broken image of Epicurus and jumped out.

Free? No. I landed smack in the middle of another fight.

I was face–to-face with a guard. I screamed. He screamed. A dozen wild zombies jumped him from no-where. I looked around for a place to run, realized I was in a courtyard. Green's men were trying to get into some kind of defensive formation, but the ferals were all over them. Freaking out, they opened fire on all of us.

The poor son of a bitch who'd been jumped went down in a hail of bullets and blood-soaked gurgling. I ducked and rolled.

On my left, bullets still flew from the shattered window. To my right, the courtyard guards were firing away. Dead ahead, near the path that led to the statue garden, I saw a swimming pool. Not having any particular need for air, I jumped the short brick wall and dived into the deep end, hoping that with all the excitement, no one had seen.

25

I slipped into the water quick and quiet. If I could move more easily once I was under, I'd have patted myself on the back. The pool was a perfect place to wait out Colby Green's private zombie hunt. Buoyancy wasn't a problem. It's easier for a chak than a liveblood to stay submerged. All I had to do was suck in the water until my lungs were full and down I went. Deadweight, right? Better yet, the chlorine would kill any mold that might be growing in the old air sacs.

I was surprised none of the other chakz had thought of it, but maybe by now, if they hadn't gone feral, they'd escaped. I hoped the one-eyed cowboy made it, even if this was his fault.

Given how clean the grounds were, the thick layer of dead leaves at the bottom of the pool surprised me, but I wasn't complaining. It was camouflage, a place to bury myself in case one of the rent-a-cops actually had a bright idea and decided to peek in. The only downside would be my soaked clothes when I eventually climbed out. The muck swirled as I lay in it. It felt pretty cozy.

I've always liked pools, not for swimming, but to go under and see how long I could hold my breath. As a kid, the way it muffled everything except the thrumming of my heart made me feel alone and protected at the same time. It even reduced my father's drill-sergeant voice to a distant gurgle. He was a real sink-or-swim kind of guy, my dad. You didn't want to get on his bad side.

Keep that back straight or I'll break it!

No heartbeat now, no angry father, but that made it easier to keep track of the fighting. The low *budda-budda* of the automatic fire registered more as a vibration than a sound. The screams, well, they were faint, but there were enough to tell me I'd be here a while.

Hess, you give me another two laps or you're walking home!

Thinking of Dad made me squirm, but then my brain did something useful for a change. I remembered the "fatherly" tone Green took with Turgeon. He must've figured Baby-head would respond.

Devil or not, he was smart. What had he said? That Turgeon didn't destroy the heads because he *couldn't*— that he wanted their approval. Christ, he acted enough like a baby. Could it be that obvious? Raised in an abusive family, he still wanted the abuser's approval, even after he cut his head off? Maybe he'd seen his father kill his mother. My mother and father got into it pretty bad sometimes. Mom swung a mean frying pan, but she was no match for Dad's thick arms. It made me want to . . .

Had Turgeon killed his father?

The idea felt important. Might make him easy to find.

I wanted to get it down, but there was no way I'd be making audio notes eight feet under. I hoped to hell the water didn't destroy the recorder. As long as it was off at the time, and dry enough before I turned it back on, I had a shot.

Soon the sounds were more distant, harder to follow. Just trying to guess what they might mean made me tired. It's not easy to keep focused for too long on a good day. Here I was comfortable and tired enough to drift off.

Next thing I knew I was lying back in a Barcalounger, a local paper open in front of me. There were slippers on my feet. I was in a bathrobe. My arms were thick like Dad's. Lenore was humming in the kitchen. I knew the song, the closing theme from *All in the Family*. I turned to look. She was just out of view, but I caught a shadow of her swaying hips on the front of the dishwasher.

A knock came at the door.

My eyes popped open. I was back in the bottom of the pool. Little globs of brown and black swirled around me in the water. How long had I been asleep?

Another knock. Was I still dreaming? No. The power was back on, bringing Colby's world back from the dead. That included the pool filter. A bare branch was dancing in front of the suction vent. Too big to go in, it hit the vent, drifted back, then got caught in the current so it hit again. Whenever it clunked, it sounded just like a door.

There was light above me, but electric, not sunlight. Other than that, silence. The assault was over. Of course the livebloods won; they always did. The crippled ferals would all be writhing in a bonfire by now. I said a little prayer for the undead.

I'm not a big believer like Misty. I just figured with all that pain floating around, someone should say something, and it might as well be me.

Green said he'd delay the swap for twelve hours. I checked my watch. At least three to go, so I waited, and did not dream, or think, really, again. Judging by the light on the water's surface, I watched morning roll around to early afternoon. It was time.

I crawled to the nearest wall, stood, and slowly pulled myself up along the tile work, surfacing beneath the diving board. There was no one in the pool area. Through the estate's windows, I saw people moving, pacing. Security guards. It didn't look like anything was chasing them anymore.

Putting my hands on the edge of the pool, I pulled and flopped out, imagining I looked like a dead manta ray. I rose into a crouch. My clothes were soaked. The dead leaves covering me made it hard to move, but I managed to reach the low brick wall. I rolled over that with a loud slapping, slurping sound, then hightailed it for the hemlocks. Better cover.

My timing wasn't bad. In under an hour, a piss yellow Humvee came up the white gravel drive. Ever since I found out Martin Boyle was alive, I knew Turgeon was my psycho. Who else could it be? But seeing it was still different from thinking it. I was angry at him for being a sick fuck, and at myself for feeling satisfied that I'd finally gotten the answer right.

I followed the car, keeping the hedges between it and myself. I expected it to head for the front entrance, but it turned. I almost lost it until, through the branches, I spotted its taillights moving along a narrower road.

Past the rear of the main building, the road curved

into an open area. I slowed down to keep covered, and crept to the edge of a circular driveway. Big enough for a truck to do an easy turnaround, it sat in front of a pretty banal section of the otherwise ornate mansion. No fountain, no decorations to speak of, erotic or otherwise, only the gravel, a flat wall, and some doors and windows. The most expensive thing there was Colby Green.

He was waiting by the door with two more brand-new gunsels. He probably had a bunch of spares behind a door marked MEN. I missed the original dogs; at least they had attitude. One of the newbies was balding, the other fair-haired, but again they wore black clothes and dark sunglasses—like they were the red shirts from *Star Trek*.

The Humvee was in the drive, hugging to the farthest spot from the building. That told me something: Turgeon was afraid of Green. Which meant he wasn't completely crazy. My clothes were a little drier, which made moving easier, and the muck left me with a nice earthy brown color that sort of matched the dirt and wood of the hedge.

I tried to stay down, on my hands and knees, but that obscured my view. Feeling a bit daring, I came forward a yard or so, but found myself staring at the rear end of Turgeon's car and not much else. I heard a power window lower, then Turgeon's eager-beaver, child-like voice.

"Where is she? Is she ready? Why isn't she here?"

Developmentally arrested or not, he sure as hell was a brat.

I stretched my neck. Green hadn't even nodded in response, but the balding dog pulled a slight figure from the doorway. Nell Parker, and she wasn't dancing now. The ropes prevented that. She was tied up tight, gagged and squirming. Her green eyes flashed from face to face like she was watching a Ping-Pong match.

I assumed she was sorry she hadn't believed me.

Green stuck his hand out and spoke two words real slowly. "The drive?"

He was using his "daddy" voice.

The window rolled back up. The door clicked open. Turgeon's expensive lawyer shoes hit the gravel a few feet from my face. I couldn't see the egghead's face, but as he came around toward the back of the car, I saw his hands. One held out what looked like a ritzy version of a data drive, silver and sleek.

"Here it is. Right here. I'm sorry, you know, Mr. Green. I did offer to buy her from you. I did. But what can you get the man who has everything?"

He wasn't very good at sounding sorry, or even pleasant. He was either afraid or trying to stifle a giggle, or both.

Green said, slowly, "Give it to me. Now."

Turgeon looked as if he were going to do exactly as ordered. As if hypnotized by a cobra, Turgeon took a few steps toward Green. That brought his face into view. At once, his expression changed and he halted. It was like he'd realized Green hadn't said, "Simon says."

"No. That's not the deal."

For the first time since I'd seen him, the careful intent that Colby Green radiated vanished. It wasn't playacting. A vein throbbed in his neck. He looked pissed. But he nodded at the gunsels and they brought Nell over to Turgeon.

As the poor thing hopped along, Green kept staring

at Turgeon with bug-zapper eyes. Turgeon kept his cool, though. It was only when Nell was squirming and struggling at his side that he handed the drive to the bald dog.

His men wasted no time trotting back to their master and giving him the drive. As soon as it was in his hand, Green relaxed so much he visibly shrank. I think the temperature dropped a few degrees, too.

What was on the drive? My guess, a "best of" video collection from the playground—more than enough to bring down the government of Fort Hammer and probably even the state.

"The activation key?" Green said.

"As soon as we're safely away."

"You know the contents can't be copied."

Turgeon winced. "I told you I didn't even try."

"And if you'd turned it over to the local papers . . ."

Turgeon would've been better off nodding and agreeing, but he gave a little self-conscious laugh that made Green's eyes flare. He was hesitant—*childish* would be a compliment—but he did start acting like he was in control. "Local papers were never the issue, Mr. Green. National, worldwide, online, on the other hand . . ."

He glanced at the struggling Nell. "Could your men help put her in the back? She's quite feisty."

Green went silent and stayed that way long enough to make everyone wonder what he'd do. If he'd really been a father, my father anyway, he'd have pulled out his belt and given his kid a whooping. But that was just an act for Turgeon's sake. Whatever else he was, Green was a businessman. He had the drive and whatever was on it. He slipped his poker face back on.

"Feisty? You don't know the half of it," he said. He nodded to his men.

As the gunsels returned, Turgeon opened the rear hatch. I was close enough that if I still had my Walther, I might've tried to grab her and shoot my way out.

To my surprise, before they dumped her in, Green stepped up, waving for them to wait. Turgeon stiffened, but Green said, "I just want to say good-bye."

Turgeon moved toward the driver's door, giving him some space. Green just looked at Nell for a bit, until something silver in the back of the car caught his eye.

"What is that?" Green asked. I knew. I'd seen it before.

The weirdest expression came over Turgeon's face. He looked half-embarrassed, half as if he wanted something from Green, punishment, or *approval*. "A head clipper, used by the authorities to remove the heads of chakz."

Green didn't react, but he sure looked as if he wanted to. Instead he turned to Nell Parker and stared into her genuinely green, pleading eyes. Gently, maybe affectionately, he held her chin with his thumb and forefinger, brought her face close, and licked her cheek. As his tongue raked her flesh, she closed her eyes.

Maybe she was thinking he'd still change his mind; maybe she was praying he would. But after making a sound that could've been a sigh or a bored exhale, he stepped away.

With that final betrayal, her eyes flashed and she struggled again, harder. She was strong, but tied up. The gunsels grabbed her and tossed her in like she was a beautiful, oversize bag of litter. Turgeon came back and closed the hatch. Good soundproofing on that car. If Nell was screaming through the gag, or kicking, I couldn't hear it.

That weird expression still painted on his face, Turgeon slapped his hands. He figured he was as good as gone. But Green wasn't going to let him off that easy.

"You know you can't leave here unless I allow it."

Turgeon tried to lose the goofy grin, but didn't quite succeed. "I said I was sorry. Once I'm safe I will call and tell you not only the new access code, but also exactly how I got the drive. Names and dates."

"Name*s*?" Green said. So there were some moles in paradise. Not surprising. A man like Green probably played with a few livebloods the same way he did with chakz. Egghead had gotten to them somehow. Money isn't everything, after all. There's also revenge.

Turgeon shrugged. "Please don't worry. Don't worry at all. Not many. Your people are loyal. Mostly."

The poker face nearly slipped, but Green kept it. Now Turgeon's grin went up to his eyes. He'd kicked Daddy in the shins and gotten away with it. All the same, he practically ran to the driver's side and jumped in. I couldn't see inside the car, but I imagined him rubbing his hands and giggling.

I had to make some kind of move or Turgeon would be gone and Nell Parker's head would be forced into a messy divorce from the rest of her. No way was I going to keep up with a car on foot. That left one option. Crazy for the living, not so much for the dead.

With Turgeon inside the car and most of the Humvee between me and Green, I crawled under the chassis. It was roomy, lots of handholds. Hoping the soundproofing worked both ways, I did my zombie death grip and latched on.

Stupidly, I thought I hadn't been seen. Turgeon hadn't noticed me, as far as I knew. The soundproofing worked both ways. But I caught a final bit of conversation from our hosts.

"Want us to do anything about that?" the balding gunsel said to Green.

The answer was whispered, but I saw Green shake his head. "No."

Of course. The power was back on. They'd seen me on the security cameras. But now that he had his hard drive back, no reason Green wouldn't root for me. He probably hated Turgeon almost as much as I did. I even thought I saw him give me a little wave.

The engine roared; the car rolled along the gravel. Strong as my grip was, I wished I had a seat belt. Wherever the hell I was going, it'd be a bumpy ride.

26

The white-gravel blur beneath me turned to an asphalt blur. We were out on the street. Hit a few potholes, but by the time we reached the southbound highway, headed back to town, the ride smoothed out. Midday, the road was pretty empty, and Turgeon had a need for speed, passing whatever cars there were. If anyone spotted me, by the time they gave me a second glance, I'd be gone.

I'd seen the clinging-under-the-car thing in a couple of monster movies, the unsuspecting driver taking someone along for a ride. I'd always thought it was ridiculous, but the underbelly of the Humvee put more than a half foot between my ass and the road. It wasn't too bad a ride. I'd been through worse on packed buses. As long as Baby-head didn't drive off-road, or over a tall rock, I didn't have much to worry about.

Or so I thought. The catalytic converter was warm when the ride started. After twenty minutes, it was oozing heat like a desert sun, the rest of the exhaust system happy to bake along with it. Once my suit dried, and it was drying fast, I could catch like a pile of leaves. Turgeon would see me then, all right, through his rearview mirror as I rolled along behind him, in flames.

I maneuvered around like a giant upside-down tarantula, desperate to find a cooler spot. Unable to find one, I headed to the passenger side, put the heel of my shoe on the running board, and found a handhold near the bottom of the rear door. I was exposed, wind whipping my hair and clothes, but at least I was in his blind spot.

The side mirror was lopsided, like he didn't use it. It gave me a good view of myself. With the crap from the pool drying all over me, I looked like a half-full Hefty Cinch Sak caught on the car. I tilted my head, trying to get a peek at the driver. I had to twist into a funny position, but it worked.

There he was, watching the road like a good boy. His lips were moving. I figured he was on the phone, giving Green that activation code, and the names of whichever employees were stupid enough to betray him. But the minutes ticked by and he kept talking. I didn't think he and Green had a close phone relationship, so that meant it was something else. Every sentence or two he glanced over at the passenger seat, like he was talking to a little person sitting there. I raised my head, angling for a better look.

The passenger seat was still out of view, but I spotted something in the back and didn't like it at all. It was the duffel bag, the one from the warehouse, the one that looked stuffed with bowling balls. It was carefully strapped in with belts and shoulder straps.

And it was squirming.

My fears about what was inside thickened in the back of my throat. I looked again, hoping I'd see that the things inside were just settling, obeying gravity. But no, it looked more like they were jockeying for position. Trying to get comfortable.

I couldn't think about that. Not now. The old electric syrup was already bubbling, tingling inside me. I blinked and looked ahead. Bad move. I realized that the shoulder strap for the passenger seat was down, wrapped around whatever Turgeon was chatting with.

Now I was freaking. Muscles twitching, dizzy, images flashing, the works.

I lowered myself so I couldn't see anything. I tried to calm down, focus on the case. I thought about catching him, saving Nell. It'd work for a minute, then slip away. I had to distract myself, keep busy. How the fuck was I going to do that while clinging to a car doing seventy mph? There was nothing but the road and the mirror.

I had to take another look. I had to know. I peered inside. Turgeon was still talking, but now he looked unhappy, alternately hurt and annoyed. Then, steering with one hand, he leaned over and lifted what was on the passenger seat.

I knew what it was. Of course I did, but, God help me, I didn't want to. I didn't want to know a damn thing.

Not a little person. A head, nothing else, still living, still thinking. Just the head.

I thought about ducking, at least, or closing my eyes, but I didn't move fast enough. As he twisted and held it toward the back, I saw it: the head, the fucking head, just the head, only the head.

I snapped my own head down. I closed my eyes, but still saw it. It'd been a fraction of a second, but that was all it took. The image had burned into me, clearer and more colorful than the cover of an old EC horror comic.

He hadn't used the chopper on this one; the neck was unevenly cut, victim of a sloppy ax job. There were thick veins hanging down like tendrils, flaps of gray flesh.

The face was older, old enough to be the psycho's father. It may have been handsome once. It had a strong, angular structure, the jaw long and bony, the chin a jutting V. The lower lips were partly gone, tear marks in their place, leaving the clenched teeth visible, still whole. The eyes were open, the mouth moving.

I shivered like a kid under a blanket. Now I couldn't even pretend the duffel bag wasn't full of them, the souvenirs, the relics, the *daddies*. And Turgeon meant for me to be one of them.

The syrup bubbled, rolled, grew, pressed against my insides so hard it felt like my flesh would pop and tear. And then, though I could've held on until doomsday, I let go.

I bounced. I rolled. The pain was enough to keep me in my body, snap me out of it, but not completely. A car screeched as it swerved to avoid hitting me. A horn blared.

But Turgeon hadn't seen. He was too busy with his friends.

27

I made it to the shoulder, collapsed at the edge of a brittle, sunbaked field. A turkey buzzard wheeled in the sky above me, coming lower and lower. Once it got close enough for a good look, it turned and flew off. I wasn't even good enough to be carrion.

Forcing myself to sitting, I fished in my pockets. I couldn't find my cell, but I did get my hands on the recorder. I was thinking I should get some of this down. Not that I was worried I'd forget, but if Turgeon had spotted me, he might be on his way back, and I wanted to leave at least some kind of record.

Crap. The recorder was still damp. I pressed a button and a set of little black LED letters flashed on the screen. It still worked. I pressed record and tried to talk, but all I could do was babble. After about ten seconds, I turned it off.

I looked up and down the highway. Hondas, trucks, and hybrids. No sign of the Humvee. Good for me, not so much for Nell Parker. Soon she'd be one of his friends, one of his *daddies*, or, in her case, a *mommy*, and he'd be reliving the death of his own parent over and over and again for the sake of . . .

Wait a minute.

Christ, I think I'd set a world record for staring at something and not being able to see it. Whatever other relationship he was having with the heads, he *was* trying to keep them quiet.

What did they know? What was the one thing Wilson, Boyle, and Parker all knew? That they were *innocent*, that *someone else* killed their spouses.

Son of a bitch, son of a bitch, son of a bitch. What if it was Turgeon to begin with? What if he'd committed the murders and set them all up? It'd be a perfect gig for a psycho. Most murder victims are done in by someone they know. Need to kill someone? Find someone with a history of domestic violence, kill the spouse, and leave the aggressor to take the rap. Brilliant. It's not like they're not going to bring your patsy back from the dead, right?

But then they *do* bring them back. You can't have them wandering around, maybe trying to find the real killer. So you find them and silence them.

And if I was on his list, that meant . . .

I grabbed my chest as if something still beat inside it. I grabbed my head. I could feel every crenellation pulse, filled to bursting.

I'd found the man who killed Lenore.

That's why he hired me in the first place, why he asked all those questions about whether I remembered what happened or not. The fact that I couldn't probably pushed me farther down the list.

The man, the *thing* that killed Lenore.

I saw my wife's face for the first time in ages, smooth, pale, Irish skin, a round moon face with saucer eyes, cupped by straight black hair. You couldn't see a single blemish unless you looked real close, but I remembered even those, even a little crescent moon scar under her jaw, half the width of my pinkie nail. She said she got it from tumbling down a flight of stairs when she was two. She had a tight body and just enough muscle to make it interesting.

The better angels of our nature aside, she was moody to the extreme and I was a shit with a temper. My father, Albert Mann, was a big drinker, a bull of a man. He'd get in your face and yell real loud until you backed down. Usually he didn't have to hit you.

Whether it was a strategy or not, the shouting worked, so I picked it up. Get me pissed enough and I'd come at you with murder in my eyes. Only, I'm not planning to do damage; I'm trying to cow you. It worked with me and with my mother. It never worked with Lenore. She always held her ground. Coming from a big family with a lot of brothers toughened her up, made her stand up for herself.

I admired it, but in a pinch, it crossed my wires big-time. I was a one-trick pony. Whenever I tried to cow her by screaming, I wound up feeling cornered. Yeah, I did hit her once, and no, I don't remember what the fight was about. Worst day of my life, not counting the one where I found her body. She kicked me back pretty good—we both had nasty bruises for days.

That one time almost ended things. I went to counseling for a year, learned to *step back* instead of forward. That helped. We still shouted. Sometimes I punched a wall or smashed a plate, but I never touched her, never again. Maybe we shouldn't have been together, but the fights were rare and, stupid as it sounds, I loved her and thought she loved me. The marriage was heaven on earth, with occasional side trips to hell, or so I thought.

By the middle of the recession, the cuts reached the homicide department. Short on staff, I wound up working extra shifts, which meant less time at home. Thanks to ChemBet, we had a string of former convictions walking around. Folks we'd arrested were popping back up on the street. It was a whole new world with all new problems. With so much going on, I lost track of her. Things seemed okay, so I wasn't worried, but I wasn't paying attention. I didn't even blink when she asked that we stop trying to have kids for a while. I was too busy resenting all the time off Booth was enjoying. He'd earned it, I guessed, five more years than me. When he retired I was next in line. Except for the fact that I wasn't well liked. Tended to be a loner, and everyone knew I had a temper.

Then came the morning the photo showed up in my in-box, Lenore's skin smooth like a goddess's, her body caught in an instant when it'd been writhing in pleasure, pushing up against Booth's muscles, her hands clawing at his hairy back. Didn't matter that it was a photo. I could see them moving. I could hear the moans of pleasure.

Something inside me crashed. It felt like my life was over, like I'd died, as if I knew what that meant. I did like my counselor said: I hit something else, in this case the wall. But it was in the office this time, and to be honest, for the first time, I was imagining it was her.

I rushed home, thinking . . . I don't know what. I don't remember. I like to believe I'd calmed down by the time

I was halfway there. I hope I was planning to talk things out, or tell her I'd give her a divorce if she wanted it. Only, that doesn't sound like me. Still, I hold on to the possibility that the last conversation I was planning to have with her would be the best I had to offer, not the worst. The fact is, the car ride's a blur. Whatever I was feeling is one of those blank spots in my soul. Message erased.

I do remember stumbling into the kitchen, stepping into her blood and wondering what was so damn sticky. I remember her crushed face, looking like a broken egg with a different palette of colors. They never found my bat and I've never been sure it wasn't me.

Now I knew it wasn't, and I had a real good idea who it was.

I got to my feet, screaming. I staggered out onto the highway, still screaming.

What a sight that must have been, zombie dirt monster raging in the middle of the highway. Cars zoomed by. I'm sure someone would've hit me if they weren't worried about ruining their finishes.

One asshole driving an old Civic must have been texting or watching a DVD. By the time he saw me, he had to turn the wheel so hard, he nearly flipped his car. Instead, tires squealing, it spun and came to a halt on the shoulder. The air bag popped and he was just stupid enough to be angry about it.

Face in a fierce snarl, he pushed the air bag away, popped the door, and stormed toward me. He was early twenties, hair baked blond and dried like the field, a football player, someone who'd kick a boulder in his way rather than walk around it.

"You stupid mother . . ."

I guess he hadn't noticed I was dead and howling until about then. I saw no reason to stop screaming for his sake.

"Holy shit!" He backed up, put the car between us. I came forward, getting louder. I wasn't feral, but I wasn't real happy, either.

He thought about getting back in his car, but I hopped up on the hood and gave him a real loud one, nearly tore out my vocal cords. He started backing up. He didn't want to give up the car, but he didn't want to die, either.

With a final, "Oh, shit!" he turned and started running.

I got behind the wheel. The engine still running, I put it in gear and drove past him.

I won't take credit for planning any of it. It just sort of happened. But you should have seen the look on his face. Wish I'd had a camera.

I did about eighty until I spotted some state troopers and had to slow down. The Humvee was long gone. No way I'd catch up, and I didn't know where he was headed. Aside from everything else eating at me, now I had the sick feeling I couldn't save Nell.

The only other lead I had was that other chak, and right now I couldn't even remember his name. I did remember the notes I'd made with Ashby, so I tried working the recorder while driving with one hand. Couldn't manage that, so I had to pull over, lose even more time.

Took me about five minutes to find it, my creaky voice saying, "Odell Jenkins, works for Hammer Rejuvenations, LLC."

Ashby gave off a little *heh* in the background. Funny, it was nice to hear him again.

After a lot of twisting and yanking at the dried muck

on me, I even found my cell phone. As I pulled back onto the road, I hit 1 on the speed dial.

Misty answered on the first ring. "Hess, where the hell are you? Are you okay?"

"I'm not so bad, considering. I figured out who killed my wife, and I've got a new car."

Rather than give her the details, I gave her the name of the remediation company, asked them to inquire about Jenkins and call me back as soon as she knew anything. The sooner I got to Turgeon's last potential victim, the better chance I had of finding him.

And then what?

As I drove, I tried to come up with a plan. Part of me wished I still had the gun. Then I could shoot Turgeon over and over until the only thing that made him twitch would be the impact of the bullets. Partly I wanted to play "good cop." I wanted to nab him, bring him in, have him arrested, tried, and fried, with me in the audience.

The missing gun mooted the first option. Being a chak put the odds against the second. By the time I reached the Bones, Misty still hadn't called back, so I headed to the office. The phone was in her hand as I walked in. There was some poster board and markers on her desk, so I figured she'd been making signs for Jonesey.

I thought she'd have a harder time guessing what I'd been up to, but as she rose for a better look at my makeover, she said, "You look like you've been sleeping in the bottom of a swamp."

"Close. Colby Green's swimming pool."

She grabbed a spork from her lunch and used it to scrape off the bigger chunks of dirt. While she worked, I filled her in on the details. By the end of it, she looked more upset than I was. I wanted to thank her for that.

Instead, I asked if she'd made any headway on Odell Jenkins.

"Yeah, he's at a job site."

"Good. Did you get a number? Can we call him?"

"Already tried. His boss said he keeps his cell off while he's working. Doesn't want to get distracted using power tools."

"Makes sense. What's the address? I've got to get over there."

"Wait. Hess, what if you run into Turgeon? You can't go."

I gave her a look. "I can't *not*. Put aside Wilson, Boyle, Parker, *and* their spouses, which probably doesn't scratch the surface of his victim list, Misty—this guy killed Lenore."

"And if you make one wrong move, he'll cut your head off and put it in a bag!"

"He's going to try to do that anyway."

"We can move out of the state. I'm still half-packed."

"I'd go feral on the bus, knowing he was out there."

"Then . . . then . . . call Booth."

I thought about that one. He loved Lenore, too. He'd want to find her real killer. But he was sure he already had.

"I'd need proof, Misty, and even then, last time I saw him, he'd hired someone to break my legs. Look, it's a long shot he'll go after Jenkins right now."

She pursed her lips. "Unless he's in a hurry because Colby Green is after him."

"Who's the detective, you or me? Fine, maybe it's fifty-fifty, but all the more reason I've got to try to get to him fast."

She shook her head. "You don't even have a gun."

"No, but I've got something else. It's the reason I came back, other than seeing your pretty face, of course." I nodded her into my office.

There, I pulled out the cash drawer, then checked the false bottom where I'd kept the Walther. I had something else in there, a little glass vial full of oily liquid as green as Nell Parker's eyes. I held it up for Misty to see, but warned her not to get too close.

"What the hell is that?" she asked.

"VX, deadliest nerve agent on the planet. Last year, anyway—I'm sure they've got something worse by now."

She took a few more steps back. "And that's been here all along, while I sleep in the next room, you crazy bastard? Fuck, Hess, how'd you even get something like that?"

"I used to be a cop, remember? Anyway, one night we raided a big drug dealer and found out he was also dealing arms, guns so big you needed three men to pick them up, missile launchers, too—and this. I thought it was some new kind of drug. Shoved it in my pocket, thinking I'd look it up later; things came up; I forgot about it. It was still in my pocket the day I was arrested for Lenore's murder. I handed it over along with my wallet and the clerk took it for perfume. I didn't find out what it was until after I came back. Always meant to turn it in; never figured out how to do it without getting arrested."

She kept shaking her head. "You're an idiot alive or dead."

I raised my hands in surrender. "Guilty as charged, but dead, I can drink the shit, no harm, no foul. One whiff would kill a liveblood, though. So, if I did run into Turgeon, all I'd have to do is put it in my mouth, get close enough, bite down on the glass, and blow. And I know how to blow."

"What about everybody else in the city?"

"Far as I know, they'll go on being a bunch of idiots." I held up the vial and tilted it so she could see how slowly it flowed. "It's not exactly a gas; it's viscous, like an oil. Maybe it was just a sample or something they'd use in a spray gun. On top of that, it's supposed to break up in the air after a few minutes. That's why the trick is getting in close. So where's Odell Jenkins doing his nine-to-five?"

"I'm going with you."

"No way, Misty. Forget Turgeon; I don't want you in the same car with this stuff."

"I'm in the same room with it now, have been for months. How're *you* going to keep it safe? What if you get into a fistfight?"

"Watch." I shoved the vial into my mouth and used my tongue to push it into a pocket in my jawbone, below my right molars. I had some rot there once. When Misty cut it out for me, which wasn't easy for either of us, it left a hole. I opened wide and lolled my tongue around. "I'm not saying I could keep a sandwich fresh in there, but it's nice and snug and would stand up to a search if he decided to frisk me or check my teeth. Okay?"

"It's crazy."

"What isn't? Where is he?"

"Everwing. The hospital complex."

"Thanks, Misty. I need something, I'll call you. Town center shouldn't be too crowded this time of day."

She frowned.

"Piece of food in my teeth?" I asked.

"Just to make your visit more fun, Jonesey's rally is this afternoon. You'll be heading right into it."

28

Not that I'm into grand theft auto, but I was in a hurry, so I hopped back into my stolen wheels and headed for the center of town. The football kid must've reported it by now, unless he was too embarrassed. If he did, the cops would be looking for the plates. In a few hours, the story would be all over the news—*Chak Steals Wheels*—another favor I'd done for undead everywhere. I had plenty to feel bad about right now, so I figured I'd feel bad about all that later. I told myself the car would be safer parked in town anyway, and, if I survived, I'd send the owner a note.

Fort Hammer's Main Street was a throwback to the days of cheap land. The grand avenue was so wide it looked like the two sides of the street wanted nothing to do with each other. The buildings were pretty much the same: Georgian brick storefronts, neoclassical public buildings, like the library and the town hall. Most were more than eighty years old, echoes of ancient prosperity. The bigger the building, the less interesting. Style gives it up to function. Our two 1950s skyscrapers were little more than boxes with doors and windows.

Generally, you don't see chakz in this part of town, maybe a messenger or two, but I was seeing lots. They're easy enough to spot; most walk pretty funny. And it wasn't only single chakz; it was groups. Five together, ten, all moving toward the central plaza. It was the beginnings of Jonesey's rally. The Dead Man Walk.

I'd thought at best he'd get thirty marchers. That *might* be okay, if they were smart ones, corpses who could keep their act together. Then the LBs could say, "Oh, look at the cute chakz carrying signs! I didn't know they could write!" But down the block one or two hundred had gathered, and there were more stepping in from the side streets. It was too many, way too many. More like people would say, "Shit, a horde!" I was inclined to agree.

The cops were out in force, and they weren't worried about a stolen car. They were setting up wooden sawhorses, all keeping one hand on their guns. The guy with the flamethrower was here, too. This was a mess that could go bad fast, in a town famous for things falling apart. Between this scene and Turgeon's head collection, I was starting to believe in the end of the world. Not that I particularly liked the beginning or the middle.

Distracted, I nearly rammed a FedEx truck. All around me, livebloods were eyeing protestors like they wished they had a weapon handy. I felt a twinge. I should do something. Like what? Find Jonesey and tell him to call it off? Too late for that. Half the marchers would go feral from disappointment, and Jonesey would go right along with them.

That's how we do things in Fort Hammer! Rush in

where angels fear to tread, then suddenly realize that maybe the angels, being *angels*, had the right idea in the first place. Send a man to the moon? Sure! Bring democracy to the Middle East? Why not? Raise the dead? Line 'em up! Jonesey, you fucking all-American idiot.

The main avenue ended at a big, all-brick plaza—the official city center. I made a sharp left and headed for the only modern construction in sight, the abandoned Everwing Hospital complex. We have so many stories like it, the basics are as worn as the plot of an old *I Love Lucy*, only with more lives at stake.

Everwing. The plans were approved after some genius figured out how to cut corners by importing questionable material from China. Two months after opening, they found asbestos in the plasterboard, cadmium in the paint, and enough E. coli in the water system to make everyone's pants want to get up and dance. One blogger suggested they keep it open, because at least folks would be in a hospital when they got sick.

Instead, it was covered up in thick plastic sheets that flapped and belched toxic dust whenever the wind blew. A giant farting corpse. All six buildings were currently undergoing remediation. That's a fancy way of saying they're trying to scrape out all the poison shit that'll kill you and take it somewhere far away, where it can kill some other people you don't know. Just what you want in your town center.

With all the cops and the pedestrians gawking at the chakz, no one noticed when I drove around the hospital barricade. Only a complete moron would go in there anyway, right? With a thick whoosh that reminded me of being in a car wash, I passed through the plastic and headed down into the facility's underground parking lot. Up to one hour of poisoning, free. My little VX capsule was less than a raindrop in a storm here. If I didn't run into Turgeon, this might be a good place to bury it.

Only, it looked like I had run into Turgeon.

The second I flashed on my headlights, I spotted tire tracks in the dust ahead of me. Maybe I was just being paranoid, but if any remediation teams came in this way regularly, why only one set of tracks? I stopped the car and got out for a closer look. Took a while for my eyes to adjust, but I waited. They looked about the right size for a Humvee.

I followed the tracks on foot, down, down, down the graded concrete and steel, along rows of empty, numbered spaces. Sunlight was a thing of the past. At the bottom levels, the only light was the glow of an occasional Exit sign above a gray metal door.

I was about to turn the last corner when I heard that boyish voice. Turgeon. I thought he'd spotted me, even though I couldn't see him or his car, but he was talking to someone.

"Please don't talk like that. I hate it when you say things that way. I'm *not* the one."

Whoever answered had some kind of speech impediment. The response came in a harsh, garbled whisper, almost like a toy train clacking on a track in slow, slow motion, or a paper bag dragged across cement, soft and crackly.

Gshhh chahhhh chhhhh.

Turgeon seemed to understand it. "That's not what I meant."

I slowed, crouched, hugged the wall, but made the last turn and kept descending. At the bottom, I made out the Humvee, parked near an elevator. The dim light made the piss yellow closer to the color of blood. A Dumpster, full of construction debris, had been plopped catty-corner in the space opposite him. Whenever Turgeon talked, I made for it.

His rounded back was to me, but he bobbed nervously, like he might spin around any second. "But it's *not* my fault. Can't you . . ."

As he spoke, he faced a heavy lump sitting on the hood. It wasn't a silver eagle or a winged angel, but I guess you could call it a head ornament. It was the one head I'd seen strapped in the passenger seat. It was making the sounds.

Shhhhkkk ggrrllll cahhhh.

Don't know why I didn't out-and-out lose it. Maybe it was the dim lighting that made everything look flat and unreal, or maybe I was more fascinated than sickened. How could it make sounds at all? I noticed it moved its cheeks before it spoke. Curious, I exhaled, pushing all the air out of my lungs, then puffed my cheeks and forced the air through my nose. Maybe it was using those muscles to draw air through its neck. Could work, I guess.

Whatever it meant by its last crackles, Turgeon didn't like it at all. His tone dived from whiny to annoyed.

"Stop it! I'll put you back with the others! I can and I will! You're not so big now!"

The others? Right. The duffel bag sat on a big flat wooden cart with a metal handle near the car. It didn't take much to figure he was threatening to stuff the head in there. He gave it a little kick to make his point.

Jssshhhh.

"Of course I wouldn't." He sounded pouty again, like the last harsh noise had put him back in his place.

I reached the back of the Dumpster and tried to focus on the sounds.

Shtpp rrr wnnnn hlp yorr.

The noises were soft, struggling, but intentional, like someone trying to play a trumpet by blowing through the mouthpiece with a straw. It was using words, best as it could. The first sentence I made out was something like:

Stop or I won't help you.

Turgeon gave it a loud *tsk* and stamped his feet on the dusty concrete. "It's not just for me! It's for all of you."

"Stop."

"You know I can't, Daddy."

Daddy? So the family-killer theory wasn't far off the mark.

"Not your father."

"*Step*father! Stepfather! Fine!" In frustration, he kicked the dolly.

Close enough. Either way, it was clear he wanted stepdaddy's approval. He was begging for it. If the pattern held true, Turgeon's stepfather must have been executed for killing his wife. That would be Turgeon's mother, wouldn't it?

Plenty of time to play Name that Sick Motive later. I had to decide what to do now, while he was distracted. If I rushed up to try breathing in his face, I'd have to come at him from the front. Too risky. I only had one shot, and I didn't want to blow it. Besides, he was still talking. For better or worse, that good-cop instinct kicked in, the one that still thought about bringing him in to justice. And he was still talking. I didn't know how far the conversation would go, but just in case, I fumbled for the recorder, pressed the button, and aimed the mike at Turgeon the Great and his amazing talking head.

Of course, the second the little red light went on, they shut up.

Not the duffel bag, though. Ever since he'd kicked it, it was pulsing more and more. Now a whole choir of scraping sounds came from inside, a jumble of sources. It dawned on me that Wilson and Boyle would be in there. Nell Parker, too? Not that I recognized any of the voices. Best I could do was pick out a couple of words, none happy:

"Help . . . die . . . why . . . murder . . . cutter."

That didn't do much to improve Turgeon's mood. He grabbed his ears and wheeled back toward the head ornament. "Talk to them!" he howled. "Talk to them!"

"No," the "daddy" answered.

"Ripping . . . blood . . . monster . . . killer . . ."

The heads didn't seem to like him very much. I wasn't surprised, but Turgeon was. He looked hurt, like he was ready to cry.

"You're the only one who can."

"No."

"I told you, it's just these *three*! Just them, all right? Just these three and I promise I'll be done. I swear I'll stop."

"No."

Seeing he wasn't getting anywhere, Turgeon forced himself to simmer down. He approached the head apologetically, stroked what was left of its cheek. "I'm so sorry I'm shouting. I get so angry. I get so upset. Ever since I saw that boy's skeleton it's been so hard to calm down. It almost got me! And that detective got away. He's dangerous. He must know by now. He must know I killed his wife. He just doesn't understand that I did it *for* him. None of them do!"

Lenore. He'd said it. There it was. A *confession*.

I couldn't let him see me, but there was a loud roar and for the longest time I thought it came from me. Took me to the count of ten to realize it didn't; it was the duffel bag. The heads in it were twisting harder, getting louder, like they were screaming *for* me. Turgeon, the idiot, had reminded us all that he was the one who'd stolen our loves, our lives, beaten them until their bodies caved.

"Killed her ... you did it ... oh, God. ... why, God ... killed him ... no, not her ... wasn't me ..."

The bag wobbled precariously. It took all I had to keep from running out and throttling him. If I was sure I'd actually be able to kill him, I'd have done it in a second.

Turgeon shouted at the bag like it was a disobedient pet. "They were hurting you! Driving you away! I was doing you a favor!" He turned back to the head ornament. "Daddy, tell them they're free now! You have to tell them they should be happy!"

It moaned two words: "Put me ..."

Relief washed over Turgeon so strongly, he looked like he shrank an inch. "Thank you, thank you, thank you."

He wiped his brow, then gently, almost lovingly lifted the head. I saw the tendrils again, drooping from the stump of the neck. What muscles there were pulsed in tune with its words, fanning air up into the throat, like gills on a fish.

"One last time," it said.

He put Daddy on the dolly and opened the edge of the bag. Using the same neck muscles that let it make noises, it *squirmed* inside the rustling bag. The weird slurred speech echoed through the space. Deferential as he'd been, Turgeon yanked the duffel bag closed and gave it a rough shake that quieted them down. Out of sight, out of mind, I guess. I'd hate to see what he'd do with a hamster.

Once they were silent, he stopped and looked around. I thought he'd seen or heard me, but no. I did get a good look at him, enough to see that his oval face was bare. The air was so thick with crap, I could taste it on my tongue, but Baby-head didn't even wear a mask. Was this a suicide run?

No, he still didn't have me. And me? I had a recorded confession, something even Booth might listen to. I had my cell phone. I was about to use it when he opened the back of the Humvee and the air filled with Nell Parker's louder, more enthusiastic cries.

My whole body shuddered with relief. Not just because there was still someone I could save if I didn't screw up, but that it was her.

Turgeon picked up the head clippers, held their big, curved blades open, directly over her neck. I tensed, ready to jump out at him, but he didn't use them.

"You're only still in one piece because I promised Daddy I would wait," he said. "But it wouldn't be the first promise I broke."

She got the idea and settled down.

With some grunting, he loaded Nell onto the dolly, followed by the clippers and the duffel bag. The last thing he loaded up was a wooden crate with some writing on it: 40—8 OZ CHGS PE4.

What was that about? Damned if I knew what. Forty eight-ounce somethings. I tried playing Jonesey's mem-

ory game in reverse, thinking whatever came to mind—
chgs ... changes, charges? And the PE? Phys ed? Pro
education?

Plastic explosives.

Forty eight-ounce charges of plastic explosive.

I could've saved myself the trouble if I'd noticed the
timer slapped to the top and the wires running down
into the crate. Nell figured it out faster than I did. She
flopped around so violently, she threw herself off the
dolly. The heads started squirming, too.

Turgeon looked like an overwrought babysitter.
"Quiet! Quiet!"

When no one obeyed, he stamped his feet, the sharp
blasts echoing through the lot. I tensed, ready to go for
him. The explosives made me think I should do something sooner rather than later. But the clippers were under the duffel bag, so rather than grab them, he pulled
out a gun. If I wasn't mistaken, it was my Walther P99.
He aimed it at Nell, too agitated to realize it wasn't that
much of a threat. Seeing it only made her struggle more.
He grabbed some oily cloths from the car and stuffed as
many as he could into her mouth.

I was starting to feel like fucking Hamlet: Should I
stay or should I go? But rushing up while he had the gun
was not a good idea. If nothing else a few slugs would
slow me down; two in the knees would bring me to a
halt.

Liveblood at a toxic site with a bag full of heads and
a bomb? The cops might not believe me, but no reason
they wouldn't listen to Misty. I crouched back down and
fished out my cell phone. Given how near Turgeon was,
I wished I could text, but instead I had to hit the speed
dial at 1.

After two rings, she answered. Unfortunately, she answered very loudly.

"Hess, are you okay?

Terrified that Psycho-baby would hear, I kept my voice low. "Shhh! I'm in the hospital parking lot, lowest level, with Turgeon. He has explosives. I think he's planning to bring the whole place down. Get the cops; tell them you have proof he's been killing livebloods. Get them over here fast."

"What? What'd you say?"

There were airy sounds behind her, crowds. She was on the street. Crap! She'd gone to the rally! At least it meant she was close.

I tried to explain again, but still kept my voice too low. After her third shrill, "What?" Turgeon heard us.

He was faster than he looked. He barreled over before I could stand and slammed into me. Before I knew what was happening, I was down on my stomach. There was no way to spit in his face while his knees pressed into my dried-out kidneys.

I saw the cell phone skitter and spin along the dusty floor. Misty's voice was still coming from the speaker, saying, "What? What?"

When he realized who I was, he started giggling.

Yeah, surprise! Happy fucking birthday. Look what I got you—me, your only missing victim! Am I a pal, or what?

He didn't have cuffs, plastic or otherwise, but he had some rope and used it to hog-tie me pretty quick. Then he gagged me with the cloth that hadn't fit in Nell's mouth. I was on my stomach the whole time, head sideways, so I couldn't get a straight shot with the VX if I tried. A minute later, I was piled on the dolly with Nell, a bag full of heads, the clippers, and a crate of explosives.

Beside himself, Turgeon wheeled us to the elevator, pressed the button, and said, "Going down?"

I think he thought it was funny.

29

If you have to be tied up, rope's more comfortable than handcuffs or plastic bands. Rope gives, breathes a little. It also gives you hope. If I wriggled and twisted my hands, pulled, relaxed, repeated, eventually they'd loosen. Eventually they'd loosen enough for me to get free. At best it would take an hour or two, long after whatever Turgeon was planning would be all over. Still, it was something to do.

I was lying near the front of the flat cart, looking up at Turgeon's back while he looked up at the elevator lights. They blinked lower and lower: basement, sub-basement, sub-subbasement, then some initials I didn't understand. It felt like I was in one of those old cartoons where the elevator goes so low that the doors open up in hell—flaming pits and a grinning devil with a pitchfork. Wrong floor. Besides, I was already in hell.

Behind me there was a frantic rustling. If it had been Nell, that would've been bearable, but the shape was wrong and the pieces kept coming apart and rolling off one another. Heads, I lose. They were shifting around like they still had bladders and had to pee real bad. I tried to stay calm, concentrate on the ropes. I was doing okay, relatively, until, through the bag, I felt a mouth close on my shin.

Electric-syrup time.

I dry-heaved. I pulled my legs in tight. I crammed my eyes shut. I stayed that way until the elevator stopped and the doors opened. When Turgeon wheeled us out, the drone of the dolly seemed to calm the heads, so the gnawing stopped.

I looked again. Turgeon was pushing from behind, so I couldn't see him at all. We were in the lowest part of the complex. Plastic sheets were everywhere, ceiling to floor, a poor man's picture windows, held by a series of monolithic concrete pillars. It looked like a buried temple to some industrial god who couldn't care less whether you worshiped him or not. As good a place for a nightmare as any.

A thin, barely visible cloud of white powder hung in the air, but there was a steady breeze disturbing its peace. The hum of vacuums sucking air through long, cylindrical tubes was loud enough to make the plastic vibrate and drown out the dolly's wheels. Part of the remediation. They were trying to take asbestos out of the air.

As he pushed us through the plastic maze, Turgeon stopped a few times and looked around. I don't think he was admiring the view; he just didn't know exactly where Odell Jenkins was. Grateful for the extra seconds, I kept at the ropes. If Egghead saw me squirming, he didn't say anything. I got nowhere, but Turgeon had some success.

He'd found an area where even the emergency lights
didn't work, and a long yellow extension cord ran to a distant hanging lamp. There were new sounds—hammering,
crunching, shredding—and the shadows shifted with
them.

Turgeon's pace picked up. He'd found Odell. Rather
than head straight for the light, he wheeled the dolly toward the gloom behind the sheets. As we rolled through,
the plastic crawled across my body, leaving a sheen of
white dust. Funny, it reminded me of Ashby.

Ahead was a dark nothing. To the left, the hammering got louder. I twisted my neck and caught my first,
plastic-blurred glimpse of Odell Jenkins. He worked
alone. Maybe it didn't make sense to give zombies a day
off. He was standing near the hanging light, where the
ends of the vacuum tubes had been set up. At first I
thought his hair was white, but when he swung a sledgehammer into the wall, a cloud of plaster dust puffed
from the top of his head.

He didn't wear a protective mask or a hood. From
the looks of the rest of him, he wouldn't go down easily.
The former brain surgeon was a bruiser with anaconda
arms and door-wide shoulders. He swung that sledgehammer like it was a feather, tore off the drywall by
hand, and then yanked the exposed two-by-fours free,
nails and all. Maybe his boss figured he didn't need any
help. Given enough time, he'd take the whole hospital
down himself.

Turgeon stopped us alongside one of the wide concrete supports. I still couldn't see him, but I imagined he
was eyeing Jenkins the way a starving hyena might look
at a distracted lion. He had all the cards; the only question was how he'd play them. He'd want to D-cap Jen-

kins, then me and Nell, set his explosives, and leave with his bag full. When the building came down, this place would make a nice mausoleum. If they ever dug us up, it'd be no surprise to find a few chak pieces. Better than the desert or the acid. The daddy head might not like it, but there wasn't much it could do.

Chk. Chk.

Somewhere above my left ear, Turgeon was testing the clippers, slowly, quietly, so Jenkins wouldn't hear. He stepped to the side of the dolly and held open the nearest plastic flap. It gave me a clear look at him, and a clearer view of Jenkins.

The odds weren't as good as I thought. Jenkins's bright orange jumpsuit made him a great target, but worse than that, he was wearing earbuds. The poor sap was listening to music, or an audiobook, trying to improve himself. Turgeon could play a trumpet and still sneak up on him. And the clippers were very sharp.

I grunted and kicked, hoping Jenkins might hear me even through whatever iThing he had on and turn around. The heads rustled a bit, but the one who really responded was Turgeon. He held the blades in front of my eyes and said, "Shhh."

I could have kept kicking. If I forced it, made him D-cap me first, Jenkins might hear something and get away. Y'know, if it'd just been about my death, I might've gone for it, but I really did not want to wind up in that bag. So one look at those razors and I clammed up tighter than a crab's ass at high tide.

With such concerns behind them, there was nothing to keep the heads quiet. They kept jostling, their twitching joined by those scraping paper-bag voices. But the vacuums were loud and their voices so soft that Turgeon only gave the duffel bag a halfhearted kick before stepping to the other side of the plastic.

Would Turgeon really take him? Likely. There was so much noise, so much concrete and hanging plastic to conceal his approach, he could get close easily and get the blades in place. One spring-assisted crunch and it'd be all over.

As Egghead crept from one hiding spot to another, Jenkins never turned from his work. The chak still had his focus, I'll give him that, but it was the kind of concentration that'd keep his back turned long enough for his head to get sliced off. Makes you wonder what the hell's worth wishing for.

I grunted and pulled. The heads started gnashing. I could see their mouths open and close through the fabric, as if they wanted to chew their way out. I might have frozen in fear, but beyond the duffel bag I caught a glimpse of green eyes. Nell Parker wasn't moving much, but she was staring at me and making noises like she was trying to talk. The gag must've been buried pretty deep in her throat. She sounded worse than the heads.

Thinking she could squirm away and hide if she was fast enough, I twisted around and tried kicking her off the dolly. All I managed was to push the bag of heads into her, and her into the handles. It wasn't happening. The only way to free her was to free myself first. So I had to do it somehow. I had to.

But "had to" is a funny thing if physics disagrees. Despite my best writhing, all I did was flop around like a fish. I stopped when my head neared the top of the duffel bag. The cord that held it closed slapped against the gag in my mouth.

I didn't like it. I didn't like it at all, but it gave me

another idea. The heads had no love for Turgeon. If I could get my ropes near those gnashing teeth, maybe they'd, I don't know, gnaw them off?

I'd rather be picking my nose in a septic tank, but that wasn't an option. I closed my eyes and white-knuckled it. I gulped, trying to swallow the electric syrup already filling my throat, and wedged my nose into the opening of the duffel bag. After some effort, I managed to wriggle my nose and then my jaw inside.

It sucked. It was so close I was already claustrophobic. Little puffs of dry air from nostrils and open mouths hit my cheeks and eyelids. I heard jaws open and clamp, teeth click. They were excited, either happy to see me or annoyed at having to share their space.

Hoping I wouldn't pass out or go feral, I pivoted my own head along the opening, trying to make it bigger. I told myself if it worked, it'd all be over in a few seconds. Just a few tiny seconds. I forced my head in deeper, widening the opening even more.

I was finished, but it turned out I'd lied to myself about the few seconds. Before I could yank my head back out, a set of teeth clamped down on a clump of my hair. The only thing that stopped me from screaming was the thought that Turgeon might still be close enough to hear me even through the gag.

Acting like a weird cyborg somewhere between animal and machine, I clamped my jaw shut and snapped my head left and right, trying to shake the son of a bitch loose. The other heads nuzzled closer. I kept my eyes shut, but I could hear their teeth grinding, clicking, chomping. I'd stuck my head into a fucking piranha tank. They'd tear me up, rip the flesh from my skull, chew my eyes, crunch the bones.

I was hungry to leave my body, like I did when the acid pool was bubbling beneath me, but before I could, no longer caring who heard, I howled the way only a dead man can. The sound startled the heads long enough for me to yank my head, and the head clamped onto my hair, out of the bag and into the dusty air.

As I came free, I felt something heavy clonk into my forehead. The sensation was followed by a sharp tug and tear on my scalp. The head went flying over my shoulder, a clump of my hair still clenched in its teeth. I heard the thud of its landing, a thrumming as it rolled, and a plop as it hit a plastic sheet.

Oddly enough, everything had gone according to plan. The duffel bag was open.

Now I just had to get the heads out and hope they'd chew on the rope instead of me. I wasn't particularly convinced they would, but I had no plan B. I kicked the bag, evening out the heads along its length. I laid my feet down on the middle of the bag, thinking I could push a few out. Flexing my tied ankles, I worked two of the heads toward the opening. As I went at it, I caught glimpses of Nell's eyes, her expression telling me what I already knew—that I was out of my fucking mind.

Of course, my brilliant idea didn't work at all. Once the two heads were separated from the others, the bag shifted and nearly rolled off the dolly. The bulk stayed on the wooden flat, but the two heads rolled off the edge. With a *crunk* and a puff of dust, the first hit the floor. The second landed on the first.

They were far from where they'd be any use to me. Their eyes rolled wildly, then settled as they took in their surroundings. One head had half its skin missing. It also had an aquiline nose and dark wavy hair that, I swear, looked recently combed. The other was younger, sporting a blond Mohawk and what was either a big scar or an ornate tattoo on a flat forehead.

They saw me, saw the dolly. Twisting toward the light, they saw Jenkins. They kept twisting, looking around, trying to find something. Turgeon, I guessed. When they didn't see him, they were either pleased or worried. It's hard to tell with heads.

The next surprise was that they could move. Not that they'd win any races at the county fair, but the one with the fancy part had enough neck muscles left to inch along as if he were being pulled by a few thick worms. Not to be outdone, Mohawk Joe, on his side, used his jaw to crawl.

As they moved, they made those scraping, hissing noises. I barely heard them, but they meant something to the heads still in the bag. Working their jaws, pulsing their remaining muscles, like the two on the floor, they all shuffled out of the bag. Some rolled off the dolly and fell to the ground. Others settled on the wood before jumping down to join the others.

Most were male, but there was one woman, a redhead with a missing eye. Some were older, with bald spots; some had neatly cropped hair. One was ugly as a prize-fighter, nose broken in a dozen places; another was still handsome enough to have a career modeling hats. I wouldn't say they were all high-functioning. More like they ran the gamut.

Daddy emerged last, as if he'd waited for the others. I took a good long look at it. Despite being the cleanest, best-cared-for of the lot, it looked the most drained, the most worried. When it hissed and clicked, the others gathered around.

As the heads arranged themselves, it turned and stared right at me. There were lines in its face that told me that in life it had been a tense, angry man, kind of like my own father. It blinked, hard, over and over, trying to communicate. I showed it my ropes, but it didn't seem to care. When I nodded toward Jenkins, though, it followed my gaze. Its hissing grew louder, frenzied. Obedient, the others started moving, rolling, crawling, under the plastic, toward Jenkins.

That could work, too. If they kept heading toward him and making those creepy noises, he might hear them. The heads on their way, I thought I'd go back to working the ropes. A scraping turned my eyes down. It was a head. Instead of going along with the others, it had squirmed up to me. It was right below my face, listing left, then right, trying to get my attention. I had to fight an urge to kick it away.

When it realized I was watching, it rolled onto its side. Mouth opening and closing, it made the same two terrible, impossible sounds over and over—*achshh bree achshh bree achshh bree.*

I knew what it meant. It was saying, "Ashby. Ashby."

It was Frank Boyle's head, asking about his adopted son.

For better or worse, I had an answer. "He's at peace."

As it took in the news, Boyle's head made a motion like it wanted to swallow hard. It blinked, huffed some air through its nostrils, then turned to join the others.

The heads moved slowly, but surely. Ten feet from Jenkins, seven. Their little noises were barely a whisper above the vacuum's rush, but they might make it. They might.

If Turgeon hadn't spotted them first.

He emerged from the dark with a wicked glint of silver, still a few yards from Jenkins, but knowing he had to make his move fast. He crept with exaggerated slowness, choppers out, blades extended. The heads picked up speed, hopping, rolling, trying to make themselves loud enough to warn Odell about what was inching toward his neck.

It definitely wasn't something you see every day.

30

As Turgeon slinked, the heads lumbered, increasing their little gasping so much I thought for sure Jenkins would finally turn. He had to. But no.

Oblivious, Jenkins turned and yanked out a chunk of plasterboard that looked like South America. It buckled against his knee with a crack and an asbestos-laden puff. The way he stood now, when the heads *did* get his attention, he'd wind up putting his back to Turgeon to see them.

I had to get into the game or it was over. I braced my elbows against each other and pulled so hard the rope threatened to tear into my dry skin like old, worn leather. I tried my ankles. There was more give, but not enough to matter. I tried to work the gag out, but the filthy wad of cloth was too deep in my mouth for me to maneuver my tongue behind it. My best efforts were as pointless as a condom in a dead man's pocket.

I thought of Ashby, how I wished I'd struggled more when he went into the vat. Was I still holding back?

Afraid to hurt myself? Being dead, it was second nature to be more careful, to keep things from getting damaged. But there was no point now in worrying about cutting some wrist skin. If ever I should break some bones, it was now.

I pulled at my wrists as hard as I thought I could; then I pulled harder. The rope's prickly fibers jabbed my skin, but I kept at it until it felt like they were tearing muscle. Still, no go. I worked my ankles like an epileptic having a fit, smashing them into the edge of the cart. I heard a crunch, thought I'd broken something. The rope was looser, but still held.

The only thing left was my tongue. I balled it up and yanked it back in my throat for all I was worth. I felt the little flap connecting my tongue to the bottom of my mouth, the frenulum, grow tight, but I kept pulling. I imagined that day at the office when I saw the photo of Lenore and Booth. I pictured myself punching a wall, harder and harder.

With a shivery burst of rage, I pulled at my tongue until I got it behind the gag. At best I'd bruised something. It hurt like hell when I pushed against the gag, but the pain was easier to manage than the rope.

Just as I saw Turgeon lunge, the wad of cloth finally moved. His face was lit with the kind of rapture a kid has when he's riding a two-wheeler for the first time.

The first sound from my throat was an airy pop as the gag flew out. The second was loud enough to make me forget I was the one yelling and wonder who the fuck was being murdered.

"Look out!"

As I screamed, I threw my head back, so I wasn't sure exactly what happened when. When I looked again, Jenkins still had his head. He'd spun in time to save his neck. Not his arm, though. The clippers were buried in his left shoulder.

With a giggle, Turgeon clamped the handles. The blades scissored; the orange suit shredded. I saw white padding, then Jenkins's gray skin beneath. Next came a crunch that almost sounded like another piece of plasterboard buckling against Jenkins's knee.

Hanging by a few orange threads, Jenkins's arm twirled slightly before it fell. It landed right in front of the parade of bobbing and hissing heads. Jenkins looked from his arm to the heads to Turgeon. To say he was shocked would be a gross understatement.

The psycho worked to get the clippers open again, but a bit of orange jumpsuit cloth was wedged between the blades. Fishing it out slowed him so much, he wasn't even looking when Jenkins's meaty right arm came up and swatted the clippers.

The D-cappers flew over the heads, hit the floor, flipped and clattered against the concrete. When he realized what happened, Turgeon's baby face went still. Then it got all puffy, as if he were going to break into tears.

I thought Jenkins had him for sure. Now he'd bash that egghead in, make an omelet, but that's not what happened. His first swing was reflex. Now he had a few seconds to think about things. Instead of belting Turgeon again, Jenkins patted the space where his arm used to be. Then he checked his work suit as if it had slipped down there somehow, like an errant set of car keys. He was going into shock.

"Snap out of it!" I shouted, but it didn't help. It also hurt like hell. My tongue was killing me.

Realizing he had a second chance, Turgeon rushed for the clippers. The heads tried to stop him, but they were no more a nuisance than a pile of glaring watermelons.

Stppp, the daddy head said. *Stop.*

Turgeon kicked it out of the way, bent over, and grabbed the clippers.

Out of nowhere, for no reason I could see, other than the universe hates me, Turgeon decided to look up and stare straight at me. He gave me a wicked, thin-lipped grin that told me I was next.

I jerked at the ropes, bucking so violently my body moved across the dolly until there was nothing under it but air. I hit the concrete sideways, earning a gash on my cheek. I flipped onto my belly, raised myself on my haunches and threw myself, wrists first, on the corner of the dolly, and rubbed my bonds against the wood for all I was worth.

I tried to cut it; I tried to use the edge to pull at the knot. The dolly rolled. I followed until it stopped against the concrete pillar and kept rubbing. A splinter the size of a steak knife stabbed what used to be the meaty part of my right hand, but the rope was giving faster than my body. Soon the knot looked loose enough for me to go at with my teeth. I chomped at it, clenched my teeth, and tried to pull an end free.

At my back, a struggle was going on. I couldn't make out the details, but it was lasting way too long for Jenkins to be winning. There were thuds, crunches, hisses, and crackles, and then the horrible snapping of those blades. I madly hoped Jenkins had retrieved the clippers and was cutting up Turgeon, but then I realized he couldn't use them with one arm.

My hands came loose, but I didn't enjoy the freedom nearly as much I'd expected. Another sound came to my ears, a steady electronic beeping. It was coming from the dolly. After I pulled the remaining ropes off my ankles, I lifted myself up to see what it was.

For the love of . . .

The timer. Somewhere along the line I'd kicked the crate enough to get it ticking. I had no idea how to turn it off and didn't have time to experiment.

I turned back to the fight, relieved at what I saw. Apparently the choppers had clamped around air. Jenkins didn't look any worse. He and Turgeon squared off. Turgeon had the clippers open again and out. His good arm poised to strike, Jenkins bobbed back and forth looking for an opening. The heads were trying to squirm under Turgeon's feet, to trip him. So far, he hadn't fallen.

A muffled moan took my eyes back to the dolly. Nell. When I tried to stand and step toward her, I crashed to the ground. In my effort to escape, I'd broken my ankle. My left foot twisted sideways, tearing skin and some muscle. Whether Misty, needle and thread, and some superglue could mend it didn't matter much at the moment. I pulled myself along the dolly's edge, yanked out Nell's gag, and untied her ropes.

This wasn't the time to ask what she was feeling, but those green eyes, glowing in the wispy poisoned mist of the air, told me. She still thought I was crazy.

"Get out," I told her. My wounded tongue made every word agony. "Bomb's gonna explode."

She sat up. "Why are you doing this?"

Now she wanted to chat? "Didn't you hear? Plastic explosive! Get out!"

She looked at the timer, then back at me. "Why ... why are you helping me?"

Was it *that* surprising? "Go!" I said. This time I gave her a shove.

Instead, she came forward, close enough for me to feel her dry breath on my skin.

"Why?" she insisted.

I could've said something about how I used to be a cop, and helping people was an old habit. I could've explained how Turgeon had killed both my wife and Nell's husband, and I didn't want the sick son of a bitch to enjoy any more success. I could have told her that there was something about the way she looked and moved that might have struck me as garish when I was alive, but now tickled some frayed and otherwise desiccated part of my being just enough to almost make me remember ... something.

But my tongue was killing me, so instead, with her so close, I grabbed her, pressed my lips into hers, and hugged whatever felt like it would fit against my body.

Was it a kiss? It sure as hell reminded me of one.

I felt the pressure, the shape of her mouth. It was hard to tell where I ended and she began. It took my mind off my tongue and my ankle for a bit. I even think I felt my heart beating, but that was probably the beeping timer.

She pulled away. That are-you-nuts? expression glowed on her face like green fire. She wiped her lips with the back of her hand, but she did it slowly, like she was remembering something, too. Then she turned and ran. Her final words echoed in the toxic dust:

"You're fucking crazy!"

I didn't disagree, but I had more crazy shit to do. Jenkins and Turgeon were still circling, skirting each other. Each one was afraid to get too close, or to back off. I picked my left leg up. The foot hung in place. As I brought it down, I found I could bounce on it long enough to bring my right foot forward. I limped past the plastic sheet.

Turgeon saw me first. And Jenkins . . . well, for all his physique, he wasn't much of a fighter. Probably just pumped iron in a gym. When Turgeon looked at me, Jenkins could've used the distraction to swat the clippers again. Instead, he looked at me, too.

Turgeon turned back first, and stabbed forward. The clippers didn't get Jenkins just then, but they made him stumble. He moved his left foot backward so it skimmed the cheek of one of the heads. If he'd had both arms, or even if he'd been used to having one, he might've stayed standing. As it was, he twisted the wrong way, looking surprised as he went down.

The dry stub of his shoulder hit the floor first. He was pushing himself up on his remaining arm when Turgeon got the blades around his neck and snapped them shut.

I heard that sound again, like plasterboard buckling, only thicker, deeper, longer. But I was too damaged and too far away to do a damn thing about it.

31

*C*runch.

They say the brain protects itself from unpleasant memories by forgetting them. This was a sound that wouldn't leave easily, no matter how bad your memory.

Crunch.

It was already crawling around between my ears, looking for a spot to lay eggs. I'd forget the texture of Lenore's skin, the sound of her voice, her eyes, her name, hell, my own name, long before I forgot that sound.

Crunch.

The heads reacted in unison, like a bottle of electric syrup hit them all at once. Did all of them remember the sound? They'd heard it before. In unison, they spoke a single, dry-whispered word: *"No."*

Odell Jenkins's body plopped back down like a piece of luggage dropped by an invisible hand. Turgeon went to his knees, not from exhaustion or horror. He was thrilled, giddy, and eager to grab his prize. He lifted the head by its sandy curls and gave it a great big smile.

Its eyes twirled, then moved in a jerky pattern, right, left, up, down. Finally, they fixed on the decapitated body. No matter what angle Turgeon held the head as he admired it, its eyes remained on the body, as if it realized they used to belong together. The mouth moved, tried to scream, but unlike the others, it hadn't yet learned how to make any sounds. It just stretched its jaw, going through the motions, acting, in Jonesey's words, *as if*.

There were only ten feet between us, tops. The clippers were still clamped shut. But you know those dreams where you can't move even though you absolutely have to? This was one. If my ankle hadn't been broken, I'm sure I could've reached him before Turgeon picked up the choppers and got them open again, but every time I took a step, it felt like my foot would tear off completely.

I always felt bad for those chakz who looked like they were in a grade-B movie, but here I was, dragging my leg, lurching just like a Romero wannabe. Instead of attacking, I limped off, heading for the nearest pillar, praying I'd blend in with the darkness behind the plastic.

Turgeon heard me, but didn't see me yet. His head was up, scanning. His voice called out above the hissing heads: "Mann?"

He put his new trophy down and snarled at the others, "Quiet! Quiet! Can't you see I have to find him!" When they didn't obey, he kicked at them. He even raised the blade like he was going to stab his favorite. "Don't make me hurt you, Daddy! Quiet them down, now!"

While he tried to get his eggs in a row, I shambled deeper into shadow. It was slow going, but I still had my one last trick. If I could come up behind him, I could still use the vial. All I'd have to do would be to pull it out, clamp down, and spray it into his liveblood face. It'd be all over, except for the running from the bomb.

As I winced and crept along, "Daddy" neared his boy. The head looked up at the killer with an expression I thought might be hatred, then clicked its tongue a few times and made a high-pitched whistling noise that seemed to come from his nose, like a steam kettle. At once, the others settled down.

Turgeon picked up the blade, then turned off the vacuums. Suddenly, dead or not, it was too quiet for me to move without being heard.

Fortunately, it was also quiet enough for Turgeon to hear the beeping timer. Eyes wide, he cursed under his breath and made for the dolly, moving away from me. As he pushed aside the plastic, he realized the ticking bomb wasn't his only problem. Nell Parker was missing. He hadn't seen her run.

He popped up like a jack-in-the-box, his funky blue eyes drilling every corner of the long funhouse maze of plastic sheets, work-light reflections, and stagnant shadows.

I knelt, with less trouble than I expected, and grabbed a small chunk of plasterboard. I threw it hard. It skittered along the ground about five feet in front of where I was hiding. Turgeon turned to it, following the sound as the plaster rolled into a different darkness.

I'd expected him to turn the timer off before coming after me, but he didn't. He just stepped back in my direction. Either he figured there was plenty of time left before the big *ka-boom*, or I was wrong and this was a suicide run. I tossed another piece, bringing him closer, then another. It was time to fish out the vial, but my bruised tongue felt like a piece of hot charcoal in my mouth. I felt like a stroke victim trying to cover six months of therapy in under a minute.

Rather than try to move it again, I shoved my index finger in my mouth. It was too thick to dig under my jaw, but I did manage, with a wild blast of hurting, to push my tongue into the hollow. From there, it scooped the vial out. I held it gently between my back molars, shivering as the ache rushed through me in waves. I was ready for Turgeon.

But he was gone.

While I'd been fussing with my bruised tongue, he'd slipped off. I looked at the heads, hoping they'd give me a clue, but they were helter-skelter, as if whatever intelligence they possessed had fled. Even Daddy lay listlessly on his side, staring up at the work light as if it were the sun and he was tanning at the beach.

I found another piece of plaster and threw it. But when it landed and rolled, Baby-Egghead called out, "Stupid, Mann. Really stupid!"

I scanned the filthy sheen of the plastic, eyed the grays and blacks, looked for odd shadows near the light. Nothing moved. All I heard was the beeping. Where was he?

A skittering on the floor caught my attention. I turned my head in time to see a piece of rolling plaster. It stopped in a pool of light on the opposite side of the pillar I was near.

"I can play, too!" he said.

If he came at me with those blades from behind I was a goner. I pushed my back into the concrete. Even if he came at me head-on, at least I had a chance to poison the son of a bitch. Not that it would do much for me, long-term. If I remembered my VX correctly, with a full dose it'd take two minutes for him to pass out, another

twenty for brain death. That was more than enough time
to lop a head off. Much as I wanted to watch him die, I
didn't particularly want a floor view.

A shadow grew along the floor on my left, distorting
against the broken plasterboard Jenkins would never be
cleaning. I saw the distended shape of the egghead, the
shoulders, the length of the clippers. He was right there,
just on the other side of the pillar, about to see me.

I inched away from the column, turned to face the
shadow, and hobbled backward, timing my steps with
the beeps, hoping there wasn't anything on the floor behind me to trip me up.

The shadow stopped moving. It lay there on the
ground, neither advancing or retreating. The shadow
lips parted. His high-pitched voice, disembodied, floated
across the dark into my increasingly pathetic hiding
spot.

He was whispering, so softly I barely heard him above
the beeping.

"Almost over now, Mr. Mann. Mr. Mann. You want to
hear something else funny? Way back when I found you
and your wife, I thought you'd be the hardest. But you
were the easiest of all of them."

What was he on about?

He went on. It was an intimate whisper, the voice of a
sleepy child lying in bed, talking to a parent. "I watched
for months, up in the trees, behind the bushes. I saw how
she drove you crazy, how she'd push you right up to the
edge. But you wouldn't jump. You couldn't. You were a
chained dog, a poor chained dog. And she was a sadist
with a stick. Do you remember that?"

Bad as my memory was, it wasn't how I recalled
things. Maybe that's how a fucked-up kid would see it,

good guy/bad guy, someone to root for, a villain to
hate.

It was obvious he was trying to get to me, keep me
distracted. He kept cooing, reciting details, telling me
what was in our house, talking about the photos on the
fridge, what we'd had for dinner, what dishes were left in
the sink.

How long *had* that son of a bitch been stalking us?

"And the hole in the wall from the bottle you threw
the night before."

That I hadn't remembered until he reminded me. It
was the day Booth denied me that raise, the money Lenore and I'd been banking on. Not getting it meant our
debt would keep piling up. It also meant we'd keep holding off on having kids. Forever, as it turned out.

In that sick singsong voice, Turgeon whispered *every*
word of the argument I had with Lenore that night.
"You said, 'Just admit it, you blame me. Just fucking admit you blame me.' She wouldn't. She'd say, 'No, I don't
blame you.' Then a minute later she'd remind you of
something else you'd put on the credit card. 'I just don't
understand why you had to get that TV set. We can live
without TV.'"

Every word brought up an ugly picture. Only now it
wasn't just me and Lenore. Turgeon was there, too, outside the window, lurking behind a bush.

As he went on, his tone changed. Something lizard-
like grew behind the sweetness. He knew it was working.
He knew he was getting to me. Smart. Smart sick fuck.
He knew I'd only hear him if I was nearby. He wanted a
reaction, any reaction, anything that'd let him gauge
where I was.

"I waited and waited and waited. You were a *police* officer. Your *friends* were police officers. They wouldn't believe you did it. They'd *help* you. But she was *so* much like my mommy. Mom did the exact same thing to my daddy, drove him away, then drove my stepdaddy away. Your wife had the same hair, the same eyes; sometimes she used the same words, so I had to keep watching. I wanted *you* to do it. I kept hoping you would. I was rooting for you. Even when I saw her fucking your boss, I didn't act. I thought maybe it was just a onetime thing. But when it happened again and again, and I realized how much she liked it *because* she was hurting you . . . well, then I knew I was right. I knew you'd be left all alone . . . like me. I don't believe in destiny, but it sure was *lucky*, don't you think?"

Something skittered in the darkness behind me, breaking the spell. It could have been an echo from the heads, a leaking pipe; it could've been nothing, but Turgeon thought it was me. The shadow moved again. He was moving toward it, toward me.

"I took thirty pictures and sent you the best. After I e-mailed it, I had to move fast. I'd timed your commute. Twenty-two minutes, and of course you'd be speeding."

He was six feet away.

"I came in through the living room window, took your baseball bat from the closet. She was in the kitchen. I was very good. When I hit her the first time, she only just started to be surprised."

Four feet.

"I hit her on the side of the head, but she fought. Even when she went down, she was still conscious. I had to keep going. I had to make sure she wouldn't scream."

Three feet. Judging from the shadow, his head was angled not at me, but at the darkness where the sound came from.

"She scratched and kicked and clawed. She called out for help, but only once."

Two. He should have seen me by now, but he didn't see me. I was a thing.

"She didn't call for *you*, though. That's how I knew this was the most *right* thing I'd done since my own mommy."

I was a thing, and he wasn't a shadow anymore. As he came around the corner of the pillar, I saw his lips moving. "'Tom,' she called out, 'Tom!'"

A wave washed over me; I thought it was nausea, or the electric syrup, but it was rage, stronger than any chak was supposed to feel. Before the sick feeling could kick in, I rushed around the far side of the pillar, thinking I'd be behind him.

He whirled too quickly. All at once there was some distance between us and I was facing the open blades. They snapped closed as I hobbled back, pinching a tiny piece from my neck.

My foot slipped sideways, off the broken ankle. The basement spun. Next thing I knew I was on my back. The capsule flew into the back of my throat and I nearly swallowed it.

Turgeon opened the blades and came forward.

I coughed, trying to hack the vial back into my mouth. The pain in my mouth got into a fight with the pain in my ankle over who'd get me killed first. I put my palms and my good foot to the floor and pulled myself away, moving backward like a big, sickly, hobbled spider.

My right hand hit something heavy, a two-by-four. It was full of nails. I knew because one pierced my palm when I grabbed it. It stung, but that didn't stop me from swinging. I slammed Turgeon in the calf. He screamed, again looked like he would cry, then stepped back. I swung again, hitting the clippers hard enough to make them clamp shut.

Nail still through my palm, I wedged the wood under my armpit and forced myself to standing. This time I didn't run; I lurched forward, toward the opening blades. I didn't give a fuck about my head anymore.

Turgeon shivered with glee at the sight of me. He had the blades open and out, half expecting I'd run straight into them. Instead, I swung the board again, knocking the clippers away. Then I grabbed his shoulder, crushed the vial between my teeth, and sprayed green poison and glass shards right in his face.

His egghead doused in the oily liquid, he pulled away, sputtering, and rushed into the darkness. I could feel a small bit of the viscous stuff clinging to the insides of my cheeks. I shut my mouth, in case he needed another whiff, and, using my two-by-four crutch, hobbled after him.

I heard steps, then silence, then that skittering again. What was he up to? Crap. I glanced back at where the clippers had fallen. They were gone. Dead man or not, he had them again.

How much longer until two minutes were up? Could he still get me? I had to hide and wait him out. I stepped along, no longer sure whether my foot was attached or I was walking on leg bone.

When I passed by one of the plastic sheets, something moved right behind it. Thinking it had to be him, I whirled, pulled the sheet away, and exhaled the last of the poison.

Only it wasn't Turgeon. It was Misty.

Somehow she'd found me, even down here, even in the dark. She gasped when I surprised her, took a deep breath, then smiled when she realized it was me, not knowing I'd just killed her.

Maybe it was the deep breath she took, but the VX seemed to work on her a lot faster than I thought it could. A few seconds later, her eyelids fluttered.

32

"**M**isty."

Her lips parted, but without a word, she fell. Too shocked to catch her, I threw myself onto the cold floor beside her. A long, stringy trail of saliva dripped from the side of her open mouth.

"Misty?"

I'd already exhaled most of the gas. There was only a little left, not even a full dose. Maybe she'd be okay. Right? She had to be.

I slapped her hand, felt her forehead, pulled back an eyelid. Her pupil was a pinprick, a distant black star surrounded by hazel. I said her name a few times more. She started twitching. I couldn't tell if she was responding or having some kind of seizure.

I hooked my arms under hers, pulled, and half crawled. After what seemed a million years, we reached the dolly. The timer was beeping its little head off, like an oven screaming that the cookies were ready and about to burn.

Fuck it. I grabbed the round plastic thing and jabbed the first button. I thought the next thing I'd see would be a flash followed by a whole lot of nothing, but the beeping stopped. No *ka-boom*. If only everything else were that easy.

I pulled the bomb off the dolly and yanked Misty on. My right foot was no longer good for much except dangling from my ankle by a flap of skin and muscle, so I grabbed the handle and hopped as I pushed. As we moved, I listed and groaned just like a zombie should.

After all, that's what I was, right? A grade-B monster.

The wheels wobbled, crunched on plaster, loud now that the vacuums were off. I pushed Misty from shadow to light, shadow to light. At the end of the maze, I pounded the elevator button like it was Turgeon's head. He had to be dead by now, but nerve gas had been too good for him. I should find his body and use the cash he'd given me to bring him back just so I could kill him again. For Lenore. For Misty. For Nell, Frank, and Colin.

For the hell of it.

By the time the doors opened, Misty didn't look like she was breathing. I wheeled her in and slammed the button marked ER. The door didn't close fast enough, so I pulled it, so hard I nearly took it off its guide. Stupid. Fucking stupid. If I'd broken it, we'd have been stuck down here.

The car jerked, then moved up, slower than a snail. Misty looked still. A kind of body memory kicked in. I pressed on her chest three times, held her nose, and blew into her mouth. It was CPR, but at the time I didn't remember the initials or what they meant.

How had she found me? Of course. I'd called her on the phone, and she tracked me through the GPS in it. I was sorry she had talked me into getting the damn thing. Did she bring the cops? No. They wouldn't have let her in here at all. The phone, where was it? Back in the parking lot. I searched for hers, but couldn't find it.

I stared at her face. She looked like she was sleeping, sleeping without air. Poor thing probably inhaled enough asbestos to kill her all over again in a year just by coming down here.

But I had to remember she wasn't like me. She was alive, still alive. She could heal. That meant there was hope. And she was strong. Crack hadn't killed her; maybe the gas couldn't, either. I kept up the compressions, the breathing.

Did it help? I didn't know. I only knew I couldn't risk doing nothing.

Forever passed before the doors opened on an empty ER hallway. There was less dust in the air here, but still enough for the sunlight to illuminate. I did my grunting one-legged dance, got the dolly to a desk, and grabbed the phone. Dead, to coin a phrase.

I had to find help. There had to be something someone could do. I wheeled her toward the Exit signs, stopping twice for more compressions and breathing. We passed the examination area: two rows of cold hospital beds, white and silver. Some had sheets so tight it was obvious no one had ever used them. Others had curtains drawn around, like they were hiding something ugly. I thought about laying her down in one to make her more comfortable while I tried to get help, but I realized no one living would want to come in here.

Windows. A way out. Or if I shouted, someone might hear. I scrambled to the nearest one and found myself looking down on the central plaza. There was a crowd, not just big, huge. It covered the brick field, the side-walks, the streets.

Jonesey's fucking rally. I'd forgotten all about it. It was in full swing. I saw an army of chakz, clothes gray and torn as their bodies, moving along the wide avenue toward the plaza. Marching would be the wrong word. With so few being "lucky," they listed and bumped into one another. They bounced, got turned around. Then they'd walk against the crowd until they hit something else that pushed them the right way. They were like a bunch of giant pinballs heading slowly in the same gen-eral direction.

Another mob had also gathered, the gawking live-bloods, all sharing a single expression—terror. Parents pulled their children into the imagined safety of the nearest store, nearly yanking their arms off in the pro-cess. If it'd looked less real, more like a wild Halloween party by night, the living might not've been so fright-ened. As it was, it was August and the sun was bright, il-luminating every patch of gray, every stub, every missing piece of flesh.

Some of the chakz held signs, but the ones I could see weren't Misty's work. The handwriting was so bad the letters looked more like multicolored blood splattered against oak tag than words. And, damn, there was Jone-sey, right at the head of the disheveled parade. He stood on a rickety float made up to look like a cemetery of broken hearts. He was using a rolled-up piece of card-board as a megaphone, and whatever he was saying seemed really important. To him, anyway.

The police were out in numbers too big for Fort Ham-mer regulars. Overweight and unshaven, a lot of them looked stuffed into their uniforms like sausage into pig intestines. The town must have called in reservists, extras, retirees, circus seals, whatever, for backup. From the looks of things they'd even deputized their sanitation people.

Male teens bobbed among the crowd like lower primates, dodging and swinging around obstacles, jostling for position, looking for a way to get past the police and in among the chakz. Some held bottles and bricks.

Misty. I snapped myself out of it and opened the window, but the sound that rushed in made me step back. At first I thought it came from the chakz. It did sound a little like moaning, but it wasn't them at all. It was the *livebloods*, their collective disapproving grunts. They were murmuring, gasping, wondering why someone didn't *do* something, wondering why they *all* didn't do something. But it hadn't gone south yet. It still might not.

My tongue still hurt like hell, but I screamed, "Help! I've got a liveblood in here and she's dying!" I thought I was being clear, but I didn't know if I was being loud enough. "A liveblood! Help!"

A few people in the crowd turned and looked up at me, but said nothing. At last a blond woman, curly hair, expensive summer blouse, pointed and screamed.

"A feral!"

"No!" I shrieked, but I wasn't sure what I sounded like. I probably looked just like a crazed killer corpse.

A cop turned from the line, thirties, fair hair, not one of the reservists. I think I recognized him from the station. Bradley? I waved, thinking for some insane reason that he might recognize me, and that it would be a good thing.

"I'm Hessius—"

"He said he has a liveblood hostage!" someone

screamed. The cop pulled out his gun and fired. Good shot. The bullet took out a chunk of plaster right near my head.

I don't know if that was what started the riot. Given my track record in supporting chak rights, it wouldn't surprise me, but I later heard a different story. Apparently a couple of the teens with baseball bats went after an old woman chak because her hair looked particularly freaky. When the other chakz tried to protect her, the LBs stepped in to help the kids. That's what I heard, anyway. The truth is as hard to pin down as it is to remember. Maybe it was one or the other; maybe it was both, or neither.

I fell backward. Screams and more gunshots, followed by some genuine zombie moans, rose from the street.

I lay on my back, staring at empty fluorescent fixtures, listening to the waves of noise. I felt that funny urge to leave my body, to desert my stupid fucking broken hunk of flesh, my long-dead piece of meat, and call it a day. If Misty hadn't been there, I would have. But she was on the dolly.

She was still twitching, but not nearly as much as she had been. There wasn't a damn thing I could do about what was happening outside, but there *had* to be something I could do for her. I was in a fucking hospital, after all. Maybe I could find an EpiPen. Lenore used to carry one of those because of her allergies. Maybe it would jump-start Misty's heart.

The ER was pretty cleaned out in terms of supplies, so I wheeled her down the hall, looking for something to shock Misty into breathing on her own again. There were oxygen tanks in the hall. Useless without a mask, and I doubted they'd help. Near the tanks was an open door to an MRI room. The giant white doughnut-shaped machine was still sitting there. Better yet, hanging in the center of one white wall was a plastic box marked DEFI-BRILLATOR.

Hoping to hell it had instructions, I wheeled Misty as close as I could and ripped the box open. Two paddles tumbled out and dangled by their coiled cords. Inside the door, bless it, were five steps printed in big type, so simple even a chak could follow them.

I yanked Misty onto the MRI platform and flipped the switch to power the paddles. Nothing. No power. I wanted to punch the freaking wall, but I had to keep my head. All those security lights in the basement were on and the elevators worked; there had to be power.

I looked around as if expecting the answer would be hanging in the air. It wasn't, but it was clinging to the walls. Thick cables led from the top of the defibrillator up to the ceiling. There they joined with a set of even thicker cables from the MRI machine. All of them headed for a junction box on the far wall. It had a single red lever, so I pulled it.

The ceiling fluorescents flickered feebly. Green and red lights glowed on the MRI. I slammed the button on the defibrillator again. This time it hummed and crackled. I didn't think there was enough time to undress Misty like the instructions said, so I jammed the paddles onto her chest and pressed the second button.

The loud *gzt* that followed reminded me of the bug zappers back at Green's mansion. Misty's whole body, thin and bony, contracted like someone had thrown a bucket of ice water on her. Her chest rose and collapsed.

Then she fell silent again, looking as fragile as glass. I watched for any sign of movement. Not seeing any, I charged the paddles again.

Gzt!

Again she contracted, looking like a broken doll being yanked upward by her chest. Again I watched for some sign of movement, but none came. And then ...

A giggle.

"The dead trying to bring the dead to life. Isn't that redundant?"

Turgeon stood in the doorway.

In one hand he held the duffel bag, its contents twitching. In the other he held the clippers. He looked like a headhunter returning home from a tough day at the office. He lowered the bag, put his arms out, and said, "Surprise!"

Got that right. How had he survived? He looked none the worse for wear. There was nothing different about him I could see, except ... one of his eyes wasn't blue anymore. A contact had fallen out. What was behind it had no color at all.

In a repulsive flash, I understood why the gas hadn't worked. "You're a chak."

He nodded. "I wanted to know what Daddy knew, so I had myself killed and immediately resuscitated. There was no decay at all, just a little complexion problem. And this way I can continue my work *forever*."

I flipped through what there was of my memory. "Didn't you ask me what it was like to be dead?"

"All the better to fool you. You're really very stupid, you know."

I'd certainly had better days. He held up the open

blades. My eyes darted around for a way out, but I was up against the MRI, as backed into a corner as you can get.

Two steps and he was within striking distance. Some remaining body instinct made me hold up my arms to protect my neck.

Disappointed, Turgeon shook his head. "Come on, now. I win. Don't be a baby about it."

Look who was talking. I didn't think I was getting out of it, but I didn't drop my arms. If I timed it right, I could make a desperation move, shove my arms between the blades and try to twist the clippers out of his hands before they got through the bone.

He gave me a second chance. "Do you really want to lose your arms first?"

I held my ground. With a little shrug, he jumped.

That was when Misty, lying on the MRI table, maybe a foot from Turgeon's ear, bolted up and let out the longest, most bloodcurdling scream I've ever heard, in life or afterward.

"Gyaghhhhhhh!"

My ears were ringing, but it was a sweet, sweet sound. She was alive.

Turgeon gasped. I dodged right. The closing blades nearly sliced my ear, but I landed on the floor behind Misty. Above me, the lights from the MRI control panel glowed red.

With a loud, rattling wheeze, she inhaled and screamed again. *"Gyaghhhhhhh!"*

I heard Turgeon coming, but I was down on my chest, no room to roll, no way to flip or kick. I reached up to lift myself, but my hand hit the controls. There was a loud crashing whir, like a miniature construction site had come to life inside the big white doughnut of the machine.

Misty screamed for the third time. *"Gyaghhhhhhh!"*

Still facing the floor, I felt something slip from my pocket. There was a clatter. A loud *thunk*.

Turgeon began cursing like a big boy. "No! Fuck! No!"

Pushing Misty out of the way, I flipped over and saw that the clippers were held fast against the buzzing, clanking machine. MRI—magnetic resonance imagery. I'd read once about a kid who'd been killed when some idiot left an oxygen tank in the room with the machine. The MRI pulled it through the air and into his body. This time it'd drawn the choppers to it.

Turgeon yanked at the handles. They wouldn't budge. They weren't the only thing the magnet was pulling. The dolly shook by its metal handles, rattling like a rocket ship ready for liftoff.

I grabbed Misty and dragged us both back to the ground. Like an animated corpse, the dolly stood on edge. It waddled a half a foot, then flew over the MRI platform toward the machine. The only thing keeping the metal bar from the magnet was Turgeon.

I'd like to say it hit him at the neck, but it was a little lower than that, around the shoulders. A lot of what looked like fat turned out to be padding, part of his live-blood disguise. As the dolly handles pressed into him, pulled by the machine, the stuffing puffed through the openings in his clothes. He was always a little pale, but the slightly pink tinge to his skin that helped fool me turned out to be some sort of skin dye. As the dolly handle tore through his clothes, patches of gray chest appeared.

Turgeon was pinned, helpless, as the powerful magnet

drew the bar of the dolly deeper and deeper into his body. It took ten, twenty seconds for the handle to travel all the way through him. When it was finished, most of his torso stayed up, held in place by the handrail. What I guess you'd call his bust tumbled to the ground.

There it twisted its head and looked around, confused.

I killed the power. The dreadful sounds of the machine stopped. Cart, torso, and choppers fell in a heap. In the sudden quiet I could hear Misty panting, the heads hissing in the duffel bag. I even heard, though it was muffled by the hospital wall, an ocean of cries from the riot outside.

Misty looked at me. Tears were streaming down her face. Her eye makeup was running. "Hess . . . what the fuck?"

I put my hand to her cheek, forced myself to speak with my hurt tongue. "Long story."

She saw me wince. "What's up with your tongue?" She scanned me. "And your foot!"

As I thought about how to explain using the fewest, shortest words, the heads forced their way out of the bag. Once they saw it, they marched toward Turgeon's split body, looking like soldiers buried up to the neck in linoleum.

One didn't join them right off. Daddy wriggled its way up to us. Misty stiffened and looked ready to scream again. I put my arm around her. It was trying to tell me something, but her teeth were rattling so loudly, I couldn't make out what.

Bbbbmmm . . .

"What?"

"It can talk?" Misty squeaked.

"Shh!"

Bbbbmmmm.

Boom? Bomb. Crap. "He set the timer again?"

Daddy nodded. My hand tightened on Misty. "Hess, you're hurting me."

"We've got to get out! Now!"

She was weak, I was on one foot, but we gave it our all. Arms around each other's shoulders, we made for the door.

Behind us, the heads surrounded Turgeon. I thought maybe they were going to greet their new member, razz him a bit. When I looked back, though, they were chewing on him. Most of them were feral. I could see it in their eyes. They'd gone fast, as if they'd held on long enough to get to this moment.

Turgeon spoke pretty clearly. Maybe it was easier because he had more neck left. "Stop! Please stop! I only wanted ... only wanted ... *company*. . . ."

"Hess . . ."

"Misty, don't look."

Daddy struggled along the floor to join them. Before it was out of earshot, I had to ask. "How'd you keep them in order? What was it you promised them?"

With perfect enunciation and a look of pride, as if for one moment it were human again, it said, "Revenge."

As it squirmed off to join the gory feast, the light of intelligence faded from its eyes.

I hoped that when the bomb went off, the collapsing building would crush them to powder, destroy them permanently. But there was always the chance there'd be just enough left beneath the rubble for something, human or not, to feel pain.

Leaving yet another bit of hell behind, we limped down

the hall like contestants in a three-legged race, dogged by the sound of chewing and Turgeon repeating his last word like it was a pained prayer: "... company ... company ..."

Before we reached the exit, the sound stopped, probably because there wasn't anything left that could speak.

33

We followed the signs to the main entrance. The automatic sliding doors were powerless, so we had to pry them open. Misty broke a nail. I nearly lost a finger. We did it, though, only to be rushed by a torrent of light and sound. The sun washed everything gray; even the colors had run away. The noises blurred and shredded.

The doors had opened at the head of a wide drive that led to the street. Beyond that, we had a great view of the plaza. Frying pan to fire.

Crowded, surrounded, attacked, the chakz gave the people what they wanted: proof that they were dangerous. Flashes of chak bodies moved in elegant waves, like flocks of migrating birds. It was as though that group mind-set the LBs worried about had actually kicked in. Maybe the ferals just never had the numbers before, or maybe you had to be far enough back to see the patterns. The livebloods, for all their higher functions, fled without grace.

The big picture pulsed and throbbed. The personal

tragedies played out in tiny spaces. It was like the two had nothing to do with each other, no trees for the forest, no forest for the trees. Near the center of the gray swirls stood the fair-haired cop, the one I'd seen from the window. Bullets sprayed from his AK-47. They tore some dead flesh here and there, but mostly he hit livebloods before the ferals took him down.

My eyes singled out a male teen, all buff and dressed to shock with shaved head tattooed and pierced. He ran halfheartedly, grabbing the spot on his head where an ear used to be. Red liquid dripped between his fingers. Eventually, he slowed down and fell.

Groups formed and collapsed like cauldron bubbles. Two families banded together. The mothers carried the little ones, forcing the older children ahead. The fathers had somehow gotten hold of some doors and were using them to shield the others as they inched across the plaza. Weirdly, two danglers banged at the doors like they were knocking. They even tried the knob.

I hoped the family would make it. Something should survive, and it didn't look good for anyone else. The elegant swarms of dead had surrounded the LBs and, as they squeezed in, began to lose their pretty shape. Together now, ferals and livebloods pushed and pulled, so many, so close together, they could barely move. Limbs tangled, the center of the blob tumbled all at once, like football teams in a joint tackle.

Somehow the mob had formed a single creature, like one of Colby Green's orgies, many limbs, many mouths, some screaming, some chewing. In my head, I heard Turgeon, or the devil, giggle.

At the edge of the mass, stray livebloods and ferals tried to pull the bodies free, but for different reasons.

The cop with the flamethrower stared at it all, unsure what to do. He tried to help. He used his free hand to grab a hand and yank. When he only succeeded in pulling a feral free, a chunk of dripping meat in its mouth, he'd had enough.

Feral in his own way, the cop let loose with the thrower, turning a dripping tongue of fire on the writhing pile. Before the cop could barbecue the whole lot, a liveblood clonked him with a crowbar, then dived into the smoldering mess, screaming that he had to find Tanya. His girlfriend, I figured.

We wouldn't be spectators much longer; we'd be part of the scene. Having reached critical mass, the blob broke and scattered. Bodies, some moving, some smoking from the flamethrower, spilled into the street, then onto the long black hospital entrance ramp where we stood. Bullets ripped the ground a few yards ahead of us. The tide was coming in.

"Hess, we've got to do something," Misty said. She was still weak, barely back from death's door.

"We have to run."

Beyond the ER entrance a service dock formed a bit of an alley. In it were several big Dumpsters, painted green, rusted at the edges, but whole.

"There. We climb in one and wait it out. It won't smell pretty, but it should be safe."

I pulled, but she wouldn't come. I wasn't strong enough to drag her.

"We can't just leave those people!" she said.

"Are you delirious or did you just develop superpowers? All we can do is try to stay in one piece," I said. "Don't look. Don't think about it. Just keep moving."

She was slow, uncertain.

"You don't move now, you'll die!"

"Fuck it; then I'll die," she said. "I was sick of it all beforehand and it just got a lot worse."

"Bullshit," I said. "Your fart is too big for your own good!"

I was so angry my bruised tongue had seized up in midsentence. Turned out it was a lucky break. Misty looked at me, then laughed. "You said fart."

"Yeah, I said fart. Can we go now? We're in this together, remember?"

She nodded and we moved. We made it to the dark of the alley, the first open bin yards away. Misty followed my lead, but it was the blind leading the blind. It'd been bright and my eyes hadn't adjusted. I saw one shadow moving on its own, but I took it for a plastic trash bag until it rose up, strips trailing from its arms. I couldn't tell if they were torn clothing or skin.

Its mouth was open, every other tooth missing, and what was left had been filed down to points. Once upon a time, it may have been a freaky fashion statement; now substance had vanquished style. When it came at us, I shoved Misty out of the way. On impact, I wrapped my arms around it and tried to bring us both down.

I put my hand under its jaw and pushed, but it wouldn't budge. Bony fingers raked my jacket, tearing the pockets off one after another, as if it thought they were parts of my body. I put my good foot up into its solar plexus and shoved. It flew up, landed on its feet, and came at me again.

On my back, I accidentally kicked at it with my bad leg. My foot flopped to the side. It was still held on by that last layer of dry muscle, but the leg bone was exposed and had a bit of a point. I pushed it deep into its gut. Yeah, chakz don't always feel pain quite the same way livebloods do, but that hurt like a son of a bitch, let me tell you. It also staggered the feral. It tumbled back, hands out, trying to keep its balance. As its feet skittered along the trash-laden floor, I hoped it might trip, but it righted, snarled, and started at me a third time.

I was trying to roll out of the way when something heavy and silver thwacked it upside the skull. It turned in the direction of the blow just in time to get another. It was Misty, swinging at it with an old wooden crutch. She must've found it among the hospital garbage.

While she kept swinging, I struggled to my feet, or rather, foot. She didn't need my help, though. Her next few blows took it down to its knees, then down. She smacked its skull again and again. As it lay there, she kept swinging. She swung so hard and so often, I winced. After seven blows, the skull cracked. After that, it twitched more than moved.

Puffing, she handed me the crutch.

"Thanks," I said.

"You're welcome," she answered.

I spoke slowly to avoid any more gas jokes. "Let's get in. The shitstorm should be over by morning."

She leaned against the garbage bin. "Then what? Go back to the office? You know once this is over any surviving chak will be locked up or worse."

I leaned against the crutch, using it as . . . well, a crutch. "Probably. I'll run from that bridge when it comes for me. And even if they catch me, at least I solved the case."

She eyed me. "Yeah, you're a regular zombie Sherlock Holmes."

"No, I've got proof! A recording of Turgeon confessing. Booth hears it, even *he'll* know I didn't kill Lenore. If it got into the press that a chak caught a serial killer, it could help things for a change . . . a little."

As I spoke I used my free hand to rifle through my pockets. Two had been torn off by the feral. Another had my wallet, some change, and . . . that was it. Where was the recorder? I scanned the ground. I got down on my knees and looked under the bins. Nothing. It wasn't there. It wasn't anywhere. I had a vague memory of something tugging free from my pocket while I struggled with Turgeon.

"I dropped the recorder in the hospital. I've got to go back."

Misty's face twisted so harshly she looked like a ghoul. She leaped in front of me and shoved me back. "Are you crazy? We just ran out because there's a bomb in there!"

"I have to! That recorder's the only proof I have. No one's going to sift through twenty million tons of debris to find a bunch of severed heads!"

"I won't let you go, Hess."

I tried to step around her. "Didn't you just say there was no point? That they're going to lock me up anyway?"

She jumped in front of me again. "And two seconds ago you said we were in this together!"

"I *have* to go! It's not just about me; it's about every life that sick bastard fucked up. If I don't go back and find that recorder, no one will *ever* know."

"*You'll* know. *I'll* know."

I didn't have time to be nice about it. Every word was another second down on the timer. I made a big show, like I was thinking about giving in. Then I knelt, grabbed her legs, and stood, lifting her against the bin. Before she finished gasping, a little twist of my hips sent her in. I slammed the lid and slid the bolt shut.

She pounded against the metal. "Bastard! Bastard! Filthy freaking liar!"

"Watch the screams, Misty. They attract ferals. Any luck and I'll be back soon."

She was right. I had lied. It wasn't about Turgeon's victims. Anyone else who might care was either dead or the next-best thing, except maybe Booth, and I wasn't going to risk my dry ass for that fuck. It was about me solving my wife's murder, chasing a shadow of what I used to be.

In case more of the riot decided to head my way, I stuck close to the walls. At the entrance, I caught a final, brief glimpse of the mad, mad world. Any shape to the chaos was gone. The was no composition to the scene, no choreography to the violence, no orchestral score rising and falling. Ferals chased livebloods; livebloods chased chakz. Cars were flipped, windows smashed, bones broken, skin flayed. Things burned.

My existence was just as pointless. The recording wouldn't change a thing. Hell, the MRI magnets probably erased the whole thing anyway. But I'd been going through the motions for so long, I had to finish the dance. If I didn't make it, just as well. If I survived, instead of my being D-capped by a psycho, the authorities would do it, or I'd be carted off to some chak camp. I didn't have the heart to tell Misty that if I were in a pen, keeping her off crack wouldn't be enough to keep me going. If I could *prove* I was innocent, then at least I'd have a story to tell myself in the dark.

I went through the entrance, down the hall, scanning the floor. Just as I stumbled past the radiology sign near the MRI room, the floor shook. I heard a sound like an enormous bubble bursting deep in the belly of the earth.

The bomb had gone off.

I tried to run, but cement floor cracked beneath me. The walls folded in like cards. Support beams shattered. Holes opened. Everything moved in on itself. Nothing under me anymore, I fell. As I spun in midair, the stench of something thick and burning hit my nose. I think I saw a fireball, a huge blossoming flower, but my eyes might have already been closed.

It went dark. The crashing and moving continued for what felt like hours. When it settled at last, I was still there. Things hurt, but I couldn't be sure if what hurt was even part of me anymore. Lost limbs still hurt amputees. They call it phantom pain. Hell, I had a whole phantom life.

I was in some air pocket, some crappy little corner; I'd be here forever. I'd go feral, I'd lose my mind, but I'd still *feel*, still see and hear. Same nightmare as being a head. It wasn't until that moment that I realized what a bad idea this was. Stupid, stupid, stupid. And the recorder was gone forever. For some reason, it didn't depress me, not yet, anyway. It struck me as funny, but I couldn't laugh.

I was lying on my side, legs stretched out beneath me, right arm stretched in front of me, my head cradled on my shoulder blade. I felt like I was lying in a narrow ship bunk on a jagged, concrete mattress. Head turned down, I opened my eyes. I didn't expect to see anything, but I did. There was mist in the air, dripping water. Past my feet, far off as a star, a security light swayed and flickered.

The hallway I'd been standing in had been shoved

into a space a quarter of its original size. I wasn't completely flat. I was at an angle. There was a space above me, maybe a foot or two, narrower spaces right and left. Ahead, past my hand, I thought I saw daylight.

Then I heard something rattle deep below. The hospital wasn't finished dying yet.

I thought I should try for the daylight before my little hollow collapsed, but I couldn't talk my body into it. Trying to get motivated, I told myself Misty would be pissed if I didn't get out. Nothing. I imagined being stuck here for good. Still nothing. Then I told myself it would mean Turgeon had won. All his victims would be gone. That did it.

With my right hand, I grabbed at the debris, trying to snag something heavy enough to pull myself along. I moved an inch or two. There was another rattle. I tried to move faster, but it felt as if the ceiling were closing in on me. I closed my eyes to better concentrate, but when I did all I saw was Turgeon's leering face. It made me angry, but I still couldn't move faster. So I kept my eyes open, even when the dust fell into them.

All of a sudden it got dark. Ahead, something had blocked my little view of sunlight. Had the way out collapsed? Was it over? No, the light returned. A shadow was wavering in front of it. It looked like a drape, its wispy shape created by the breeze. Then it got thicker, longer, larger.

Something was moving toward me.

Some*one*. Too big for a head. Chak or liveblood? Couldn't tell. It came near as it could and knelt right in front of me but I still couldn't make it out. It vanished again, but a few seconds later it reappeared and shoved the back end of a fire hose at me.

"Take it," a rough voice said.

Someone was saving me. Had Misty gotten out of the bin?

I wasn't going to complain. I grabbed hold. Whoever was at the other end pulled. I pushed with my good leg until I passed into a larger hollow. There I got up on my elbows to get a look at my benefactor.

It wasn't Misty, but it was a woman. At least, it was shaped like one. I stared, trying to focus. When I recognized the pale skin, black hair, and green eyes, I was startled and confused.

"You came back?" I whispered, pushing myself up on my knees.

It was Nell Parker, silhouetted in the gloom.

She took a step back as if I were a dog that might bite. "I was hiding when I saw you run back in. I heard the blast. I couldn't leave you in here. Not after you . . . after you . . ."

Turns out maybe some of the dead do have feelings.

34

I didn't have the recorder, but I had something else, maybe something better. Nell wasn't like Misty. She was definitely lighter, despite the remains of dancer's muscles. She was hesitant, too, unsure if she wanted to touch me. But side by side, we staggered into a smoky day.

The firemen found us before the police, saving us some trouble. They were more concerned about the collapsing building, so it was easy to convince them we weren't feral or interested in putting up a fight. They even believed me when I told them Misty was trapped in a bin. Not right off. I had to beg them to listen, to let her out. I didn't care what it looked like to Nell. She already thought I was nuts. Anyway, they'd never seen a chak beg before, so it worked.

A stocky first responder, Thompson, I think, who seemed to have sweated through to the surface of his black rubber coat, headed for the garbage to let her out. I hoped he'd tell Misty who sent him. I wanted her to know I was still . . . whatever it is you call what I am.

While he was gone, two cops came by. Their barely fitting uniforms gave them up as auxiliary. The regulars handled the more important stuff. These rubes were left with the cleanup work, like rounding up the rioters. Each led his own row of chakz, all shackled at the ankles like a monster chain gang. We were not so politely asked to join the line. I tried to refuse, but they insisted. They didn't bother sorting men and women or children and adults. There were only two kinds of chak: those who obeyed and those who wanted to eat them. Lucky for them, I wasn't hungry.

"It'll be okay," I told Nell as they clamped the iron on my good ankle. She gave me that look again. I imagined there was some fondness to it now, like she was beginning to think of me as a mentally challenged younger brother.

They led us, leashed, to the plaza. The fires still smoldered, but it was relatively empty now, except for the piled bodies. Show over. Buses lined the street. Any chakz who'd somehow kept themselves sane through this mess were being herded on.

It was pretty orderly, considering. Orderly enough for me to spot the master of ceremonies, Jonesey. His left arm looked shot to shit, but his sandy hair was intact, and he still wore a bit of that smile. It didn't quite match the dazed look on the rest of his face. I was surprised he hadn't lost it, and wondered how long he had left.

They were about to shove him on a bus when I thought I'd say hello.

"Jonesey!"

He saw me and stopped, nearly pulling the chak ahead of him back out of the bus. Like a windup toy, the chak, not one of the smart ones, kept trying to climb in, unable to turn, unable to realize what held him back.

Jonesey raised his good hand. "Mann! You still hiding out among the living?"

"So far," I said. "Looks like you made it, too."

His smile widened. "Have to keep a good thought, right? I mean, it was a start, wasn't it?"

I furrowed my brow. "A start?"

A cop pushed him into the bus. Good thing, too. I was about to tell him what a fucking idiot he was. Well, he'd figure it out soon, or give new meaning to the word *denial*. Made me wonder, though, if I'd let him go feral back in that alley whether it would've been better for everyone.

Unfortunately, I wasn't the only one recognizing faces in the crowd. Of course Tom Booth was there; it was his job, after all. He must've heard Jonesey call my name. Puffed up like a fighting-mad turkey, clipboard stuffed under his arm, temple throbbing, he stormed toward me, ignoring all the men asking for orders.

"Hi, Tom."

He pointed at me and barked at my walkers.

"Where was it found?"

The auxiliaries looked like startled fawns. One fumbled for words. "At the hospital. The firemen found him."

Booth looked at the thick dust on my coat, scraped some of it off with his finger, then rubbed it, looking like he was touching someone else's shit. "You were in the blast."

It wasn't a question, but I nodded.

"That bug, Jonesey, the terrorist who organized the attack, he's your pal, isn't he?"

"Terrorist? He's an asshole. And it wasn't an attack. It was a rally."

Booth sneered. "And I'm Miss America."

"Maybe if they left out the swimsuit competition."

"*You* set the bomb."

Nell, who'd been quiet all this time, grabbed my hand and squeezed. She may have been afraid, or she just wanted to let me know she was there.

I met Booth's eyes and tried to glare back.

"That's lame even for you," I said. "It was a fucking psychopath, the one I was after. Those two *contractors* you hired to do that work on me? They were his. He was after Odell Jenkins, a remediation worker down in the basement. There must be some record of him, at least. Tom, this psycho, *he* killed Lenore."

As soon as I mentioned her name, I knew I'd gone too far.

"Shut up."

"He saved me," Nell said.

He looked at her with equal disgust. "Take them out of the line and bring them back to the station."

"Both?"

"That's what *them* means, shithead," he said. "I've got you now, Mann. This time we're going to figure out a whole new way to kill you."

He stomped off, a dust devil twirling through the dry, flat, smoky terrain.

We were unshackled, taken from the line, and put in the back of a squad car. Nell and I didn't speak much during the drive. I was afraid that anything I said would earn me another condemning stare. We did hold hands. Hers were cool, white and smooth beneath the dirt, like some kind of cotton. Mine were gnarled and gray, like tree bark.

At the station, we were separated. I was put into holding and left to sit there rotting for days. No reason to let a chak out to stretch his legs, right? They didn't offer any medical care, but they did let me keep my foot. To be fair, it was still attached by a little flap of muscle, so it probably would've been too much trouble for them to find a pair of scissors.

My old partner, Jimmy Hazen, came by once. If he was sorry he'd betrayed me to Booth, he didn't say so. He just shoved a needle and thread through the bars and walked away like he'd done all he could. I wished I knew how to sew.

Better yet, I wished I had that recording. If only . . . At least I had Nell Parker to think about. Ever since she saved me, I figured I might as well try to stay saved, at least until I understood why.

As for the rest of the world, I didn't have access to news, but my guards talked. Over two hundred feral chakz had been put down "humanely"—though there was a bullshit rumor that they'd developed some kind of virus that could spread to livebloods. I'd heard crap like that dozens of times, whenever the LBs got scared. We could walk through walls, bend steel in our bare hands.

I did believe the rest—sick and tired of waiting for the feds to do something, the state was passing its own legislation. Meanwhile, all the chakz were being rounded up and put in camps. At worst we'd all be incinerated. At the liberal end of things, we'd be forced to register and undergo monthly exams. Somewhere in the middle, we'd be stuck in those camps forever. Liberals, unfortunately, are worse at organizing than chakz. They'd do well to hire Jonesey. Didn't matter much. Thanks to Booth, I was already in my very own special five-by-five camp.

My mind had little else to bounce off of other than itself, but I kept thinking of Nell, and Misty, and the fact that I finally knew what had happened to Lenore. Once, as I sat there, I even remembered, I think, what it felt like to love my wife. It was possible, I guess, that if I got out of here I could convince someone what'd happened even without the recording. Colby Green would want to know, but I wasn't about to write or call him. If he was my best bet, there were times during the long, slow days when I thought those camps might not be so bad.

About a week later, they let Misty in to see me. She was so worried about the broken foot and all the tears in my skin, she forgot to be angry with me for locking her in the Dumpster.

"Nice dress," I said with my best grin as the guard locked the door. No lie. It was sleek and auburn. Was it already fall? She'd carry it nicer if she wasn't weighed down by the heavy bag. It threw off her posture, made her look like a schoolgirl struggling with too many books.

"They wouldn't let me bring you new clothes," she said apologetically.

I shrugged. "Be like lipstick on a pig anyway."

She *tsk*ed, put the bag down, and opened it. "You don't look so bad. Nothing I can't fix."

Inside I saw books and papers. I started to ask, but Misty made a face like she didn't want to talk about that yet. Instead, she pulled out her own sewing kit and some Krazy Glue.

She started with the foot, checking pictures in an anatomy book to see where the pieces should go, then using the glue on the bone. Whenever she got a piece together, she'd hold it tight for a slow count of sixty. I knew better than to make a peep until it set. It might dry wrong, or get stuck to Misty's hand.

Half an hour later, the bones roughly in place, she was the one who started talking.

"New law was passed this morning," she said, threading the needle.

"I heard the guards grumbling about something. Camps or fires?"

She shook her head. "It was a close vote. Everyone had to compromise."

"Camps, *then* fires? The other way around would be ridiculous."

"All chakz have to register, carry photo ID. They've got a test worked out, supposed to tell how likely it is for a chak to go feral. You take it once a month. Pass and you're free for another thirty. Fail and you're . . ."

"In the camps."

"Yeah. Or the fires."

Triage of the dead. It was almost like the cells in Green's basement. I tried to whistle, but that trick never worked. What I managed was more like blowing a raspberry.

"Doubt I'd pass now."

She looked up from her work. "I'll help you study. We're in this together, right?"

I smiled, tried to make it warm. "Right. Thanks. Sorry about the Dumpster."

The muscle reconnected, she stitched the skin. I felt the needle go in and out, but there wasn't much pain to speak of.

"Was it worth it?" she asked. "Nearly getting yourself buried?"

"Got any easier questions I can answer first?"

"No."

"Fine. Yes and no. I didn't find the recorder, but if I hadn't tried, I would've gone crazy."

"And that girl chak pulled you out," she said. Now it was her turn to smile. Finished sewing, she waved at my foot. "Come on; try it out."

The little flap of muscle still working, I managed to move my ankle. I even stood and circled the cell. I didn't say anything, but my foot didn't feel exactly right.

She nodded. "Better stay off it for forty-eight hours until the glue completely sets."

I sat on the cot and tried not to look disappointed, but Misty could read me.

As she loaded up another line of nylon thread for the smaller gash in my neck, she said, "They say if a chak gets ripped a second time, old wounds can heal. Even bone." She looked up at me. When I didn't say anything, she added, "We do still have some money."

An image of Ashby's powdered bones shivering in the moonlight popped into my head, along with a thought. Maybe Boyle had saved enough to get the kid an extra RIP, hoping to fix his brain, and that was the unexpected result.

"I'm already worried I can't ever really die. Why push it?"

She *tsk*ed. "I can't keep patching you up like this. Could you think about it, at least?"

"One crisis at a time, okay?" I answered, indicating the jail cell.

The neck only took a couple of stitches. "How's your tongue?"

I clucked it against the roof of my mouth. "Dry as chalk, but working. Any idea what happened to *that chak-girl*, aka Nell Parker? Unless, of course, you're jealous."

"I have half a mind to stitch your lips up."

"I wouldn't blame you. But . . . ?"

"She was released last week. That's all I know. The police have been trying like crazy to connect you to the bomb, but they can't. Every time they try to make a circumstantial case, there're articles in the paper tearing them apart."

I was about to ask why, but she put a finger to her lips and shushed me. She lowered her head and whispered, "I can't let anyone hear this, but I think I figured out Turgeon's real name."

I nearly bolted to my feet, but she held my shoulders and kept me down. "Hess, they can't know I'm telling you this. I didn't exactly get the information legitimately. I had to get friendly with one of the guys in records."

I flashed her an angry look. She slapped my forehead. "Don't judge me! He was nice, treated me with some respect, and I've done worse for lots less. We're even going to NA meetings together. Anyway, that's why I'm not supposed to know what I know. I don't want him getting in trouble for letting me use his computer."

She'd already done whatever it was she'd done, and I didn't feel like I was in a position to lecture her. Besides, the part about the meetings sounded good. "What did you find?"

"Took me a while, going through records of spousal murders. There're thousands, Hess; it's like everyone gets killed by their lover."

"I know, I know. Get to the point."

"Fine. About seven years back, this guy James Derby was executed for beating his wife to death. He had a history of abuse. There was a bloody golf club with his prints and DNA all over the handle. He pled guilty, so no one looked too close. His stepson, Lamar, inherited his business. Inside of a year Lamar sold everything and vanished with a shitload of cash."

The next part, like it usually happens with exonerations, was almost an accident.

"Then a university crime lab class gets ahold of the case for practice. A student notices some bruising on her neck, like strangulation. Those wounds were swabbed, too, but never tested. They gave him the extra samples, thinking he'd just find more James Derby DNA. Maybe he started choking her and moved up to the club. But it wasn't *his* DNA. It belonged to Lamar. Hess, the bastard murdered his own mother, then planted his stepfather's golf club at the scene. Why would someone do that?"

I whispered back, "Because he blamed her for driving away the men in his life, his daddies. At least, that's what he said."

"But it still doesn't make sense. Why would James Derby go to the death chamber to protect him?" she said.

I shrugged. "Guilt? He abused the kid's mom, right? Probably felt responsible, even if it wasn't him. Didn't realize the boy was a sociopath. Or maybe he'd just given up on life. It happens, y'know."

"You think it's him?"

I nodded. "Sounds like it. It fits. Good work. No, great work. Lamar Derby. Shit, no wonder he changed it to Turgeon."

I sat up and gave her a hug.

"So maybe you can double back? Find the same evidence and get Lamar convicted posthumously?"

"It sure as hell is something to do. But first Booth would have to let me out of here."

She made a face. "I'm trying, Hess. There isn't a lawyer in the city who'll take your case, and the bail is more money than we've got. I could sell some stuff, try to borrow."

"Don't. Save the money. They can't keep me here forever, and it turns out I've got more patience than I thought."

She nodded, but I wasn't sure she meant it.

"Misty," I said, grabbing her wrists. "You've done a lot for me. More than I can say, but stop now. Don't you spend that money on bail. And no more being 'friendly' for favors."

She seemed offended. "I told you, it's not like that. He was nice to me."

"I don't care if he's Prince Charles and plans to make you his queen. Sleep with who you want, but not for favors. Promise?"

"Okay! I promise."

I still wasn't sure she meant it.

35

I thought about that name a lot over the next few days. Lamar Derby. Lamar. Derby.

I recited it slowly, quickly, all sorts of ways, as the light from my little cell window grew long and then receded. Was there still a way? Short of getting the DNA from the other cases retested, I was thinking probably not. I went over it again and again, trying to find an in, but the easiest plan I came up with was to dig him up from the hospital rubble with a teaspoon and get him to confess again.

I could've gone on like that for months, but what Misty thought of as fate had other plans. About a week after her visit, the lock on my cell clicked open. One of the guards stood there, shaking his head.

"Social visit, Max?" I asked.

"Nah. Someone posted bail. You're free."

My thoughts went to the obvious. "Fuck. Misty. I don't want it. Give the money back."

"Seeing how much I enjoy your company, I'd love to, but it ain't up to either of us."

"No choice?"

"Not even if you were a liveblood. Out you go."

I followed him down the hall, through some doors, and into the property room. They handed me my wallet and the spare batteries, then asked me to wait for another surprise. I didn't think they were going to throw a party for me, but I also didn't expect Tom Booth to step in.

"You got friends I don't know about?" he said. As usual, he didn't look happy. Only now he looked so unhappy, I was starting to think my luck really had changed.

"You mean the bail? I tried to give it back," I said.

"No, not the bail. The newspaper articles, the editorials. All three Fort Hammer papers were hammering away at the case against you. Conspiracy this, conspiracy that."

I had no idea what he was talking about, but I decided not to let him know that. "Tom, you getting jaded? Don't believe in reporters trying to uncover the truth? Can't be much of a case anyway, seeing as I'm not guilty."

He sneered. "Not jaded, Mann, just not stupid."

Part of me wanted to get while the getting was good, but I couldn't help trying to learn a little more. "These newspaper stories. They must be saying there was another bomber, right? Anyone starting to believe them?" I asked.

The sneer on his face all but disappeared. "Maybe."

I straightened. "Enough to get the DA to consider dropping the charges?"

He hesitated. I twisted my head and gave him a good hard look. Finally he said, "Maybe."

Under the circumstances that was better than a yes. "Tom, I know you hate me and I know why. But do you really think I'd blow up a building? For what? Forget everything I've been trying to tell you. You're a decent cop when you pay attention. Does it make *any* sense?"

His eyes darted away. Shit. I was impressed.

"Okay, then. Are you so wrapped up in making this about me, you'd ignore the real crook?"

"Your imaginary psychopath who D-capped the chakz he loves? He's buried anyway, isn't he?"

Like him, I wasn't stupid. I knew why he was talking to me. The investigation had gone sour. He was hoping to trick me, get me to reveal something he could follow up on. Even so, it was the most civil conversation we'd had since Lenore died.

"Yeah, but there were seven or eight heads in that bag, and I only knew about four: Wilson, Odell, Boyle, and the one he called Daddy. Forget me, okay? I'm getting my chak card and going off to summer camp. What about the families out there still thinking Mom or Dad or daughter or son is a killer? Or if there's a liveblood on death row right now?"

"You're full of shit."

He was about to walk away, but I was in for a penny and going for the pound. "I've got a name, Tom. Lamar Derby. Some kid in grad school pinned his mother's killing on him. Just check it out. Couple of fun calls, you could match that DNA to the other killings."

"Lamar Derby? That's a new one. You've been locked up. Where'd you get the name, from that crack head who stitched you up?"

Fuck. Misty would kill me. "If it checks out, who cares?" I said. "Two and two equals four? Didn't you teach me the rest didn't matter?"

I went into a little speech about everything I knew.

Without the recording, it was a bunch of dangling threads, but if he bought it enough to check the DNA, it could change things for both of us.

I had to give him credit. As I spoke, he turned his head sideways and looked as if he was thinking about it. I was only about halfway through when he raised his hand to stop me.

"Give it up, Mann."

To anyone who hadn't studied Tom Booth, that might seem like the end of things, but this time, for a change, I remembered. It was a phrase he'd used back when I was alive and trying to get him to follow some lead that seemed thin. *Give it up* really meant that he *was* thinking about it.

For a second, just an instant, as I stood there, I didn't feel like a chak; I felt like I was a homicide detective talking to his boss. I wasn't angry with Misty about the money anymore. The moment was worth twice the price. I was even thinking I might *deserve* what I imagined could happen with Nell.

But there are no happy endings.

His shoulders relaxed. Booth was ready to leave again, but I had to go and ruin it all by asking one more question. "Tom, the woman I was arrested with, Nell Parker, what happened to her? Do you know?"

He looked puzzled, then surprised, as if something with an awful smell had been shoved under his nose. "The stripper chak?"

Not wanting to push it, I only said, "Yeah."

"It was picked up by Colby Green. It gave him a nice big kiss when it saw him."

Something collapsed in my chest. "A kiss?"

"If you can call it that. There was enough tongue involved to tell me I shouldn't bother pressing charges on it, either."

"Colby Green?"

"You gone deaf?"

The thought of her back there, dancing for him again, after I . . . when I thought . . .

Before I knew it, I was pounding the wall, just like when that photo of Booth and Lenore popped up on my computer. Only now it didn't take one punch to break the plasterboard; it took three.

Booth remembered it, too. He grabbed me by the shoulders and shoved me out, kicking me along the way. "If you *ever* say you're innocent again, I'll destroy you! Do you understand? Do you? I'll D-cap you myself!"

By the time I was sprawled on the sidewalk in front of the police station, yeah, I understood.

36

A week later, the heat wave had broken; the air was cool and dry. The threat of decay receded. It was September. I'd just woken up from a dreamless sleep. A pleasant gurgling came from the other room along with the smell of coffee. It smelled kind of nice.

"You're up early," I called to Misty.

"So're you," she said. She stuck her head in. "Got a ten-o'clock with Chester."

I slumped into my chair, both it and my bones making little cracking noises. "Another? Didn't you just go to a meeting yesterday?"

"Ninety in ninety when you start."

"And you already told me that, right?"

"A hundred times. Put it on your new recorder."

Another way of saying, *where the sun don't shine.* New? I stared at the recorder on the desk. The silver strip on the side was wrong. I didn't recognize it. How could she afford that?

I was about to ask her when I glanced at the mail

piled under it. A manila envelope stuck out from among the delicate whites of unpaid bills. I figured it was a credit card offer gone astray, but then I eyed the return address—*Revivals Registration Dept.*

I knew what that meant. Thinking I might as well get it over with, I tore it open. Nice, new, and plastic, my registration card plopped out. Funny how people used to think plastic was fake. There was nothing more real than that card. It was embossed with a name, two dates, and a number. The name was mine, the dates my execution and "revival."

The number was mine, too, now, and it meant that unless I reported to a designated chak center within the week, I'd be arrested. If I failed their test, or didn't have the card's magnetic stripe updated properly, well, then I'd be arrested, too. After that, who knew? I might be sent to a camp, tossed in a vat of acid, D-capped, buried in a pit, or whatever. There were lots of stories, none of which I liked.

I called to Misty, "Aren't you the one who said meetings were crap? Not for you?"

"No, Hess, that was you."

"Was not. What changed your mind?"

She poked her head in again. I covered the card with a file just in time. Her hair was combed, her blouse clean. The shirt barely covered the spots on her chest where the defibrillation paddles had left small circular scars.

"There was something about being dead I just didn't like, no offense."

"None taken. Hey, I never asked. No white light, no welcoming relatives?"

She shook her head. "Nope."

I held up the recorder. "How much this set you back?"

"Twenty bucks, maybe. Why?"

"Nothing. Just surprised we could afford it after you paid my bail."

Her face dropped. "Hess, I told you when you got out, and I've told you a dozen times since, I *didn't* pay your bail."

I felt a shiver. Something told me I shouldn't ask, but like an idiot, I did. "Who did?"

"Nell Parker."

I slumped in my chair. Misty stepped farther in. "She went back to Colby Green...."

Memories swarmed me like a bunch of fat mosquitoes. *Nothing to suck here*, I wanted to say, but they don't care. I tried to keep them back. Feebly, I raised my hand to keep Misty from repeating what I'd already recalled.

"Right. On the condition he'd get my ass out of jail and have the charges dropped. That's where the newspaper articles came from. He planted them. I remember."

She came closer. "Seriously, Hess, how can you keep forgetting that? She saved you. You could at least go see her."

"I can't."

She made a face. "Is this because she's a stripper? Spoiled? You still talk to me."

A big memory with green eyes landed on my soul and started sucking. "It's not that."

"Then what?"

I rustled in my chair like dead leaves in a wind. I waved in the air as if trying to swat the words, but really I was trying to swat the memory, kill it once and for all.

"Fine. It *is* that. Lenore was a good woman, aside from Booth, I mean, but Nell's . . . she's just . . ."

I didn't think Misty would buy it, but she did, or at least she was polite enough to pretend. Her face, fuller than it used to be, twisted in disgust. She rushed out to her meeting, where I was sure she'd share beautifully about what an asshole her dead boss is.

I couldn't really tell her why. If I did, I'd also have to let her know how close I was to the abyss, how even thinking about Nell Parker made me want to fall in.

Misty had been doing so well, there was no point in her worrying about my wrinkled gray ass. Better she should hate me. It'd make it easier if . . . when . . . I go feral.

I thought about forcing myself to do some legwork, try to find out more about Lamar Derby, look for one of those sympathetic attorneys trying to protect chak rights. Instead I sat there and smelled the coffee until a breeze from the cracked window took it away. I was still sitting there when my cell phone beeped. A message from Jonesey. I played it back.

"Why you been avoiding me, Hess? I got plans, big plans. I'm going to start a new *religion*, just for chakz! We gotta believe! We gotta act *as if*, right?"

I erased it, like the others. If I ever saw him again, I didn't know if I'd be able to keep myself from ruining his little *as if* big-time. As if. The idiot didn't even remember the riot he caused. Crap. He was my friend, and all I could think about was hauling off and . . .

I clenched my hand into a fist and the rest of the memories came flooding back.

Nell Parker. Back in the property room, when I smashed my fists into that wall, I was ready, able, and willing to kill her. Why? Because of what I thought she'd done to me.

And that meant I must've been ready to kill Lenore, too.

Two plus two equals four.

Oh, Turgeon, or Lamar, actually did it, but I would have. I'd wanted to.

I wasn't staying away from Nell because of anything she did. I had to keep away because I realized who I was. It was a magic moment, a fucking epiphany, a cruel crossroads long after I was supposed to have left all the crossroads behind.

That's what I couldn't tell Misty.

The biggest difference between my memory and the future is that if I wait long enough, the future comes to me. So I tried to forget. Sometimes I succeeded. When I did, I hoped to hell Misty wouldn't remind me. I prayed she'd leave me alone so I could get through one more day, like Jonesey says, *as if*.

ABOUT THE AUTHOR

Born in the Bronx, **Stefan Petrucha** spent his formative years moving between the big city and the suburbs, both of which made him prefer escapism. A fan of comic books, science fiction, and horror since learning to read, in high school and college he added a love for all sorts of literary work, eventually learning that the very best fiction always brings you back to reality; so, really, there's no way out.

An obsessive compulsion to create his own stories began at age ten and has since taken many forms, including novels, comics, and video productions. At times, the need to pay the bills has made him a tech writer, an educational writer, a public relations writer, and an editor for trade journals, but fiction, in all its forms, has always been his passion. Every year he's made a living at that he counts as a lucky one. Fortunately, there've been many. His newest work, *Ripper*, which is sort of like the Harry Potter books but with no magic and with a serial killer, will be out in March 2012 from Philomel. He's also at work on the next Hessius Mann novel.